For Uwe.

The Amber Ark
Book five, in series
Ark of Hoof Prints.

Bibliografische Information der Deutschen Nationalbibliothek:
Die Deutsche Nationalbibliothek verzeichnet diese Publikation in der Deutschen Nationalbibliografie; detaillierte bibliografische Daten sind im Internet über http://dnb.dnb.de abrufbar.

Illustration: **Evelyn G Lohmann**

Herstellung und Verlag: BoD – Books on Demand, Norderstedt

ISBN: 978-3-7347-6826-2

Ark of Hoof Prints. Book Five

Amber Ark.

The Iron Man wants to make the Old Emperor pay for the death of his father and for banishing his family. He's plans are twisted by She-With-The-Sight, she uses her own kin to take her revenge on the Iron Man cruelty. She let the Iron Man take the boy, but ReeMara has the power, she will carry the amber stones to the city to place under the temple.

The girl does not know she has been manipulated till the sward is in her hand pointing at the Iron Man' hart. He killed her family, destroyed her village, he took her brother. The real danger to the city and her and those ReeMara loves is She-With-The-Sight!

She-With-The-Sight wants the twins ReeMara's younger children. She-With-The-Sight wants to disgrace ReeMara and ReeArk, put the twins in their places as Emperor and Empress.

Control the trading city or destroy it as she wishes.

There is no Future without a Past.

The beach curved into the blue horizon both sides of the midday sun. The sea washed the band of open sand as the wind caressed the sea grass that grew on the dunes before the twisted pines. The pine trees held the sea's playful winds from ReeMara's village.

ReeMara's feet were not quick enough to stop the sea splashing her; it did not even try to stop her from knocking over her brother as they tried to run away from the playful water. The sea's white waves mixing with their laughter, ReeArk was back up on his toddler's legs ready to splash ReeMara, he was not going to wait for the sea to knock over his sister again.

The two children's mother and aunt were too busy to enjoy the youngsters' games. The men were fishing out in the bay. They were hoping the last storm had sent big fish into their bay. From the amount of seaweed and shells there should also be many of the floating stones for the women to collect.

The children were supposed to help find the flashing bobbing stones but the storm had kept them hemmed in their huts for two days and their held in energy could only be set free on the open beach.

Reed baskets already had many of the light stones held in them, the driftwood only need to be dried before it could be used to heat the village's fire. The kale weed was used to feed the horses in the lean winter months, there were other seaweeds the folk could eat. And, as long as storms did not stop them from setting out in the long boats to cast out their nets, there was fresh fish. The last storm had thrown many of the villager's daily needs onto their white sand beach. It only needed willing hands to collect it.

Hooves pounding the wet sand did not stop ReeMara and ReeArk from splashing in the shallow water. ReeArk was the first to be frightened; so many horses were galloping towards them, screaming into the rising wind! ReeArk did not know there were men lying low on the strange horses' backs now disturbing the village grazing hard. He did not see the cold steel held in the man's hand till it had struck his mother.

ReeArk's little body twisted in the air, the hard hand held his ankle; he could see the white water swirl before his eyes as he was swung over the back of a horse.

ReeMara grabbed at his dangling feet as the sword swung again. It missed her; she felt it passing like a leaf from a tree.
The blade caught ReeArk's up turned face, a cruel red line ran from over his eye and down his left cheek, his flaxen hair was   soon matted with his blood.

The sound of man and women shouting, their screams mixed with the water that pulled ReeMara under into an incoming wave; it drew her away from the beach into the deeper sea.

Losing the sand from under her was the last thing ReeMara could remember. Only the image of her brother's damaged face and the pleading look in his frightened blue eyes came with her as the sea dragged her away from the beach.

Why the sea spat ReeMara back onto the beach, ReeMara did not want to ask when she tried to brush the sand from her eyes and spit salt water from her mouth.

A woman's body lay, not far from where ReeMara lay, if her mother looked the same ReeMara did not want to know. If she had turned the body over, she would have known it was the body of her mother's sister.

ReeMara stood up the beach was as empty as it had been that morning when they had come to comb the beach. If tears had not been running down her face she would have seen the sand smeared with blood and the blood merging into the sea.

Deep patens of hooves and feet had scuffed the wind smoothed dunes ReeMara did not understand the meaning of the marks, not even when she then saw smoke rise above the dune.

A strong smell of burning wood did not cover something ReeMara did not want to try to comprehend.

The smoke was black and thick and chocking as ReeMara came out of the trees guarding her home from the winter's cold wind from the sea.

If the huts had still been standing the smouldering mound in their midst would not have been noticeable. They had so often cooked their meals in the communal coals; it was not fish backing in the glowing charcoal. The blackened hand lost its hold in the embers; it could only crumble into its reddened bed.

ReeMara sat shivering where she was; she could not move it did not seem right. It was her folk ashes that were blowing away in the sharp wind heralding another storm from the sea.

"If you are going to sit there any longer, you may as well sit on top of the fire."

ReeMara jumped she turned to where a pair of black eyes peered out of a black feathered head set on a sleek gray body with his wings folded like the village alder when he was scolding wayward youths.

ReeMara was still too shocked to understand what she was doing but she fallowed the crow's instructions and rose to her feet and let the bird lead her away from what once been her home.

To take the human back onto the beach as not a way the crow could lead the little girl. Great waves were pounding the beach as if it wished to punish the open sands for what they had aloud to happen there that day. The other way was to take her through the salt marches; its tall reeds would hide her from the wild men that had destroyed her folk and home. She was small it might be too defalcate to get her to move through the reed's curtains.

The storm took that route away from both of them. It had picked up the fire from the village, and taken hold of the reeds in the salt march. That only way left open was between the flaming reads and the twisted pine trees; that was the way others were taking.

The wild cat, C'raw did not like the look of it. If they had not been hurrying out of the path of the fire he would have had to worry about its' presents.

C'raw had too worry about the speed or lack of speed the young human was making; he dipped his wing at her to get her to hurry, her short legs did not cover the ground as well as his wings could.

A horse brushed past ReeMara, she fell to the ground C'raw could not get her up before another's hooves pounded past.

ReeMara saw the bird fly in the face of a horse, it had to slow down or hit the bird; the one behind it collided with the slowing mare, pushing her into the way of a leaning pine. C'raw had to peck ReeMara to get her to cling to the mare's mane, she heard him say, 'She would have had to learn to ride sometime!' When she could catch her breath she would have words with that bird. She had been cling to horses' backs since she could crawl, so had ReeArk! That bird pecked her again!

The mare picked up speed once she freed herself of the tree C'raw had used to slow her. Her hooves covered the ground better than the small feet of the girl, but not to the satisfaction of the worried bird; he helped guide her as the smoke whipped them all before it.

Flames were hidden in the leading smoke, no one had to be told, had they stopped the flames would not have waited to burn them. The mare did see the flames devour a familiar horses' solute, as it sank into the smoke.

C'raw was in the air over the strip of land that leaded to the higher ground, hidden from those trying to out run the fire were humans with their spears pointed, waiting for the meat being driven towards them!

She-With-The-Sight would not except any excuses if he did not get this last remaining human to her. Why it was so important he got the last remaining human to her, he had not been told. For his acceptance trial C'raw would have like a less taxing test than the one facing him now.

Spears were pointing at the frightened animals racing before the wind driven flames, towards the strip of land held by those holding the sharpened points. If he was going to carry out her wishes he was going to have to think of something soon.

The mare turned suddenly she pushed the youngster following her towards the darken bank above the water reflected the leaping flames; they jumped into the living waters with the little girl still cling to the mare.

The mare and her son swam away from the shouting men and the devouring flames. C'raw rose above them to search for a point on the opposite bank where they could set hoof onto dry ground and be safe from the hunting humans.

Wherever C'raw looked the chalk banks would not let a horse climb out of the water.

"You will have to swim past that point." C'raw was saying as the mare and her youngster were holding their heads above the cold water. If you can make it there you can get out of the water and rest, the tress are too thick and the over hanging bank will not let you set hoof on safer land, but it will give us time to work out what we should do next."

Two horses found the shallows took their weight and the covering chalk bank took the wind away from their wet coats. They were also glad to have the overhanging bank to hide them and the girl from the humans prowling among the trees above them.

The humans did not take any notice of the watchful bird. They were not even interested in the carcass of a goat that they could have fished out of the water easily with a stick. If they were not hunting for meet, than what were they hunting for? While the humans were about C'raw was not going to try to move those hiding under the bank.

The first light of dawn was creeping over the still water, salt water, fresh water did not make much difference wet was wet! ReeMara was cold, wet and hungry and they were arguing? The mare and the black bird were heatedly disusing how they were going to get out of this uncomfortable hiding place.

A child could scramble through the roots if she stood on the mare's back but to get the youngster and his mare through the over hanging roots was just not possible. The only way out for them was to swim, and that was not the only the problem!

The mare was saying she wanted to get back to her herd, the youngster need to be weaned and the time was coming, when she could enjoy the stallions attentions, she would like to foal again this coming season.

The black bird's argument they should get this human to She-With-The-Sight with all the speed their hooves had!

That did not impress the mare, why should she worry about a crow's problems? He had to remind her, without him she would have ended her life on 'the end off a spear.' and her foal as well!

The decision to swim out into the lagoon had to be made before the new days' light could brighten the water, C'raw was worried if there were still humans about they would be easy to spot in the clear waters mixing with the chalk bed of the lagoon.

C'raw felt in the tips of his wings it was important to get this small girl to She-With-The-Sight.

The humans had not been hunting! They had let too much meat just float by; he should know as he was a crow and crows did not kill their meat, they scavenged seeing meat was not wasted. The humans last night had prowled the woods; they had not been dragging way carcasses. That really puzzled C'raw; it could not all be part of his acceptance trial?

To C'raw's horror the young horse would not get back into the water, not even when C'raw pecked his rump would the youngster move. The girl seemed to be making a decision, was she going to climb out of the chalk dell? She was soothing little colt:

"There is only one way out of here, hooves are not made to crawl their way through chalk banks." her voice was calming and reassuring. "If we just swim over there, I am sure we will find just the right spot to get onto dry land!"

The little girl swam with the young horse, helping him keep his muzzle free of water; the mare let C'raw lead the way to where he had spotted a place where the swimmers could get out of the water. What did trouble him was as they swam the water mixed with the chalk, leaving a white trail! If anyone was looking out over the water would see the white chalk slick with a dark hart. A black sheep would have had more chance of not being spotted in a herd of white sheep!

C'raw knew he could not hurry the swimmers, he could see they were tiring; standing with your fetlocks in cold water all night cannot have been be pleasant. The skies were brightening, the normal early morning flyers had taken to the air. If C'raw had not seen the humans attack the fisher folk with his own eyes he also would have enjoyed the warming thermals, now last nights' storming winds were worrying some other place.

At least the horses looked happier with their hooves on solid land; the mare did not seem to mind the girl on her back. Maybe the girl did not have to learn to ride; she was not disturbing the mare as she trotted over the turf, with the youngster close to her.

They did not stop to take a close look at the smouldering remains of what had been a village.

ReeMara did not want to see any more evidence of the horrors she had seen the day before; it must have been repeated here.

ReeMara thought she had been to this place before, but it had looked so different. ReeMara remembered cling to her mother and hiding her face in the woven wool robe, to shy to look at the other people there; ReeMara wanted to feel her mother's warmth.

It was not her mother's warmth she felt, it was the mare's mixed with the sun. They could not apologise for what had happened. ReeMara buried her head in the mare's mane, not caring if her sobs were heard. The mare made sure her hooves did not jar the little girl, she needed to cry, whatever has happened to her?

No one had spoken since they had left the smouldering village. They were crossing open land C'raw was worrying as he circled above them; the land was too open for his liking, there was nowhere he could hide the two horses and the girl.

Humans had horses when they were hunting or trading with others; could the mare and foal out gallop the human hunters? C'raw was happy to reach the tall beach trees even if the rising hill was making the horses puff.

Now C'raw was worrying that he had not seen any humans! The woodland fringes were where the folk came to collect firewood and they must need firewood after last night storm.

There were normally many humans here but now there were none! C'raw did not feel comfortable even though the forest was where he had been hatched, where he had leant to fly, where his family had lived since the first egg of time.

The beach trees were mixing with taller pines, the ground was clear for the horses to move easily, the twisting brambles did not start to grow thickly until the worn tracks lost their way in the Old Forest.

The Old Forest was where the undergrowth would be too thick for those on the ground to follow.

C'raw had not thought of how was he going to get them to She-With-The-Sight? Her dwelling was only assessable from the air, he had never had to think about it before, he had flown in and out without having to think about bring a human or other ground bound!

C'raw did not have time to think about it, anymore! Three members of his flight were heading towards him through the swaying pines.

C'saw was always sparing with his words; C'raw was not offended with the lack of normal greetings:

"We are to escort you all into She-With-The-Sight presences."

The other two crows dipped their wings in greeting as they turned to lead the way.

"Hay, we can't follow you as fast as you are leading us."

The mare's voice sounded cross from the ground. C'raw fluttered down to land on her withers; the girl was asleep on her back. He would have to wake her before they reached She-With-The-Sight. C'raw had not had to think about finding a ground bound way to her dwelling, when he had been required in her presence he had just landed on the old tree; from this level the forest looked very different.

C'saw was in charge of escorting the strangers, his directions were sparse as his speech, the other two birds had to drop down now and again to check those on the ground were going the right way.

Thick walls of brambles grow out of the ground, weaving the tree's saplings into its mass. ReeMara did not know how they were going to get through it or round it, sleep was still trying to call her back, she would have fallen asleep again had three strange crows not stopped her party and C'raw asked her to drop to the ground.

"Here, take a stick, you will need it to open the way." C'saw's short words were not enough to explain what ReeMara was supposed to do, was she to beat the brambles away?

A crow drop down to explain, ReeMara was to pull to one side an over hanging curtain of straggling strands of the massif bramble plant.

Behind the hang was a tunnel large enough for her to stand, the mare could squeeze into the opening of the tunnel, she had pushed her youngster in behind the little girl. The mare did have a lot to grumble about, the dangling brambles caught in her mane and pulled at her tail and scratched her back. Her grumbles could be heard as their group emerged into the clearing.

The clearing was dominated by a tree, a tree so knolled and twisted, if the top most branches did not have leaves to show it was an oak, it would have been hard to tell what it was or what it could have been.

ReeMara had not seen anything so impressive, she was standing in the way as the mare shook herself free of the last arms of brambles trying to keep hold of her.

"I don't know how I let myself get talked into this!" Was all she was aloud to say; C'saw announced they were to stay there, food would be brought to them and water could be found stored in the roots.

C'raw would have joined his flight brothers, but C'saw told him to stay with those he had brought here. C'raw was surprised and a little hurt when he had to stay down with the land bound.

Berries and grass were delivered as promised, but not words were exchanged, his arrivals were tired just glad to rest and eat the feed that had been given them. Why the crows delivering the food had been told not to talk to them annoyed C'raw; he had been looking forward to at least catching up on what had been going on.

She-With-The-Sight had to wait till the daylight slipped into the night; her pale eyes did not like light. She did not know how old she was or how old the tree was. It was as if she had never left its inner cave; never left its' protecting cover, the sun would only hurt her.

It did not mean she did not know what was going on around her; every Flight of Crows reported to her the land under the mists busyness, for her use.

That it was a child asleep in the curling roots did not fit her plan. If one human was to escape the shadow that had befallen the sea surrounded lands she controlled; she had not thought it would be a child and a girl at that! She was not pleased with the crow that had managed to find the survivor that had slipped away from the men with the long metal arms.

She-With-The-Sight would have preferred one of the crows from an older flight, further along with the doctrine of her thinking; still the youngster was keen to serve!

"My eyes, what do you have to tell of maters in the land ringed in water?"

The old woman was twisted like the roots around her, asked the large crow that had entered the inner space through a hole where a branch had once been.

R'Taw was a large bird his feathers and set of wing told of his leadership and command of all the crow flights.

"The only living human from the peninsula is that young human. The iron clad man has seen to the destruction of every living animal, except for the two horses C'raw used to bring the human here."

R'Taw knew She-With-The-Sight would not be pleased with the little human, too young for whatever she had in mind.

It was not for him to guess at what She-With-The-Sight was planning. As long as her plans kept him in command of the crows and skies over the Islands in the Mist, he would see she got the things she asked for.

"What of the humans living on my land's skirts; has the iron clad man kept his word?"

"He has taken villages not in your argument."
Was all R'Taw could say as She-With-The-Sight was laughing! Any warm hearted sole would have felt its chill deep in their bones, R'Taw could only smile.

"See that the child has what a child needs." She-The-With-Sight seemed to except the child. All hatchlings needed care till they were fledglings. The girl was of an age that She-The-With-Sight could pass on the knowledge the girl would need.

A flight could only be as good as the knowledge of their leader. R'Taw acknowledged her last remark as he swooped out of the old tree's massive trunk; he would see She-The-With-Sight's wishes were carried out, personally.

ReeMara did not know what to make of the nuts had been given her; there did not seem to be a way to open them, but the fruit, she could eat. Thankful for something to eat and drink she rocked her body to sleep in a blanket of leaves, in the base of the tree's roots.

Sleep was still in ReeMara's eyes as a small female crow pecked her to follow her. It soon became clear that she was not going to be able to fly into the tree as the little crow had hoped. The darker hole was too high, and the knurled wood was too smooth for such a small person try to climb. Cam was at loss as to how she was going to get the visitor to She-The-With-Sight!

The little crow watched ReeMara crawling in and out of the roots legs as she and C'raw tried to puzzle away to get the child to She-The-With-Sight. Crows could carry messages but not heavy humans!

The little human solved their problem by exploring the spaces under the great trunk. A visitor did not usually squirm their way into She-The-With-Sight's presence from under the tree's roots!

As ReeMara's eyes got used to the gloom inside the tree, a figure as bent and twisted as the tree its self appeared to move from the inner stem towards her, ReeMara had not expected to see a pair of white misty eyes following her.

ReeMara did not want to trust the root to support her, she did not know if it was her child's mind that saw such a twisted body, or just a trick of the tree's gloomy shadows?

"Child, take my hand." She-The-With-Sight's voice commanded ReeMara to come to her side. ReeMara took the hand to find it was not made of wood, though the skin was white like the eyes; it was as if gnarled bones were taking her hand. ReeMara wanted to pull her hand away but did not want to break the fingers like twigs in the forest.

"Let me look at you." For eyes that did not see she could see into the sole of this child, it surprised her to see the strength behind the little girl's expression. She could use this strength! The child did not look away, nor did she try to take her hand back.

"What did she say to you?" C'raw wanted to know, she had not been away long.

"I have a lot to learn. ReeMara said. "I am, to return to her as the sun sinks tomorrow."

C'raw could only turn to the little crow that held her head on one side as she said:

"We had better see to more mundane needs, if they are going to be staying longer."

C'raw could hear Cam discussing with the mare, the mare did not sound happy at the idea she should let the child suckle.

"Your youngster is ready to stop suckling, to keep enough for this hatchling would not be troublesome, we do not have another possibility to provide for a young human needs.

You have saved her life, the responsibility lies with you to see she thrives!"

Sea Spray was finding it hard to argue with the little crow, she did not like to be told what she had to do. Her youngster decided to allow the human's head rest on his warm flank, as he sleepily rested in the protection of one of the roots, how she could have thought to refuse to help to nourish the human?

The crow had taken to the air promising to see more feed suitable for horses was made available.

Cam returned later with a flight of crows, all carrying well chosen grasses for the horses, berries and nuts for the child. C'raw had the idea to drop the nuts from a high branch, in hope their husk would brake so the girl could eat the flesh inside. ReeMara had to duck away from the dropping nuts while trying to grab their flesh.

From inside the tree it was strange for She-The-With-Sight hear a child's voice.

The days and weeks that followed saw as the sun went down a little human wriggle into She-The-With-Sight's presence. At first she let the girl play with the stones that held the day light, wonder at their difference in colour, enjoy their warmth, peer into their depths, to see spiders on their webs, or leaves and the drop of rain balanced on it.

There were green moss stones like shadows in a green summer forest, and there were stones like mares' milk and stones holding misty and rainy days. Little secrets ReeMara could find to play with in the woods were held in some of the stones that ReeMara was aloud to play with, as she played with them, She-With-The-Sight told her stories.

"There was a great village alder; he was not only the alder of the Village of the Sun but of all the villages in the Isle's of the Mists. He had many horses that run with him in the winds that drive the sun onto the next dawn.

One day his son asked if he could run with the winds and horses as his father did. Proud to see his son wanted to match his father, the alder agreed. But, the horses did not like the extra weight on their backs, they bolted with the wind.

Without the wind the sun was left alone, it burnt the earth and scorched the trees! As the sun did not move the villagers covered their skins with ash from the earth, so the sun could not scorch them. When the horses had been gathered and calmed by soft returning winds; the villagers thought the winds would blow away the scorched earth they had used to protect themselves, but the softer winds could not blow away the earth's colours from the humans' skin.

The humans had as many colours on their skin as the horses had in their flowing coats. The herd stallions carried they pride with their colourful flowing manes and tails, stamped their anger on the newly burnt earth, to protest at having to share colours with the villagers.

With the might of their many hooves the ground broke up and splashed into the sea sending spray of protest to the sun. The sun spat fire at the spray turning it back to the sea, the sun laughing as the spray copied all the colours that had made the stallions so angry.

In the colours were parting gifts from the trees and plants the sun had scorched, animals, birds and insects added their memory to the spray the sun sent back into the sea."

She-With-The-Sight waited as ReeMara turn one of the sun's stones over in her small hands.

"The sun and the sea remember the day the Alder and his son tried to run with the horses of the winds. The sun and the sea like to through the spray holding the memories back onto the beach, to remind the village alders not to let their sons try to ride the wild horses of the winds."

ReeMara remembered the beach before the men had come with the horses. Similar stones to these in her hands, her mother and aunt had been collecting. She as a child had never been aloud to play with them. Now She-The-With-Sight had told her their story, ReeMara could understand why they were not for babies to play with.

ReeMara turned another one over in her hand that looked like it was holding a little of the sea's spray! ReeMara put it into She-The-With-Sight's twisted hand; the old woman was slumped in sleep as ReeMara left to join the others that night.

She-The-With-Sight told ReeMara more about the sun and sea holding little secrets from the trees, animals and birds in their stones. The sun kept some of its light in them and the sea kept them in its depth to throw at the land so the horses would not forget they did not own all the colours.

She-The-With-Sight took a rough stone and she struck it to light a small pile of brush wood, in its flickering light she through a handful of sparkling dust, like the sea throwing some of the stones for the sun onto the beach. A smell filled the hollow tree, telling of plants and flowers! ReeMara did not want to leave She-With-The-Sight alone to enjoy the senses in the fire's dancing light, that night.

ReeMara did not understand how could the stones be so old? They had come from a time long before her folk lived in the Isles of the Mist! That much her mother had told her.

ReeMara rubbed a stone on what was left of her clothing, she set it next to the cold fire of the night before, so she could rubbed another, ReeMara saw a flack of wood ash move towards the stone and then another!

"When you rub a true stone, it can draw little things to it. Folk think a stone that can do that will gather good fortune for them. Good fortune they need in hunting or the kind of good fortune folk like to have when they build a dwelling. If they place a piece under the fundament of the dwelling, they think good fortune well be attracted to the life they lead there."

She-With-The-Sight hand stirred the ashes so ReeMara could see more flakes move towards the stone she was playing with.

ReeMara's days were spent with Sea Spray and her foal Sea Soul, were watched over by C'raw and Cam. In the evenings ReeMara was with the old woman, She-With-The-Sight.

ReeMara liked to play with the stones She-With-The-Sight showed her, she peered into their depths delighted in the creatures captured there, and wondered at the way the fire light played in stones and at all the colours they showed.

She-With-The-Sight would often through chips of the stone into fire, from a bag she kept tucked among the roots of the old tree, their smell mixed with the warmth from the fires embers, it help her twisted body to find comfort as she told ReeMara her stories.

C'raw surprised ReeMara when he said he was going to take them to a beach by the lagoon, were they could enjoy the shallow water. And the grazing was undamaged by the resent season's storms.

ReeMara did not know she and the others had been sent to the lagoon beach, so they would not see the man, who was to visit She-With-The-Sight.

He was different to the folk that lived in the Isles of the Mists. The folk here were fair skinned with flaxen hair and blue eyed. To see a man with dark skin and squarely built, his did not match the pale faces of the island folk. Black leather and iron did not match the folk of the Isles dress; they used woven wool from their sheep and ponies.

When ReeMara saw the man moving alone through the trees she was curious. The man was so different that ReeMara did not move form the tree trunk she had slipped behind, she had not intended to hide from C'raw. He had tried to persuade her from leaving the fun of the beach, C'raw had been so insistent they should go to today.

Not even Sea Soul wanted to retune with her to the strange tree. But ReeMara wanted to play with the fire stones and listen to She-With-The-Sight tell her tales and stories about the stones; they were not like the cold stones she had played with on the small beach.

Thank goodness ReeMara did not move thought C'raw as he was cling to his perch, if the man saw the girl, he would kill her.

C'raw had not been told why he was to bring one of the humans back to the tree. He had not been given orders as to who he was to bring there, only the last he could find. A good flight member did not question his orders.

C'raw was worrying that the two horses would want to follow ReeMara, if they were to make themselves known trotting through the trees while the Iron Man was heading towards the old tree, he did not know how he was going to warn ReeMara!

The Iron Man cut his way through the guarding brambles, his sword flashed in the evening light as ReeMara watch fascinated despite fearing the man. ReeMara saw the Iron Man climb the twisted tree to where the branches would let him drop into the tree's center.

ReeMara wriggled her way into the trees' roots; she did not use the route she used to visit She-With-The-

Sight. There was something she did not like about this man! She did not like him visiting She-With-The-Sight.

C'raw did not like what he saw! It R'Taw knew what was happening he would peck his eyes out, for sure! He could not stop ReeMara crawling into the trunk; he could only perch in the branches opposite to were he knew ReeMara would be watching the Iron Man and She-With-The-Sight.

"You did not keep your word Iron Man. My eyes have been dimmed with time, but I have seen you have destroyed the folk on my islands, without them how are you going to harvest the amber you came here for?" C'raw heard She-With-The-Sight say.

"Old hag, you have not understood my intention. I want to control the amber, stop it leaving the islands. The amber will fetch a better price when there is not much to be had."

The Iron Man's voice sounded false in the restricted space of the tree. It also rang false in C'raw's mind. Had so many humans died, just to please the Iron Man? C'raw had thought the human wanted the horses bred in the islands as they are sure hoofed over rock and sand and in sea foam.

Horses were exchanged for goods with the humans behind the mists. C'raw had known that, he had not known the seas' stones were used in exchange as well.

When the sea allowed the humans to cross to the land beyond the mists, they would take other live stock as will as the sure hoofed horses; salt and wool were also among the things they traded with.

C'raw had enjoyed the human gathering he had attended with his flight. Food had been easy to find and chatter had been exchanged with other Flight of Crows.

She-With-The-Sight voice cut into C'raw thoughts:

"You think if you control the amber you have power over your people."

"You have taken revenge on your people; they did not put you here because you are abhorrent to look at. Their fear of your foresight has made you captive in this tree. Your knowledge has been their down fall. That, and their foolish belief there is magic in the fire stones. I well use their belief to rule the lands on the other side of the mists. The Isles in the Mists will be as you wish; shrouded in magic. They well believe death is all that awaits them on this side of the mists.

This land is yours, held behind the mists. The land beyond is mine to do as I please! Civilisation ruled from the Seven Hills will know of my power!"

The sword returned the light from She-With-The-Sight's fire. ReeMara did not wait to see what he did once it was free to swing over She-With-The-Sight's head. She through a hand full of the stone chips from the bag She-With-The-Sight had shown her into the fire. The fire spat at the figures in the tree.

C'raw talons struck at the Iron Man's eyes as his sword swung towards the twisted woman hart! ReeMara pulled She-With-The-Sight away from its sharp point as C'raw talons caught in the Iron Man's black hair.

Had the Iron Man seen ReeMara? How could he protect the two humans? His cry was answered, other talons were tearing at the air above the Iron Man. Cam pulled ReeMara away from She-With-The-Sight, she shooed her into the safety of the old tree's roots.

Crows were tearing the Iron Man away from She-With-The-Sight; his sword could not control their beating wings. As blood and feathers hissed in the fire's embers ReeMara's voice was lost in the crow's wild cries, then she was held in the silence that was left behind when the Iron Man climbed into the branches above her.

ReeMara had been screaming her words were covered by the wings beating the air above the Iron Man. ReeMara hated his retreating back; her rage did not stop when her arm was held by She-With-The-Sight. ReeMara kicked at the fires red ashes, her anger turned on to She-With-The-Sight.

"He took my brother from my arms, he had killed my people… my mother… he was sent by you?!"

ReeMara sank to the ground tear stained and lost, not able to believe what she had just said. She-With-The-Sight sat slumped opposite her.

ReeMara was unable to speak; her feelings would not let her move, till Cam tried to lead her to Sea Spray. Cam did not knowing what to do with the sobbing child.

"You heard what was said when the Iron Man was here. You well know I had you spared from his and his men's swords." She-With-The-Sight was saying ReeMara did not want to hear what she had to say.

ReeMara had not at first obeyed when she had been summoned into the tree. She had refused to enter She-With-The-Sight's domain up until now.

"I place a command on you; you are to see that the Isles stay hidden behind the mists. If you refuse my command your people well have died for nothing." She-With-The-Sight saw ReeMara shrink away from her.

"You are to take the one thing the Iron Man fears the most, place these in the temple at the hart of the Seven Hills."

She-With-The-Sight place next to ReeMara an amber stone, the stone was like an eye, an eye that seemed to look into your soul with its orange sun rise colour. The next stone She-With-The-Sight placed next to it was a deep red, the deep red of blood. ReeMara's took it in her hand not wanting to look into its depths. The smoky form of a proud horse's head held high with its mane lifting in the unseen wind. Deep in the stone was a milk tooth; like the one Sea Soul had lost on the day they had been to the cove C'raw had insisted they go to. May be that was a twist of a foal's woolly mane mixing with the proud horses flying mane. ReeMara put it down, not wanting to enjoy looking into it. It was not the last stone She-With-The-Sight was to show her.

The green stone's flat side looked as if it had sat in the dying embers of She-With-The-Sight's fire, the deep green stone showed shadows that were like the sun in the trees of a great summer forest; such invitingly cool shadows in a summer's heat, and their leaves offering shelter from a summer shower.

ReeMara did not know what a temple was, nor where the City of the Seven Hills was. Into that twisted woman face ReeMara did not want to look, though she could feel She-With-The-Sight was trying to draw her to look at her:

"Their lives have been taken so the Isles will be hidden in the sea's mist. Should you fail, you will have wasted their lives and lose the Islands its secrecy."

ReeMara was trying to understand what She-With-The-Sight wanted, what she was saying. Her child mind was clouded by the thoughts that were holding her. Her

mother's face was flickering in She-With-The-Sight's
fire, then the face of her brother, her father and aunt the
other folk in her village. She was to be made responsible
for their lives being wasted? Why did the island have to
be secret?

Sea Spray did not know what to do with the sobbing
child, she was sobbing as if her hart would brake, Cam
insisted ReeMara scramble onto the mare's back. Cam
told Spray to take ReeMara out into the forest, she hoped
the sun light and shadows would calm the little human. It
would be hard enough for anyone to have heard what
ReeMara had just heard!
If Cam's fledglings had been whipped out of the sky, she
did not think she would be consolable.
Sea Spray was glad to feel ReeMara relax as she was
lulled to sleep as they moved through the trees, Cam did
not leave her watchful position on Spray's crest.
C'raw was gliding above them, Soul did not really
understand what was going on no one seemed to want to
answer his questions. Not even when they had stopped
did anyone want to talk. Sea Spray encouraged Soul to
keep ReeMara warm; her little body still shook with
passion when they rolled her closer to Soul's comforting
body.

C'raw was concerned he had not received any
instructions!
What were they supposed to do now? ReeMara would not
go back to the tree. One day had rolled into another and
there had not been a word sent from the tree. C'raw could
see the massif tree from the hill top they had made their

camp. He had not seen any of his flight even start to fly in this direction, he was more than puzzled.

The sun was warm and the winds kind, ReeMara was enjoying being away from the tree. She and Soul were running in and out of the trees shadows. Neither crow had heard her laugh since she had left the tree, but to see her run freely with Soul was a good sign and Cam was happy now the little girl was eating again.

Summer turned into autumn, the trees took on some of colours that ReeMara had seen in the stones. Storms started to announce winter was on it way. The two crows decided the hill was not a place a human could stay the winter's season. A more suitable place had to be found. Sea Spray was all in favour of the cave the birds had found, it at least offered shelter from the harsh wind.

If the Iron Man was still in the Isles to let ReeMara start a fire would not wise but in the cave a small fire would warm the child; and ReeMara could be kept busy collecting wood!

Cam was not in agreement with C'raw plan to take ReeMara to the remains of a humans' dwelling. She did not want to see the little human so upset again. But, as C'raw pointed out the little human need things the woods could not provide. For instance the rag of cloth did not reach her knees any more! To sleep with a foal for warmth at night was one thing; a human cover would help her on a cold winter's day.

She-With-The-Sight had Flights of Crows to collect
fire wood for her and the berries and nuts she lived from
were collected by them as well. The two crows and two
horses and a child had a cave for shelter, it was better
than nothing as Cam liked to say.

The next weeks were spent in gathering nuts and
wood. The trip to the human dwelling did not upset
ReeMara as much as Cam had feared. The things that
ReeMara brought back with her would make her daily
life more comfortable.

The wooden bowl meant there was water in the cave
and soft skins were drawn together, held nuts the child
could eat. ReeMara had insisted she would gather arms
full of dried grass, at first they had thought it was to make
a bed, as Soul was always being shooed away from the
pile ReeMara had made:

"You well be sorry when the snow comes if you eat all
this now!" Soul's answer was to turn his rump to her and
skip away before she could slap his bottom! Sea Spray
knew what ReeMara was trying to do.

The little human looked funny raped in a sheep's skin
and the woven garment she had found amongst the
humans' things; that had not been burnt by the attacker's
fires. Bits of sea rope and leather thongs hang in the cave;
Sea Soul did not see how ReeMara would find them
useful. Unlike the flint fire stones, they made lighting the
fire with cold little hands easer as did the dried twigs the
crows had taken upon themselves to bring with them
every time they came back to the cave.

Cam had worried that the cave could give them away
to the Iron Man with its piles of twigs and piled grass and
the bags of nuts stored in every corner.

A bit of fishing net, ReeMara had found on the beach
was stretched at the mouth of the cave; she had woven

ivy and bracken into it. Soul was not as clever as Sea
Spray when trying to slip past it. The net had got caught
over his ear, he was seen trying to shack it off; it would
not let go not even when he bucked strongly. Those
watching had to wonder why he was cantering around
and around, if a tree had not been in the way he still
would be!

A lower branch got caught up in the fun and snatched
the net and its decorations out of Soul's face. As he was
trying to thank the tree for enabling him to see again, he
fell over his own hooves landed in an untied a hep!

The hep stood up shook himself free of the reddish
coloured leaves sticking to him. Soul found the others
laughing too much. He kicked at the net that had tried to
ride him, before he decided to go and drink at the stream;
he hoped the others would stop laughing soon.

The sea's white foam mixed with the flakes falling
from the dark snow laden sky. It was quite on the beach
they only heard the wind playing with the lapping water.
It was as if the anger in the storm from the night before
was forgotten, if it was not for the amber stones lying on
the cleaned sands, it would have been.

ReeMara stooped to take into her hand one she spotted
caught in sea weed; it reminded her of the summers' sun.
Sea Soul warm muzzle puffed hot air at the back of her
neck. Soul was trying to tell her it was time to play; his
hooves were splashing the shallow water at her.

C'raw and Cam looked up from feeding from the
remands of a fish the storm had thrown out of the water.
They could only smile as the two youngster race along
the beach.

Sea Spray had to agree with the two crows, Soul had
grown and ReeMara had as well! Sea Spray could see

ReeMara's bright mane mingle with Soul's dark mane as they ran together.

Before ReeMara could ride on her son's back they would both have to grow; persuading them to eat was not difficult, ReeMara like to put the fish she found into the embers of the fire in their cave. Soul found the seaweed Cam suggested to try to his liking. In fact the dried grass ReeMara had collected for the horses was only used if the winter storms made going outside the cave imposable!

When they could not go outside their cave ReeMara would play with the stones she had found on the beach, they were like many, She-With-The Sight had shown her.

It did not worry her, no one had heard from the old woman, in fact she did not think it was strange, but not to have heard from the Flight of Crows, C'raw and Cam did.

C'raw had flown back to the tree only to be told to return to the group at the cave and wait till She-With-The-Sight had instructions for him.

Of the Iron Man and his men the instruction C'raw had been given, was to see those in his command did not wander to where the human's boats were sheltering from the winter's worst weather.

Had the humans left the amber the Isle folk had stored in their dwellings, they would have been able to drive the horses they had gathered over the causeway. But their greed for the gathered amber had cost them their chance to cross over to the main land till the viscous winter storms past.

C'raw had seen the camp below him! If Cam had been had been assigned to the Iron Man's men, the men would have faired better and the penned in horses would not have hungered. The pair of birds was glad they were to look after their ReeMara. Both birds enjoyed looking after their group now playing on the beach.

Sea Spray watched as the snow, whiten the path they had made to their cave, when Soul appeared among the trees with ReeMara close behind him Cam and C'raw were not any where to be seen.

ReeMara took a branch and mixed Soul and her tracks into the snow, Sea Spray did not need to tell them to duck quickly into the cave.

C'raw was frantic; the humans were too close to the cave!

Cam did the only thing she could think of, she dropped the half eaten fish into the pack of hounds savaging among the trees above the cave. If it had not been snowing the men behind the hounds would have seen the track to the cave.

C'raw had turned away from the hounds he was preparing to swoop low over them in hope they would chase him. The fish Cam had dropped was distracting them, their hungry mouths were showing fangs. The fight that broke out between the hounds stopped C'raw from trying his plan. Men were shouting trying to stop the hounds from tearing themselves apart.

A horn sounded, the men whipped the hounds apart and sent them towards the horn sounding through the falling white storm. C'raw and Cam rested on an oak as the sound of danger faded into the snow covered forest.

If the sound of the horn had led them over the cave the men's whips would not have been for their hounds. The two crows decided not to think about what could have happened; it was now safe to fly back to the others.

Though the snow fell thickly for the next few days no one grumbled at having to stay in the cave. If the Iron

Man's men were hunting for food, they were going to have to be very careful.

C'raw and Cam decided to keep an eye on the men camping not far away from the bobbing boats in the bay. In the trees above the men's camp one of the two birds could perch when on watch.

The men were going out every day the weather aloud them. From what the crows could see there were not enough provisions stored for man or live stock to take them through the raging storms. Cam was glad they had managed to collect the stores they had.

The fish they had found on the beach packed in snow soon became as stiff as the ice ReeMara broke from bank of the stream that was for every trying to run into the sea, could be melted in their cave by ReeMara's fire for them to drink.

C'raw and Cam could not fly over to the cove where the Iron Man and his men were, as the storm did not let any bird get safely in the air nor could any sane horse wander in the blinding snow, they all had to be content with sheltering in the cave.

ReeMara did not need to be told not to go outside even if Soul did. Soul was not happy playing with the amber ReeMara had found, though he was happy to comb the beach with her. ReeMara could always be persuaded to gallop with him, if those crows would let them, they were always stopping their fun and shooing them back to their cave.

C'raw came one day to say the men had eaten the last of sheep they had stolen from the isle' folk, Cam had looked worried; she had said it would be safer not to go out today. Soul and ReeMara had both grumbled Soul knew ReeMara did not feel like playing with her stones today, he had been so looking forward to combing the beach with ReeMara.

When they heard a hound barking everyone stopped grumbling. Everyone held their breath; it was not long till the bark was answered by another.

A ferret's face appeared under the fishing net holding the snow and chilling wind at bay, dark eyes blinking in the surprising light from ReeMara's embers. Sea Spray tried to hoof the little intruder away, but it was too quick, it ran into the wool rap ReeMara was wearing. If ReeMara had not been so surprised she would have giggled as the little intruder tickled!

A hound barking stopped anyone moving, their protecting cave was now not allowing them escape from the hounds sniffing at the entrance.

ReeMara forgot the little intruder in her rap; she kicked hot ashes at the mussel of a hound trying to enter their cave. Its howling complaint rang round the cave, but it backed away. Scorched by the embers the hound's second howl was suddenly ended as the snow above the cave entrance slid down forcing the hound and the one close behind it to back away.

From inside the cave they could not know the bank had let all its frozen snow cover the entrance; they could hear muffled human voices:

"Dam hound, going after a ferret!" a hound yelped, had it been kicked?

"Pull the bitch out of the snow." An angry voice ordered.

"We lose, any animal, we will wish we were one!"

"I don't want to feel his wipe, or his sword."

"It won't be his wipe or sword you will have to fear, it will be, mine!"

No one could hear anything it was as if the outside world had been cut off! The silence in the cave was broken by the squeak of the ferret in ReeMara's clothing.

A neat face with bright eyes wriggled to the floor of the cave. The ferret had black points over a sleek red coat and her red tail was extenuated by long black hairs.

ReeMara's fingers could not help but smooth the red fir; the little ferret arched her back with pleasure. The others did not know what to make of the little intruder.

"That was close!" said the little intruder. "I thought they would get me. Good thing I popped in here!"

"You could have given us away!" Soul could not help pointing out.

"How are we supposed to get out of here? Now all this snow had blocked entrance!" Sea Spray tried to muzzle the snow wall away. Before she could put her shoulder against the wall, the sound of a horn reminded everyone the Iron Man's men were still in the forest!

"We well have to wait till we are sure they have gone." C'raw was just as concerned as to how they were going to get through the fallen snow.

"Don't talk the hounds may hear us!" Cam said softly.

"What are we going to do?" ReeMara asked she did not want have to wait to talk with someone new.

The day must have ended it was so still outside the cave, they heard an owl hoot sometime later but any sound of the Iron Man's men did not reach them.

Cam was the first to ask the ferret her name.

"Piper!" said the ferret, "Why are you hiding in here, the snow was not falling that thickly?"

"It is a long tale, though time does not seem to be our problem right now!" Sea Spray was just as interested to know what a red ferret named Piper, was doing running around in the snow when most ferrets had changed their coats for ones that matched the white country side?

"My red coat is why I am here; the others thought it was a good idea to play on the other side of the bank opposite to the entrance to our hole. It is ok when you are their colour but I do stand out!

When the hounds from the hunters found their way to where we were playing, it was my coat that caught their eye. Not that anyone tried to distract them; they left it to me to draw the hounds away."

It sounded a tall story to C'raw, but as there wasn't another ferret about to ask, he had to let Piper's story stand as it was. It did not mean he would not be keeping an eye on this red furry thing amusing ReeMara. A ferret was a ferret even if it was hanging upside down from the roof, she was trying to pull Soal's ear as he dozed.

ReeMara found Piper's game funny but had to hold her self to stop herself from laughing as Soul first twitched one ear and then the next. When Piper's tail brushed through Soul's whiskers making him sneeze, ReeMara was not able to hold in the giggle any longer, not when the lose snow near the entrance was blown into air at the command of Soul's sneeze, covering everyone!

As it happened, Piper's game with Soul made the horses stamping their hooves as they were trying to shake the lose power snow from their coats, loosened the snow blocking their way, letting it sink enough to allow a horse of Sea Spray's size slip out, though it was decided to stay in the cave till the following morning.

That their scent in the cave had not attracted the hounds was surprising the crows remarked and added; to make tracks for humans and hounds to follow; was not worth risking.

No one was board waiting for the dawn, as Piper told them about her life with her siblings.

Everything had been normal till the time when the others pointed out Piper had not changed her coat for the same winter white coats as the ones they had.

Piper said it was one thing to be different with a bright coat, but it was another when the coat stuck out so much you caught the eye of other animals that thought you were only interesting as convenient snack!

Soul was head to ask, when would Piper be running back to her friends? But ReeMara would not hear of it and insisted Piper stay with them; she liked having Piper's warm little body next to hers. Soul was still not so sure when they all settled down to sleep, ReeMara's arm was over his shoulder as usual but in her other arm a ferret slept.

When the season through snow over the land and the wind blew the cave kept them warm and safe. When the frost made everything stiff they could collect water from condensation at the mouth of the cave. ReeMara's fire could melt enough ice for them all to drink and as its burning embers kept the cave warm.

When the sun shone on the white world they ran along the beach! They gathered all, the sea weed they could carry and any fish they could find.

The crows found they could open the shells ReeMara had said she liked to eat the flesh inside and they found the meet to their liking as well. When the tide was low they would collect as many as they could bring back to the cave and pack into the frosted snow, for the days they could not leave the cave.

ReeMara found if you dropped them into bubbling water heated by the fire she did not have to ask the crows to open the shells for her and the water changed into a soup she could share with Piper.

Piper made her self useful; she was a clever hunter despite her bright coat. Mice and other rodents she would often bring to share with the crows, she helped gather fish, see ReeMara was warm when her raps were not able to keep the wind from trying to freeze her.

Soul and Sea Spray found living in the cave had comforts to offer them. Without their herd to run with, to hide from the winds cold fingers, to group together for warmth, the cave was a good alternative. They could also contribute to the welfare of their group. Their bodies were enough to see the cave did not chill when ReeMara's fire was slow to respond after it had burnt down when they had been salvaging for too long on the beach.

C'raw and Cam were always on the look out for any of the hounds the humans used to try to hunt for their meals.

There was a sunny lull in the winter's weather when C'raw decided to fly on a higher thermal with the idea to see where the Iron Man and his men were.

A question that had been worrying Cam and C'raw, was, why had the hounds not been a greater problem than they had been?

That question was answered when C'raw saw how the men tied the hounds to stakes in the snow. The wolves found this idea saved them the trouble of hunting for their meat! The humans did not like having wolves around their camp put men to watch over their hounds. The wolves did not mind which meat they had to eat, they took any man that was not watchful and a hound as well!

Cam was shocked, but as C'raw pointed out while the humans were occupied with hungry wolves, they would not be hunting in the woods by their cave.

The humans were not doing as well as Cam and C'raw charges were. C'raw was glad they were not his responsibility! All the humans had to do was take their hounds into their sleeping shelters with them, for the hounds comfort as will as theirs and set fires around camp, most of the folk knew, wolves did not like fires.

ReeMara did not let herself think of She-With-The-Sight, not even when she played with the amber she had herself colleted from the beach. It was C'raw that could not forget the old woman in the tree. He had been brought up to follow the Flight's orders. The order to look after the child had not been cancelled nor had Cam received other orders, she was to see to the little human's welfare.

How C'raw was supposed to persuade ReeMara to do anything She-With-The-Sight wanted, he did not know.

Spring would come as soon the storms stopped blowing; then they would be free to wander away from the cave. What the humans had planed to do when the spring came was not all together clear to a crow. But when the sea was calmer they could drive what was left of the live stock they had stolen over the causeway to the land beyond the mists.

What C'raw was not expecting, was the humans would try to leave before the causeway was safe to use! Nor had C'raw expect to find a small bag of ground amber dust lying beside three sea stones that had been left on a scrap of soft wool outside their cave.

The sunlight and green shadow stone and the red fire of the horse, and the golden eye in its amber coloured stone, looked up at ReeMara from her hand.

ReeMara was too quite for Cam's liking, her face too pale! Soul and Piper could not brake into ReeMara's thoughts.

ReeMara put the stones and a little bag on a ledge in the cave. Soul and Piper had to hurry to keep up with her as she urged Sea Spray to test her hooves in the sea freed from the frosting ice.

The humans started to roam the woods again, the humans were looking for the animals that had not stayed to enjoy the humans company in the storm's seasons. The humans could not burn the forest as they had before, it was to wet with the winter's frost! C'raw and Cam saw the humans digging deep pits to catch earth bound animals.

Trying to keep ReeMara and the horses from roaming among the sparking trees was proving a nightmare for the two birds. Had the humans been more careful when camouflaging their pits in the still frozen ground, C'raw and Cam would have had to help more animals escape before the humans came to take away their captives. Piper's sharp eyes helped the horses avoided the human traps, but she could not sooth the crows' nerves.

C'saw was waiting for C'raw to make his usual aerial surveillance. C'raw had been the right choice for this mission; he had paid attention to his flight training. As C'raw and Cam had managed to get the little human through the winter season storms the two crows were the right members of his flight to send on the next part of She-With-The-Sights plan.

'You are to see the human places the amber under the human's temple in the city on the seven hills.' Were the words she had used, C'saw was to command C'raw to see ReeMara carried out She-With-The-Sight's orders. How C'raw was supposed to undertake such a command? He did not even know what a temple was let alone how to describe a human temple to a junior member of his flight.

Maybe the little human was not such a strange choice as C'saw had first thought. Humans always find humans, they gather together as flights of crows do. The temple could be like the place where She-With-The-Sight lived.

She-With-The-Sight had ruled over the folk before the Iron Man had destroyed all but one. She commanded the great Flight of Crows. She ruled the Isles in the Mists and it was she that would command the mists to rise to hide the isles from any human that wandered on the main land.

As She-With-The-Sight did not want humans on the Isles of the Mists, the stories the men with the Iron Man would have to tell would scare most homely folk. Sending the wolves to worry the humans' camp was a clever plan! Scattering the animals; in his opinion the humans had stolen, had distracted the humans from finding the little human and her companions.

It was not among his duties to ponder why She-With-The-Sight had made such orders all he had to do was give C'raw his orders, before he took the tree's younger flight of crows for training in spring's fresh thermals.

C'raw flew towards his flight commander not knowing what was wanted of him. To receive the orders to accompany ReeMara to the City of the Seven Hills was not what he had expected to hear!

C'saw knew he did not have the answers to any of the questions C'raw had.

The problem concerning C'raw the most how was he could persuade a little human to leave the Isles of the Mist? Would the horses carry her? At least Cam would support him! C'saw did not have orders for Cam to leave ReeMara.

"Those are the orders of She-With-The-Sight." C'saw was saying but the look on his face was not one of confidence:

"Of all my fight you are the one crow I can entrust with this kind of mission." He wanted to tell C'raw he was the only member in his command that had enough imagination to attempt to survive beyond the shrouding mists.

As the crow before him head hung in thought, the flight commander did not want to add to C'raw's dilemma by reminding him, if he did not follow the directions She-With-The-Sight had given him, he would be driven from his flight.

The two crows circled around each other each dipped a wing in salute. An upward thermal took the Flight leader away, leaving C'raw to watch as his commander became a dot in the sky.

Sea Spray had realised that she and Sea Soul were the only horses on this island! The Iron Man's men had seen to the rounding up of all the herds of horses on the Isles of the Mist.

Not all had survived the harsh winter in the keeping of the Iron Man's men. Other livestock had been greatly reduced in their numbers, just to feed the needs of men and their hungry hounds had caught many of the deer the wolves relied on in the cold season. Sea Spray noted.

Now the season was turning towards spring, a mare's thoughts turned to other things, but the herds had been taken away along with their stallions, Sea Spray realised how alone she was. For the time being she did not have to worry about Soul, but she knew the coming season would not see the herds and their stallions returning, as the humans had taken them away. The remaining deer had the season to breed kids to insure their survival here.

C'raw had confided with Sea Spray, the orders his superior had given him, from what he had said it all sounded a mission without a stable hoof, though it did offer her the chance to change her and Soul's isolated situation. It seemed sensible to her to help C'raw. But, if the little human did not want to go she did not see how they could make her! Watching Soul and ReeMara playing on the sweeping beach with Piper, Sea Spray did not see how they were going to persuade ReeMara to leave.

"You know Soul we could cross the causeway, not like the Iron Man's men did, we could stay dry! All we have to do is watch the tides!" ReeMara sounded excited.

"You want to gallop along that beach?" said Piper she was standing on Soul's withers staring over the waters to the shore on the other side.

"If I stay here I will go mad. She is still in the tree I want to get as far away from her as I can. If this island becomes a secret then no one can disturb their memories."

Piper looked at ReeMara; that was a funny thing for a pup to say! Soul did not want to be the one to tell her what had happened to ReeMara. Soul could feel ReeMara's was not going to say anything so Soul decided to tell Piper what had happened to ReeMara's folk.

"I thought I had had it bad!" Piper said under her breath, "I thought it was not being white like them was the reason they through me out but…." Piper could not say anymore.

C'raw and Cam were flying towards them at an alarming speed, they chased ReeMara and Soul into the undergrowth as two men rode through the shallow waters of the causeway.

From the cover of the undergrowth Piper could see the horsemen head towards the forest she wandered why they were carrying bundles of twigs tied to the horses' saddles! Why are they travelling so fast?

"Thank goodness their horses are galloping or they would have seen us, for sure!" Cam breathed into ReeMara's ear. C'raw had flown off to see Sea Spray did not come looking for them and get into the path of the two horsemen.

C'raw realised they were heading towards the tree She-With-The-Sight had as her own! The Flight was in the air wings were beating the air. The men were cutting their way through the tangle of brambles surrounding the massif twisted tree; their swords did not let the crows to stop them.

S'caw saw C'raw, to C'raw surprise S'caw ordered him to return to his charges! C'raw turned to comply too the order, as he rose to take a thermal he saw C'saw dive into the tree. He hesitated uncertain what to do, serving the She-With-The-Sight was the very bases of his training as a flight member, but he had just been commanded to be on his way!?

One of the two men was trying to climb into the tree, the crows swiped past his head stopping him from finding safe hand holds to scale the bark.

C'raw saw the second man set the twigs a light the flames sprang into life licking at the knurled bark.

C'raw had to swerve to avoid a formed winged flight, he thought they were heading for the man fanning the flames; to his horror they were aiming at him!

S'caw repeated the order he had give C'raw earlier. The Flight flying behind S'caw hissed at him as the flames around the tree grew higher!

Black beaks and beating wings stood out above the flames as C'raw turned to comply with his enforced orders, his heart was torn he knew he could not turn back. He did not see the humans that had started the fire were searching for their horses.

The horses had not waited to see what the humans had intended to do once they had disappeared into the thick brambles. The one idea the horses had was to get back to their heard. The horses of their herd and their humans were travailing away from this cursed island with its swirling mists.

When the smell of smoke reach their nostrils the two horses picked up speed, flashing through the shadows the spring sun made in the woodland.

C'raw decided to drop down in front of them to shock them into stopping; they might be able to tell him how the land lay over the water as they were not from the herds of horses that had run on this island.

At first the horses did not want to answer C'raw's questions they would have liked to canter off had C'raw not blocked their way.

"It is not everyday humans come to this place to burn a great tree nor is it normal to see the horses that brought them hoof away without their riders! You could explain what you are doing."

The first horse did not like to be held up by a crow!

"Bramble, tell that bird to get out of our way!"

"You tell him!"

"You are a season older than me."

"You don't use that excuse when it comes to chatting to the mares!"

"I have more experience than you have…"

"Well, use your experience now and tell that bird to get out of our way!"

"Cane! You tell him!"

"I don't intend to get out of your way till you have answered my questions." C'raw was getting annoyed with these two chaps. They stood there looking at him like fledglings not sure what they should be doing:

"You have left your humans to fend for them selves?"

"Our services were no longer required." said Cane, "They did not tie us to a tree."

"Did not tell us to wait!" said Bramble, "They did not give us any orders."

"You have your saddles and bridals on!?" C'raw pointed out. They did not seem to have an answer for that comment, and as they did not look like they were going to reply, C'raw decided to lead them to where ReeMara and the others were.

The smell of smoke was on the breeze as he escorted the two runaways to the hill where the winter cave was, what he did not expect was to see ReeMara urging Sea Spray to speed up the hill towards him.

ReeMara was holding on to all the possessions she had kept in the cave. Piper was clinging to Sea Spray's mane unable to help ReeMara hold on the flapping cloth that she was trying to gather together.

C'raw did not waste time to ask what was on the two horses' minds; he encouraged them to pick up speed. Now there were four horses moving fast towards the causeway. The strip of sand offered a dry passage to the mainland as ReeMara urging everyone forwards. Cam and C'raw did not have time to wander at ReeMara's urgency they were flying above the group worrying, there would be humans watching for two horses and their riders, they could see ReeMara and her friends!

S'caw had said ReeMara leaving the Isles of the Mists should go unnoticed! Now a human was starting to cross the sand causeway, Cam drew C'raw's attention to the human. C'raw could not let the human reach the mainland, how was a crow supposed to stop a human, scratch his eyes out?

Cam and C'raw circled round the human, his sword kept them away from his head. He could not move forwards with the furriery of the birds blocking him.

The horses had left him and his companion; his companion had been blinded by more crows than bothering him now!
If there had not been so many grabbing talons flying over the flames they had set, he would have been able to help his floundering companion. A companion he could use now with these beasts flapping at him, their sharp talons were pushing him into the water lapping at his feet, the sand started to swallow him.

C' raw would have stayed to watch the man sink but Cam was climbing to catch up the others. He did not feel responsible for the human foundering in the returning sea. What they had to do now was see the horses and their passengers got to the mainland.

A horn sounded C'raw was near panic; that meant humans were about! They would be able to see the small human on Sea Spray's back form wherever they were in the trees on the cliff! He could not see any humans on the long beach, only the sea joining together over the causeway.

The sand on the beach did not show any prints from man or horse, only the paten the water had made greeted the group.

C'raw flew ahead to see if he could find away up the crumbling cliff, the cliff's steepness C'raw knew the horses would not be able to scramble up, another way had to be found.

"If I were you, I would go the other way to where the cliff allows horses like us to trot up."

"Quite right Bramble, I could not have said that better my self." Cain said agreeing with Bramble.

"Why did you not say before you know the way up from the beach!" C'raw was irradiated they had not spoken up before, letting him fly around wasting time. Cam landed on Bramble's back:

"If you would be so kind to lead the way, we would be happy to follow you."

Bramble was pleased to be asked turned to lead the way, he and Corn had used before.

Once up on the cliff ReeMara could see the sea had covered the causeway it was as if it had never been away.

Sea Spray stopped a little way along the cliff her eye was held by the curling smoke hanging above the isle they had left.

ReeMara had seen the smoke too. The tree was burning, throwing sparks above it; they dominated the sky line till the sparks and smoke were swallowed by the sea's mist as it rose to cover the island.

The mist swallowed all ReeMara had known is if it did not care, it was as if the mist was laughing at her, she thought she could hear the sound of She-With-The-Sight laughing.

ReeMara did not want to look again, if Piper had not remarked, she thought she had caught the sound of someone laughing as they had started to move along the tree covered cliff ReeMara would not have looked back to see the tree's black shape lose its power to the mounting mists.

The mists shrouded the forest as well as the Isles they had left. The sound of water dripping from the leaves could be heard among the sound of the horses' hooves on the forest floor.

No one wanted to travel through the dark mist swirling in with the night, even if Cane and Bramble seemed to know how to find their way through the forest's trees.

To make a camp for the night was all they could do; Cam and C'raw would not let ReeMara make a fire, the thick mist took way the night's sounds but would not hide a camp fire in its folds.

The crows worried about the Iron Man's men, if Cain and Bramble had been sent with the two humans to burn the tree and its inhabitant, might mean the Iran Man and his men would not have travelled so far ahead that the two men could not catch them up.

When C'raw training with his flight members it had been a rule, to be at all times in contact with his leader, he could remember his leader's crow reminding the younger flight. 'Scavenging in the forest was an advantage of the individual, not for the good of the whole flight.'

Cam was worrying also; she had studied the herbs that relieved the ailments the Flights could suffer, she had assisted in looking after She-With-The-Sight. Cam had learnt to understand the twisted old human needs but this little human had other needs. What ReeMara needed now was to sleep as did the horses. It would have to be the crows that would keep watch this night; Cam did not trust the ferret to stay awake.

The two crows were chilled in the damp of the fog slowly sinking to make way for the new dawn. Humans' heads and shoulders showed above ears and heads of horses the crows did not know. Cam dropped down to warn her wards not to move, keep as low as possible; she did notice the ferret was fast asleep next to ReeMara. To wake the ferret could mean her chatting would give them away.

C'raw did not dare to move from his branch as the humans and their horses passed under him, the cold of the morning slowed the pace of the humans and their horses. It was not to the liking of the commanding Iron Man, his voice whipped them as hard as a leather wipe could:

"It dose not serve me to hold back any longer. To wait for two stupid men." he said under his breath. "Too much time has been wasted already!"

"I only wish to return to the men at the winter camp, we have as you say, been away too long. We did not plan to be held up by the winter's harsh season."

"She had to be destroyed?" asked another voice from in the fog.

"She did not say, she wished to 'live', hidden by her mists. Just, she wanted to have the Isle in the Mists to herself. To keep her alive to take control of the amber again would not serve my planes."

The voice of the Iron Man laughed before he said:

"Control the amber, control the belief of the people. Control the people; take the riches and rule the land!"

C'raw did not fully understand what he had just over heard the laughing men say! But he knew he could not ignore the words the humans had said. He had to repeat them to the group hidden below him.

"We have to know what the Iron Man is up to! We do not want to be caught in his way. ReeMara has a lot of amber with her."

Cam could not help but agree with C'raw's opinion; ReeMara was playing with some now, and Cam had not forgotten She-With-The-Sight had placed strange demands upon the little human.

To take away fledglings protectors had been a crime in the flight where Cam had been hatched. Cam had not understood what She-With-The-Sight had been planning; the pain of loss was still to be seen in their little human.

C'raw was right; it is not what She-With-The-Sight had planned they need to know now, but what the Iron Man was going to do in this forest. Just how they were going to find out?

"Piper!? You have been lessening to what we have been saying!" Cam was taken by surprise when the ferret appeared on the perch the two crows were using.

"I have just been hunting I have a good catch, is anyone hungry? There are humans camped no far from here Sea Spray knows not to let anyone make a noise. If you want to know what they are planning, we well have to get as close as we can!"

The two did not like to be told what to do by a ferret, but they had to agree she was right, trying to guess what the humans were planning while they sat in a tree, would not provide any answers.

Birds flying over a human's camp did not look suspicious nor did a ferret, hunting among the humans' belongings.

Piper noticed the humans provisions were low, good thing the season was providing for the live stock they had with them. There were swords and knives and shields, leather bags for water, there was one that smelt so strong it made Piper's head swim. One of the bags must have held dried meet, but it had nuts in it now.

The humans did not seem to as clever as the group Piper was with. Providing for one's self was an art Piper had learnt long a go, good thing those two stuck up crows had enjoyed the mice she had brought them for their breakfast.

Piper did not mind looking after ReeMara; in fact it was a lot more fun than living among her siblings and the idea of travelling was to her liking too, she was sure the Isles they had just left were not the most interesting of places.

Someone was coming so Piper slipped into a bag, she was not expecting to be lifted into the air and swung onto a human's back.

"Ah, Sim we well need more water than that to day. They will want to move on to Crossover as soon as possible. If I have to eat another feathered bird I well cry."

"A mug of ale is all I want; mind you I could eat a leg of a lamb straight from the grill. Hope they know where they are going, they don't ask for my advice. I would go south to the river then east to Crossover."

"They were not born here to know that Sim, unlike us, but we have sworn to do as they command. For the riches we shall receive I don't mind wandering round these woods."

"You did not complain when you were eating from the plundered live stock. The riches we are owed will also be paid in whatever livestock is still standing."

"It was a cold season, was there another choice? The stores we had could not take us through such a winter."

Piper was dropped to the ground with the other bags; rough hands sank the leather bags into the cold water of the stream.

Piper was thankful to slip away as the two men's attention was taken by the third human grumbling at the two men's slowness.

If the place Crossover, was where a river ran over a shallow bed of stones that was easy to ford by the horses and ReeMara. If it was the place the men collecting water for their journey had been talking about, it had only taken their group most of the day's light to find. They might have found it sooner if Bramble and Corn had not argued about which of the crisscrossing tracks they should take.

ReeMara wanted to play in its running water her little hands splashed water at everyone. Soul's hooves were also involved in the game of sending water everywhere in the evening sun. Cam did notice ReeMara did smell a lot nicer after her dip, maybe the little human need to wash more often. It would not hurt her, now the days were getting warmer.

Cain and Bramble were drawn into ReeMara's and Soul's game, Sea Spray watched with Piper from the river bank. Piper did not want to bath again; cold water was not for her, even if it was fresh unlike the stale water lingering in the leather bag.

The sun invited the group to dry themselves on the hillside above the river, just as well as everything they had with them was wet! ReeMara took of the saddle pads from Corn and Bramble's backs, their bridles had been used in other ways long ago. The saddle pads had been useful, Cam had used one to make sleeping for ReeMara more comfortable when the ground was hard and the other ReeMara had tied her belongings to.

As they lay in the morning's helpful sun Cam noticed ReeMara had a little bundle of cloth on a leather thong tied round her neck. Cam did not have to think which stones ReeMara had in it. Cam could only shake her head and feel her heart cry. To think a little fledgling was being made to see her family did not died in vain. Fly out into an unknown world without enough experience to look after her self.

If it had not been against her oath of elegance to her Flight she would have liked to scratch the twisted human that had done this to this little child.

The horses had to press themselves into the bushes' shadows and ReeMara with Piper crawled under them as the crow watching from the sky warned humans were coming towards the Crossover.

Simple landsmen herding sheep appeared on the way to the running water. Piper was not expecting to see the men she had seen in the Iron Man's camp ride the other humans down! They slaughtered them like they would slaughter the sheep they drove. The sheep's blood did not join the human's in the river, they were rounded up and driven to join the livestock they all ready had. Humans usually scream war cries but this had taken place with out such cries, only their swords had flashed warnings in the sun's light.

ReeMara drew Piper close to her; Piper could feel ReeMara's body stiffen. Piper had been told what had happened to the little human. As a hunter herself, Piper had been shocked by the way the humans had taken the livestock. To swop some of the feathered foul they had hanging from their saddle pads would have acquired the fresh meat they wanted. That was the way the humans on the Isles had gone about their busyness.

Having just seen what those men had done Piper could understand why ReeMara was shaking now. The little human had not been caught and slaughter like the others C'raw had spoken of. Was ReeMara the only human to have survived the Iron Man's men!?

The fun of the day had gone; though the Iron Man and his men were moving away from the ford. Only the ground showed that men and livestock had travelled this way.

Piper looked down the hill at the smoking village, the smoke told of homes burning, not of meats cooking.

Maybe ReeMara was right to want to go down there, the little humans' rags did need replacing. Having a fir coat did have its advantages, even if its colour was not the same as your siblings, it grew with you.

Cam and C'raw circled down to the stricken village to check it was safe to wander around. Cam did not think it was good for the little human to see what the Iron Man's men had done. But she too realised the little human need to replace the cloth she was using to cover herself, the sun could be just as harmful as the cold and the wind.

The crows signalled to ReeMara and the others it was safe to come into the village, any live human had long gone.

ReeMara decide not to look at what the men's swords had done instead she stared to hunt through the villager's scattered belongings.

They needed a leather bag for water; ReeMara found in one in a smouldering hut and some dried meat, she pulled a bag of nuts from under a pill of small stones that had kept the fires heat away. There was some milled corn in a bag that Piper found, as Piper did not know what to do with, but as it smelt as if you could eat it, she took it with her in case ReeMara could use it.

Smoked fish hanging from a beam that had been charred but had not burnt through caught Piper's eye. Reaching for the fish Piper nearly fell off the beam; swaying with a beam over glowing ashes was not her idea of fun, if the fish had not smelt so good she would have left them.

Piper did not see why ReeMara was more excited with the things she had fond than those Piper had found. The burnished metal comb nor the knife was not in Piper mind, such a good find as the food! But if Cam was right ReeMara wanted her hair to look as nice as her ferret tail. A human's tongue could not smooth their hair as a ferret's could, then the things ReeMara had found might help.

The strange bags that let ReeMara's feet stick out were tied with a leather thong to stop them from slipping below her waist. ReeMara was especially pleased with them as riding on any horses' back was now much more comfortable, as for the soft wool strip of cloth she had found she wound across her chest. Her flaxen hair she smoothed back and twisted with a band of leather, hang neatly down her back. A strip cut from a woven blanket hung over ReeMara's shoulder. She had cut it with the short knife she had found with the comb, it now hang in its own bag at her hip.

Piper was as happy about her finds as ReeMara, though Cam could understand Piper's ferret's mind, food was the most important commodity.

Cam had noticed ReeMara liked to bath as often as she could. She could see ReeMara was growing so was Soul, though he was not as tall as Cane and Bramble he was as tall as his dame. ReeMara eyes still peered over his withers as they had done when he was a foal, as Sea Spray liked to tell Cam as they watched the youngsters splash in the stream.

Cain was complaining as ReeMara tied to his saddle pad even more bags, Piper was standing on his withers over seeing ReeMara's work and to make sure she did leave behind any of the food she had found.

Piper would have questioned ReeMara had the girl not stuck her tongue at her. The reddish mettle pot was coming with them no mater what Piper thought.

ReeMara remembered her mother had one like it, and nice things to eat had come out of it. The sun and the sea had their power, but this pot did not, she guessed she would have to find out how to make use of it. A large tear rolled down her cheek, she whipped it away, why did she have to think of her mother and brother?

ReeMara was in a hurry to leave the village, not that anyone grumbled it was not a pleasant place to stay, the smell of wasted life hung about the place.

C'raw did wonder why the humans had not striped the village of all its assets, the things ReeMara had found meant the raiders were in a hurry.

The first part of the legion was crossing the river where the grassland started after the old Fallen Forest ended. The clang of iron and the crack of leather mingled with the sound of iron shod hooves on the river beds stones. Foot soldiers hang their sandals over their shoulders with their swords to keep them dry.

The second half of the legion would be reaching the same crossing in the next few days. It would take both parts of the legion to see to the end of the Barbarians that had been causing so much unrest in the lands the gods had forgotten.

The legion's commander plume fluttered in the wind as he watched his men cross the river. He was not interested in his men and horses pulling the heavy wagons through the water. He was more interested in the cool wine waiting for him in his tent. He did not like having to camp this side of the river, the other bank would have pleased him more. The thick trees offered better protection for his men. If the other part of his legion did not need as much place to camp as the first, he would not have had to make the crossing.

The meadows on this side could be used to graze the live stock. The legion's primus pilus was going to have to send out parties in the next few days, the meat the men needed would not be covered by the animals they had with them. That problem could wait till the morning, that challis of cool wine was waiting for him.

"See them down there?"

"Hard not to with so many tents lined up in the meadow."

"Think that he must be in command. His plume is longer then the other men around him."

"We don't have uniforms like that!"

"We don't have uniforms."

"We had better tell the 'Iron chap' of what we can see here."

"Do you think they are waiting for more men?"

"How would I know! They don't look as if they have enough to eat, look at the live stock they have brought with them. "

"Good looking pair of oxen, my old dad would like them; they don't breed their like that, where I come from!"

"I thought all you did was breed!"

"We try to… Are you talking about oxen?"

"Would I talk about anything else!?"

C'raw had found the men without uniforms observations interesting. He was flying over a landscape he did not like, it was all too wet. The lake over towards the setting sun was not the only obstacle that blocked his charges passage; this marshland was just as impassable!

C'raw had been directing them south, for no better reason than, any crow he or Cam had talked to had not spoken of any large human settlements on the northern thermals.
To try to get the land-bound through the hoof dangerous marshes was not a risk he was willing to take.

Now there were large numbers of humans camping on this side of the river, how was he going to get them past them?

Cam dropped down onto C'raw's thermal, he was glad to see her, but the news she brought with her did not please him at all!

C'raw should have guessed by what the two humans were saying that the Iron Man and his men were in this part of the world! They had not seen or heard anything about them since they had seen what the Iron Man and his men had done to that village! With Cam's observations, information of the presence of the Iron Man's men though some flying time away from their present point meant humans were still in a position to stop them from travelling on.

It was a long night for the two crows as they tried to decide what they should do. To try to move tonight would not be safe even with the horses' good night sight; they would not know what dangers they could be walking into!

Cain and Bramble were not keen to meet up with any of the Iron Man's men, as all thoughts of trying and catch them up, to return to being hobbled riding horses again, was no longer an appealing idea. They were much happier jogging along with ReeMara and Sea Spray and playing games with Soul.

Cain and Bramble did not think, to try and skirt round the men and horses that might know them as something they should do, the risk they would be recognised was too great, and how were they to explain ReeMara's presence, not to mention a ferret?

C'raw had told them how the land lay behind the trees and where the uniformly dressed men were camping. The land was quite different to the lake side, where the horses had chosen to graze while the crows had a look around.

C'raw was right they could not just run around at night between the lake and two bands of humans. The unknown men C'raw had seen carried swords, they were not here to trade C'raw was sure of that!

ReeMara woke when the sun played on her eye lids, Piper was still asleep on her back with her legs running with her dreams. She was not dreaming as human shouts and blood curdling screams broke the early morning quite.

There was the sound of swords hitting swords, hooves pounded on the turf by the lake. ReeMara managed to grab the upside down ferret and run to where tall rocks rose out of the ground like broken teeth. ReeMara managed to climb one to hide on the top. Piper was impressed at ReeMara's quick thinking she was glad to be out of the way of the men fighting below them.

The men on horses had a chance, but those on foot had to fight with feet in the soft muddy banks of the lake. ReeMara did not watch how the mounted men took advantage of the men on foot; she hid her face in Pipers coat.

Cam pulled at ReeMara's hair; the horses were waiting for them at the base of the rock. As ReeMara's hands wound in Sea Spray's mane, she could feel Soul press against her leg when the horses picked up speed.

There were many other horses moving fast, along with other animals of the forest, their way to the river that feed the lake was blocked by more men and horses then ReeMara had ever seen and more were at the river crossing!

Wild cries rang in the dark forest as men started to charge out of the trees!

Sea Spray pushed deeper into the mass of frightened animals, the others kept close to her. She could only hope the unformed men did not see there was a child cling to her as their banners and drawn swords were pointed at the mass they were caught up in, they were being driven at the men standing in the shadows of the forest.

The Iron Man sat on his horse in front of his men waiting for the unformed men with plumbs on their heads to gallop into the trap he had waiting for them. The trees were thick and the branches were low were his men were ready to take on their opponent.

When four horses split away into the marsh, the Iron Man did not see them, he would not have cared as the marsh did not allow safe passage. He did not know that two crows would guide them back to the river crossing.

The Iron Man's thoughts were concentrated on the battle in front of him. It was in his grasp; the foot soldiers were no longer in the tight paten they had been before they entered the confines of this woodland.

Men had swords and were well trained and experienced in warfare, were as the folk around here only had starves! But they knew the land well; this kind of knowledge was very useful to him as he was planning to whip fear into those that had sent the battalions after him! He had no intention of losing control of this land, not now he had stopped the flow of amber.

The Barbarians from the north had fired the folk to fight an enemy normally so well armed that men with only staves could not have taken them on. The Old Forest was their homeland and they were light and fast footed men that could run skilfully over tree roots. Their simple staves helped them keep to firm ground and keep a soldier's sword away from their unprotected bodies. The prise they had asked for their local knowledge was salt!

The woods rang with the shouts and screams of men. The foot soldiers had to fight among the roots and lower branches with their restricting uniforms; that handicapped their trained ability to fight their opponents! Swords could not be swag in the thick lower branches.

The red sunset mirrored the stained water that had settled in the marsh's pools. Cam was glad ReeMara did not ask questions, the little girl was more concerned that Piper did not allow Sea Spray to put a hoof on unsafe ground, Soul was right behind her. Cain and Bramble did not want to show they were nervous in the woodland marsh, they were happy to have Piper on the ground and Cam as look out.

C'raw was way above them trying to see what was happening ahead, he had to get his charges out of the red marsh somehow! Behind them was a battle that they did not want to get involved in. The men on horses were being pulled off by men with long wild hair and those that got by them had to face the Iron Man's own horsemen.

The marsh held its water away from a tree edged glade were wagons of stores the unformed men must have brought with them, stood unattended! ReeMara took some of the smaller packages with her; she would have eaten some of the cheese she found in one of the wagons but the others would not let her, they wanted to move on. ReeMara insisted on packing as much as she could into a saddlebag she had found.

Cam could not grumble with her, ReeMara had to learn to look after herself, things crows liked to eat were not what little humans should eat, not when they were growing.

The sound of men coming closer sent everyone into the cover of the trees again. C'raw could see an ox unwillingly being lead by two men. The ox had to pull a wagon as the men commanded but the ox did make their task an easy one.

A small pouch had fallen into the trampled grass left by the puffing humans with a jingle that the human scavengers had not heard, but C'raw had; he was quick to pick it up as the others came out of the trees. He did not know why he had done that but if it belonged to the men that had taken the wagon it must be of use. The sounds of men and their battle stress were beginning to echo among the trees C'raw knew it was time to move on again.

The only safe way out of the forest was to take the trodden track C'raw had seen from above. They could try to push their way through thick trees or worry they would sink into a trap the marshland had hidden.

They had to use the trodden track and ran the risk of confronting any humans travelling along it as the marsh was no longer skirting the forest, the forest trees was standing with their roots in the wet marsh. The two crows could watch the road from above; a raucous cry could send the ground bound into the shadows. Their plan was not put to use, as no human's were moving to where the uniformed men must have marched.

When the track opened onto rolling grassland all were relived, the mash and forest had held them in its shadows to long.

C'raw took to a higher thermal, he returned with the news there was a village over the hill.

"From what you say it is not a place we should allow ReeMara to see. All she has seen is how cruel humans can be. To have to see another human dwelling wasted like her own village. No we will not take her there!" Sea Spray was adamant.

"The smell alone would turn you away!" Cam looked at C'raw.

"Did you have to say that? Even sleeping humans have ears."

"The uniformed men must be responsible, their handy work could be seen everywhere!" C'raw said in a low voice: "We had better move away from the open way to rest. Those humans have war on their minds."

"We all could do with rest, time to graze." Sea Spray started to follow Cam.

Sea Spray had to shake ReeMara awake, men on horses were pounding their hooves along the way four horses with child and a ferret had just come. Their own hooves were soon pounding the turf to get them away from the speeding horsemen.

The uniformed men riding fast did not notice them slip behind a hillock. The side of the hillock offered them shelter for the night; the hillock also separated them from anymore signs of the war the humans were waging.

The next morning was warm as the season started to show the first signs of changing to summer. Everyone felt lazy, they grumbled as C'raw guided them, he was still travelling southward for no other reason than the birds he talked to had not spoken of any large human dwellings that could be described as a city!

In the first few days after leaving the marsh filled forests the only living animals they saw were wolves, they were not hungry their scavenging must have been successful. Cam was glad to see, she did not want to have worry about hungry wolves.

With the summer sun warming them they all but forgot the humans and their wars. One rolling hill led to another, grass waved and played with the pleasant winds. As the hills rolled one into another so did the days.

C'raw could see a camp set in the folds of the rolling grassland, that the camp was for trading he could see from the thermal he was hovering on. C'raw was not sure it would be safe to take the little human into the trading camp or any trading camp! The little human's flaxen hair did not match that of the humans he could see, he did see humans were tethered with the cattle and horses. A pen was surrounding sheep and goats. There were also tents offering things humans found important, he did not need any of the human things offered to look after his ReeMara.

The stand that court his eye was loaded with the very stone ReeMara liked to play with!

A man was telling those standing close to him about the stones. 'When chips were grounded and added to a drop of wine they would take away pains of the stomach.'

"Good Sir, the measure of your ample girth tells me; after you have eaten your rumbling stomach disturbs the sleep of your wife! Let the lady rest in peace, slip this powder into your wine and the peace of the night is yours!" The trader of sea stones was saying.

"Do you have anything to keep the wife awake?"

"You would not know what to do with a wife that is awake!"

"If the wife was awake she would not lie with the likes of him!"

The laughter the friendly banter was cut short as a shadow fell across the trestle table!

The Iron Man's sword tip rested on the table cutting the sea stone trader away from the humans he had attracted to his stall. The other humans turned away when three other men placed their swords between them and the trader, he did not want to make any more jokes from the look on his face as he was on his knees, his body shaking as the sword pointed at his throat.

The Iron man kept his eye on the frightened man as his men swept all the sea stones on the trestle table into their leather bags.

The tent was searched without respecting the owner's belongings; everything was torn apart on the point of their swords. The sea stone the trader had left in the back of his tent was taken along with the powders he had prepared for his customers.

C'raw did not think their swords should have been pressed into the trader's belly; he had not tried to stop the Iron Man nor his men.

"Let this be a warning to all! Amber is for men of power not for people like you! To have amber, sea stone in your dwellings will cost you, your lives!"

C'raw was not going to forget that commanding tone the Iran Man used to shock the humans from helping the luckless trader.

"He won't have to worry about his overfed belly disturbing his wife again!"

The laughter did not come from the humans that had come to look at the amber the trader had but from the men following The Iron Man as he walked out of the trading camp.

C'raw had watched the scene from the peach he had taken on the top of the trading tent offering tanned hides. His little ReeMara had stones like that with her… if he had brought her to this trading camp!

C'raw took to the air he wanted to get back to those waiting for him; to have ever thought of bringing them here was mad! The flaxen haired girl would have been cut down with the trader and the horses sold like those that had been tethered and penned.

Other than the trading camp the four horses and the two crows and Piper along with their little human did not see other humans on the rolling plains, though there were cattle and horses roaming on the grassland.

A pack of wolves disturbed the peace of one evening; they were chasing a pair of calves that had strayed to far away form their heard. C'raw would not let them stop for the night till they had left the hunting wolves well behind.

ReeMara was the first to see the horizon had changed its form. No longer did the grass roll to the horizon a blue land seemed to rise towards the sky.

C'raw took to a thermal that would take him over the new land. What he saw was impressive; rock rose towards him out of a river that looked deep and wide, running towards the side the sun returned to bring the new day. From what he could see the rock folded into cliffs and perches, some wide enough to stand four horses on, if they could fly up to them!

The cliffs had set spicks like teeth spitting out on the both sides of the river then, the cliffs gave way to higher pecks, shining white in the evening light. It was a sight C'raw had never seen before, snow covered mountains were not to be found in the Isles of the Mists.

"I don't know how we are supposed to get horses and ReeMara with her ferret over the mountains!"

"They are everything you said; magnificent, like nothing I have seen!" Cam could only hang on the thermal next to C'raw and wonder.

"They might be able to climb round trees but not these rocks!" said C'raw: "We cannot lead them back the way we have come; we need to take a longer aerial view, fly both to the east and then to the west before we decide what we should do."

Cam knew they had to find away forward, but for now they had to find somewhere safe to leave their charges while they used the thermals. She and C'raw sank to join a lower thermal that would to take them down to where the group were grazing.

"Let's take a look beyond the rocks' teeth I cannot see the river from here." Cam said.

The river swung in curve that cut into the mountainous rock, it made two beaches one for the mountain side and the other sloping gently to the grassland.

"We don't need to look for a better place for our friends." C'raw said as he dipped a wing to turn into the wind that would drop them onto the thermal that would bring them back to where the land bound were waiting for them.

ReeMara and Piper liked this place as much as the horses did, the grazing was good and the grassland winds could not reach into the river's curve and whip them if it had a mind to.
To have to wait for the crows to return here would be a pleasure!

ReeMara lay in the grass with the sun warming her body as she dozed; Piper was by her side with her legs in the air, she was enjoying the sun as much as ReeMara was; till ReeMara sat up suddenly! They both could hear the sound of horses moving fast.

Soul was the first horse they saw with Sea Spray close behind him. Corn and Bramble were galloping for all they were worth with more horses than they could count, not far behind them!

Sea Spray almost through ReeMara onto her back, she was glad to feel the little humans fingers weave into her mane as she picked up speed. Piper had to grab Bramble's tail as he passed.

The horses were crowding around them, their breath mingled with theirs. For the four horses to try and out run the large herd was no longer possible nor was it possible to turn to the side. The teeth of rock prevented them from escaping that way and the weight of the moving animals stopped them from cutting across the other.

All they could do was to gallop with them! Piper did wonder why they were going towards the river!?
The cold water did not stop them as it splashed into the air as horse after horse jumped into the river. It was not as deep as Piper had thought, if it had been she would have been washed away, not had the chance to scramble onto Brambles back.

Piper could see ReeMara on Sea Spray's back the other two horses were close to them as the water splashed with pounding hooves and tossing manes.

The herd stopped to shake water from their coats, Piper was not pleased, to stay on a wet back was not easy. She would have grumbled at Bramble if he had not moved on to keep him place in the herd. Sea Spray was being pushed forward, Soul was beside her. Piper could not see Corn anywhere.

Corn was being swept along, he did not get a chance to look for the others; the rock seemed to swallow all the horses he could see around him, now the sun light had gone!

When Corn could see again rock rise on both sides of him, the other horses were beginning to slow down. Inside the towering rock sweat rose in clouds. He was breathing as heavily as the horse next to him.

"Why we have to do this every time they say wild humans are about!?" said a mare with a round belly.

"You want to be taken?"

"There were more humans than before!"

"Do they want to take more of us?"

"There are more strange things going on the in the Grasslands."

There was whinny that stopped the horses talking near to Corn.

"We have a human among us!"
The horse that had whinnied did not sound alarmed, more surprised!

"What is a small human doing on your back?"
Sea Spray would have tried to answer but another voice remarked 'she' was not a horse they knew.

Bramble was standing in a circle his saddle pads marked him as stranger. Sea Spray and Soul with ReeMara found them selves pushed forwards to join him.

"Are they from the wild humans?"
Piper stood up to answer, but before she could a mare screamed:

"A ferret!"
Horses stamped their hooves, clouds of dust rose in the air of the canyon it made everyone cough and sneezes.

"Here is another stranger!?"
Corn was aloud to join his friends.

"Anymore strangers among us?"

"Their not strange, they are my friends!" ReeMara slipped to the ground. Piper thought she was seeing things, her ReeMara confronting all these angry animals! She moved to jump down to ReeMara but the very moment she moved a mare let out a scream that made everyone nervous again.

"We are not from the wild humans; we are trying to get away from them!" ReeMara's voice sounded very small in the large canyon, but the voice that asked her from where she had come from did fill the horse's canyon.

ReeMara had not been afraid of any of the horses but the woman standing on the rock shelf made her shake. The woman was as round as she was tall, she was not taller than ReeMara.

"Welcome! You will have an interesting tale to tell, but for now would you like something to eat? We have not had many ferrets as guest but you are also welcome.

My horses will look after your friends so don't worry about them. Shall we take off their saddle pads? They would be more comfortable without them."

The round woman helped ReeMara with the saddle pads. ReeMara had stopped shaking somehow the little woman's slow movements were reassuring. None of the horses were nervous of her, they were just not sure of Piper!

"I hope you can tell me about some of the strange rumours coming from the Grass Lands?"

The round woman chatted as she leaded ReeMara into the rock, Piper had to be helped to find away up the steep steps by the round woman. Piper noticed the way the woman smelt; she smelt like many of the sweet plants in the rolling land they had come across.

"Don't worry about your friends the canyon open's into a basin were feed and water is waiting for them. There is a lot you well find interesting here."

ReeMara sat at a table, food was being placed on it, but ReeMara did not know how she was supposed to eat it, there were knives and bowls placed in patens on the table, more folk were coming to the large cave with the long table and the cooking fire.

ReeMara could only sit where she was, there was too much she did not understand; to sit at a table was something new to her, as was how the other folk were dressed! ReeMara felt she was dirty compared to the folk moving around the long cave.

The folk were smiling and chatting to each other, sometimes hugging each other! Had folk in her village been like that? ReeMara felt so far away from all she knew, had Piper not been close to her she would have cried.

The round woman sat beside ReeMara and offered her food; Piper was the first to except an offering of cooked meat. ReeMara saw Piper was enjoying the food took the next piece offered her, she took the bowl of soup with both hands, the slurps she made were so loud that folk near her looked round, and again to see the newcomer except another bowl, ReeMara want to eat it quietly but her hunger slurp the soup just as loudly as before!

"The young newcomer likes your broth Mattie!" said someone farther down the table.

"So do I, can I have some more?"
The cook looked at the youngster that had asked for more and waved his ladle at him:

"You will get fat!"

"It will take me sometime till I am as fat as you!"

"You won't live long enough if you speak like that to your elders and betters!"

ReeMara thought the ladle would not give the youngster any more soup, but it did and it put some into her bowl as well. The bowls were taken away and a mug of something sweet and hot was placed in front of ReeMara.

"We have a newcomer at our table a full belly can tell good tales. And a good tale is worth hearing with a full belly and a mug of mead!"

Piper could tell ReeMara would not be telling anyone anything after eating so much! It was Piper that stood on the table to tell the folk there, how a ferret and a child with four horses came to be sharing a meal with the folk sitting at this table!

"I did not tell them of the stones She-With-The-Sight gave ReeMara to take to the City of the Seven Hills; I only said that was where she had to go!"

Piper had found the horses just where the round woman had said. They had food enough to keep them happy and a waterfall fell into a pool that sparkled in the evening light.

"We can get back onto the Grass Land whenever we wish; we only have to go over there. We won't be where the crows left us grazing." Bramble was not as worried as Corn was about what Piper had or not told the folk that lived here. He had done what he could to see there was a way, if they needed to a way out.

Sea Spray wanted to know where ReeMara was.

"She is asleep, she eat so much she fell asleep as I was telling them about our travels. As she will probably sleep for along time I thought I would come and find you."

"You better get back to ReeMara I don't want you to leave her alone, alone with those humans."

Was Sea Spray cross with Piper?

"Sea Spray we needed Piper to come and tell us how ReeMara is. If the humans here want to harm her they would not have feed her so well and then let her fall asleep!" Bramble pointed out.

ReeMara did sleep deeply more deeply than she had for a long time! The bed she had slept in was so comfortable and soft, even if Soul had been with her she could not have been more comfortable!

ReeMara may have been nervous to step out of the safe bed but the sounds coming from the room next to hers were inviting. Laughter and shrieks of pleasure and the sound of water splashing drew ReeMara into a room full of bubbles and kids of her size.

Tubbs were filled with water and bubbles, legs and arms waved and wriggled, happy voices called her to join them. ReeMara was not quick enough taking off her clothes, as hands full of water were showering her!

If she had felt dirty at the long table the night before she was squeaky clean now, she had pink arms and legs like the other children.

Piper did not join ReeMara even with all the fun the children were having, Piper enjoyed all their fun from the safety of the door way. When larger humans than the children came into the room with large raps to rap around the wet children, Piper followed the happy crowd to where a table was laden with a breakfast Piper could only have dreamed of!

ReeMara went with the children after they all had eaten; there was still mare's milk around her lips as they burst out in the morning sun light.

ReeMara saw the herd of horses in the canyon basin with the waterfall filling the pool. Someone took her arm and she was pulled along with the other kids. Before long she had arms full of clean cut dried grass and was running after the mob of kids down to the waiting horses!

It was not difficult to find her friends so ReeMara went back for more of the dried grass. ReeMara would have gone again for more but the kids took her with them.

The benches and tables were not like the table in the long hall. The benches and tables looked towards a bench large enough for a grown human to sit on.

ReeMara was not as comfortable in this hall she did not know what to expect as she was pulled to sit down on a bench.

The only difference between the girl and ReeMara was they had different coloured hair, now ReeMara's hair had dried after the bath did it show its golden colour, next to the girl's dark head. ReeMara was not too busy to notice even though there were so many strange things going on in the hall.

The children had things in their hands and flat things were on the tables before them, it meant something to them but not to ReeMara!

ReeMara wondered why the kids were so quite, maybe the woman sitting on the bench had something to do with that!?

The woman did not look like someone you argued with, if Piper had not been with her she would have been frightened.

"There you are ReeMara, I have been looking for you!" the round woman from the evening before came into the hall, she offered ReeMara her hand:

"Let us find you something better to put on than the towels from the bathing room."

ReeMara found her saddle bags waiting for her in the place where she had spent the night. She only had the comb and a small mirror of burnished mettle that pleased the round woman.

"We had better get you one of my robes." Then the fat lady laughed as she looked at ReeMara and then at herself, ReeMara laughed too despite her self, she liked this human.

"They call me Beana I look after any new comers."
The round woman said as she turned to find something
more suitable for ReeMara to put on.

With the comb and the help from the mirror ReeMara
smoothed her hair. Beana returned with a soft woven
cloth she dropped over ReeMara's head, Beana had a
blue band which she tied round ReeMara's waist, she
stood back to look at ReeMara.

"You look like a little princess; who would have
thought the herds would have brought me a little
princess!"

ReeMara found herself in Beana's arms and she was
hugging Beana back!

"We had better go and see The Sage, she is waiting for
us."
Beana put ReeMara down and smoothed the cream
coloured rob and straitened the blue band.

ReeMara was not sure she wanted to go and see
anybody, she was happy to be in Beana's arms.

Beana had not expecting ReeMara to bust with such
emotion as soon as she saw The Sage. There was fear and
anger mixed with love in the rage that a child as young as
ReeMara was not able to control.

Beana was not able to console ReeMara nor could
Piper, and as ReeMara was so upset Piper did not have a
chance to say, 'The Sage looked like She-With-The-
Sight!'

Piper did see The Sage wave Beana and ReeMara way
with a sad smile.

Beana sat the sobbing girl on her bed; she wanted to
put a mug of warm mares' milk in ReeMara's hands but
she was still sobbing too much.

"Tell my, what has happened to you?" Beana saw Piper was going to speak. "Let ReeMara tell me, I don't want to hear about iron men in the forests!"

The ferret looked as upset as ReeMara, Beana took both ReeMara and the ferret in her arms to wait till ReeMara could tell her what was breaking her hart.

The Sage sat with her chin resting on her chest as Beana told her what was behind the newling's tears and screams. ReeMara had fallen asleep after drinking the warm milk Beana had given to her.

Beana did not expect to see tears in the old woman's eyes.

The moments seemed to pass slowly till The Sage spoke:

"She speaks of my sister! Of that I am sure! That her hart had turned so cold I could not have guest."

"How can you be so sure?" Beana was astounded.

"How many people do you know with twisted bodies and skins so white they don't like the sun to warm them?"

Now Beana was silent, The Sage was The Sage; she lived in the highest hall in the cliffs. The Sage looked out over all the folk in her charge. The herds had benefited from her leadership and had increased their numbers; The Sage was mother to them all.

No child had ever been sent away, no traveller was ever sent away. Those that lived here prospered under The Sage's guidance. That she had a sister, Beana knew and she had often heard the tale of the two sisters.

'Two white skinned girls that had been thrown out of their village because of their twisted bodies and white skins! Even if their bodies were weak they could serve their people with their clever minds. But the people hid from them, they believed to look at the two white sisters would mean their bodies would twist and their skin would lose its colour like theirs.'

The Sage wisdom had solved many of the daily problems the folk that lived in the mountains' cliffs had, and she had seen that when winter and storms came, food was stored in the mountain caves, for folk and horse alike.

No one these days thought about where The Sage came from or were troubled by her white skin. She was here.... Beana's thoughts came back into the small hall and she looked into the eyes of the old woman she trusted. How was she going to get ReeMara to trust her and The Sage?

"ReeMara is young, the gift children have is time." The Sage answered Beana's unspoken question.

There was a knock on the door; it was Mattie he had a wriggling bundle under his left arm and under his right a ferret was trying to spit at him. He set the angry pair on the floor in front of The Sage:

"This young lady was in my larder with that ferret, they were filling their saddle bags as fast as they could!"

ReeMara and Piper sat on the floor with their backs to everyone.

"ReeMara, tell me why you wanted so much food? You only had to ask Mattie when you are hungry." Beana said quietly to the pair of backs.

"Why do you want to go? The herds only come to the cliffs when there is danger in the Grassland. Look from my windows and tell me what you see."

At the voice of The Sage ReeMara did not move but Piper did, she scrambled onto the first sill.

Piper had to wander at the view, the canyon were the horses were resting, the waterfall splashed below. From the next window the Grassland rolled away into the horizon, it was the same view from the next, only flags fluted in the wind. Tents were set in straight lines that reached as far as Piper's eye could see!

Mattie's cooking smells made Piper's nose twitch, he had come to stand at the window with her.

"I thought the horses spoke of wild men trying to herd them away! Those straight lines can only suggest a Legion from the City of the Seven Hills!" Mattie scratched Piper's back as if tickling her would help him think:

"What brings them to our door?"

"ReeMara, I don't think this is the right time to be out in the Grasslands." Piper turned at the sound of The Sage's voice to see ReeMara standing in front of The Sage:

"We are going to the City of the Seven Hills!" her clenched fists were on her hips.

Mattie left The Sage's hall, the little girl was not going to be easily persuaded not to travel!

In The Sage's hall was not where ReeMara want to be, to have to see the old woman again! Piper was telling her there were humans in lines as far as the eye could see. C'raw and Cam would not find them here; would they be able to find the horses among the others in the canyon?

Beana and The Sage could only watch the little girl standing defiantly in front of them. Piper broke the stale silence:

"ReeMara, we could wait till C'raw and Cam return, it has only been three days since they took off, to find away around the mountains."

"You are welcome to stay till your friends return." said The Sage: "A day or two will not be too disturbing to your plans. I know Mattie will be pleased to see you have all the provisions you need."

Piper was nodding in agreement:

"We could have another bath and breakfast; it was such fun this morning!"

Beana took ReeMara in her arms, ReeMara was not given anymore time to make up her mind. As Beana was hugging her tightly, then Beana took her hand, they were running from The Sage's hall with Piper scampering after them.

There were so many men with the Iron Man that camp fires burnt day and night. Cam and C'raw hang on a thermal watching the humans moving below them.

How many human leaders had the Iron Man called to come to this camp? The banners by the camp fires showed different colours, and the humans had different clothing. One thing was for sure they were not here to exchange the time of day.

"Do you think this camp had something to do with the warring in the Marsh Forests?" C'raw wanted to know, there was so much going on; the humans down there were planning something. Cam picked up on C'raw's thoughts:

"Whatever they are planning, we cannot bring the others here. The river will bring them too closes to this human camp."

"We had better forget this way, we should settle for the night so we can make an early start on a fresh thermal." C'raw could only agree.

The night had cooled the air over the river; the cliffs were still warm from the day before. The two crows were able to lift to a thermal taking them towards were the sun rose.

They were not expecting to see the lines of ordered tents stretching over the grassland! Cam wanted returned to ReeMara and the others, but as C'raw pointed out there was more to this, it would be better to continue to fly along the river. C'raw did not think they could take the land bound back onto the Grassland, safe passage was no longer possible!

Cam was the first to see the men marching; they were almost hidden in the dust their feed raised!

C'raw was impressed by the columns of men mounted on horses; there were more horses with humans in one place, than he had ever seen! And! There were replacement horses with cattle being herded behind support wagons matching the columns of the horsemen and men on foot.

C'raw and Cam did not wait to discuss what they should do; they turned to return to where they had left their friends.

Cam was worrying about them, more now after what they had seen. Where were they going to find a place of safety?

C'raw and Cam circled around at ground level over the prints they had seen from above, they could see they lead towards the river. Between them they could not find any sign of a little girl or ferret.

C'raw could see they were horses that were not under the control of humans; a ridden horse's hoof print is not so even when they are carrying humans.

C'raw and Cam rose to make another survey from another birds' eye view. The Iron Man's men must have been the reason for these horses being on the move! Cam had to see what had happened to the horses once they had got to the river, the cliff's teeth did not let them see where horses could have crossed the fast flowing water.

Searching the beach on both sides of the river did not revile anything that could tell the two birds where to look next, now the evening's darkness was going to prevent them from continuing.

The perch they chose was on the cliff, they could not see the beach on this side cut into rock below them. If an owl had not flown past and spotted the two sad crows on a ledge, they might have thought to fly away the next dawn.

"There has been so much movement on the Grassland; hunting has become difficult most of my meals are staying underground after dark! She back at the cave keeps grumbling at me, can't blame her, young chicks are always hungry.

Haven't seen you around here before, thought crows liked wooded lands, mind you if the pickings get any less I think I well have to fly farther."

"You won't have to, not if the humans camping out on the Grassland cross swords."

The owl did not seem to understand what the C'raw meant.

"They are not out there for fun!" C'raw did not know how to make this owl understand, till Cam said:

"There are so many humans out there with war on their minds. We saw humans driving others into swamps in the marshes or suffering at the point of a sword."

The owl's all ready large eyes opened wide:

"So the rumours are true!?" he would have fallen from the perch they were sharing if C'raw had not helped him regain his balance.

"Want to tell me what else you know? It would explain why hunting has become so difficult."

"We are looking for a little human and a ferret; they were travelling with four horses." Cam wanted to end the silence that had fallen between them.

"I tried to get a ferret running around outside the door to the place where the best smells come from! But a human showed me away with a broom!"

The owl had to explain what he meant. Did he mean humans lived round here? Cam wanted to know, how could humans live in the rock? Was there a human dwelling in the rock they were resting on? Living from the river and the Grassland's bounty, and using the canyon to protect their livestock from winter storms and now war!?

Cam would not let the owl go; he had to tell all he knew about the folk that lived around here.

"Glad that owl did not get the ferret he was after, or we would not be looking at our friends." C'raw said to Cam as they sat on the windowsill. ReeMara was asleep and next to her was a red ferret as deeply asleep on her back with her legs running in the air! When she should have been looking out for any danger!

Cam was going to wake the ferret but a soft voice told her not to.

"We have been waiting for you." said the soft voice, Cam span round to look at the woman standing in the doorway; the likeness to the woman they had left in the tree was as strong as a storm's lightning! As the woman stood there, Cam could tell she was not She-With-The-Sight.

"Can we offer you both something to eat you must have been in the air for sometime?" said another woman.

"You are safe in the cliffs over the river." said the old woman, so like She-With-The-Sight.

"You are as welcome as they are." The other woman went over to see the sleepers had not been disturbed.

Mattie was not sure he wanted two crows sitting on his kitchen table, but his early morning guests were enjoying the delicacies he was offering them.

The Sage and Beana sat at the other end of the table their breakfast was in front of them; they were watching the crows hungrily eating theirs.

Having heard what the two crows had to say about the humans camping on the Grasslands, The Sage knew the war the intruders planned was going to affect them all!

The little girl had been so insistent when she said she wanted to go the City of the Seven Hills, it had made Sage wander why? If the lady in the tree was her sister, her sister would have had a plan. What had She-With-The-Sight done to this little girl to make her leave her homeland? The sobs from ReeMara had not told Beana what had upset her so.

Both crows were helpful when she asked questions, but there was something they were not saying. That the crows were trained flight members was clear to The Sage. That ReeMara trusted them and they had sworn to stay with ReeMara and accompany her to the City of the Seven Hills was clear. But, they would not say why.

The Sage was saddened to learn her sister had been living in a tree; she must have had her reasons! Had she been burnt with the forest fires? The mist in the Isles of the Mists could cover many secrets.

It would be sometime before ReeMara would tell her what her secrets were, but time was what they had. There was no way she could allow anyone to travel through a battle field!

The crows knew it was not safe to travel; if they were going to stay then plans had to be made. Four horses were not a problem, nor was another child even if she had a ferret that would not leave her side!

The Sage saw everyone in her care leant skills, the young were kept out of trouble studding the skills need to understand the written word. Other skills like using a sword or a bow and arrow were also among the skills she saw the young were taught to survive in a human world.

C'raw and Cam were busy keeping an over all view of the constant battles on the Grassland, if the Legionnaires thought they could prevent the Iron Man's Barbarian warriors from advancing over the Grasslands or thought it would an easy victory; the supplies being brought into the area, told of a long engagement.

The herds in the canyon benefited from the information the crows brought in, the daily information as to where it was safe to graze, or if it would be better to remain in the safety of the canyon.

Others that lived on the Grassland were able to benefit from those warring, scavengers were often to be seen prowling.

The owl the crows had met also brought news to the folk in the cliffs, not that there was much movement when the sun went down from the humans of the Legions.

The only Barbarians used the night to move their positions to confuse the other side!

The war was still being fought when the season had completed a full turn. The humans battling had still not brought a victor, Cam and C'raw decided to nest, their conclusion was this human war would take another turn, time enough to see hatchlings mature and see ReeMara grew with the schooling and good food available here!

Both birds kept a bird's eye view on what was happing on the Grass Lands. To find men that had fallen and were wounded was common sight. But when Cam found a man with a festering wound lying in the grass though she did not want to be away from her fledglings for too long, she felt she could not leave this man without trying to help him, there was enough of the herb he needed about.

The man did not try to push her away from him, he was muttering:

"The Legion should have returned from the North Marshes by now! Only a hand full of men, have come, only a hand full!"

"I would not have understood him if we had not seen with our own eyes what had happened in the 'North Marshes'

From the look on the man's face the herbs I used will not bring the relief he needs, though the wolves will." Cam said sadly as she left the kitchen to take titbits to her fledglings.

"A third Legion would make a difference!" Mattie was trying to work in his kitchen around the currant battle being mapped out on his table. ReeMara was moving pieces to match C'raw's instructions. The boy opposite her watched intensively, as ReeMara finished moving less reliable young troops to a safer position, the wheat she had used to represent them did not hold their formation either.

The carrots she used to represent the Legion's prime warriors did not mind when the stringy boy banged the table because ReeMara had not placed the uniformed men where he thought they should be.

ReeMara shook her head, from what C'raw was saying where the watercress was, was where the heavy infantry were.

Harron put the feathers he had plucked from a chicken waiting for Mattie's oven, where he was sure the heavy infantry would better used.

"I don't doubt you are right, but they don't have the benefit of a bird's eye view." Mattie said from by the pot he was stirring on his fire as the two children bent over their battlefield.

Harron was a favoured friend of ReeMara she often played with him under Mattie's kitchen table it was the best place to show him her stones. Harron wandered at the stones, their warmth, their colour, the sun light in them made him laugh as much as ReeMara. Though Harron did not utter sounds most people understood, ReeMara did not find him difficult to understand as others did. She admired his ability to understand all the markings the quill made. Some of those quill strokes made sense to her now thanks to Harron's help.

Harron could also read words from other's lips and he would make hand signs, telling her what some else had said, it made boring lessons more fun, but did not keep them out of trouble, though they could not be heard chatting in class and the teacher had tried to see they did not sit next to each other ReeMara always knew what Harron wanted to say.

Beana was proud of ReeMara's progress; she seemed to enjoy her lesions, she could use a bow as well as any of the others, outride most and now thanks to Harron was making headway with the use of the quill!

The battlefield's conflicts the children were always constructing on Mattie's table were lost thoughts for Beana; she just saw nuts, wheat and vegetables and now feathers! Beana saw Mattie was enjoying along with the kids, the crows' reports of the battles the two sides were engaged in, even though he lost the use of his table so they could map it out.

"That man Cam told us about, the one dieing. Cam said he muttered about the Legion that had not come down from the north marshes, could they have been the solders they are waiting for?" signed Harron, "Another Legion would tip the balance."

To make his point he swept the hapless barbarians on to the floor, as they were represented by hazel nuts they made Beana jump! She sent them off to see to the herd after they had picked up all the nuts.

Corn and Bramble, Soul also enjoyed the crows' daylily reports, Sea Spray enjoyed chatting with a group of mares much more than listening to the crows chatter.

Corn and Bramble were galloping around the canyon pretending to pull a chariot. Their game did not amuse Sea Spray to day and their game was annoying the other mares as well; their chatter was turning towards next season's foals and which of the stallions they fancied.

Corn and Bramble along with Soul were pleased to see ReeMara and Harron, a game, like pulling a chariot they would enjoy!

"We cannot think to start towards the City on the Seven Hills today, not when the battling humans are so close!" Corn remarked.

"We will have to wait till they move away then, but we could show them how to gallop and make kids laugh!" Bramble was hopeful of some fun, as it was dull not being able to go out on the Grassland.

ReeMara and Harron were not going to be any fun, they were busy bring arms full of hay to the horses in the canyon, under the watchful eye of Beana, and she was making sure they did not waste time talking to any horse or human.

Had they displeased her? Soul wandered as he took another mouth full of the sweet hay.

The two men astride flashy chestnut horses who held their heads high to let their manes flow free in the wind were on the mountain over the Grassland. They would have gone unnoticed had they not each had a trained hunting bird on their arm.

An eagle was not a bird Brilla had seen on a man's arm before, as for those horses by the way they held themselves Brilla could tell they did not come from the herds the humans had in the cliffs caves farther along the river.

Brilla was interested in these strangers they were not wearing the same clothing as the Barbarians nor did their robes mach any of the flapping clocks the legionaries had.

The humans in the cliffs were always interested in anything unusual. Brilla had not expected to see two humans on the mountain rock looking over the Grassland; she had to try to get chooser to them, if only they did not have eagles sitting on their arms!

The sun would sink soon below the horizon, Brilla's owl eyes would be better than an eagle's in the gloom.

The strange group were making a camp on the lip, this would give Brilla a chance to get close to them; the rock above them would provide her a discreet perch.

Brilla had planed to sweep the lower cliffs for nourishing nightlife, to have to sit hugging the cold rock was not her idea of fun. As much as she loved hunting, her owl instinct to gossip about what was going on, got the better of her.

Brilla was surprised to see the humans did not light a fire; they took food from their saddle bags. When darkness fell Brilla could see why the eagles were so quite; hoods of leather covered their eyes and straps held their legs. Brilla had never seen anything like that before! Her tummy rumbled but she was not going to move away, what she need to do was get even closer so she could hear what they were saying.

"I could use the warmth of a fire tonight."

"There are enough fires out there; we don't want anyone to join our meal tonight."

Brilla wondered why they laughed. The heavens stars burnt a bright as the warriors fires did below.

"We have been able to cross the mountains with our horses; all we need to do is get down there!"

"We are but two men, you want to bring many horsemen with the stores you need through the mountains!?"

"We pack the stores onto the backs of the donkeys! They don't need to carry silk here. The silk can go on in wagons to the markets to be sold to fill our coffers of cause."

The men's laughter rang around the rock.

"Keep the donkeys to carry our stores!"

"I had thought your plan to come over the mountains unworkable, but now I look down on the Barbarians and the City of the Seven Hills Legions battlefield, I see your plan could work!"

"They have sent three legions to destroy the Barbarians and yet the Barbarians are still holding them here. We are to hold the legions here while others to destroy their capital."

Brilla did not understand what they meant; who's capitol? What was a capital anyway?

"Cut the legions from their capital and they will be like a spider without legs"

The men's laughter made Brilla's feathers quiver. Brilla would have flown away then but the men took the hoods of the heads of the eagles, she had to sit still, as they were feed.

If her tummy rumbled any louder it would give her away!

Maybe that was why she took the thongs of a bag into her beck as she stepped off the cliff as the dawn began to light the sky.

The table in Mattie's kitchen was once again supporting the battle field. There had not been much movement between the two sides as far as the two children could see. What were they waiting for? Harron wanted to know, the Barbarians supplies to run out? If he could have told the commanders of the legions that the Barbarians were being supplied by the folk living in the land behind their camps and others from the north, brought them fresh meet, maybe the legions would go home, wherever that was!

Harron saw only C'raw was flying out to day on his scouting missions as he called them. Cam was sitting on their clutch of eggs; they would hatch soon, she was just happy to sit on their nest when C'raw was flying. They would have much to do the young when they hatched even though ReeMara brought her food while C'raw was underway.

The last time C'raw had flown over the Legions encampment he had reported seeing wagons moving in long lines, constantly moving to and from their camps.

Harron had remarked when C'raw made his report. The legions would not be going hungry. If he was in charge he would see that the wagon lines were stopped from delivering their supplies. If their old scribe was right, 'An army could not march on an empty stomach. Just as he, as their scribe could not cope with young students when his stomach was empty.'

They had heard him say it so often, not only did their scribe use the comment often, so did anyone that were responsible for the children's meals. Only their version was to do with growing children. 'Growing children cannot study on empty stomachs!'

Harron did not waist time chattering like the others did at mealtimes, he would practise the subjects he had been studying in the morning lessons on a slate in his lap.

Chatting at meal times was fun; ReeMara liked chattering with the other kids just as much as the other children did, after all they were not aloud to talk when lesions were being given.

Lessons and meals were not on Harron's mind as he was pointing at the long lines of wagons on Mattie's table. Where they passed close to the river he would ambush them, there, as the rivers water prevented them getting away from any swift attacker, and the land before the grass rolled on towards the horizon was too wet to take a laden wagon.

Today discussing the tactics of those battling below them did not interest ReeMara; she was dreamily looking out of the window.

The owls liked to fly at night, the dust and dawn saw owls flying about too, in daylight it was not normal!

Brilla was in such a hurry that her landing was not as tidy as it could have been; she skidded on the kitchen table right through Harron's planed complain. The bag she was carrying fell free from her talon; ReeMara had to jump to catch it!

"That is an egg, I was going to eat it but I heard funny sounds coming from it!"

Brilla had other things to tell the surprised folk trying to put the battlefield back on the table.

Harron feed the hungry owl bits of bacon as she told him about the two men and what they had said.

The bag in ReeMara's hands were holding her attention, she took it out of its bag. The leather was so soft, but it did not stop her from feeling how smooth the egg's shell was; it had a mottled paten. It could have lain in the sand dunes fringing a beach, no one would see it, or it could have been on the rock of the mountain and just looked like a lose stone.

It was warm and somehow busy with the life held in it. ReeMara held it to her, rapping it in her robe. Piper would be coming into the kitchen soon; Mattie kept the best titbits for her. Owls, ferrets and children often found their way to his door, someone was always hungry.

Things in the kitchen started to get out of hand. Harron was so excited at what Brilla had told him, he was bubbling like the soup in the pot Mattie was attending to, or trying to.

Beana rushed in, to say the first egg of Cam and C'raw was hatching! And the others would soon be! Where was

C'raw? That he was perched next to Cam with a smug smile on his face Beana had been too excited to see.

Harron was trying to tell Brilla to go and tell The Sage what she had seen, but Mattie's tempting bacon was stopping her form leaving the battlefield table.

Beana ran back into kitchen to tell them there were now two hatchlings in Cam's nest! She nearly trod on Piper as she ran out of the kitchen again, taking some of Brilla's bacon with her for Cam and the hatchlings.

Mattie's soup was bubbling over, the hungry owl was bubbling over because her long awaited breakfast had just been taken away by Beana. Harron was determined to get the now screeching owl out of the kitchen and up to The Sage's hall. The hungry owl's flapping wings sent his battle plan to the kitchen the floor!

Mattie's wooden spoon flew through air to hit Beana as she ran into the kitchen to say there were two more hatchlings demanding to be fed!

ReeMara could not move as the egg was cracking in her hands! Piper had to help her take the bits of shell off the little wet hatchling while it chirped loudly trying to move its featherless wings.

The hatchling was no more than a snack for a ferret but Piper could see, 'It' and ReeMara was fascinated with each other. If she had known she would have to wet nurse the hatchling when ReeMara had scribe lessons she might have eaten it then. But as it was, it was requesting food from ReeMara.

Trigary, said was a name he liked, he was trying to eat a chunk of meat much too large for him, ReeMara thought he would burst trying; all she could do was hold him in one arm and try to find meat the size he needed with the other!

ReeMara was so involved in looking after Trigary; it was a full time job with just one hatchling. ReeMara had to wander at Cam and C'raw they seemed to cope easily with all their hatchlings!

Beana seemed to cope with them all, and saw ReeMara had the right food for a growing eagle. If ReeMara had to run around to find food for Trigary she would not be able to attend her lessons nor see to her friends with the herd.

Soul was concerned ReeMara was spending so much time with the fledgling. Fledglings did not seem able to graze on the grass covered lands as he could.

The Sage was strict about anyone going outside; food for the herds and folk had to be collected. They were not to be seen by warriors of either side, not to remind folk living on the Grassland of the caves caverns on this side of the river. It would be better if they forgot folk still lived in the cliffs.

That two men had found away over the mountains was worrying enough. That the men had another colour to their skin asked another question! Their noses match those of their eagles, their dark hair suggested they came from and other regions, other lands than the Barbarians or the Legions.

Good thing about the owls she could trust them to report everything they saw. But they could not tell her, just what seeing the two men and their horses on the cliff meant.

Brilla had told Harron everything she had told The Sage. It was Piper that pointed out that Harron's nose could be described as matching an eagle's beak; When Piper said that, Brilla turned her head to look at the boy.

Harron was as tall as ReeMara. Brilla could describe him as thin, even bony. His hair was dark as the night it hung around his face, his nose stood out under his dark eyes.

As owls had been living in cliffs dwellings for more turns than she could remember, Brilla was used to seeing folk but not from this point of view. An owl was an owl, as a human was a human! Now Brilla come to think of it, Harron was a human hatchling as was ReeMara. Her flaxen hair and pale skin did not match Harron's hair or skin it was not the ferret round her neck or the hatchling on her arm that made her look different!

Harron was making Brilla describe the strangers again, he was wondering, what were they doing here?

Whatever they were doing now Brilla could not say from her perch in Mattie's kitchen; Harron could see Brilla was not interested in going and have a look not after all The Sage had said, nor would she miss the bacon Mattie had sizzling over his fire. Harron was interested in the strangers. Why would they want to cross the mountains with donkeys?

The season turned a full curricle, no more had been heard of the two strangers with their eagles, the only evidence they had been there was the young eagle on ReeMara's arm. Trigary spent the time ReeMara was at her lessons watching Piper watching him. There was always a rush of red fur and feathers to greet her when her lessons finished.

Everyone had got used to their strange games but this morning they could not rush at ReeMara. As ReeMara and all the students and their teachers had gone to stand on the cliff top, from there they could look over the land by the river flowing towards where the sun sank at night.

Brightly coloured tents could be seen in the morning haze. Every bird that could leave their nest was sent out to report on what they could see. C'raw would not let birds with newly hatched fledglings fly, as their young had to be looked after as well as their humans.

C'raw pride for his flights could only be bettered when he looked at the hatchling in his and Cam's nest. The human battle had brought other crows to the cliffs, and now the cliffs had Flights strong enough to look after the Cliff Roost. With the cliff owls to cover the skies at night and his Cliff Flights by day, the humans living there could count on them. But the mountains had kept a secret. The unexpected lines of tents shocked him.

Harron's table battlefield on Mattie's table was marked with the new arrivals! He could see that the balance had changed, even if he was not sure what the unknown party had in mind. When they engaged, who were they going to engage with?

The Senators were trying to bring the Emperor to discuss maters of grave concern.

"We have all ready sent three legions to the area! How can they request more assistance?"

"Should we send another Dux to take command?"

"The Dux we have employed is the wrothest of men we could send."

"I think the empire has sent more than enough men to deal with the Barbarians. I think we should address the other problem! My ladies are requesting silk; it is bad enough not to have enough amber available. As for the taxies the Senate are not receiving while building has been slowed down due to the shortage of amber to put into their foundations. Who would have thought people still need to continue such a tradition!"

The Emperor was finding daily life tedious, his senators were complaining, his women were complaining, at the lack of silk in the city's markets, and there was the unexplained lack of amber in the city. He waved his advisers away.

He had sent men to other cities to get the silk his women needed. As for amber, his store had not been aloud to risk his private believes. And, any man with such a troublesome belly could not allow his supply to dwindle. Without the amber powder his attendants made, he would not be able to enjoy his food.

If his head had been clear he would have spent this day in the Senate instead of asking his advisers to attend him in his private apartments. The wine had left its spoor from the fest the night before. Why did they expect him to worry about their interests as well as his own! He was glad when the great doors swag shut behind the irritating senators.

"Senator Markus, we have to discuss what we should do, the Emperor is not attending to serious matters as he should. The Senate will not be happy to leave things as they are!"

Senator Markus muttered to Senator Clod as the doors of the Emperor's private apartments clang loudly as they shut to hide his words from the others.

"The shortage of amber is serous. It has also come to my notice that the silk trains have not been coming regularly into the city."

Senator Clod was responsible for their trading permits. He had seen his coffers- the city's coffers were not as full as they should have been.

Senator Markus was saying the Emperor's frail health was preventing the Senate from acting in the City's best interest.
He was thinking they should continue their discussion in the baths the other Senate members would be easier to talk to in its relaxing atmosphere.

Should the Senate send another legion to the north, if only to end the tiresome problem of the Barbarians? Amber could be brought from farther a field; other countries also had large supplies of amber.

"The Amber from the north has captured the belief of the people for as long as I can remember, the new religion believers have not disregarded their old traditions."

Senator Clod interrupted Senator Markus:

"The new religion has taken to using amber as pray beads!"

"They like their crosses of gold!" remarked Senator Markus. Was Senator Clod laughing behind his hand? Trading of gold had to be registered with his office.

"Good thing you don't have you finger on the amount of wine that comes into the city, Citizen!" Senator Clod's arm patted the back of his well feed friend: "There are deals we have to talk over; a glass of wine would make our discussions more sociable."

"They have not engaged either opponents what are they waiting for?" Harron wanted to know, the lack of movement was frustrating him.

ReeMara was so frustrated! The Sage would not let her leave. ReeMara had not trusted herself to tell The Sage why it was so important to go the City of the Seven Hills, with the stones She-With-The-Sight had insisted she take there. Those stones she held tightly in her hand.

"She just said, 'I could not travel while a war raged in front of our door!'"

"If we were to go north, back the way you came, it would take us away from this battle, but not to the City of the Seven Hills. The river is guarded by both the Barbarians and the Legions. And now, the men that fly eagles are using the only way through the mountains. How do you suppose we are going to get to where we want to go?"

ReeMara turned away from Harron and his table! He could be so infuriating at times! And what did he mean by 'We'?

"A trip like the one you want to make will take a lot of planning!" Mattie said and he was right. "No army can march on an empty stomach…"

"No student can learn on an empty stomach!" sang the two children sitting in Mattie's the kitchen.

"Have I said that before?" asked Mattie as he waved them away to their next lesson with his wooden spoon.

"The eagles I have talked too, speak of a silk road leading right to the City on the Seven Hills, it is on the other side of the mountains." CC'raw said, he was a hatchling from C'raw and Cam first brood, that was over two turns ago. He, like his father, took his flight duties seriously, as he did when it came to helping Harron and ReeMara in anyway he could.

CC'raw had been to see for himself the entrance of the way into the mountains. He found it was very busy with donkeys moving one behind the other; they looked like a brown gray snake as they descend to the Grassland.

CC,raw's father C'raw was too busy to take scouting flights, the running of his 'Flights' took up all his time and this season's hatching was not that far away.

"The way in the mountains will be watched by the humans attending the donkeys. And, we know the legions are constantly receiving supplies from behind their lines!" CC'raw pointed out before flying off; he had to catch up with his other duties.

"The Barbarians are not short of supplies, folk from the north are seeing to their needs." Harron said, "The man, who brought those small children, was telling our scribe at the meal last night."

When the man in a boat had slipped past the Legions, he had offered himself as a scribe and he was skilled as a bowman. He had come as he needed to find protection for the children with him; their village had been destroyed by the warring parties.

ReeMara did not question how Harron had learnt that, when he had not been sitting close to the man when he had been talking. She knew he could read the words from folk's lips. His strange talents had got them into and out of trouble, many times!

ReeMara did understand Harron when he said she needed the skill of a bow to hunt, thought Trigary was proving a better hunter than she was. Trigary was growing into such a handsome bird and he could fly higher than any owl or crow.

Hunting for food was difficult on the Grasslands, with men engaging in battles or horsemen charging at surprised opponents disturbing the grass edible inhabitants.

The cannon did not offer much space for play or practice, Soul was always willing to carry ReeMara as she tried to shoot a bundle of straw with her bow. Harron had to laugh ReeMara's arrows did not always hit the intended target. She had not hit anyone yet. Though neither, horse or human had let themselves get between her and her target.

The new man tried to teach them how to use a curved bow, he was also a scribe. His style fascinated Harron, it was so different to the one he had learnt before; it was as if a spider had run over the soft clay they used to practice on, not at all like their sharpened feathers could write.

Harron fascination was not felt by ReeMara; she did understand this was a place of learning, she felt at home here. But, she still had to go to the City on the Seven Hills. Her parents had been taken away from her. 'Their death must not be wasted.' She-With-The-Sight words rang in the depths of her mind.

It was not that ReeMara wanted to leave the cliffs; there was much more she wanted to know about the cliffs that had become her home, and Beana was like a mother to her and Mattie fussed over her and her friends.

"ReeMara, it is no good wishing to make a journey when warring men are sitting at our door step. The Sage would be out of her mind if she let you go! You still have so much to learn." Beana did not stop at seeing the look on ReeMara's face: "You are two young to be about alone."

Beana did not want to hear ReeMara point out that she had got here without human help.

Since ReeMara had been here, not many folk were able to get to the Cliff Citadel. Though folk form the Grasslands still wanted to bring their children to the teachers in the Cliffs, they were kept away by the war disturbing the grass land's normal life.

"ReeMara, you got here before the wars started!" said Beana pleased with her point, till Harron broke in:

"She would not be going alone, I will go with her!"

"From the mouth of babes!" Beana turned on her heal and left the kitchen.

"Ok, ReeMara, now you tell me why we have to make such a journey?" Harron was not going to let her leave the kitchen without telling him what was behind her longing to leave and go to an unknown city. Were they not good enough for her here?

Harron did not expect ReeMara to grab him nor did he expect to be pulled under the table, under their battle field!
He was surprised to see her pull from her robe a pouch of leather and three stones slide into his hands.

The eye looked at him it held him till the green sunlight came through its shadows to remind him of the sun in the woodland's trees, then a deep red with the proud horse and his swirling mane. Was that a horses' tooth he could see deep in the stone? Those three stones ReeMara had not shown him before.

When Harron heard what ReeMara had experienced, he said:

"To make such a trip will take much thoughtful planning; we have a lot to do. ReeMara we cannot go out there, as babes in the woods!" Using the same expression Beana had used as she had left the kitchen.

"Is there a battle going on under the table, under the battle table?" Mattie said as he came into the kitchen, his friendly face smiled at them form over his ample belly. Mattie did not see ReeMara slip the stones back into their leather pouch and flip the edge of her robe to hide it.

Harron did not see ReeMara for some days as he was in the halls where mysterious maps were rolled and stored in racks or stretched on long trestles. The Legions came from the City on the Seven Hills, Harron had heard. ReeMara nor he could not travel through the Legions nor roam round the Barbarians!

If the men living in the coloured tents had come over the mountains with horses and donkeys had carried stores. When they could find away to across the mountains, Harron was sure!

Harron did not know who had brought him here. So many came to the teachers in the cliffs, most folk knew from where they had come from. Harron thought he had been brought here was because his speech was difficult for most to understand. That ReeMara understood him was like rain on dry ground, she had befriended him even when others had tried to step out of his way. That his nose marched the eagles on the men's shoulders had often been remarked on, more so now Trigary was flying around. Harron's dark hair, his dark eyes and his dark skin matched the soldiers from in the bright tents. There were questions he needed answers to. Maybe accompanying ReeMara to the City on the Seven Hills would bring answers to his questions that could not be answered here.

How to cross the mountains must be shown on these maps. When Harron had found a possible route he was going to ask Trigary to take a higher level look. But Harron did not know how he was going to talk to the eagle with out ReeMara knowing what he was planning.

There was not a moment to discuss anything with anyone! The Sage found everyone work to do, hay had to be brought down from the high meadows, and the snails from the cliffs green ledges were ready to take into the drying boxes so they could be eaten in the days to come.

Elder kids went down to the waters edge for watercress as the sun sank low as the owls kept watch as the darkness fell.

Contact with the warring parties was not to be encouraged. The folk in the cliffs would not be safe if it was known by the warriors, there were teachers there. But daily life still had it needs and the needs of the folk in the cliffs were many. While the war raged some of their supplies had stopped getting through.

The horses had provide their hair for their clothing when the fine wools of sheep could no longer be brought by the river from folk whose life had been disturbed by the long war. The horses helped keep the Cliff dwellers warm in another way, their waste could be dried by the sun and winds on many of cliffs' tops, ready to burn in their fires places and heat cook pots. Hay was made from grass taken from under the noses of the warring parties with the help of the Cliffs' owls and crows.

Herbs were collected to top up the ones that everyone grew in their dwellings, and the seeds in the hay were used to make bread.

The river saw water was always fresh and fish could be caught to see there was other food on the table. Goats were happy to live on the mountains cliffs; their milk was helping the folk in the cliffs through these hard times.

The hardest problem for The Sage was she felt cut of from what was going on below her and from whatever plan her sister had for the child standing before her.

"ReeMara, I am only one half of a pair of twins; my feelings are not her feelings, my pain is not her pain, her fear I do not feel. But her life is half of my life. When life was not in her body I would know as half of me would be gone.

I can only tell you that she lives; whatever her wishes are I do not know.

She-With-The-Sight has placed a command on you, a command you wish to fulfil. You want to take her command in the name of your parents."

The Sage stopped what she was saying to look at the three pieces of amber in ReeMara's hands. The Amber Eye looked back at her, deep into her soul. The Sage had to turn her head away from its stare. She covered it with her hand to look at the wild horse held in the next stone, what was hidden in its' windswept mane?

The Sage's mind wandered in the woodland summer shadows or was it cool water running over a stream's bed?

The Sage looked again at the girl standing before her in her hall in the high cliffs. When ReeMara had come to the Citadel in the Cliffs she could not tell her what had happened to her. Beana had held the child as she had cried. How could she have known that her sister was behind the pain the child carried!

Looking at the amber in ReeMara's hands The Sage realised her sister must have made plans to find a carrier for such amber!

She-With-The-Sight had a reason for wanting those pieces of amber placed under the temple at the hart of the City on the Seven Hills. The child believed placing the stones would give meaning to the death of her parents, her brother, and the folk of her village. But, The Sage was sure, that was not the only reason behind her twin sister was plan, she wanted something more.

The three pieces of amber told The Sage of a stronger power. Whatever was on her sister's mind, amber with such power had to be taken to the hart of the City on the Seven Hills!

The Legions came from there; they were chocking the grassing lands with their solders, putting the balance between the Grassland and the Forest of Marshes at risk. Also the damage to the Grassland threatened the mighty herds of horses, and threatened the lively hood of her people here in the cliffs and the folk living on the Grassland; if the balance was to change here it would also affect the Great Forests to the North.

The Barbarians were here to keep the Legions from advancing any further, but that did not explain why an army from the Spice Regions was also here.

Somehow ReeMara was involved in all of this!? That little girl was standing defiantly in front of her and an eaglet was watching ReeMara confront her, The Sage! With a problem much larger than just a child with a childish wish.

This child had brought three pieces of amber all the way here and she was now demanding to be aloud to take them over the mountains to the largest city known to mankind!

Outside the safety of the Cliff Citadel, warriors were engaging in a bloody battle, men's screams rang off the cliffs rock walls.

The men from the Spice Regions had taken advantage of higher ground. Their bowmen rained sharp arrows onto the ranks of sword carrying legionaries and stung their horses' sides as they pulled chariots over the trampled earth.

Horns blew and whips cracked, in the air above the men bearing spears were burning balls of turf that were flung with sizzling flames from catapults at the advancing Barbarians.

Harron was sure the Legionaries were being held back by the Barbarians. The Barbarians would not have been able to hold their ground without help from the men camping in the bright tents!

It was their arrows that stopped mounted legionaries riding down men in the first lines and their arrows were aimed to burst the fireballs, so the hot oils did not burn those its fire was intended to reach.

Harron was watching the current battle from the window in the passage outside the entrance to The Sage's high halls. His attention was torn between what was happening out in the grass land below the cliffs and the frustratingly closed door that The Sage and ReeMara were behind. He could hear the battle raging outside but from behind that door, nothing!

C'raw and his sun, CC'raw landed on the sill of the window:

"Are they still talking?" CC'raw wanted to know, "They have been in there for an age. When The Sage caught ReeMara trying to hide provisions under her bed, I knew there would be some talking, but not so much!"

"It is not often that one of The Sage's charges wants to leave, and leave at a time when egg-lings are about to hatch! Cam is flying around keeping an eye on every nest. It is a joy having new members to the roost, if only the young were not so time consuming!" C'raw ruffled his feathers to make himself look larger than his son; his dark hood and smoky body were matched by his son's feathers, all Cam and his' hatchlings had black hoods and

smoky bodies. Cam's and his fledglings contrasted with
the black crows from the forests.
Though the crows from the forests had black feathers,
C'raw had to admit they made excellent flight members.

The Cliff Citadel had trained flights that any flight
leader would be proud to boast about. For the disciplined
training C'raw thanked those that had schooled him and
Cam when they had lived in forest round the tree She-
With-The-Sight lived in the Isles of the Mists.

After ReeMara had been accepted by The Sage into the
Cliff's halls and though Beana had tended ReeMara like
any crow tending their hatchlings; the two leaders of the
Crows Flight knew ReeMara would want to leave the
Cliff Citadel to continue the journey she had begun with
them.

The pair of crows had been living in the cliffs for many
seasons with ReeMara; they had taught their hatchlings
and commanded the wild crows that had joined them.
They saw to the daily running of Flights of Crows of the
Cliff Citadel.

C'raw needed to talk to The Sage; the Cliff Citadel's
welfare had to be taken into account. She-With-The-Sight
had commanded Cam and C'raw to accompany the little
girl.

Now ReeMara was not the little child they had
watched over as well as any hatchling, she was now
much stronger and had taken advantage of the lessons the
kind humans had offered her. They loved her as much as
any hatchling; they felt torn between her and their
responsibilities in the cliffs.

The passage outside The Sage's hall strained silence
was disturbed by Beana; she was slightly out of breath by
the climb from the library where the citadel's maps were
stored.

Harron recognised the map rolls Beana had in her arms, he had been studying them; if the donkeys were bring stores to the bowmen and their supporters, there had to be away over the mountains. The Legions blocked the way Harron would have normally advised ReeMara to take.

"Are you all waiting the see The Sage?" Beana did not wait for anyone to answer she was through the door to The Sage before they could.

"Young Harron and Flight Leader with his son are waiting in the passage" Beana set the maps onto the table in front ReeMara.

Trigary was perched on the window sill as CC'raw brushed past him, to take a perch close to ReeMara. The Sage could see C'raw hovering outside her window, not daring to push past the eagle that was always to be seen with ReeMara.

"Can you ask Harron to enter my hall; I don't want him to try to attract my attention by trying to reach me through my window!"

Beana went the door Harron almost fell into The Sage's hall. He had pressed himself closely to the door trying to hear what was going on inside. Beana did not have to ask him to enter he was across The Sage's hall and by ReeMara's side before she could!

"I have studded those maps!" Harron did not wait to greet those around the table. "The best way is to use the same route the donkeys use. There are often horses among them and we could travel unnoticed among them…"

"We!" ReeMara was surprised Harron had said 'We' before, but that he wanted to come with her! In fact she had not seen him since she had said she was going to try to get to the City on the Seven Hill. If she had not stored the bacon titbits for Trigary and Piper under her bed she would not be here now trying to explain to The Sage why she had to go, even though part of her hart was braking at the very thought of leaving a place she had come to love.

"Yes WE, you did not think I would let you go on your own did you? You…"

"I got here by myself…." ReeMara started to say.

"We got here, with you…" C'raw would have said more, but Piper running up the table leg made Beana start:

"How did you get in here?"

"That ferret can always find away into the food stores when she wants to, so why not into my halls?" said The Sage glancing at the ferret.

Harron ignored them all, he unrolled the maps; spread them out to show The Sage and ReeMara what he had in mind:

"When I saw how different the people look that had come over the mountains it occurred to me there must be other lands beyond the mountains! So I went to talk to the donkeys, they did not seem to be staying around the bowmen's tents for long before being sent back into the mountains with new loads, this time with hay.

The donkeys I spoke to told me their lodes had been change from bails of material to arrows. They would have rather carried the bails over the mountains, as they were lighter than the stores the bowmen needed.

The route they had taken before had not taken them through the mountains. They had taken away through open grass land between human dwellings and waterholes, before entering a high walled place, with many more human dwellings than they had ever seen before. Where, they said their bales were exchanged for other things. It has to be the city we are looking for, and seven hills are marked on this map."

Harron did not use words to explain further he let his long fingers show everyone what he had found among the scrolls.

ReeMara eyes were fixed on the point on the aged map where Harron indicated the City of the Seven Hills was.

The city must have a great river running through it. Harron hands were telling them the river was like the one below The Sage's halls. From the number of maps now rolled out and placed end to end the City of the Seven Hills must be far away!

Trigary was not helping his head was in the way ReeMara tried to push him to one side. If The Sage was cross at having a young eagle hanging upside down from her lamp she did not say so. He was studding the maps from a bird eyes view; he did dryly remark. If Humans could see the land the way he did their maps would make more sense! Now there were two birds hanging upside down!

CC'raw was trying to see what the eagle was grumbling about, it was obvious those squiggles were rivers and that must be a mark for a hill, that mark meant a city or at lest a meeting place for humans.

C'raw made the third bird hanging from the lamp attached to the halls ceiling:

"The way to go is away from the river that leads to the sea."

"If you turn this way you will see that is not a sea but a lake fed from the mountains."

Harron head of dark hair and with his nose like Trigray's beck did not look out of place with his feathered friends hanging from the lamp in The Sage's hall.

The discussions in The Sage's hall did not fade with the day's light. Beana was not happy, the very thought of ReeMara leaving was making tears swell in her eyes even when she busied herself seeing that food was brought to The Sage's hall.

C'raw was both happy and sad his son was going to accompany ReeMara and Harron. The Sage had acknowledged he and Cam were of important to the running of Cliff Citadel. That his son was going to take on the command She-With-The-Sight had given him filled his chest with pride. A pride Cam would mirror, she was not present as new hatchlings were eminent.

"Sea Spray has decided to remain here as her awaited foal will be foaled next spring. Soul has stated he has decided to continue travelling with ReeMara." C'raw reported.

"What did he say, really!?" Piper asked.

"What he really said was, 'I go where ReeMara goes.'" C'raw was not hanging upside down anymore he was perching on the table's edge next to the questioning ferret. He had to ask the ferret whether she was planning to go with ReeMara or not, as the ferret did so like the titbits she could get from the kitchen!

"I go where she goes." Was all Piper would say as she helped herself to more of the food Mattie's kitchen had sent up.

"Your plan is to attach yourselves to the trains of donkeys taking the mountain route?" The Sage was asking.

"We don't have to go down to the Grassland to take the trail, we can cut through the canyon, there is away through the lower caves that allows us to take the trail this side of the river. We can then slip out from behind the rock and mingle with those in the trail." Harron said,

"Soul say's we will be travelling with Bramble and Cain, they have been arguing as to which one of them will come with us, till they realised they did not want to be parted from each other!"

The Sage looked at Harron's face with his nose and dark hair, raped in a robe like the Bowmen he would go unnoticed but ReeMara would be noticed! Her hair! They could cover it, tie it back. She was the same height as Harron; put a robe on her and you would not be able to tell she was a girl. Not that ReeMara could be described as feminine; she was as likely to exchange fighting fists with any of the youths, mostly on behalf of Harron it had to be said.

The Sage had decided to let them go, even though apart of her did not want them to leave and Beana considered ReeMara and Harron as her children. But her sister, She-With-The-Sight, had a plan that she The Sage did not understand, could only try to guess at. She, The Sage of the Cliff Citadel did not want to be responsible if the plan were to falter at her citadel.

Both Bramble and Cain had decided to make the planed trip with Soul and their little human, Piper was coming as well and ReeMara's new friend the eagle. They thought it was the best compromise that CC'raw was coming with them in place of his mother and father, Cam and C'raw. They were not so sure about Harron, he is too full of new ideas.

"We have been made to feel so welcome by the herds of the Grasslands and the comfort the canyon offered and thanks to generosity of the kind humans in the cliffs." Bramble started to say, but Corn had stopped him by saying they needed mores stories to tell. While they were grazing they had bored everyone silly with their old tales, they now needed new tales to tell.

Whatever their reasons were for going with her made ReeMara happy, it also meant there would be a horse to carry the things they needed to take with them, as Harron had pointed out.

Things as well as packets of food that Mattie had given them were in piles in her room. What he had given them it was better than the food ReeMara had taken from the kitchen Beana had wanted to point out, if they had not found the bundle of bacon rinds ReeMara had hidden under her bed she would not have known ReeMara was planning to leave the Cliff's Citadel.

Beana did understand what drove ReeMara; she had held the little child when the tears of sorrow had flowed down her cheeks. Beana had known from that day, in her heart, that this day must come. She and The Sage told ReeMara and Harron over and over again there was always a home for them here, whenever they wanted to return.

The Sage had thought it was better if they did not tell everyone what they were planning; ReeMara and Harron were to write on scrolls their goodbyes.

The Sage also saw ReeMara wrote down her account of how she came to the Cliff Citadel and the command She-With-The-Sight had given her, her scroll was then placed in the deepest cave of the Citadel libraries.

The dawn's light was not to be seen on the planes as ReeMara and Harron woke; the breakfast Beana had prepared for them was as she said to carry them through the day, from the amount ReeMara remarked there was enough to carry them all the way to the City of the Seven Hills!

Piper and CC'raw took advantage of the food their humans could not eat, Trigary watch with look of impatience from the window ledge. He was looking forwards to taking to the lightening sky; he looked sideways at the packs and bundles waiting for them in the corner by the door, but his gesturer did not make anyone eat any faster.

The Sage did not ask them if they had everything they would need. She had helped them with their plans, she was still worrying about letting two children go into the mountains alone. But, if any one was going to have a chance to make such a journey it was the pair sitting staring at the breakfast Beana wanted them to eat.

It was time to go; the horses were standing waiting on the clip leading to the donkey trail. Bramble and Cain were arguing as to who was to take the packs and who was to carry Harron. Soul did not help by saying he would only be taking ReeMara, and Trigary was grumbling loudly, 'this was not the best way to start their trip!'

Piper and CC'raw thought the eagle was making a fuss, but when they saw how upset ReeMara and Harron were when The Sage and Beana came to see them on their way, maybe this was not a moment to say so.

Cam and C'raw watched with pride and sorrow the group waiting to join the donkey train. They were proud their son was accompanying ReeMara in their place, and proud to be among those training the Flights of the Citadel, but that did not stop them feeling deep sorrow at the departure of their friends.

The Sage did not say anything as she hugged the children to her she only let them go so Beana could take them into her arms. Donkeys were starting up the path from the river they soon would have to slip between the donkeys carrying hay; their driver must not see there were others joining his donkey train.

The Sage and Beana were hugging each other:

"Wherever this trail leads you, however your journeys end, you are always to think of the Citadel as your home."

Then they were lost behind the rock as the path cut into the mountain.

ReeMara felt as if she had been torn from those she loved. She did not take any notice of the chatter around her.

"No, they are known to me, that's Bramble. He and I have grazed on the planes behind the human encampment."

The donkey that had asked who the strangers were had been in the last train coming to the humans' encampment. She was grumpy at having to make the return trip so soon after getting here. She only had to carry hay without the difficult to balance materials that made the arrows or swords the humans seemed to need. If she had to carry human feeds she would have had even more to grumble about!

"If you had stayed with your group you would have to put up with the driver's sharp tong and stinging whip!"

The speaker was all ready fed up with the old jenny complaining so much and they had only just started their trip. He would have pointed out if they had been farther back they would have had to carry heaver feeds to replace feeds the donkey train had used on their way here.

Harron already knew about the stores of feed and provisions kept in caves along the trail. Trigary had seen the donkey drivers drop supplies from their donkeys' backs and drag them away out of sight into the rock.

The eagle and the crow were circling above then as they turgid up the every steeping path and it was getting so narrow only one donkey could walk behind another. The three horses found the pace too slow for their liking. Only Piper was enjoying the ride on Corn's back, the packs made a comfortable place to watch the rolling planes grow smaller; then disappear into the blue horizon of the Grass Lands.

The day was slow and boring winding their way between high cliffs, ReeMara did not look down when the cliff's walls fell away, the falling drop made her feel sick, she could not even ask Soul how he could walk so close to the edge without getting nervous.

The donkeys never seemed to trip, get nervous or upset, not even when rocks fell from above or the wind blew cold blasts at them, or the rain washed the warmth from their coats.

It would have been a cold night on the mountain platform if the over hanging rock had not saved them from the worst weather the clouds could through at them. Harron and ReeMara were happy to have Soul and Bramble with Cain to keep them worm. As they were hiding in the sea of donkeys they could not light a fire as the drivers could, nor could they warm some of the food they had with them.

Whenever the dark night had stopped the donkey train on the trail, they were thankful then the twisting path hid them from the drivers leading the packed donkeys and the drivers in charge of the end of the train, it gave them the opportunity to heat their food and warm themselves.

The Bath House tall columns threw dark cool shadows over the baths of hot water waiting for bathers to sink into. Armnell saw to the fresh towels for the senator she was going to massage. Her strong fingers had been prised for many years for relieving strains and pains. She had been much valued in the gymnasium of the gladiators, till she had been bought to work for the senators in their parlours.

Armnell was proud she had a status not many slaves had; her skills had made her mistress of the Senator's Bath House and the teacher of other slaves providing the services the bath house offered.

Senator Clod did not look at her as he rolled onto his stomach waiting for the strong fingers to work into his tense muscles.

"You do not have to let your body carry so many problems."

If Armnell had not been an old trusted slave he would not have let her talk to him that way.

"If you only knew what problems I have to face! The Emporia's ladies are raging over the lack of silk for their togas! And now there are problems when starting foundations for any new building due to the lack of amber. No amber has been brought here since the Legions were sent to prevent the Barbarians from taking control of the North.

The amber from the north has the reputation of being of the best quality; so much so, the religions are demanding more than has been agreed."

He did not know why he was telling Armnell, she was a slave despite her soothing skills:

"The Dux is to be called back; another man is to be made Dux of the Legions. The Senate want to send another legion to end the continuing conflict, but our other legions are dealing with problems of security on our sea border between the Olive Island and our main land."

Armnell did not have to hear what this senator was saying as many had been grumbling about the lack of silk, not that it was a problem for her, for her work she did not need silk togas.

Silk was not the only shortage Armnell had noticed the city was suffering from; many of the spices the cooks need were difficult to get, they were usually brought by the silk trains. As were some of the medicines she used to ease the senator's complaints.

'Maybe, it would serve the city better to know why the silk trains have not brought their wares to the markets.'

Armnell could not speak aloud what she was thinking, as a slave she may not suggest such matters to her masters. It had surprised her that none of the senators thought to question the absence of the silk trains. All the talk was about placing the great Legions in the regions that would best benefit the Senate's pockets.

Armnell large body was no longer young or thin like the young slaves the masters played with, but she still had her wits about her and knowledge in her fingers. If anyone was to ask her to counsel the Senate, she would bring their attention to the Emperor's failing heath, his loss of judgement had been often remarked on. And, the Barbarians were not the only threat to the plans of the Senate, there was more behind the missing silk trains.

It was not her place to talk, but she could listen to the lose talk she heard when the members of the Senate that made use of her skills.

Armnell had once planed to run away, though she had gold enough, her black skin would always betray her if she was to enter the world of the free man! There weren't any free slaves in this city with dark skins like hers. She knew her key to survival was to wait, hear whenever the Senators had to discus. There were those that would give a piece of gold to hear what was being said in private quarters.

No one knew Armnell could read and write, none of the dark skinned slaves were taught such things, she had taught herself. As a white male eunuch had always been employed to write downs the amounts of goods the Bath House needed. Armnell had only to ask for goods to be replaced was why the skill she had learnt had not been discovered by her masters.

The man's body began to relax under Armnell's fingers; she took warm towels from the heated stones and laid them over the Senator's legs as a man hurried towards the Senator rapped only in a towel.

"A messenger has arrived in the Emperor's palace! The Emperor's is refusing to see him. I have brought him here, the Senate is not open. He has news that should be heard without delay!"

The man that had disturbed the quite of the Bathhouse was pale with shock; he was as pale as the marble columns. He worried that he would suffer for being so indiscreet. But, the most powerful senators were to be found gathered in the comforts of the Bathhouse.

The columns of the bath halls had not seen such a scene! Senators clutching towels rose from their rest as the messenger was made to stand in their midst.

The senator that took control of the disturbance asked the men to explain what mater was so urgent it could not wait for more formal surroundings.

"The Dux sends the Senate-."

"Now young man, the formality of the Senate dose not fit the surroundings of the Bathhouse, you shall speak more directly!"

The impatience in the voice told of the impact of the disturbance the man had caused.

"The Dux." The man tried to start again: "Leader of the Legions for the Empire of the City of the Seven Hills sends his greetings-."

He was stopped again by another irritated voice.

"If our peace is to be disturbed then tell us what is so important?"

"The Barbarians have crossed-."

The Senators did not want to hear more, they had presumed the Barbarians and their accomplices had been defeated, sent away like a dog with its tail between its legs, the long awaited revenge for the loss of the Legion in the Northern Forests.

They fell silent as the words of the messenger rang from the columns:

"The Barbarians and their accomplices are causing grave concern. Their place on the field of battle has been deserted."

In the silence the poor messenger was able to tell the astounded senators of the smoke of the many fires that had hidden the withdrawal of the opponents.

Leaders had heard the cries made for the dead greet the morning sky; when their smoke had risen to the Gods, it left the Grasslands bare!

No explanation could be found was to why they had disappeared, nor where. The dwellers of the Grasslands and the folk heading horses with those found living in the cliffs, did not have the answers to questions asked of them.

The women and children found in the cliffs above the battle fields could not provide answers. Questions about where the other worriers came from or where their companions had gone could not be answered.

Armnell could not improve her store of gold with this information, that was her first thought. The fact the Legions stood alone on a battle field without a component struck her as funny till she realised the City on the Seven Hills was without protection. To have their armies so far away was to have the city exposed to any enemy took the welling humour from her heart.

ReeMara and Harron were enjoying the freedom form the daily routine they had been used to. For Piper travelling was not so different, she was always was hunting! Hunting in the kitchens or hunting among the rooks was all the same to her; the only difference was fresh meet or cooked!

Piper enjoyed shearing her catch with CC'raw and Trigary; Trigray helped with his high altitude rodent movement reports. Piper and CC'raw were surprised to find they were after a bear! Trigary had spotted movement from his thermal way above the hunters. It was not that he could not tell the difference between a bear or a mink or any of the smaller rodents, he just had not thought a bear might be a little too big for a ferret to take on, even with the help of a crow.

Harron found the ferret's favourite catch attractive; the mink tails of his friend's meals had caught his eye. The white thick fur with the black tips were at first hanging from his belt; when he had enough he hang them from the neck of his over robe. ReeMara thought it was a bit flashy at first, but she had to admit they held the cold wind away from them; Piper could not hang around her neck all the time.

The three horses were the ones with something to grumble about, the way was narrow and wound forever upwards!

They found the donkeys were far cleverer than the horses had been told when they were foals. The donkey's hooves found safe ways through the mounds of fallen rock. They did not panic when rock rained down on them, they calmly lent into the wall till it was safe to go on.

Wild cats tried to make the donkeys run blindly, in hope of catching an easy meal. Piper would have been an easy meal in this for ever whitening world, if CC'raw was not about to keep an eye on her.

Trigary could not see from where he was there were other travellers on the mountain; his friends were climbing among the donkeys along the narrow route below him! Trigary would have had to climb to a higher altitude to observe the men moving along the track far below their donkey train. He might have seen the men and horses, had he not sent the ground bound after that bear!

Harron a ReeMara were not at risk from the men climbing behind them, it would have taken weeks for the men to reach them and that was only if they stayed where they were.

The donkeys did not wish to stop even when it was dark they just kept walking and chatted intently with one another. They did not like changing places, to get them to change places was a trick ReeMara a Harron had to learn, when the weather close down on them the horses were reliant on the hay on the backs of donkeys.

Corn was fond of saying, 'I could eat a donkey!" What he really meant was he could eat all the hay a donkey could carry. Then the horses eat the hay from one donkey, another had to be placed so the horses could reach the hay a donkey was carrying without reaching over another, risking slipping from the path and falling from the mountain.

When the track passed through a gorge or a cliff offering space enough to juggle the gossiping donkeys, Piper and CC'raw would start a conversation with a jack or a jenny.
Then all ReeMara and Harron had do was step in and carry on chatting so the donkeys with out hay in their packs were distracted and did not notice they had been moved along the line.

Corn was also fond of saying, if anyone talked too much! 'They could talk the hay off a donkey.' What he really meant was if he wanted to get a donkey to move, all he had to do was talk, a lot!

Should a chatting donkey notice they had been moved along the line, the rock rang with their braying disapproval. Not that that stopped the other donkeys talking or their long ears form twitching, but for human or horse, ferret or bird the sound of disapproval set their nerves on edge.

The route had not looked like this on any of the maps Harron had studded. It had not looked to be so vast, nor did it show how high the path went. Despite Trigray's higher surveillances did not tell them of the vastness of the white field stretching before them, with a single line of donkeys cutting a dark line on its white face.

It was cold, so cold that the air was still, white flakes cut into their half closed eyes; this was not a place for donkeys. Their chatter told the accompanying group that donkeys did not like the cold that greeted them on the white field. Having to listen to a stream of complaints from grumbling trudging donkeys brought down the listeners sprites.

The three horses trudged with their heads low matching the donkey's short strides as well as their depressing mood. The humans cling to their backs were not spotted by the drivers, for some reason there was a brake in their line, something was holding back the trailing donkeys and their drivers.

For the first time their group were starting to travel downwards or slide downwards! After all the climbing upwards and now the sensation of going downwards did not help the three horses control their hooves. The slide down the snow covered path showed the humans in the tented camp the value of clever donkeys and their better way of putting foreleg before hind leg; were as the horses behind them could only spin round making the humans cling ungracefully to their saddle packs.

ReeMara sank to the ground with her head spinning. A rough voice accompanied a large hand caught her arm.

"I feel like that after a drink!"

"I wish I felt like that after a drink, I need a whole skin to feel like that!"

"The last time you drank a skin you were sick and had to stay in your tent for a week!"

"That's what you think; I can drink a skin and still stand up in the wind."

"All you are is wind!"

Harron took ReeMara away from the support of the first man that had spoken. They had just walked into, slid into a camp, without warning! Why had the birds not warned them? Harron did not have a chance to find them and scold them; the two men were leading them towards their camp.

"We have not had word from the outside world; I have not seen your faces before."

Harron would have said something, but he could not as the man's words were flowing faster then even a donkey could!

"But we have not seen other faces or any faces for so long! One face here looks the same as another, after spending so much time here."

"As he says we have been here for months!"

"He wants to know what news you have."

"He wants to know how long we are going to have to sit here."

Harron's expression, somehow make the two men admit they had enough to eat and drink, and would the travellers like to join them in a warm meal.

Without waiting for an answer the longer one started to build up their fire while the shorter one prepared fresh meet for their unexpected guests.

If ReeMara thought they would give themselves away as the sound of their speech did not match the two men's, she need not have worried, as Master Long and Master Short did most of the talking, when they did ask questions they answered them, themselves.

"You will be travelling to Base Camp. We miss the home comforts we had there."

"Always something going on."

"Not like here."

"Where nothing happens and when it dose, it is only donkeys and more donkeys!"

The two men did not stop talking even when they had their mouths full. If Piper had thought the donkeys could talk, she had not met these two men!

Harron did manage to say in answer to one of their questions:

"Something must be holding them up, could be the weather; it was clouding over when we started to cross the white field."

"That could be it; donkey trains are expected to keep together, though we don't mind when there is a break."

"We don't have to unload so much hay." the short man said.

Harron thought quickly:

"How much hay do you think we need to get us to Base Camp?"

"Don't worry; we will see you have all the return supplies you need."

"We are skilled seeing to supplies!" interrupted the long man.

Harron was interested to hear that the donkeys had been expected, their loads of hay were to be stored, but the two men did not say for whom. That they were here to see the large cave was stocked with supplies must mean something.

As if to answer ReeMara's puzzled look the short man said they did not up their tents in the storage cave, the risk their fires could set the hay a light was too great. That was more than their lives where worth. Even if they jumped off the highest cliff they would not be able to get away from a revenging sword!

Piper could not imagine a sword doing such a thing, not after two humans had jump of a high cliff! ReeMara tried to keep Piper hidden and give her some of the cook meet. It was as well roasted, but not as good as Mattie's, Piper wanted to say, but she was in ReeMara's robe and in a tent in the mountains and not under Mattie's table.

To try to travel on in the low cloud that had spread a shroud over this part of the mountain was madness, not even the surefooted donkeys were willing to travel on. The cloud offered an explanation as to why other expected donkeys did not need the store masters attention.

ReeMara and Harron had to stay two days with the store men; if they had to stay any longer they would have wished they were donkeys. Corn's new saying was, 'the store men could talk the hay off the back of a donkey!'

Trigary had kept an eye on the white field as Mister Long and Mister short were expecting others to come this way. The others, ReeMara and Harron did not want to meet, not here anyway!

There must have been other people travelling with the donkeys as Mister Short, Mister Long had asked why the leaders of this train seemed to be in such a hurry. Harron signed to ReeMara to say they were hurrying to go to a wedding at Base Camp.

"Dark old fox, who would have known!" said Mister Long.

"He has gone for that little widow." Mister Short seemed to know.

"How do you know that?" Mister long wanted to know.

"I had an eye in her myself!"

"You old dog! I was going to through dice for her when I got back."

"Looks like that dark old fox has beaten you to her!"

For awful moment ReeMara thought they would be travelling with them, to find out if it was their little widow!

It was not just that they talked too much that worried her. Up until now they did not know she was a girl.

Sometimes Harron could be too clever and now Harron was deliberately ignoring her worried signals.

Though they never did tell them their real names as they were talking too much! Store Master Long and Store Master Short saw to their groups needs. The horses were happy to get two days rest from the ups and downs of the mountain's track.

Trigary needs were seen to but when one of the store masters brought out a hood for him, thinking maybe he had lost his. They were just as upset as he; they had not expected the bird to make such a fuss. ReeMara had to come and calm him. On seeing she did not have a proper glove to protect her arm from Trigray's talons they scurried back into the cave without drawing breath or taking a brake in their constant chatter to bring her a glove.

ReeMara was glad to have the glove they brought her, it soft leather kept her hand warm and the long sleeve made handling Trigary when he was upset easer.

In the volume of words exchanged between the two men ReeMara heard one of the horsemen had dropped it, as so many men had passed this way they could not say to whom it belonged. They could not see such a fine glove going to waste not when the youngster could use it. They must have noticed the horses did not have bridles, as they also brought three new ones. ReeMara thanked them, she would have said they did not bridle their horses, but thought better of it. ReeMara had noticed the horsemen used bridles, but she had not thought of themselves as horsemen!

Piper was not happy at having to keep hidden it was easer for CC'raw find a perch. Piper sulked off on her own she had found the cave an interesting place to explore. She told Herron about the other stores that could be found in the cave. He did feel guilty after he had helped himself to a bow and a quiver of arrows, but, the bow was much finer crafted than the one he had. No one would miss the bow, Piper was sure, nor would they miss the two tightly woven robes from the piles stored in the cave. Nor would they miss the mice Piper had found among the stacks of hay.

ReeMara like the robes as the colours were as bright and the wool was tightly woven against the winds that chilled them. Though the cloud had lifted it had not changed the colourless mountain track or the gray backs of the donkeys.

There was one mater that their group agreed about as soon as they had taken the first turn on the track; that was, as helpful as the store masters were listening to the donkey chatter was relief!

Trigary report offered no relief; he reported the white field above them had many strings of donkeys and horseman crossing it. Piper remarked that store Master Short and store Master Long would have many to talk at. But, as Soul pointed out their constant chatter would speed the hapless men quicker down the mountain after them.

ReeMara remarked, lest with these robes they would not look like kids from the Cliff Citadel. CC'raw said he would try his best to look like an eagle as he sat on ReeMara's shoulder.

"Good thing you are not trying to look like a donkey!" Bramble said.

"I have never seen a donkey sitting on a humans shoulder!"
Corn remarked from behind him.

Harron signed to ReeMara maybe talking too much was catching! Piper saw ReeMara pull her robe over her head in answer, so Piper said:

"Let the donkeys do the talking while we do the walking."

"That's rich coming from a ferret that looks like a fur rap!" said Soul. CC'raw was trying to imagine something Soul could look like, other than a likeness to his mother he looked like a horse! And, as a horse he could not tuck himself in the comfort of ReeMara's robes as a ferret could.

Herron was also hiding in his robe; the grayness had got to him like everyone else. The track crossed the mountain turned back on it self only to cross back again, the wind tried to whip them every time they made a turn. Now everyone was trying to be like store Mister Long and store Master Short!
Herron could not get away from their chatting even inside his robes.

The travellers could only catch glimpses of the land below; it was as if the clouds did not want them to know how vast the new planes were. Now that the morning sun had warmed the cold clouds travelling with them, they had drifted out into the wide valley they had been hiding. ReeMara had caught her breathe when she saw how vast the planes below were.

Greens and yellows seemed to strip the land far below them and blue lines crossed over to join the two colours. The view was like the maps at the Cliff Citadel only much larger. CC'raw was cling to Soul's withers in front of ReeMara, she did wonder why he was not interested in the wonders the clouds were revealing. Trigary was playing with the mountains thermals and swooping in and out of the clouds now drifting towards the new land cape.

Trigary was annoyed CC'raw was not watching him, not even when Trigary tipped a wing at him did the crow respond, he just sat all hunched up not looking at anything.

Bramble was chatting to Piper they were discussing whether or not the new land would have as good grazing and hunting possibilities as the familiar lands they had left. CC'raw would not be drawn into their chatter.

ReeMara and Harron were fascinated by the land below them, they were beginning to understand Trigray's world.

"Not often you get a chance to see the world with an eagles' eye." said Harron over his shoulder to ReeMara. He was as surprised as ReeMara to see CC'raw fall to the track; he lay there in front of Corn. If Corn had been chatting to the donkey behind him, as he was a moment before he would have hoofed the fainted bird off the track, off the mountain!

Sliding off a horse to get to the track, were CC'raw lay was not as easy as Harron had at first thought. Where they were the track was only wide enough for a horse to stand, had CC'raw swoon to the ground in the middle of the lines of donkeys, to get round those without hay and rescue the crow would have been a lot easer.

It was ReeMara that slipped out of her warm robe, she wrapt her arms around Soul's neck and slide to the ground, she then crawled between his front legs and out through his hind legs. Soul's dark tail hung over ReeMara's head hid her face when she reached for the prostrate crow. CC'raw opened his eyes to see a dark haired apparition before him; he let out a squawk that ran like a whip crack around the mountain. The donkeys wanted to move sharply forward before anyone was ready; their normal chatting was interrupted when they all started braying at the tops of their voices as if they were trying to wake the mountain!

Their noise did not disturb the crow he was now safe inside ReeMara's robe, ReeMara had to struggle to get back on Soal's back without falling of the mountain or disturbing the poor bird.

CC'raw did not know how to explain he did not like great heights, his fly expertise were in the lower thermals. When the donkeys heard this, they laughed so much that the mountain track rang with their braying for a second time that day.

Piper would have teased CC'raw about his vertigo but as he was still so upset she decided to bring him a mouse to calm his nerves. Piper did not mind peering over edges of ledges or taking vertical decent short cuts to get in front of the leading donkeys. The mountain rodents were more wary of the donkeys than they were of the hunting ferret, just as will as Piper was not happy with the food the store men had given them, much to dry for her liking.

Good thing they did not have to carry water, streams saw to every ones thrust, the donkeys had carried enough up and over the mountain, and then all that hay to the store cave. Those carrying enough stores to get them all to Base Camp were only to glad to share their loads, every mouth full of hay eaten was one less to carry the next day.

Piper would have been happy the share her catches with donkeys as well as with Trigary and CC'raw. But, they like the horses preferred their hay.

The mountain became almost friendly, the track sloped less unkindly and there were grasses offering tempting fresh snacks for eager muzzles. The weather was warmer than it had been, as for the wind it puffed sweet scents from the unfolding land below. Even the donkeys were moving with a spring in their hooves.

Once every ones hooves touched the springy turf the donkeys would not move on! They had only one idea and that was to indulge in the high slopes' good grass, they did have some hay left, if they had to go though another rocky mountain pass they all would have gone hungry. Strangely no one was chatting they were to busy taking advantage of the good vegetation.

Before the two young humans with Soul, Corn and Bramble could come up with the idea of travelling on without the donkey train, Piper and CC'raw diced to go on a hunting trip.

Trigary was left on guard above everyone; it suited his mood to hang on the gentle thermals. He was the first to see the long awaited Base Camp, if that human camp was Base Camp.

When they all were ready to travel on a few days later the many lines of tracks were for hooves to follow. The donkeys did seem to know were they were going, but they did not seem to want to get there.

When Piper asked a chatting donkey why they were not in a hurry to get to Base Camp, the little jenny's was answer surprised him.

"It is a, every loud place, everyone talks so loudly and there is so much going on. If we are unlucky we get repacked and sent away without even a muzzle of oat as a thank you for our last trip."

Once a donkey was chatting it is hard to stop them. The little jenny was telling Piper about a jack she had her eye on. To be sent on another trip without him would break her heart.

As for the other travellers, they were looking forward to seeing where all these tracks lead to and other tracks were coming down the gentler slopes and merging with theirs.

Harron did think to ask Trigary to see if the part of their train that had not crossed the white fields with them were on the mountain track.

He did not like to ask CC'raw, remembering the crow suffered from vertigo, but the CC'raw's commonsense would give him a better idea about what Trigary meant by.
'Many men on horses were threaded between the donkeys.' When Harron asked Trigary to describe the men he had seen the eagle remarked their noses matched his.

"Why are the men with the coloured tents coming back over the mountain?" CC'raw wanted to know when he heard Trigary's report. "They were supporting the Iron Man's men!"

ReeMara and Harron thought of Mattie's kitchen table and how they had positioned warriors from both side, but it did not help to explain why the men with the coloured tents wanted to cross back over.

Piper thought it was better not to know, her hunting trip with CC'raw had not been disturbed by the warriors farther up the mountain. But they had to decide what they were going to do now they were close to Base Camp.

Base Camp had all the colour the mountain track did not have when the donkey train with ReeMara and Harron had been travelling over it. Tents of many colours made their lines seem less regimented. There were more banners fluting in the almost warm breeze with every animal or bird they could think of, suns or moons or other symbols they had never seen before, fluted over each tent.

The lines with tents were only replaced by lines of tethering places for horses or donkeys; they were tended to by scurrying attendants. The lines were camels were being attended to by more scurrying attendants fascinated ReeMara and Harron, one of the donkeys had told them they were camels, when Piper had remarked they had never seen their like before.

Piper did not like the idea that camels could spit and when the donkey she was chatting to told her, 'They, the camels, never missed their targets!' Piper decided she would keep well out of their range.

Pens for cattle made more lines all leading towards a centre. But before the centre could be reached there were tents where trestle tables with goods matching the banners hanging above them, to catch the passer's eye. Everything a modern person could wish for himself or his horse, bird, camel was on display! Nothing for ferrets! Piper noticed.

Fine weapons, cooking pots, materials so fine you could see through them rippled their colours from their tables.

Voices rose in the air bartering or advising those passing by the virtue of their goods. They were so loud Piper would have preferred the donkeys chatting.

If the voices were not rising to mingle with the banners, rich smells were. Spices and herbs mixed with foods cooking, tempting hunger from those that had just eaten!

Scents to flatter any woman or make any man attractive teased every ones noses, except Pipers, she was annoyed.

They were supposed to have discussed what they were supposed to do once they got to Base Camp not just walk in!

That is just what they had done, walked in without thinking, just followed the donkeys. The donkeys did seem to know their way round, Piper had to admit and many of the humans had birds of prey accompanying them. A crow hovering above, no one noticed, not that anyone noticed a ferret in ReeMara's robe annoyed Piper too. The only sensible thing they did was to see that Soul, Bramble and Cain put on bridles to look like any other ridden horse.

What fascinated ReeMara and Harron were the folk themselves, they were just as different as the goods they sold.

ReeMara was used to Harron's darker skin but to see some of the folk had skins even darker than his and then turn her head to see folk with skins as light as hers.

ReeMara kept her head covered to look as if she and Harron were in charge of the donkeys they were with.

There were others with their donkeys distributing their wares to many of the merchants behind their trestle tables.

No one had asked them to say where they were going or who they wanted to make a deliver too, left them free to take in the sights and sounds new to them.

Piper did not get a chance to suggest they find away from the ever increasing crowds of humans. She could not just pop her head out of ReeMara's rob and tell them what to do.

There was a small man that reminded Piper of a wrinkled nut, sending younger humans with packages in their hands in different directions; his tong was as sharp as any whip.

'What were they going to do walk round in this hubbub for the rest of their days?'

Piper was not a happy ferret; that much ReeMara could feel.

But there was so much to see in Bass Camp, ReeMara did not want to stop and ask what was on the ferret's mind.

They were passing a large tent, so large it was made of many tents joined together. Where the tent flaps were left open they could catch glimpses of its inside, it was like looking into a clearing in a forest. The tent was the one place were folk were not filling its shaded places; it was quite and somehow a place to be respected.

"It is a place for meetings!" Harron singed to ReeMara.

If he knew any more about the large tent he did not have time to say. The donkeys had turned away from its large form into a line of tents where trading was just as vigorous as it was before they had seen the Meeting Tent.

ReeMara and Harron were once again wondering at colours and merging smells. A group of horsemen were riding through the clambering crowds, those close to them melted out of their path, no one spoke when the horsemen were passing.

Their banner Harron had seen on the battle field:

"They are men with the Iron Man." Harron signed, they did not make him feel comfortable and ReeMara face was pale. Soul felt ReeMara stiffen so did Piper, she poked her face free of ReeMara's robe so she could see better what was troubling ReeMara.

A face not unlike ReeMara's passed before her. That was a nasty scare running down his face! He must be important the other men around him were seeing the way was free for him to pass. ReeMara's robe fell in front of Piper's face when she could push it to one side she could not see the men anymore, though she knew they were not far behind her group.

Someone was shouting, not with banter of the traders but with authority of the man in command of the horsemen that had just passed them.

"Show more respect to the son of commander of the Barbarians."

A woman and her donkey were trying to get out of their way, but the man with a camel carrying what must have been rolls of wool rugs could not move the loaded animal without the rugs getting caught in a tent's guy ropes. The woman's donkey had had enough for one day he twisted sideways abruptly pulling the woman with him, if it was the donkey or the woman that upturned the heavily laden trestle table. Piper was not sure but the sound of copper pots landing on the ground added to the commotion.

The Commander of the horsemen were shouting, the trader with his trestle table upturned was shouting and banging his pots. The man with the camel was shouting, the camel stood still as his loads unrolled themselves at the feet of the horsemen.

The woman was shouting! Piper was not sure at whom, it could have been at her donkey; his braying did not charm anyone! What was to happen next, Piper did not see as Soul moved forward to follow Corn and Bramble.

Harron's back was all she could see. More razed voices did not announce the end of the commotion.

"Just be glad we are not in the middle of all of that!" Corn said as noises and smells returned to normal. Bramble nodded he was trying not to trample on a chicken that was not keen on being someone's meal.

Soul wanted to jerk his head way when a hand took holed of his bridle. He was only wearing it, as were Corn and Bramble to fit in better with the other horses being ridden around Base Camp.

"My lads, how can you wander around in the middle of camp with all these donkeys? You should have taken them to their places by going round the outer ring, not through the middle! Why don't youngsters ever follow orders?"

The plan robed man did not wait for an answer; he slapped the donkey just in front of Soul, on his rump sending him forward smartly:

"You, you old jack should have known better than to come this way."

The old jack gave the man that had interrupted their tour around Bass Camp a look that would have melted snow.

Piper wondered if his look was close to that of 'spitting camels'?

If the others were wondering why the man had taken Soul's bridle? Piper was not, she had seen the man react when he spotted ReeMara's glove, the one the store men had provided for her.

Piper had not looked it before it was just, a thick brown leather glove. But now they were being guided away from the tents and their trestle tables. Piper could see the glove was embossed with an eagle holding a ball in its talons.

A similar eagle and ball banner fluttered in the breeze in front of lines of tents matching those they had seen on the Grass Lands in the Iron Man's camp.

"You can help unload the donkeys." ordered the man in a plain robe. "If you had come straight here we would have had time to see to your beasts. But with so many expected to be returning soon, my men have enough to do."

He pointed at lines were the donkeys could be tethered; hay and water were waiting for them. It was plan to see many more places were prepared than their group needed.

Piper wanted to know what they were going to do now!

ReeMara and Harron were arguing, and were still arguing as they saw to their horses and the donkeys with them, as they had been told to do!

Corn and Bramble did not say 'no' to a feed of oats, they told Soul to tuck in.

'You never know when you will get a chance to try the like again.' The pair had said, what they did not say was oats can go to your head. Any thoughts of travelling on that day had to be stopped as Soul was doing strange things. He found cantering small circles, funny. Jumping in the air funny! Standing on his hind hooves was also as funny.

When Soul tried to sing the man with plain robe interrupted his fun, he called for an attendant to see to the foolish horse. When the attendant would not let him drink, Soul did not think that was at all funny. Nor did he think it was funny to be lead around like a silly donkey. Piper had to tell him to behave, neither of them found that funny!

When Piper had heard Soul trying to sing again she left ReeMara and Harron in one of the tents, the food they had been given was tempting, but instead of enjoying it with them she had to tell this silly horse to behave himself. And, if that was not enough one of the attendant had mistaken her for a rat! His broom, mist her by a whisker. Where was CC'raw when you wanted him?

That eagle was of no use, he had been brought fresh meat; Piper would have enjoyed some of that too. But no, she had to see to silly Soul, and hear Corn and Bramble laughing at the young horse. He would not be laughing tomorrow, his head would hurt. That was the only pleasing thought Piper had as she scurried back to the tent where ReeMara and Harron were.

That ReeMara had seen the embossed paten on her glove was the same as the banner fluttering in front of the lines they had been brought to.

The food they had been brought was not to be wasted, it smelt so good, the taste of the drink they pored from the jug suited ReeMara well as it did Harron.

Piper was horrified to see they were becoming as silly as that horse! Had she known it was a trick of the man with the plain robe she might have been less cross with them. In his opinion it was better not to have youngster returning form the mountain tracks lose in the camp. They could get mixed up in all sorts of trouble.

'Young men can be as silly as horses.' Piper heard the man say. By the time the man in the plain robe had past on to see to other duties, Piper's two humans were rolled in the beds provide, leaving Piper free to enjoy the rest of leftovers and give that silly eagle a piece of her mind for not taking better care of their humans. She did not take a drink from the jug she did not want to be as silly as those now sleeping.

ReeMara's sleep was not as peaceful as the drink in the jug was supposed to bring, she kept seeing the pale face of her brother in her dreams.

The next morning was the right time to discuss what they should do now, that is what Piper had thought. But the sleepy heads woke to headaches and were grumbling so much that Piper decided to get out of the tent. She was hoping to find CC'raw; that he was sitting on one of the polls of the tent opposite was a good thing, but he was not in a good mood as he had to sit outside all night on watch.

No one had thought about their security! It had been left to him. He was not listening to Piper when she complained that she was the only one that was looking out for those in the tent. He was complaining about how he was the only one concerned about their safety.

Somehow their agreed to leave the horses alone after all the oats they had eaten they would not want to talk to anyone. CC'raw did understand when Piper told him it was the same with those in the tent, what he did not understand was why oats had given them headaches! It was known that oats could cause horses problems if they did not have it in their daily diets, but did oats have the same effect on humans?

Piper and CC'raw decided to explore further the Base Camp. Piper was to concentrate on a ground exploration were as CC'raw was to take to the air; they were to meet back here when the sun was at its highest point in the day.

CC'raw did sweep over the horses to see they were alright; he was not surprised to see their heads hanging, fresh feed had been provided they had not touched it.

Bramble did flick an ear at CC'raw carefully so not to have to move his head. Why had he and Corn not listened to their own advice? This headache was not worth oat treat. From the look on Soul's face he was one horse that would not be indulging in so many oats, for some time.

The air was warm and the smell of horse and donkey with the new sent of camel were drifting on the breezes. The same breezes were fluttering banners on tall polls. The eagle with its talons around a ball banner was at the head of the line of tents CC'raw had left his humans in. Another line had an iron fist on its banner. Had he seen the iron fist before? It had hung over the Grass Lands... the Iron Man!

There was little movement along the lines, only a few humans bring things to place inside tents. That there were more tents being added to the lines, that was interesting now he came to think about it, there were more places for horses that there were horses.

CC'raw took to the air he had decided to take a look from a higher thermal there was a mater he needed to investigate.

The first lines of men riding down the mountain tracks did not tell him how many more to expect, but their banners did tell him the eagle and the iron fist had followers. If only the length of their trailing line could tell him how many there were. Their lines curled back into the mountain; from one side to the other their lines crisscrossed the broad side of the slop.

'Where is an eagle when I need one!?'
To take a higher thermal did not please CC'raw's stomach, but if he was right there were two armies coming to Base Camp.

Piper could confirm there were many more expected at the Bass Camp. The tents she been exploring had huge amounts of human and animal food stored in them. The men outside them called each other 'Store Master' of this or that; just as the two talkative men had at the mountain cave. Though the men here did not talk as much as they had! What she had heard was, there were more stores expected and they were worried the store tents would not be ready when the donkey trains coming from the East arrived. Wherever East was Piper did not know, but it must be big, if they were bring it here, Piper reasoned.

When Piper saw a tent with men, standing stiffly outside she had to look inside.

Soft glowing metal standing in piles, one piece stacked on top of another like flat stones from a river bed; were the first thing that met Piper as she wriggled under the tent hanging side. There bags of stones she had never seen before even though their colours matched the sky or the grass they were just cold colour to her. But there were bags the smell told her their contents were stones like ReeMara had. As to why there were folds and folds of soft flowing stuff among the guarded stores Piper could not work out.

When Piper got to the part in her report about seeing bags of stones like ReeMara's, Harron had sat up and taken the ferret onto his lap. He asked so many questions and at such a speed Piper could not keep her replays to match his thinking.

"We should not think to move on till we know what is going on here." Harron was adamant. Even though they had heard they only needed to take the way leading south, it would take them to where seven hills had a large city built upon it.

ReeMara was not the one arguing. The ferret was; Piper was just as adamant Harron was. If CC'raw would at least back her up, and not just sit there with his head on one side. As for that silly eagle, if he put his head over to the other side his expression would mach that crow. Why were they huddled in the tent when they should be moving away from Base Camp!

"Look if they are expecting the Iron Man and his men as well as those that joined him on our side of the mountain.
We should try and answer a few questions." Harron looked so like one of their teachers, ReeMara was grinning. Piper did see the likeness but she was not in the mood to enjoy such jokes.
Before Piper could remark sharply about this was not time to make jokes Harron said:

"Look, ReeMara has stones like the ones you have just seen and from what you have said, it must be gold they have in the storage tent you pop your nose in. Why so much?

A legionnaire is a well paid that much I know; the only use for so much gold could be to pay the worriers coming here."
It made sense to ReeMara but Piper did not see how that could be used as a good reason for not travelling on.

ReeMara remembered something C'raw, CC'raw's father has said. But his words faded as a memory older than that filled her mind. She-With-The-Sight was with the Iron Man as she remembered his words
'The fools believe there is magic in the fire stones. I will use their belief to rule the Land.'

ReeMara did not know what he had meant then, nor when C'raw had repeated similar words he had over heard on their way to the Cliff Citadel. It felt so long ago, now. ReeMara repeated the words again to Harron not expecting him to find them interesting. He sat up abruptly almost knocking Trigary's stand over. Trigary's flapping wings did not stop Harron wanting to run to the library, forgetting there was not a library in the city of tents:

"We have been playing with amber ReeMara, we are going to the City of the Seven Hills to put the pieces in a place She-With-The-Sight said you should do. How it all fits together I don't know, but it is amber they have in the tent with guards around it. You don't use amber to pay soldier!"

"I think my people exchanged it for…" but she could not remember. ReeMara could remember her family, their faces, their open arms and running to them with her brother.

On seeing ReeMara's sad face Piper could only try to console her, she made ReeMara take her in her arms, trying to dissuade them from staying, to move on. All would have to wait while ReeMara was so sad.

No one really understood the rumours circulating around Base Camp. That they were talking about the burning stones, amber was clear, but why there was so much decision was puzzling. As ReeMara and Harron wandered around they over heard remarks like.

'They can't do that!'

'I have always had that with me!'

'But, these are my pray stones'

'I did not come here to have my possessions taken from me!'

The remark that must have meant something to ReeMara was, 'If they took the trouble to stop the sources of amber stones, you can understand why they don't want any getting through from here.' But the remark only shook memories in her mind.

It was not easy for humans to move around the camp as so many more people were milling about. It was then CC'raw over heard a man in a plain robe like those worn by the attendants say to some ones retreating back:

"How do they think they can search everyone? How are they going to explain to members of the new religion they can not have their rosaries! They are going to have trouble explaining that to me!"

The man whose back was walking away from the speaker only shrugged. When he raised his fist it was clear to CC'raw that he was one of the Iron man's men. CC'raw's opinion now matched Piper's. They had to get out of Base Camp.

When CC'raw flew down to the horses he was pleased to hear them say it was time they all moved on.

"The chance they will try and search us is growing even with so many humans moving around; the lines for the new arrives are filling up." Bramble said.

"We were not shooed away when we went to help ourselves this morning, they don't have enough men to see to all the new comers." said Corn.

"Yesterday Soul was lead away from the feed store. I thought they did not know where to bring him, they started to lead him to the Iron Man's lines…" Bramble was interrupted by Corn:

"Till one man said 'he', Soul could not have come from there as he was too good a looking horse, for the Barbarians camp…" Now it was Bramble interrupting Corn:

"They never said we were good looking!"

"You have never been good looking!" remarked Corn.

From the look on Bramble's face he did not like that remark, he went back to telling CC'raw how Soul pulled way from the man trying to lead him, and how Soul trotted off faster then the man could run. That Soul had entered a storage tent and pop out the other side. As the man tried to follow him the tent had collapsed leaving Soul free to return here without bringing further attention to his self, or us.

Soul would have liked to have told this tale himself, that much CC'raw could see, but all of this was not dealing with the problem he had come here to discuss:

"I am going to find the others and bring them here. You lot stay here, no more wandering about! Keep your heads down, don't call attention to yourselves."

As CC'raw flew away he did notice that Soul's coat was free of the winter wool he had had in the mountains, his dark coat shone it the sun, were as the other two still had a good amount of shaggy wool still hiding their summer coats.

If CC'raw had been asked before about finding a girl with an eagle on her shoulder, he would have said easy! But now he was flying round the tents and their trestle tables he was not so sure, so many humans were humming around the goods on show and with similar robes as ReeMara and Harron had. Any number of the tented army had a bird on their shoulders.

ReeMara did not show her hair even if there were others with light coloured heads, as for Harron his dark head nor his nose was unusual here. But! A ferret poking her nose out of a robe was!

CC'raw normally would have swoop down and redirect his youngsters, but the birds sitting on their human's shoulders were not going to let him drop down so easily, if they did not see him through their hood their handlers would. Trigary had shown him just what an eagle can do, and he was a friend!

The question why humans found tents with things on trestles interesting CC'raw did not wait to ask, he had to think of something! Men with spears were pushing their way through the crowded humans. Their orders did not go unnoticed, nor did the look of resentment from the humans when they heard what the armed men wanted.

'All the stones known as burn stone, amber, the sun stone. In anyone's possession were to be brought to the tents with the mark of the Iron Fist. Were it would be exchanged for gold to match its weight. This was the order of the leaders.
And should the folk disobey this order the direst of consequents would be bestowed upon them.'

Those nearest to the men did not grumble so they could be over heard, but those that were out of ear shot had a lot to say.
ReeMara knew that the weight replace by gold was not a fair exchange; she only had to look at Harron to know he knew that too. ReeMara wanted to say, how, could they put a prise on a piece, when the stones were so individual? But this was the moment when people started to move away from the armed men.

Harron a ReeMara were being pushed along with them, Piper saw there was away between the tents that they could squeeze through. That was CC'raw chance to drop down to direct them away from the humans that were getting increasingly cross.

Back in the tent they had been using, on one spoke Piper and CC'raw were on watch as ReeMara and Harron hurriedly put to together the things they had.

From their tent to where the horse where was not far, but the amount of people standing around grumbling about the unwanted declaration hampered anyone in a hurry.

Maybe this was the moment to try to leave there were so many humans about, the folk were discussing angrily they did not have time for two young fellows that had pulled their robes around them to cover they were carrying all they owned.

No one challenged the three horses and their pair of humans moved towards the outer rings of Base Camp.

The people that should have been watching out for the animals in their care were distracted by others from closer to the middle of the camp. The news they brought needed to be discussed. Both ReeMara and Harron were surprised to see how upset everyone was.

CC'raw found a small group of donkeys that were taking advantage of their handler being involved in the discussions taking place. He directed his group towards where the handler's donkeys were enjoying a drink from a small pool.

CC'raw did not have any trouble persuading them to take them to where the best grazing was said to be.

Then the hill hid them from the outskirts of the camp CC'raw and Trigary decided to take to the air, if only to know if they were being followed. It was soon clear they did not need to worry about that, what was interesting was Base Camp had made it very difficult for humans to leave.

Darkly robed men were erecting blockades at the ends of all the ways out of the tent city. Humans were shouting and starves were waving at the men with spears, standing watching the darkly robed men as they laboured.

Trigary wing told CC'raw he was going to return to ReeMara and Harron, CC'raw had to agree they had seen enough. Had they left it any later to leave the camp they may not have got away! What danger they would have been in echoed in CC'raw mined as did the angry shouts from the humans below.

There was an unusual uproar in the Senate; men were trying to control their tempers as the Emperor's back was turned away from them. The Emperor lack of interest could no longer be hidden. Those close to him were at a loss as what to do about the arising situation; maters could not be left as they were.

It was clear the city had been left exposed, with so many of its legions away. The legions serving on the cost were not able to return without losing the ground they had gained at great expense and much of the gold needed for that campaign had come from the senators own coffers.

The reward that had been promised was the increase of trade due to the ports being kept open and in their control. The city merchants could bring goods to the city more efficiently than relying on the donkey trains. Even if it was possible to bring some of the legions and their resources back to the city, the city still had its belly exposed from the north east.

It had seemed commonsense to see the city's needs were not neglected. Therefore the need for amber had not been ignored; the religious leaders did not approve of the peoples pagan use of it, though they used it to enhance their services.

None of the player in the coliseum would come before the crowds without the stone to enhance their costumes; even the popular gladiators had amber sown in their clocks, to flash in the sun light or torch's flames when they were excepting their rewards.

The building of houses had slowed down not due to the lack of building materials, nor from any of the religious points of view, but from the pagan habit of placing amber in the foundations of any new structures.

As the donkey trains had stopped coming down from the north the amber they had brought was lacking. The lack of the medicine, amber powders provided was also causing problems. The shortage of amber was not the only shortage the city was suffering, silk and spices were becoming an increasing problem.

Many wealthy citizens had noticed the much acclaimed wine from the lands rising before the Alpine mountains had for sometime not been seen in the city's wine houses.

In fact every household was disturbed by the lack of commodities. The commodities had been promised by the funding of the legions, those legions were now employed in maters no common citizen any longer understood.

What the citizens did not know but the Senate did, was that the three Legions that had been sent to deal with the troublesome maters in the north. One Legion of the three had been completely destroyed. How that could have happened to such a formable force had not been explained by the Senate nor had they explained how they were going to get the remaining legions they had sent there back here! If the rumours were to be believed they were going to be needed. But to return from the lands behind the Alpine mountains would take many months!

It was obvious that the Emperor did not care about such maters. That husbands, sons and lovers were missing around family tables was not that he cared about. He had planned to leave the city, he had planned it for sometime all his wealth was all ready in stores, he alone knew about. The Emperor had had every slave in evolved slaughtered to silent their knowledge of his business. He did not need to hear nor wish to hear any of the senator's speeches.

Senator Markus stood up as he watched the Emperor walk out of the Senate without even looking back. This moment did not surprise him; he had been the man that had warned those that should have taken action long ago. From the moment he had talked to Senator Clod he had known this moment would come. Had others paid more heed, what good were their private matters to them now? Now there was a large army advancing in the City!

The advancing army did explain the city's shortages, but as to why they would want to prevent trade along the amber road and hamper the silk trains, was not at that moment clear to Senator Markus; he had feared a shift of power among the people of the lands of the north, but he could not explain why that was connected to the silk trans from the east. Now he knew he should have invested his time in finding out the answers to the questions now in his mind, instead of trying to canvass the Senate to take heed of the lack of goods coming to the city. He was one man of many men that should be asking the same questions of the disgruntled Senators here.

The Abor's entrance was over shadowed by the fact the Emperor was absent from his seat, the plinth where he should have been was an empty stage, the Emperor's attendants had followed their emperor, only the fire baskets and incense smoking verses told he had been there.

The Abor's cloak with its clashing bright colours hang in his hand instead of challenging the sombre robes of the senators. The feathers in his head band quivered with his annoyance as did his voice as he turned to address the Senate.

The Abor's presents had not be requested, but the Senate could not refuse to hear what he had to say, even if the Emperor was not there to command order:

"Had amber been speared from being turned into rosaries the winds of fate would not be blowing in our faces!" the Abor's cloak was fanned out as his arms razed to take hold of the senators attention:

"Taking heed, the religion's fancy words have brought this trouble to you! Put them outside the city's walls..."A man stepped forward to interrupt the wrath of the Abor.

"We protect the people from the burdens life has placed on their souls, not with the trinkets you offer, but with prayer." The man's quite voice was penetratingly against the loudness of the other man in his vulgar costume.

The older ways of some of the people in the city clashed against the new religion, the new religion had divided into two groups. They were again divided by those that felt having slaves was to follow a false god. They argued work had to be carried out by every member of their household for the good of every household. Others countered with the question; were their ladies and concubines supposed to undertake those daily tasks?

Another man from the splinter religion, Senator Markus knew would want to discuss such maters moved towards the two men confronting each other. Before Senator Markus could decide if this was the right issue to bring up at this troubled moment, another member of the Senate thought it was his place to steep in between the two men before they locked together like wild beasts.

After the spectacle of the Emperor's retreating back! To have fractions fighting, all be it verbally, their differences were not in the best interest of the city. The city was under threat, decisions had to be made, and made now!

"Brothers we don't have to take such issues to heart at a moment when we should be discussing maters of greater emergency. There is an army, an uncountable army travelling the roads leading to this city!"

Other voices were joining the three leading voices:

"Take the lead of your Emperor leave the city to the coming heathens." rang from behind the Abor's swishing cloak.

"I claim the protection of the God of the new faith!"

"Claim the protection of the Legions. I have paid my gold for their protection…"

"My soul has the protection of…"

"My property has need of protection; the loss of business is prohibiting further development."

"We should be condemning those that have aloud this situation to arise."

"The wrath of the gods, are upon you!" the Abor's voice chilled the senators close to him. Others moved towards the man that had challenged the Abor's words, his secretary had never had so many marks pressed into his hands. He would never remember who had placed their marks with him. If they wanted their souls protected maybe it was not to a god they should looking to.

Senator Markus could not gain control of the senate meeting not even with the help of Senator Clod the

different factions of the Senate were too concerned with
their own business to hear   they had the same problems.

Senator Markus was ashamed to leave the Senate his
wish to find compromises were lost in the shameful scene
of Senators batting each other to except blame that no
one would admit too.

Armnell's bathhouse was strangle quite only the sound
of water heating in their pots over the fires Armnell kept
alight, even though she knew the likelihood any of the
Senate would becoming to bathe was unlikely. She had
seen for herself the wagons carrying their households
past her steps and pillars, their worried faces had not been
hidden behind fanes and fancy robes.

This was her chance of freedom; Armnell knew all of
her hidden gold would not buy her from her slave hood,
not while those that lived here knew she was a slave;
even though she had been for many years in charge of the
bathhouse used by the members of the Emperor's Senate.

As a young slave, she was a slave to the whims of …
what part of her life had been ended when the ailing
Emperor found relief in her soothing hands.

Armnell knew this was her chance, if there was going
to be a new ruling senate she could make use of her
acquired knowledge. What was awaiting the city she
could not tell, there had not been a word that had reached
her, she could make sense of!

The Emperor had deserted his people meant those that
stayed behind to defend their homes would be more
likely to corporate with whoever, she did not know.

Till she did, she would see the fires did not go out
under the water coppers, that old slave they had left
behind could help her, even with his twisted limbs. There

was not much else he was good for now, but he was easy
to pay for his work, all he asked for, was for her to ease
his pain with her skill of her fingers.

Till there were strangers in the city Armnell would sit
in the shadows of the bathhouse and watch and wait. The
new silence of the bathhouse was not to Armnell's liking,
the hustle bustle of daily running was missing; just the
old man shuffling from shadow to shadow with fuel for
the coppers' fires did not help her to wait, to wait for
whatever fate had for her and the city she had spent all of
her life in.

ReeMara and Harron found the road almost boring
compared to the breath taking views the mountains tracks
had to offer, though the horses were happy to trot on its
even surface. The road was straight as an arrow's flight,
no stream could have cut such a line in the landscape;
men must have had their hands in its making.

The county side was a pleasant mixture of fields
growing wheat and beats and there was land set aside for
hay and more was free for grazing. Sheep and goats
herded by folk that did not seem to be surprised to see
ReeMara and Harron with three horses nor did the two
birds accompanying them cause concern.

Most of the folk let them ride on by with a wave of the
hand were as others continued to attend to their work.
The travellers had the feeling all was well with this land
and its people.

Harron did not think the folk around here had any idea
there were two large armies camped some five days ride
from here. Nor did he think even if he asked; anyone
would know what the armies business was.

No one said they could not drink from the wells along the road nor did anyone challenge them for forging any streams that crossed their way.

ReeMara remarked it was somehow strange to be riding through a normal homely landscape. Harron did ask if ReeMara would know what a normal homely landscape was. He could have asked the same question of himself, he might have done if Bramble had not been discussing with Corn the same thing.

Food was easy to find for their mixed group, ReeMara was not always sure they could help themselves to vegetables they found growing where folk must be attending them. Harron pointed out if she did not want to go hungry she could always try the grazing the horses were enjoying.

Piper and Trigary with the help of CC'raw saw that fresh meet could be roasted over their camp fire.

The travellers were enjoying the warm weather and the straight road, a hollow would offer them shelter for the night, and the trees growing along the way shared their shadow in the midday sun. Only Soul was to be heard grumbling, he would rather be galloping along the road he found their pace boring. But as Corn said, it was better not to waste horse power!

The sound of a trumpet sounded shapely in the sleepy heat of the afternoon. Another joined it as well as drums beating a rhythm that clashed with the lazy mood the travellers were enjoying.

The trumpets' sound were not like those that had sounded on the battle fields below the Citadel of the Cliffs, nor were the drums beating massages like any they had heard as the armies had battled against each other.

The sounds reaching them were somehow attracting their attention in another way as they would have done if they were on a battle field.

Soul took ReeMara to the top of the small bank that was between them and the makers of the attraction. Corn would have suggested caution if the others had not so promptly followed Soul. Trigary and CC'raw took to the air not that any warning they could have given would have helped anyone, Corn wanted to point out.

From the top of the bank they could see from where the noise was coming from, the sceptical was more surprising than the sound they were making.

Eight large oxen were harnessed to a solid double axle wagon. Men in drab robes with their heads covered with hoods walked beside each animal; in their free hand they held a staff like those shepherds used. The men with the drums were naked to the waist, their mussels pulsing with the beat.

Those with the trumpets flanked the heave wagon; they had short robes with two red lines that crossed over their chests.

Behind the wagon were men with chains wound round their bodies, others carried a wooden plank with a shorter plank bound across it, the weight of which bowed their backs.

The men holding whips swing them over their own backs with every beat of the drum. It did not make sense to ReeMara or Harron, anymore than the main seen set on the wagon.

On the wagon stood a vast table, more like a slab of stone from it a wooden plank rose to point to the sky where another crossed it to match the bands of red the trumpeters bore and the planks of the bowed back men carried.

The man standing before the altar seemed small
against his stage, but when he razed his arms the
whiteness of his robe bellowed open, like the wing
stretch of a great bird.

What he was saying was hidden in the trumpets and
drums pulsing sounds, other human voices were woven to
follow his secret rhythm.

People were turning from the fields they had been
working in to watch, as Harron and ReeMara were. Some
bowed their heads others fell to their knees lifting their
hands to in a gesture that looked like to Harron, they
were asking for forgiveness!

Strange as the show was Harron did not understand
what it was all about, to him it was just that a show. A
show like no other he had ever seen. They had made up
plays at the Cliffs and laughed at each other as they tried
to impersonate teachers or Mattie their cook. ReeMara
had done an impersonation of how she thought a teacher
should be; Harron thought she was copying the old
woman she had talked of long before they had met.

But this was different this was a show; if this was to
bring folk to religion he had heard folk talk about; he
would have planed it differently. To whip one's self or
drag chains to pay for one's sins seemed to him a bit
dramatic! Not that he knew what sin was. ReeMara
pointed out, she has seen so much in her short life to
make her think there was no place for a god like that in
this land.

The wagon rolled slowly past, the folk from the fields
that had remained standing watched it in silence. It was
as if their strength was being drawn from them, when
they too sank to their knees.

"I don't know how you can be-wonder that!" Piper said. Her remark made everyone jump, had they been caught up in this spell? Piper wanted to know.

Piper was the one to insist they move on their way, when the birds returned. Piper made the two of the horses grumble with her insistence they should hurry, only Soul was pleased to be moving more briskly than they had been.

It was sometime later when those in the group found their voices, other than to grumble with. What they had seen had left a deep impression and the two humans did not have answers to any questions they had.

But one thing Harron was sure of was it was a show they had seen, why he thought so he could not say. ReeMara and he had spent so much of their time watching the battles fought below then, seen how they their leaders arrange their men trying to get the better advantage. One attack had started from behind a hill on the outer flank of the opposition; the attack had been a ploy as the real force had come from the other side.

Harron reminding ReeMara of this manoeuvre, ReeMara did not see how it was connected with what they had seen earlier, her sharp remark sent Harron sulking in his robe not even Corn could make him talk.

Piper said, Harron could be trying to point all is not what it seems, ReeMara wanted to say he had a point, but there were moments it was better to leave Harron sulking.

Productive fields sent lines of green and soft golden stripes to paten the rolling hill sides, the road rose and fell matching the undulating hills.

They were all enjoying the slow, comfortable tempo as they travailed along the road lined with shade giving trees. How many days had past after seeing, 'The Show,' as Harron liked to call the strange happening, no one could say.

Trigary flapped lazily over head; he had left CC'raw to keep watch on a convent thermal while he did a spot of hunting. The fields were not reviling if they had any edible rodents, out of respect to Piper he did not look for ferrets; a mouse would do for CC'raw. A chicken, his humans could enjoy, Trigary rather fancied a chicken, his self. There had been enough chickens scratching about for him to choose from, but now he could not see any, even when he swooped low over the fields.

Now Trigary came to think of it, he had not seen any movement from animals or humans, other than his ground bound group for some time. Smaller birds did not cross his flight path, not when they knew he was hunting; would they know what was going on around here?

Trigary was hoping to have answers to the questions forming in the back of his mind. As he landed on ReeMara's waiting glove. Harron was saying to ReeMara:

"The cultivated fields must need many humans to look after them. These fields are much larger then the gardens we had to tend to. I wonder why we have not seen anybody." He had to pores for a moment. When had they last waved a hand friendly to someone, working or anyone walking along the road? Not even a wagon or cart had passed them. They had become used to seeing folk in the weeks they had been travelling along this way.

Maybe they should have talked to those along the road, not just asked the way to the city when roads crossed. Maybe they should not have been worried about drawing attention to themselves. When huts had clustered by the road they had skirted the outer fields to pass by, even though they had seen the horses and their humans and would not have looked out of place.

Harron was always nervous others would find his speech hard to understand. ReeMara's voice would make folk wonder; it was not how young men usually sounded.

"Why have we not seen anyone? They cannot all have followed the, 'The Show.'" ReeMara hesitated to use Harron's name for the strange way the men had behaved. There had not been any women among the followers of the wagon.

Trigary could see there were more questions than he had thought of, he interrupted ReeMara's thoughts:

"Maybe CC'raw had seen something, he is flying towards us."

ReeMara would have laughed; CC'raw looked so like his father as he landed on a branch close by his group. Had he not spoken of how he had flown over the fields; he had not seen any humans or beasts, nor birds land bound.

CC'raw reported, human huts had been knocked down and their animal pens pulled apart. Food stores had been empted and made unusable. Which was strange as the fields would soon need to be harvested!

The shade giving trees had stepped away to leave the road alone to rise with the hill. The birds rode with their humans as they slouched on the backs of the horses. The horses put their hooves in front of each other as if the hill was steep.

Only Piper was watchful of the passing surroundings. Piper had pushed her way out of ReeMara's loosened robe before the sun had taken advantage of the absence of the trees. Piper saw Harron had let his robe swing from his waist his dark skin glistened under his sweat. Her humans, Piper noticed were not longer the pups they had been when they had started their journey. She noted that no one spoke, or even looked at each other; everyone had sunk into their own thoughts.

The line of the road was as straight as the flight of an arrow, it pointed to where the hill met with the sky; the sun had heated the air to shimmer a blue haze over the road and the surrounding fields.

The three horses and their humans became part of the blue haze; it silenced the sound of their hooves, their thoughts, their will, left them drifting within the haze's will. It held them till it cut them free as the hill new side dropped sharply away. The hill cut away to leave a landscape that held seven hills in a basin.

A river flowed under cliffs; bridges span its water holding the city in its arms.

Buildings boasting columns and pillars and walls that circled to hold secrets, roofs that shone with the sun. Buildings that clustered together like wise owls, telling tales of homely things. Buildings that had to hold knowledge of past generations!

The sign that had crossed the chests of the men flashed on the dome of a building that held the highest place on the hill marking the center of the city. There was a building whose magnificence challenged with powerful pillars and pride, the building with its high dome, from its place on another hill top.

"It is a wonder what humans can do!" Corn said, as he studded the city stretching below him.

"It is a wonder what horses can do." said Piper. Corn stopped staring over the city on its seven hills to look at the ferret balancing on her hind legs on Soal's withers to get a better view: "Without you how do you think we would have got here?"

"Nice of you to say that, to hear a compliment from a fellow traveller is very heart warming." Corn looked at his small friend. Bramble was about to agree with him when he noticed ReeMara slip to the ground without disturbing Piper's sight seeing. She walked to where the road had been cut into the ground before it started to descend to the City.

ReeMara could not say anything, she had come so far, here was so far away from the beach she had played on, from the island where the stones that were in the leather pouch under her robe came from. She had come this far and still did not know how to complete the mission She-With-The-Sight had given her. The city may look like one of Harron's maps from here, but once they entered its walls what was she supposed to do?

Bramble wanted to blow warm air into her face, to blow away her sorrow, but Soul pushed him out of the way, had Corn not had the same idea ReeMara would not have had to stand up smartly. Three horses blowing hot air at her had the affect of blowing her robe over her ears! She tried to hold the flapping robe around her and stop her horsey friends from blowing so much warm comfort at her.

Harron turned around to see Piper swing on ReeMara's robe trying to get hold of it, three surprised horses wondering how so much hot air and concern can cause a robe to behave so wildly!

Harron was not able to explain that air from the basin below was mixing with the still air on the hill that it was not just three horses playing with ReeMara's robe. He could not hold himself together, he was laughing so much. Her hair, her robe and a ferret flying in the wind and an eagle and a crow flapping about, as will! Thank goodness there weren't folks about to see this show!

No one spoke to Harron as they settled down for the night; to travel on towards the city could wait till the new day.

Once ReeMara had steeped away from the playful winds everything took on a more normal way of behaving, horses grazing, ferret and crow grumbling about having to eat vegetables! ReeMara holding on to her robe encase it took off again as she enjoyed the vegetables they had found.

If they had been talking, Harron might not have noticed that the city on the seven hills was lost in the dark of the night, the only lights were the stars in the sky.

Harron had seen worrier's fires spreading out below the Cliff Citadel. How could a city be without fire or light? Harron could not sleep.

There wasn't any one to greet them or deny them entry to the city. Harron and ReeMara sat still as Corn and Soul carried them through the arched stone way, Brambles hooves rang with Corn and Soul a hollow echo greeting.

The buildings they passed were for living in; Piper could see wells in pleasant shady yards, the doors that must lead into comfortable dwellings were closed as were their windows, but there were flowers in pots to show there was order, or had been. Piper did not see anyone, but she did feel there were dwellings that were hiding their humans.

CC'raw and Trigary could not see if there were humans moving about the side streets from their higher view. Trigary took up his position on ReeMara's glove; CC'raw chose to stay at roof level. He was the first to see a building that must have been used as a store. His wings sounded like a stranger to him in it was emptiness. The only thing left was the smell of the stores they had held. The next warehouse had another smell but it also was without its goods.

Where there should have been stalls and tables for merchandise, was now deserted not even the white preening birds were taking an interest in the market place.

The road was no longer taking them past dwellings or store houses; they had seen other places where tables could be set up. The buildings they were wondering passed were growing grander and larger, impressing dominating magnificent!

Figures of humans and horses had been made of stone not of flesh, stood tall and proud on columns. Menacing animals with open mouths and shaggy manes protected vast entrances.

A wall held worriers with swords and spears battling the enemy, their vanquished lay at their feet. It was so like the battle fields they had seen. It made them walk past its length trying to look the other way but they were not able to take their eyes of it; even though it was cut in stone it told of realty.

Piper pointed out that they could not stay in the city, as the horses could not feed on house flowers, CC'raw lead them from the road to where trees offering shade and grass grew among stones laid in lines. The symbol they had seen when 'The Show' had passed by; stood to watch over the stone slabs, as did figures of sorrowing women weeping behind their stone veils.

Harron lay on his back, sleep would not come to him, he did not understand city around him. The Cliff Citadel had been his world, he understood its way, its rooms, it was a school, but it had not taught him what he needed to know now! He could almost smell there were places of learning here, what would the scrolls in their cellars have to tell?

ReeMara had heard Harron turn sleepless during the night as he had grumbled he had not slept the night before she slipped out of her bed roll without disturbing him, but to sit and wait for him to wake was not on her mind. The city was calling to her curiosity. The place they had spent the night seemed to her dead, the stones lay marking something gone. The magnificent stone figures she had seen had told of something powerful.

The horses were dosing and grazing among the lying stones, Trigary was sunning his wings on one of the upright stones. CC'raw had tucked his head under his wing, was Piper supposed to be on duty? If she was, she was on her back fast asleep next to Harron. Her legs were running in the air in pace with her dream.

ReeMara was not content to look around the lying stones, when she saw a small arched way in a building; it tempted her to enter to see where it would lead her. She had expected to find a small inner courtyard not an open squear where grand buildings with pillars stated their importance.

When had she last smelt soap? She could almost feel the hot water with its bubbles wash over her body. Her feet were carrying her up the wide steps, past the pillars into the wonderful smells that soap and hot water had! It was not dark in the bath house wax lights softened any darkness turning the water blue as reflected is self on the walls.

ReeMara dropped her robe to step into the welcoming water, she took soap from a dish; it was scented with flowers,

She splashed it into the water to make it bubble, rubbed it into her hair; shook it out of her eyes, laughing, her laughter rang around the walls.

How long had they been underway, with only streams or cold waterfalls to wash in? ReeMara could only lay back and enjoy this wonderful bath house, dream with the scenes on the walls.

Armnell put her finger to her lips; Alois was not to disturb the young woman enjoying her bath. The bathhouse had served the senate and their ladies, to find combs and scented oils and soft towels did not take Armnell long. Alois was busy seeing there was more hot water in his coppers.

Armnell washed the soap out of ReeMara's hair raped a towel around her. Why they did not speak was lost in Armnell combing the tangles out of ReeMara's flaxen hair.

ReeMara remembered Bean, who had nursed her back in the Cliff Citadel, what fun baths had been then, when she was a girl! Armnell was used to young women and their wants, it had amused her to tend ReeMara after the long weeks that had past after the senators and their families had left.

The robe ReeMara had been wearing was discarded, no amount of soap would make it look as fresh as the one raped around her now. How was she going to thank this woman for showing such kindness?

Harron stood in the archway that lead back to where they had spent the night. The question as to where ReeMara was, was answered when he say ReeMara start to decent the flight of steps. ReeMara robe pressed against her body, he saw her as if he was seeing her for the first time. Her hair was picked up by the playful wind; it farmed her head like a golden cloud.

Harron was not the only one watching ReeMara coming out of the Bath House, other folk were be wondering ReeMara, they drew their breath when Trigary landed on her out stretched arm.

A point of a spear invited Harron to steep into the squear; he was pushed among the folk that had been watching ReeMara flounce down the steeps.

Spears were pushing the people away from the bathhouse Harron was forced to go with them. The last member of his group he saw was CC'raw, the bird was hovering uncertain who he should follow.

It was dark in the place where Harron found him self being confined, he had found a corner where he could set down.

The others being kept in this place voices were held in low whispers:

"I thought all the fine people had left."

"They cannot help us now."

"Maybe we should have gone with them."

"What! Carry my old bones away from the City!"

"What do those men want with us?"

"We should have gone."

"The fine lady will help us."

"If she is one with of those that left the City, she won't care you are here!"

"Follow the true God."

"The Gods of our fathers are angry with us."

Harron would have preferred listening to others whispering than the silence he had to sit in. A sward had clung a warning on the iron bars of the door.

Armnell had taken a cloak and placed it around ReeMara's shoulders. The man that had commanded the soldiers had not commanded them to be taken to join the people he had driven out of the squear. They had been lead into grand house behind the Senate. The rooms were lavishly decorated but everything that could be carried way had gone.

Armnell looked at the young woman; the young woman that had enjoyed bathing had changed into one stunned and shocked.

It was hot and sticky with so many folk huddling together, and more people had been pressed into the dark silence. Harron lent against the wall its stone offered him support. When the barred door open the light from outside blinded him, but he did see a figure of an elderly man bent over a staff enter.

As no others had been ushered into the grim prison Harron was interested in the elderly man. The man's frail form told of years of hard work, but his manner told of something else. Harron could not put his finger on what this old man had.

"Had I known this was my fate, I would have gone with them!" a woman's voice sounded in the dark.

It had been sometime since anyone had spoken. Their guards had left the door barred, but they were no longer standing before it.

"I don't want to stay here."

"Well leave them!"

"Do you think they will bring us water? It is so hot in here!"

"Had the Emperor thought for a moment about his people?"

"The Emperor has only thought for his gold."

"The Empress has stayed by her people." It was the elderly man's voice that told them that the young woman they had seen in the squear would protect her people.

Harron would have spoken out but he was interest in what else this man was going to say. ReeMara had astounded him, but she was ReeMara! Why did he think she was an empress?
ReeMara would find the idea funny!

"No, no the Empress that will see no one suffers at the hands of the armies entering the city." another voice said.

"I have seen there are many legions of men camped on the hills."

"They are not our soldiers, not our men."

"Where are our men?" asked a woman.

"It was a sad day when they left the City. I heard their wagons. No one came for me; no one wants an old woman that cannot see."

"You did not see the lady?"
Harron must have slept. Those near him were worrying; they should be given water. Why had they not been given food?
Harron looked for the elderly man he must be near the door but the gloom did not show where he was, nor did his voice betray him. Harron was puzzled, now he too needed something to drink.

When ReeMara tried to leave the empty room a guard stood to attention, his salute also barred the way.
ReeMara could only turn back to the other woman in the room.

"There is a garden through there, but there is no way we can get out, the walls are too high."

ReeMara looked at the dark skinned woman, her skin was darker them Harron, she whished she had woken him this morning. ReeMara did not really know what to say, if she had thought a bath could cause so much trouble, she would have gone without!

A bird fluttered past the door leading into the garden, Armnell thought the bird looked into the room. The eagle drew the girl's attention to the passing bird; Armnell was surprised when the crow walked across the floor.

ReeMara greet CC'raw:

"I am glad you have found us! Do you know what is happening?"

"The leader of the Barbarians has brought his combined armies to the City of the Seven Hill. Those of the Tented Army are among the men controlling the City. Humans that did not leave with the Emperor are being gathered together.
The Iran Man's soldiers are looking for the riches they say they are to be rewarded with."

"The Iran Man is here!" ReeMara look of horror was plain to see.

CC'raw had not seen the Iron Man as ReeMara had seen him. CC'raw had seen the Iron Man on the Grass Lands below the cliff's where he had been born. But his father, C'raw, had seen the Iron Man use his cruel hand and he had told him what the Iron Man and the Barbarians had done.

CC'raw did understand the hate ReeMara must feel for this human. He was a human that had destroyed ReeMara's childhood and this human had destroyed a Legion.

CC'raw he had seen for himself how the Iron man's men had held another Legion on the Grass Lands below the Cliff Citadel.

Why had the silly girl gone off like that? And then come out of that place so changed even he had to look twice! Trigary had flown to ReeMara at the moment Harron had been pushed into the crowd. ReeMara had been rapped in a cloth by that black woman. With the white cloth to follow CC'raw could see ReeMara among the humans that took her to the house behind one of the grand buildings.

CC'raw took Piper to the garden within the tall walls; at least Piper could keep an eye on ReeMara, Trigary might be able to guard ReeMara if any one attracted her. CC'raw needed Piper's cleverness to protect ReeMara, while he went to find Harron. How was he supposed to find Harron among these buildings, so many were large enough to hold large numbers of humans! Harron was among the humans that had seen the twit of a bird land on ReeMara.

As the sun went down CC'raw could not continue to investigate from the air. He had to really on flapping to any window showing light.

The next day CC'raw took to the air, looking through lighted windows had not helped; he had only managed to disturb the pigeons roosting for the night. CC'raw had found trying to describe Harron difficult as there were many men that had recently come into the city, with eagle noses and dark shins.

Two days had passed since the group had been split up. CC'raw got Bramble, Corn and Soul to hide in a building with other horses. Grazing among the lying stones would attract attention. The glove ReeMara wore, CC'raw had tucked in Souls bridal; the mark on it had helped them at the camp the donkeys had lead them through, CC'raw hoped it would help them now. He warned the horses not to draw attention to then selves. 'Don't let Soul eat any oats!' were his last words as he took to the air to continue his search for Harron.

CC'raw sat on a stone figure, resembling a shrunken human with stomach ache. He was at a loss as where to look next, the only comfort was the sun worming his tired wings.

A man came out of the grand building where the figure CC'raw had chosen to rest on was. The man was elderly and needed a staff to support him as he walked, he interested CC'raw.

The elderly man must have been living in the city long before the Barbarian armies came, reasoned CC'raw. Why were there men from The Iron Man's circle following the elderly man? With no better ideas CC'raw decided to discreetly accompany them.

What uses the building had had before, was not clear to CC'raw, the way into the building was helped with a ramp. The elderly man was finding the slope steep, he would not except help from the men. A sturdy wooden bridge passed over deep ditch and an archway large enough for wagon and horsemen to pass under took the humans CC'raw were following from his sight. CC'raw had to fly over the steep walls to find the men he was watching in a courtyard.

A flight of pigeons did not notice CC'raw swoop with them; he wanted to get closer to the humans waiting in the courtyard without being noticed, luckily for him that his black head and gray body did not look out of place among the native birds.

CC'raw fluttered past the men standing around the elderly man but it was not until he had passed with the pigeons a third time did he hear something that could help him.

"The people you need to inform… they saw the Empress…a girl…are being held here. We are waiting for a suitable escort to take you down to the cells."

CC'raw did not flap passed with the pigeons again, he chose a perch that he could watch what was going on below.

Two men looking as if they had been disturbed form their sleep came blinking into the sun light from a door just below CC'raw.

CC'raw through himself among the pigeons swooping past, he wished he was an owl he needed to see into every shadowed corner the courtyard had, if he was not to lose sight of the old man!

Why did the pigeons have to get upset now, he was a stranger among them, the silly birds swooped and span as if he was a hark. CC'raw was not worried that the humans would see him; he was more worried that he would not see which door the old man was taken through.

The silly pigeons continued to swirl around and round the courtyard, there were so many doors and dark ways into the walls.

The two men lead the elderly man towards the door they had come out of, the other men stood watching the strange way the pigeons were flying about.

CC'raw dropped to the ground; he walked behind the small group that had just entered the darkness inside the wall.

Once CC'raw's eyes got used to the darkness to follow the humans was not difficult as he could walk outside of the light from the torch they carried. He had to duck into a passage as the humans had stopped, the torch was flashing light back up the tunnel.

The door was slammed shut; the two men stomped back the way they had come, leaving CC'raw in another darkness, what now? There was a barred door between him and wherever the elderly man was. He could hear voices from the other side of the door.

"I don't want to stay here!"

"The Emperor has only thought for his gold."

"The Empress has stayed by her people."
The elderly man's voice had spoken the words. 'The Empress has stayed by her people.' of that CC'raw was sure, what the elderly man meant he was not sure.

'You saw the lady?' was asked by someone that had not seen the lady. CC'raw was at loss what was meant by, 'They are not our soldiers, not our men.'

There were many humans the other side of the door; they were sitting in the darkness as he was. Could they be the humans the Iron Man's men had gathered before the steeps ReeMara had started down?

The humans were grumbling behind the door, they did not have any water, it was warm in the tunnel CC'raw was waiting in; it must be warmer behind the closed door.

CC'raw jumped at the sound of the two humans grumbling at having to leave their breakfast to take the elderly man back to the courtyard.

"There are many humans being held, I can only think they are the humans the Iron Man had taken from the courtyard after you came out of the building." CC'raw finished his account.

The rooms ReeMara and Piper were held in were presently cool and there was food and drink that a crow could enjoy. It was a contrast to the place where CC'raw had been waiting in the dark.

The light hurt every one's eyes as the door was banged open. A voice ordered everyone out, a torch light the way they were to go. But the torch's light did not warn them of the power of the sun. Blinking and feeling faint Harron was pushed into the courtyard. The steep ramp drew him down into the street. The others he had been held with scurried way.

Harron realised he too had to leave the street he found himself standing in, he walked as fast as he could to where a side way took him out of eye contact with the blank menacing place he had spent the last few days.

The sound of marching feet rang from the surrounding walls the clang of a spear on a shield made Harron turned round to see armed men herding a large group of frightened people towards the ramp he had come down.

Harron moved away from the street where the prison was, he hurried up a narrow way, he did not want to be herded back in there.

Some how Harron found his way back to where they had spent their first night in the city, he had not expected to find anyone, but he was still sad that no one he knew was waiting for him. He did fined his and ReeMara's things, but it did not stop him feeling lost.

The day started with trumpets, the city was hung with banners, banners like those ReeMara had seen at the Base Camp and others she had not seen before.

ReeMara had asked to see the city from the top of the tower she had climbed with the armed escort. That she and Armnell were prisoners ReeMara understood, though they were not treaded as prisoners like those on the battle field below the Cliff Citadel. Food and drink had been brought to the guarded rooms with is walled garden. Fresh robes and comforts were brought to the room; Armnell had dared to ask for hot water.

To have Piper with her and to know CC'raw was keeping an eye on the horses. To have the black woman, Armnell, from the bathhouse with her made the prison less lonely.

ReeMara believed Armnell when she had said she did not know what was going on. When they had asked their captors they were met with shrugs.

Those comforts did not stop ReeMara from worrying about Harron. CC'raw had reported more people had been taken to where he expected Harron could be, but CC'raw could not say if Harron was there, he did not have any other ideas were Harron could be.

ReeMara had hoped to help CC'raw find Harron, the city stretched in all directions below her. It was not hidden in blue clouds of dreams as it had been from the bend in the road.

ReeMara's fingers felt for the stones She-With-The-Sight had given her. 'Place them in the temple at the hart of The City of the Seven Hills.' She-With-The-Sight had said, what has she to do with this world? To revenge her parents, to see they had not died without purpose, the old woman said.

ReeMara's guard coughed, she had to turn away from the city and start down the twisting steeps inside the tower till a sound stopped her, a great clanging penetrated the stone of the tower. The guard did not stop her from climbing back to look out over the city, the first sound was joined by more clanging coming from different buildings all round the city, threads of smoke were curling into the sky.

The guard could only grunt and direct ReeMara to start to decent the twisting steeps again, when she asked what was meant by such signs.

Armnell was agitated when ReeMara returned to the rooms, Piper was sitting on top of a pile of fine robes looking just as agitated.

"Have something to eat ReeMara it is going to be a long day!" Armnell was looking at the ferret and Piper the ferret was looking at Armnell. What was so was so important about the robes, and why were they looking at each other in such away?

ReeMara let Armnell comb her hair and place a deep red robe and tie a golden band at her waist. The finest of white silk veils ReeMara refused to cover her head with; Armnell hide her alarm when ReeMara refused to wear it. Armnell had been told to dress the girl in the finery they had brought.

The door was opened by their guards and a man whose white robe looked as if it had been cleaned so often ReeMara decided he must an official, that he wanted them to follow him was clear but why he would not say.

Uniformed guards formed two lines for ReeMara to walk between. Piper was annoyed to see Armnell walk behind ReeMara and she was annoyed as she had to stay behind.

If ReeMara had expected a drawn wagon the four flashy snow coloured horses standing harness to a matching chariot, they would have imprested her. The driver was dressed in white leather, he was squarely built no one would doubt his strength even if he lacked height.

ReeMara was offered help to mount the chariot. She refused to hold onto the chariot side as the small drive indicated she should, as he sent the horses forward.

ReeMara was not aware what effect she was having on the people lining the road. The snow coloured horses, the matching drive and chariot, her blood red robe, the golden belt, her flaxen hair free in the wind.

Harron had heard the trumpets and had wondered at the tumultuous sound clanging all over the city. He tucked their possessions under a flat stone; he needed to be able move unhampered.

Harron was soon swallowed into the crowds of people walking through the squear in front place where he had last seen ReeMara. They were excited as if expecting something, from what they were saying Harron tried to piece together what could be happening.

"The Emperor left the city to anyone who would like to take it!"

"You don't have anything worth taking!"

"You don't think life is worth keeping?"

"You don't have to push we will not miss anything!"

"What will we not miss?" asked Harron.

"What dose it mater, we are to feast!"

"Will there be wine?"

"How long has it been since wine was available?"

"The Emperor took it all with him."

"He took everything with him."

"Why did he forget you?"

"How much wine would if have taken to keep him?"

"Why have you stayed in the city?" Harron risked asking.

"The Emperor took those that he had a use for the rich families did the same. Folk like us do not have the resources to leave."

"Where is there to go?" asked a gray haired woman. "The Barbarian armies are in the city, around the city. The Emperor has left us to our own fate."

"The Conquer has proclaimed a feast."

"He only had to walk through the gates!"

"That makes him a Conquer!?"

"You want to argue with his worriers?"

"No, I want to enjoy the feast!"
Harron and the people he was with were made to more out of the middle of the street as soldiers rode in two lines escorting a chariot.

Harron could not stop to get a better look at the woman in the chariot; he had never seen ReeMara in such finery! What was she doing there? Harron shouted and tried to sign to ReeMara if she heard him over the folk around them he could not tell, her head turned towards him, them she was lost in a sea of people and horses.

The chariot stop making ReeMara open her eyes, hands helped her step down, she had good sandals on her feet they would help her to run, but the large squear was full of people and soldiers were standing marking the way up a great flight of steps, she was supposed to mount!

ReeMara looked for CC'raw to help her, but he could only watch from among the pigeons perching on grand arches. It was comforting to have Trigary fly towards her, she did not notice how the people below them astounded at the sight of a great eagle escorting a fine lady in red silk.

ReeMara was wishing Trigary could carry her away, till she saw the Iron Man standing next to a young man, the same young man she had seen in the Base Camp. Her heart mist a beat, he did not look as if he had recognised her, he did not know who she was.

A man wearing white and gold robes with the crossed mark on it brought Armnell to smooth down ReeMara's robe and fix a cloth of red silk to match the robe about her shoulders in length that flowed over the steps as she ascended the steps.

Another man who's staff had to support him waved his free arm in the air, he trough amber dust over ReeMara it sparkled in the sun light, then over the young man.

ReeMara looked intently into the young man's face willing him to remember her. He did not look at her as he placed a string of creamy white amber around her neck, he did not want to know he was her brother.

The Iron Man struck his sward on his shield, then again and again, the men standing on the steps took up his beat. The people in the squear began shouting. Harron could not get near enough to hear what had been said by the men on the platform on the top steeps. He was to fare way to read their lips, though ReeMara did not appear to be in danger, she did not look as if she was part of what was going on.

The younger man took ReeMara's hand when the Iron Man started to walk down the steeps still banging his shield with his sward. He mounted a waiting horse waved the man that had been holding it back to make room for the chariot to move forward to take the pair descending the steeps.

ReeMara's flaxen hair matched the hair of the man beside her. The blood red robe with its blood red silk train seemed to cut the stone of the flight steps in two from where Harron was.

"Trigary will keep an eye on ReeMara." Said CC'raw, he had not expected Harron to be annoyed with him. Without sight or sound of Harron for days, he might have been a bit jubilant when greeting him.

Harron wanted to keep ReeMara in his sight, with a crow landing almost in his face he had not seen where they had gone:

"Yes, yes it is good to see you, but are we going to be able to find them?"

"With the noise they are making, I don't think I will have any trouble in locating them."

"It would be better if you stay with them; I cannot follow them fast enough with so many people about. I can find my way back to where we spent the first night here." was all Harron could say, the people had started to move forward after the soldiers, taking him with them. Harron did see CC'raw tip his wing at him as he strove for a thermal over the city.

Soldiers were directing people into doorways of a building so large that Harron could not say what it was at first. The tunnels were dark and the steps steep; everyone around Harron was nearly out of breath when they stood again in day light.

The gallery ran around the inside of the building and there were others above and below the one Harron found him self on. Food and drink were waiting for the people filling each of the galleries. They must have taken everything edible from the fields they had ridden though, thought Harron.

In a gallery held separate from the others Harron saw ReeMara; she was sitting beside the young man and the Iron Man was also seated in the separated gallery. There was another man with a cross on his robe! Harron might have wondered at the golden seats had he not spotted the elderly man that had been in poisoned with him! What was he doing standing behind ReeMara?

What had the old man said in the place where they had been held? Empress! Was ReeMara to play the part of an empress? Harron had not thought the elderly man could have meant ReeMara!

Harron saw ReeMara stand up the people around him
became still, waiting to see what was going to happen.
ReeMara razed her arm to the eagle flying towards her, in
her other hand the elderly man placed a challis. ReeMara
had to raze it to counter balance the large bird.

Harron saw a sentry make room for a man to stand on
the parapet close to where Harron was, as he watched he
saw the man draw breath:

"Hail! Hail to the Empress!"
It was not what Harron had expected; this one voice
encouraged others to add their voices. 'Hail the
Empress."
The whole coliseum rang with 'Hail to the Empress.' was
to change to 'Hail to the Emperor.' when the young man
stood next to ReeMara, in an up stretched hand was a
cross, in the other he held a sward.

Harron did not add his voice to those around him, how
could he? They were shouting to ReeMara! Who the
other was standing next to ReeMara, he did not know!
The man with a cross marked on his robe was shouting
with the people. The elderly man was holding his staff
stiffly to point at ReeMara.

The Iron Man remained in his seat, he like Harron was
watching the scene being performed. Harron had seen
often enough the consequence of this man's leadership on
the Grass Lands. ReeMara had experienced The Iron
Man's harsh acts before she had come to the Cliff
Citadel. He, the Iron Man was sitting on a golden seat, as
if he was the benefactor of the fest.

Drummers took up the rhythm the crowds voices
hailing the Empress and Emperor, the drummer's dark
skins were glistening under animal skins as they beat

their drums. Horses were being lined up in front of chariots, each team had four horses.

Trumpets sounded when ReeMara stood up to lift a golden belt for all to see. The voice of the man that had hailed the Empress informed the drivers that it would be awarded to the driver of the wining team.

Harron was not surprised to notice the man that made this announcement, beside the gallery where ReeMara stood was the same as the man that hailed the Empress from the parapet close to him.

A team of black horses were racing next to a team of horses with fire coloured manes, their wheals seemed to touch as sparks flew and sand showered the people in the lower galleries. Women's voices changed from complaint to excitement when the team of snow coloured horses got their noses in front of the team of brown stallions, with black manes.

The driver of the snow coloured horse was knocked off balance when the driver of the brown stallions with the black manes took his whip and hit him across his shoulders, forcing him to pull his team to one side allowing the brown stallions to pass by.

Harron was not happy when the driver received the golden belt from ReeMara; it was a mean trick to use to win the race!

More wine was brought to the galleries, Harron did not drink as the wine smelt as if it had been strongly fermented; he needed a clear head, though he did help himself to the food that was offered.

The folk around Harron did not thank the men that brought more wine; their attention was taken by the sound of swards banging on shields.

The Worriers with the swards and shields showed off their skills, they were good natured no one was hurt. The crowed shouted for their favourers. Harron was impressed when a man with nothing but a net managed to unarm a swards man.

Horns announced men from the Tented Army, they sent in bowmen to shoot at targets too small to see let alone hit! When they shot small apples in two Harron had to admire their skill. The Empress, ReeMara gave a gold arrow to the best bowman. He offered her the two halves of the apple he had shot as he received his prise.

Three men sitting on a donkey entered the coliseum dressed as worriers; their heads did not reach their donkey's withers. Harron had to wander if their swards were not too long for them and their shields were so large they could sleep underneath them. The folk around Harron were laughing at the three worriers tripping over each other.

Harron found it funny when they tried to copy the bow men, their arrows landed in the sand missing the apples waiting for them. One of the little men speared an apple on an arrow and gave it to ReeMara.

Now the donkey would not take the three small warriors out of the coliseum; he just stood there, the three men had to dismount and push the stubborn beast. The crowed laughed as all the men's attempts to make him move were rejected by the Donkey.

Horses were lead into the arena; their riders had cloaks of different colours. The donkey had been persuaded to leave as the start of the ridden race was about to start. The nervous horses stood on their hind legs when their riders dropped their cloaks to the ground. Wages were being made between the folk around Harron as to which colour would win.

The young man next to ReeMara razed his sward to start the race. While the donkey had entertained the people; men had placed barrels to mark where the riders were to direct their horses. Their manes and tales flew in the wind and their hooves pounded the ground the people pounded their feet as they shouted for their favourite to cross the line a head of the others. The victor received a golden bridle from the Empress. The black stallion that had won the race was shamefully showing off.

Trumpets, drums and horns sounded; three men rose out of the ground tall as the donkey's men were small, their swards matched their height, they razed their swards to point to the sky as their shields rested on the ground of the platform still rising out of the sand.

Harron found the effect most impressive! The sand arena was pulsing with the marching feet of the Iron Mans worriers, the Tented Camp were mounted on their horses, their birds on their arms.

Every one around Harron was on their feet shouting, 'Hail the Empress. Hail the Emperor!' To add to their voices they stamped their feet. Harron was not the only one that was stunned by what was happening around him, but Harron could only stand there!

CC'raw was just as stunned at what he had seen from his perch, the pigeons had taken to the sky when the drums had started to beat but CC'raw could only sit there, he saw there was another that was not moving with the other people starting to file down the stone steeps.

Harron's hair had covered his face; he was waiting till most of the people had descended the steep steps.

"What did you think of all of that?" CC'raw settled beside Harron.

"To see the Iron Man here has given me given me a lot to think about. CC'raw, stay with ReeMara till we know what they are going to do with her. I will go back to where the flat stones are."

CC'raw did not want to leave Harron, he look troubled. Even though Trigary was with ReeMara, that silly bird was to blame for involving ReeMara in whatever is going on.

CC'raw told Harron to take as much of the food as he could, they were not longer able to take food from the fields they had passed through.

ReeMara was sitting on a comfortable bed a low table was laden with all sorts of foods and drink. Armnell was placing more food on the all ready laden table. They were in a room not unlike the one they had lived in since ReeMara had had a bath. The difference was the room had furniture and the lights were much grander than they had been in the rooms they had been kept in.

The Iron Man and ReeArk were in the other half of the large room sitting on beds and taking food off their laden tables.

ReeMara could only sit and wonder, Armnell made her eat, but she could not take her eyes of her brother and the Iron Man.

ReeArk must have asked a question, it was not he that spoke nor the Iron Man but the Elderly man. Armnell seemed to know him but he was not taking any notice of her:

"As Abor of this city I can tell you. The people that have stayed in the city are mostly women and their children. The others are too old to fight with the armies or are crippled."

The Iron Man turned to ReeArk to say:

"There is no need to brutalize them, they are brides for our men and the work force the City needs."

The man with the cross on his robe moved so ReeMara could see him:

"Give them a beautiful empress and strong emperor and do not let the people here starve."

"Show them we have power they won't think to buck!" ReeArk sound impressed and enthusiastic at whatever the future plans were.

"What they have seen and heard, they will pass onto others outside the city saving our men the trouble to build a reputation!" The last man that had spoken ReeMara could not see as a curtain blocked her view. A bird on his arm fluttered its wings as he spoke. The Iron Man took more food from the table and sank onto on one of the beds:

"Well said; I could not have explained it better my self!" He waved a hand full of cooked meet at ReeArk and then pointed at ReeMara with it:

"Emperor and Empress!"

It was not clear to ReeMara what the Iron Man meant but ReeArk was laughing with the Iron Man.

ReeMara did not have a chance to hear what they were planning as she and Armnell were ordered to leave.

They did not return to their rooms with the grandeur they had left them, the guards escorted them on foot, the guards did not seem too happy at having to guard them, most people were in a festive mood and it was their luck to be on guard.

"It was wonderful the other horse could not keep up with me! What do you think of the bridle I won? " asked Soul.

"You are as bad as that bird!" CC'raw said perched on the stall wall. "Bragging! Why were you taken to run in the race?

Did I not tell you to keep your heads down?"

Soul was not allowed to answer, CC'raw was so angry he could not explain that a man had shouted, 'The black stallion was to be brought out to be saddled.' That the man had not known which black stallion the man that had shouted wanted, had just grabbed the first black horse he pasted.

If CC'raw had worried he might not have been able to get back to Bramble and Corn, it had not been problem as the man that had picked him out had handed Soul's rains to a youngster, telling him to return him to his stall. Soul sensed that the youth did not have any idea where to bring him, so he had lead the poor boy to where Corn and Bramble were.

"Don't draw attention on yourselves, Harron can hide in the place were we spent the first night, but you are too big to hide behind the stones that stand. You have to stay here till I can find somewhere else."

They heard him muttering under his breath as he flew way: "A stupid bird and now three stupid horses!"

Harron was lying on one of the flat stones when CC'raw came.

"You are lying on top of their dead humans." CC'raw remarked as he landed on one of the stones that stood upright. "The pigeons from the squear told my, here they lay their dead." He had not expected Harron would jump up so quickly from the bed the stone was offering.

"Do you know where ReeMara is now?"

"They have brought her back to where she was being kept before."

Harron nodded, he was thinking he should find away into where ReeMara was being held. CC'raw read Harron's thoughts when he said:

"You could climb the wall but once inside the stone has been polished not even a spider can climb it."

"She is safe for the moment; with the show they have put on no one will harm her. The question is why do they want ReeMara as an empress? I would have puzzled why chose her, but, I saw her coming out of that building, she did look wonderful." Harron could not say. "Why Trigary flying to her was so impressive?"

"Silly bird, he did not realise what he was doing; the humans in the coliseum found him flying to her most impressive! Why the humans liked such a show of power, if they knew Trigary is just a pet."

"The Iron Man has created a show to…" Harron stopped he was deep in thought.

"Did you notice that most of the humans here are women and their hatchlings? Any male is either aged or crippled."

Harron had seen for himself what this man could do, why did the Iron Man want to impress so many people? He would have still been wondering, but for a pair of pigeons fluttered passed, billing and cooing at each other; all those warriors had marched into the coliseum. Warriors that the Iron man had marched over the mountains; the image of ReeMara hand in hand with the young man flashed in Harron's mind. Then a pain passed through him, it was so strong he had to draw breath sharply!

Harron had been friends with ReeMara for so long, from the time she had arrived at the Cliff Citadel and taken her first bath! He had seen her enjoy that bath and splash with the other children. They were older now; Harron could understand why ReeMara had slipped away if there was a place to bath. Harron saw again ReeMara's hand in someone else's hand.

CC'raw was telling him about that 'silly horse'! To win a race was not CC'raw's ideal way of keeping a horses head down! Harron was at first confused CC'raw had spoken of a 'silly bird.' When CC'raw had finished telling him about Soul taking part in the horse race they had watched in the coliseum, and that he had won it, made Harron laugh!

Piper did not know what to do with ReeMara; she seemed to be in a trance! Armnell would have liked to shoo the ferret away, but ReeMara pulled the ferret to her.

Piper was frustrated she did not know what had happened after she had been left alone in their rooms, and now ReeMara was about to burst into tears. Piper could only ask Armnell what she knew. Piper was not sure if she had understood all she was being told, not even when CC'raw told her what he had seen. Piper had been a red ferret in a white world; ReeMara was now an empress in this new place!

Piper was glad the horses were all right, good place to hide them with other horses! It was also good to know Harron was not fare way. What Piper was not sure of was how much they could trust Armnell; Piper did not want CC'raw to bring Harron here till she was had a chance to think about all that had happened. That Armnell knew her way around the city she had managed to bring ReeMara back here. Their escort had only grumbled they were not with their comrades, enjoying the wine they had been promised.

Armnell stood before the Iron Man; she looked into his hard eyes. What had this man in mind for the young woman she had left back in the rooms? Why had he called her here?

"You will be well rewarded for you services."

"I had planned to use my freedom for my own purposes."

Armnell did not take her eyes way from the man's face; she was trying to decide how to talk to this man. That he wanted something from her was obvious, she had the feeling she would have long been put to death.

"You have long controlled the Bath House of the Senate." The Iron Man stated. What else had the old man told this man?

Armnell had recognised the old man was acting as Abor when the young women had ascended the flight of steps.

"With your experience I wish you to see the young woman has all that is required for an empress. I will make available funds need for this purposes." The Iron Man turned his back on Armnell to pick up a leather pouch, he handed it to her.

"There will be times when I will require the girl I will inform you of such duties. You are to see she is dressed befittingly."

"It is not just cloths that make a lady."

"I have already said, all required. Here is my seal giving you the right to obtain a fitting house hold."

Armnell felt her ordinance was about to end, what she had not expected was the words she heard the Iron Man say.

"See that the union between my son and the girl is fruitful."

ReeMara sat in the walled garden, going over in her mind what had happened. The Iron Man had called Armnell to him, what did he want from her? What did he want with her? To recognise ReeArk; to have her hand was placed in his! She had thought to run away but where was she to run; there had been so many people!

If she had run she would not have seen her brother. That he was live was beyond any wish she could have ever made, but what she was to do now was weighing heavily on her mind.

Harron was not even hear to talk too, ReeMara hands covered her face; she did not want even Piper or Trigary to see her cry.

Piper ferreted her way into ReeMara's arms:

"Piper I saw ReeArk to day." ReeMara had to explain who ReeArk was. Piper had first met her ReeMara when he had had to leave her siblings due to her red coal and found shelter in a cave ReeMara was hiding from the old woman and then from the Iron Man. She had heard the story of how the Iron Man and his men had slaughtered ReeMara's family, burnt their village. How could she have seen her brother today?

"It is not his hair or the colour of his skin or his height, not even the scare on his face, how could I forget his eyes?" ReeMara's hands covered her face again.

When she dropped her hands she saw a brown leg dangling over the top of the wall, then a hand with fingers feeling for a firm hold. When ReeMara saw Harron's face appear over the wall, all her self pity melted in the joy of seeing him.

Harron did not heed any warnings he dropped and ran towards ReeMara, she was quite happy to fling herself into his arms.

Trigary did not understand what CC'raw and Piper were fussing about, he was just as happy to see Harron as ReeMara was. Piper agreed with CC'raw, how were they going to get Harron back over the wall? The wall on this side was so smooth they were not going to get him back over it. And they did not know when Armnell would return, if she would return. When they had last seen her she was being escorted by two soldiers across the squear until the door was pushed shut by their bored guards.

Harron waved way their arguments by saying he could no longer sit on the flat stones in the cemetery. Had they heard what Soul had been up to?

"We can hide Harron from Armnell; he could slip under the bed when she comes back." said ReeMara not wanting to let Harron go, not now!

"She may not come back!" Trigary was hopeful not that he had anything against her, she had brought him tasty titbits as she did for Piper.

Harron's brown legs slid out of sight as the door opened and Armnell returned with food and a worried expression. She looked up to see a crow sitting on the wall, that he had a gray body under his black head marked him as unusual. At least the girl looked better than she had done when Armnell had to leave. She needed time to think over what the Iron Man had asked her to do. Asked! Was he a man that asked? Armnell knew if she was not prepared to do as he asked she would not live long, even with her knowledge of the City!

Had Harron kept his foot still Armnell would not have seen it as it slid under the bed ReeMara was sitting on. The movement could have been the ferret, but it was in the girl's arms, and a crow with a dark cap was sitting on the wall watching her. Now she came to think of it, she had seen that bird flying around the garden before:

"You don't come from around here, do you?" Armnell said looking at ReeMara, "If you don't want me to pull you out by your ass, come out from under the seat. As for you, crow you can come in and help explain what you are all doing here? I have never seen a ferret as a pet; I should have asked you before."

"But other events have rather taken control." Harron said as he straitened himself to stand before Armnell and ReeMara.

Armnell stood waiting for Harron and ReeMara to start explaining themselves. ReeMara did not know what to say, how to start, Harron looked at the food the dark woman had brought with her:

"It is much easer to talk with a full stomach." Armnell could only laugh the youth had a good point there!

Harron had to wait, and wait under the bed as there was a bang on the door. Men were labouring under, a marble table and matching benches and beds more fitting for an empress, and drapes to enhance the room. A wonderful mirror lent against a wall. The figure of a woman in a robe that left nothing to the imagination was placed in the middle if the of the things the men brought. Thank goodness they did not ask to take the bed ReeMara was sitting on!

Armnell was pleased with the things that made cooking meals easer; if the way to loosen their young tongs was to feed their tummies, so be it.

ReeMara was not sure what they should tell Armnell. Harron told Armnell of the battles below the Cliff Citadel where the finest horse were bred. Of the alliance with the men that had come over the mountains with their bright tents.

There had been talk of a legion that had gone to the far northern forests to counter troublesome barbarians. No word had ever reached the city as to what had happened to them, not one man had returned to say, Armnell remembered.

Other legions had been sent to stop marauders on the grass planes on the other side of the mountains. Were they talking about what had happened to them? Where the two youngsters talking of the lost legions?

More legions could not be sent to help as the Senate had spoken of needing legions to control the ways to the sea ports.   Shortages had interrupted everyday life, silk and amber were hard to get and the men of the senate had complained the good wine from the north had not arrived in the city.

The Senate could not protect the city to many men had been sent to support the legions. The City had been left to whoever wanted it. Those left could not hold the City against an army.

Armnell told of how the old Emperor had left the City to defend its self, taken all his wealth with him, other wealthy people had followed him. She had thought to leave the City, but where was she to go? She had decided to supervise the bath house as she had done, that old fool had been glad to help her.

Harron asked Armnell, who she meant when she said, 'That old fool.' He was not surprised to hear the Abor the Iron Man had used in his ceremony was the same old man. And, he was the same man that had been where Harron had been held.

Harron had wondered why send the elderly man to talk to folk the Iron Man had chosen to confine, if they were released in the name of the Empress they would run home to tell of the good thing 'she' had done for them! Then show a lady richly dressed with hair of gold and place her on a chariot. He had been there and seen the show the Iron Man Had put on to please the people.

Now the dark skinned woman knew they did not come from with in the City. It did not matter to the Iron Man where ReeMara came from. When ReeMara had come out of the Bath House with her hair blowing in the wind she had all the Iron Man needed for his plan. Whatever the Iron Man was planning Harron did not want to think about right now. Right now he and ReeMara had to decide what they were going to do.

They had come to the City to place the stones She-With-The-Sight had given ReeMara in the temple in the heart of the City. She-With-The-Sight had told ReeMara her parents would have died for nothing if she did not do as she was asked. Now they found themselves in a wall garden with a dark skinned woman, who had dressed ReeMara as an empress!

Armnell was also wondering what she, they should do now?

"I can only try to calculate the Iron Man's power!"

"I know of the Iron Man and his ways. He destroyed my family, my village." ReeMara out burst did not surprise Harron, but it did surprise Armnell. Harron did not stop ReeMara telling the dark woman what the Iron Man meant to her, of his cruelty and his command in the battles under the Cliff Citadel, where she had met Harron, and had been accepted as a pupil. Look after by Beana and The Sage till she and Harron had left to make their way here. The one point ReeMara did not tell Armnell was about the stones She-With-The-Sight had commanded her to bring here.

Armnell told them about her life such as it was, as a young woman how she had been used until her youth faded, till they found her massaging fingers could ease their aches and pains. She had been found a place in the bath house; where her skills had allowed her to become matron of the baths.

One of the advantages of working in the Bath House had been, to know what the Senate were discussing. She had known amber was in short supply; for one thing, those that believed it should be placed in the foundations of any new building were complaining; they could not build without it.

The new religion had wanted amber for their prayer beads. When silk had also stopped coming with the donkeys the wealthy ladies had made their men's life very uncomfortable.

Armnell had heard them complain as if she was the one at fault. Now she was sitting opposite to a young woman with the finest string of white amber given to her at the joining with the young man. The young man was one of the Iron Man's men, of that Armnell was sure. That he had the same colour hair and skin as the girl Armnell had noticed, but did not know what if anything, that could mean!

Harron was the one that spoke next.

"What we have to decide is what do we should do now!"

He could not say to Armnell why ReeMara and he were here.

Those that had stayed behind in the City were the ones that had been impressed by the show the Iron Man had provided, he too had enjoyed the food provided, as if to explain why he was here, he told them, he had eaten all he had been able to carry with him and he was fed up with waiting for news in the cemetery whenever CC'raw had a mind drop in on him.

"We cannot undo what has been done!" Armnell said, while she put more food on their new table, Harron looked as if he could eat his own weight. "The facts are I have not been able to leave the City and make use of my freedom as I had planned. I had not expected to be made a lady to the Empress!

What do you plan? If you chose to leave, I will have to leave with you as the Iron Man is not the type to let me live if his empress wishes to leave."

Armnell could see ReeMara was not comfortable with the title empress; it did need explaining what the Iron Man had meant by such a title! Harron picked up Armnell's thought by asking what the Iron Man wanted; she could only retell what he had said to her and it was food from his larders, they were enjoying now.

ReeMara was in tears for the second time that day, Piper and Trigary started to fuss around her, CC'raw and Harron could only show concern as flapping wings and a red ferret were covering ReeMara. Armnell hurried away to get some herbal tea to comfort the young woman.

"We should think about getting out of the City, ReeMara. The dark skinned woman has a mark from the Iron Man we could use to our advantage!" Harron did not want to stop to look at ReeMara he continued to say, she, the dark skinned woman might know which place She-With-The-Sight meant you should place the stones she gave you.

ReeMara was crying even harder when Armnell returned with the tea, Harron was beginning to need some tea himself, ReeMara's tears did not make sense to him.

Harron decided to leave ReeMara in the care of the bird and the ferret, he and CC'raw sipped tea with Armnell, it seem a good time to ask the dark skinned woman to repeat exactly what the Iron Man had said and could she explain the meaning of the show on top of the great flight of steeps.

Harron had not expected to hear ReeMara had been
united with the young man, and that the Iron Man had
made it clear that he wished that their union was fruitful.
Armnell did have to explain to Harron what was meant
by that! He could not understand why ReeMara did not
want to leave the City, but when he repeated this idea
ReeMara sobbed even louder than before. Harron had not
seen ReeMara so upset since he had seen her sob in
Beana's arms all those years ago, when ReeMara first
came to the Cliff Citadel.

Armnell dashed out to make more tea, Harron tried to
ask ReeMara what was upsetting her so, before Armnell
came back, but what with ferret and now two birds
fussing around ReeMara and Armnell hurrying with a full
pot of herbal tea, he could not make sense of ReeMara's
reply.

They would just have to wait till ReeMara stopped
sobbing enough to explain what was upsetting her so.
When she blurted out that the young man her hand had
been placed in was her brother shocked the other's in the
grand room as much as it upset ReeMara.

Armnell had noticed a resemblance but never would
she have thought that such resemblance could have meant
that they were siblings. Armnell wanted to ask ReeMara
if she was sure, their faces had the same look and their
hair colour matched, not many people had such light
coloured hair in the City, the senator's ladies would have
coveted such hair!

Harron thought ReeMara would want to leave the City;
he did not think she would want to stay now she knew
she was united to her brother! ReeMara's voice was
steady when she said she would not leave now she knew
ReeArk was alive!

Harron knew it was no good arguing with her, if he could not persuade her to stay at the Cliff Citadel, how could he persuade her to leave the City?

"What we have to decide is what do we should do now!" Had he not said that before? Only now instead of planning to complete the task She-With-The-Sight had given to ReeMara, they had to plan how they were going to keep out of trouble here? And, from what he had seen since he had been in the City that was not going to be an easy task, not now the Iron Man was commanding the City!

When Harron had seen the Iron Man's mark Armnell had been given he had hope to use it to enable them to find ways to slip out from under the Iron Man's nose.

"This mark entitles us to anything an empress could require?" Harron asked Armnell. "We can use the position of scribe to explain my presence. The Iron Man cannot know of ReeMara or me, he just took hold of the first girl he saw."

Remembering how ReeMara looked as she started down the steeps of the Bath House.

It was strange to think they had been travelling across the mountains and strange new lands with the Iron Man and his armies behind them! What did the Iron Man want here?

This mark entitles us to anything an empress could require; Armnell took the mark from Harron's hand.

"An empress needs a scribe!" Armnell could read and write though she had not let her past masters know; it did make sense to have a scribe in an empress's house hold.

It they were going to survive in the City then they were going to have to work together; she asked Harron if he could read and write? He would have to be skilled beyond a child scribble as the Iron Man would not be easily fooled. It was CC'raw that in formed her that the teaching in the Cliff's was of the highest standard.

There was the small mater of enlightening the guards that the Empress household had a scribe! Armnell found that the Iron Man's mark enabled her to get food and materials for robes but it did not entitle her to appear in front the Iron Man.

Harron had to remain hidden till they could find away to explain his presence, he was not happy as he had been confined one way or another ever since he had arrived in the City. If it was not the hot dark place where he had been herded too, it was the flat stones and now he was confined under a bed whenever there was a bang on the door!

It was not until Armnell thought to go to the place where the market used to be held did she find away out of their problem. The market had not only supplied food brought in from the surrounding fields, it was the place where silk and amber used to be sold, the merchandise had been brought in by the donkey trains. The market was where the rich brought and sold their slaves. Those that had households where slaves were needed had taken their slaves with them, so it did not surprise Armnell to see there weren't any slaves changed to the sale places, but she did see people standing about, Armnell asked a woman why she was there, the woman offered to wash her robes or tend to any household needs in return for food or marks she could exchange.

There were others offering their services, so Armnell could argue she had found a scribe offering his services, when there were not letters to write then, his services would be helpful in daily maters, she was thinking about firing up the coppers in the Bath House. She had not seen the old man since the day ReeMara had fond her bath house.

Armnell had to get Harron out of their rooms to get him back in! ReeMara and Armnell tried to push him over the polished wall. But it was so smooth that he could only slip down faster than they could push him up. Harron squealed when Trigary tried to help by pulling Harron up by his hair, they had to stop the great bird from helping encase the guards were to hear Harron complain about having his hair pulled.

Armnell thought to roll him in soiled robes and take him to the market for the women to wash, but he was too big to hide that way! The next plan involved dressing Harron in a woman's robe covering his head with a veil, but he could not walk like a woman! A young man with bed sheet over his head would not convince anyone.

The simplest way was to distract the men on guard ReeMara decided, and through their stomachs. Armnell made them bread; as she was offering them the bread fresh and steaming. ReeMara pushed Harron out behind their backs!
He did not stop to listen to Armnell say, 'It must be tiresome standing around all day, would they like some bread, she had just made it and little wine to help it go down?'

Harron was back in the cemetery again, where he had to wait till Armnell could come and get him. Then they could walk in through the door with him as servant.

The only part of the plan that did not workout as Harron would have wished was when Armnell was stopped by their guards and he heard her say: 'Eunuch.' as they were passed them.

Everyday life was made so much easer with the mark of the Iron Man. There were shortages in the City but when Armnell or ReeMara showed the mark they were offered the best the seller had.

Soul and Bramble, Corn were better stabled when the stable manager learnt that they belonged to the new Empress. The stable block for private horses were not far from the Senate's main assembly hall, and could be reached through outer rooms. If it was not for the guards ReeMara and Harron would have been very comfortable, it was somehow disconcerting to have guards follow them to the stables or the Bath House.

When ReeMara wanted to ride they had to be content with the coliseum where the Iron Man's show had taken place. It was to the relief of their guards as they did not have to run behind her horses, just stand by the entrance.

There was still the question as to which temple ReeMara should place the stones She-With-The-Sight had given her.

Harron was exploring maps and scrolls he had found when exploring the Senate's corridors, he did not have to have a guard watching him so he was free to move around the City without being followed.

Harron did not know where to start looking, there were maps and drawings of buildings great and small. There were plans for new waterways underground and other maps for those all ready supplying water for the City's population.

There were scrolls of names that looked like families that had lived in the City long before Harron and ReeMara got there. The lists had signs like the one on the glove ReeMara had been given by the store masters in the mountains and names listed under them. How that was going to help him, Harron did not know.

The lists of those entitled to bring food for sale in the City's markets did not help him either, though it was interesting to see how much they had to pay to the Senate so they could sell their goods. That sale of silk was taxed as was the exchange of ownership with amber, wine and horses.

Whenever Armnell dressed ReeMara in fine robes, Harron had plenty of time to explore the Senate's halls were scrolls were stored.

ReeMara was often taken to feasts; all she had to do was look pretty as she sat next to ReeArk. ReeMara told Harron of the folk that were invited, they had another look to the people they had seen on their way to the City. He had laughed when she had tried to explain how the other folk looked. Some were like Armnell, not as round as she was, but their skin was as dark. ReeMara could not be sure but she thought their leaders were offering warriors. The men looking like Harron talked a lot about bring silk to the City and compared their birds, not that they were as good looking as Trigary!

ReeMara had the most difficulty describing to Harron, the folk that had another look. Harron could not believe folk had eyes the way ReeMara made Her's look. And, he laughed when she described their skin as yellow! They had horses of a type they had never seen before.

There were changes in the City Harron noted. When they had moved through the streets for the first time it was clear halls and stores were empty of their goods, but now with the supervision of the warriors, goods like silk and bales of cotton were being stacked. One house stored spices that filled the air with strong and interesting smells.

One house had guards standing in front of the doors, as there was not a smell of food, Harron had to think precious stones or mettles could be being bought and sold.

Laughter was often heard coming from houses where food and wine was offered. Men from both armies were enjoying the welcome from the women that had not left the City.

Harron could understand why the Iron Man would be pleased his men were staying in the City's confines; Warriors taking their pleasures outside the City's walls were more likely to cause trouble.

Harron's fascination for old scrolls helped him to see why the Iron Man wanted to have command of this city; it was built on both sides of a river, a river where large boats could dock, unload their goods before taking on new merchandise. The sea the river ran into, offered passage to traded with other nations.

Harron remembered the donkey train they had travelled with to the Base Camp. The donkeys must come from lands with goods to offer; the donkeys had talked about carrying bales of silk before they took weapons to the men of the tented army below the Cliff Citadel. And, the Iron Man had gone to a lot of trouble to stop amber from come out of the Islands in the Mist. She-With-The-Sight had gone to a lot of trouble to make sure ReeMara would bring the stones she had been given to this city! Harron could, and then could not understand why ReeMara did not want to leave the City now she knew ReeArk was here.

Harron found that the whole city was mapped on scrolls he had found. It was the waterways under the City, Harron had found interesting they could offer away out under the noses of anyone wanting you to stay!

When Harron came across older scrolls that showed underground ways where passages crisscrossed each other and there seemed to be passages on different levels passing underneath.

Harron found a way into one of the marked passages he had seen on the old scrolls. It had not been hard to find, a low dark arch in the corner of the cemetery he had slept in had suggested to him that he should start to explore from there. But his enthusiasm was dampened after he turned the first corner. He found there were stones like the ones he had sat on in the cemetery! He would have turned back into daylight had the light of his oil lamp not lit a sign cut into the stone. It showed a closed fist, like the one the Iron Man had on his banner!

ReeMara was busy being pretty, fussing with Armnell over silk robes and how to wear her hair, it made Harron feel sick! If Piper and CC'raw felt the same they did not say, Trigary was happy to preen himself, he would never say a word against ReeMara, so it was no good asking him.

"All this fuss for ReeArk!" ReeMara turned when Harron said that, as he came into the room.

"If you found someone that belonged to you, you would want to find out about them."

"I belong to you; we have been through so much together." Harron did not look happy sitting on the bed.

It was as plain as the nose on her face to Armnell that Harron was jealous of ReeArk, from what she knew of the two young people, they had up until now loved each other as brother and sister. But now they were living in the City among other people, things were changing for them. Armnell could see Harron was not happy when

ReeMara was needed to attend some event the Iron Man had planned.

ReeMara was happy to see her brother even though he did not speak to her, though ReeMara had cried on the way back when he had not even tried to talk to her. ReeMara had said when she had whipped her tears away. 'If He won't talk to me how can I tell him I am his sister?'

Armnell decided not to worry about the Iron Man's remark about the child he wanted them to have! If the young man did not want to talk to ReeMara what could she do? Probable the Iron Man's attention was concentrated on running the City. He had not said anything when he had seen Armnell attending to ReeMara's robe.

"I found a stone with the iron fist on it, like the banner the Iron Man has." Harron's remark would have gone unnoticed had Piper not squeaked loudly, everyone thought she was chocking!

"The leader of the Barbarians has his sign on old stones in this City!"

"What is so strange about that?" Everyone wanted to know.

"A man like the Iron Man, leader of the Barbarian armies; lead his and the Tented Army against the Legions coming from this City, has his sign on old stones, for Harron to find when he is snooping around. I find that strange!"

"You think the Legions came from this City?" Harron was not really surprised Piper thought the Legions came from here. He had not thought till now to question from where they had come, but to say they had come from here made sense. But it did not make any more sense of seeing the Iron Man's sign on an old stone in the maze of tunnels he had started to explore.

Harron started to explore for scrolls with the sign of the iron fist. Under the sign were names of family members going back to the time where the scrolls were first started. But the list of names did not tell what had happened to those living under the sign. Harron took scrolls from other families to see if they could tell him anything, but they too had lists of who had begat who and who had which children, when they were born, but not what had happened to them, other to state when they had died.

Harron did not real know who he could ask, as Armnell had pointed out most folk had left the City that might know how to answer his questions.

The day the man came to see Armnell; Harron did not like to ask him what he knew about the Iron Man, after all he was known as the Iron Man's Abor. And Harron had seen him when he had been kept in that horrible place that had been so hot and dark. Where the man had gone to a lot of trouble to tell those held there that the Empress would see they would see daylight again!

Harron tried to eavesdrop on Armnell and the man, all he could learn was the man's name, Alois; that he was enjoying Armnell's fingers work into his tense mussels, Harron could see. But as to whether he knew about the Iron Man history their conversation did not make clear. Alois and Armnell knew each other from the Bath House, had he been one of the Senate members?

Armnell could answer that question; she told Harron the old man had been in service to one of the families that had left the City. They had not taken him with them was because they thought he was too old to be of any use where they were going. How he had caught the Iron Man's eye she did not know, but his airs and graces were from his imagination not from any rank he had held.

Trying to think what the Iron Man wanted to achieve, Harron had spent a lot of time pondering over when he had watched the battles from the Cliff Citadel. Harron had admired the battle plans the Iron man had used against the Legions opposing him. Had he kept the Legions occupied on the grass planes so he could take this City? Were the people so frightened of the Iron Man's army they had just left the City?

Armnell had said the Emperor had refused to rule the City; he had let the Legions engage in maters too far away from the City, they could not get back to protect it and its people.

ReeMara mind was occupied by ReeArk's lack of interest in her. Why would he not talk to her? When she had to attend a feast the men among the Iron Man's guest's eyes followed her when she took her place beside ReeArk.

The other women at the feast did not speak to ReeMara, mostly because she had to sit at ReeArk's side; the ladies could not approach the table of the City's leaders. ReeMara would have liked to be able to talk to them, but ReeArk was more important to her that the prettily dressed ladies, even if he would not talk to her. She had to accept she was going to have to wait till the right moment offered its self, where she could confront ReeArk.

To try to engage her brother in a conversation that told him of his past was not going to be easy at a feast! There was so much going on, music for the dancers and drums to accompany fights between men representing their armies. Bets were made loudly by the Iron Man's guests; their shouts of encouragement mixed with the clang of weapons on shields, and calls for more wine did not make for congenial conversation.

ReeMara had to be content sitting next to her brother wait and watch what was going on. Harron would ask her about who was at the feast. Harron was always interested when the man with the cross on his clothing was attending the event; he also had men to represent his sign. The men fought as though their god was at the feast! ReeMara had reported, as the men from the Barbarian army laughed as they swung their swords, the Tented Army's men fought with light swards and confused their component by moving at speed.

Harron was more interested when the man with the cross and the Abor decisions grew into an augment! The augments were about whose beliefs held the most power, which places the men with the crosses could use to worship their god and where the pagan could follow theirs!

ReeMara told Harron about the argument they did not even try to hide from the other guest. Why they were arguing about the amber stones? What was so important about them? Why did they want to have more than they should be assigned?

ReeMara had seen the Iron Man's anger rise when their arguments disturbed the fest.

It was while the two men were voicing their unsettled busyness ReeMara found herself alone with ReeArk. They were supposed to enter the great room that was used to feast and fights were staged.

The two men were facing each other at that point in silence when she arrived. Armnell was fussing about the folds of the robe and smoothing her hair when ReeArk

strode into the outer room where guests waited to be seen
to their places and the two men were facing each other.
The small room was filling up with men, some stood
behind the Abor; men with the same crosses on their
robes backed their leader.

ReeMara arm was grabbed by ReeArk's strong hand,
she found she was standing in front of a curtain; he pulled
aside the curtain there was a door he all but pushed her
through!

It was dark when the door swung behind them; his hand
was no longer holding her arm. ReeMara wanted to move
but did not dare in the black darkness. Then she had to
cover her eyes when the small oil lamp lit the room.

ReeMara did not have words ready she did not know
what to say:

"ReeArk."

The young man did not say anything but he did turn his
face to look at ReeMara. ReeMara repeated his name.
The coroners of his eyes told her he knew the name, there
were memories flickering behind them? Did he know
her? Did he see the beach where they had been playing
that day? ReeArk's fingers toughed the scare that run
down from his left eye over his cheek.

"I was there when you got that scare!"

ReeMara thought for a moment that ReeArk would leave
her standing there as the sound of men fighting reached
them. He just stood there looking at her.

"I did not lay a sward on you, you are my brother."

It was as if the world had stopped as ReeArk stood in
front of her, she did not know what to say she could not
know what he was thinking. ReeArk hand again toughed
his face but he did not say anything.

It was quite outside the hidden room when ReeArk
lead ReeMara out and through the reception hall where

there had been fighting and into the grand hall where guests were waiting for them to enter. ReeMara did notice there were more of the Iron Man's men than usual standing behind the men that had been fighting.

Harron was most interested to hear that two of the new factions in the City were not in agreement, it did explain why the Iron Man wished to control the amber, and maybe why he destroyed the main source coming from the Islands in the Mists where ReeMara came from. To have amber to offer the two sides in dispute would give him a governing hand. And there were those that were making request for buildings, they need amber to put in the fundaments.

Why the tradition of placing amber was being continued now the Iron Man had taken control of the City, Harron did not know. But it had something to do with the two parties; the man with the golden cross on his robe and the elderly man, the Iron Man's Abor. Not that Harron trusted him, from what Armnell had said he could not be the leading figure of the pagan followers as he insisted he was.

It was more than two weeks after ReeMara had told ReeArk she knew from where he came. She had expected he would come and talk to her, why was he not as curious as she was to know her sibling?

Sitting in the shade in the walled garden outside the room Armnell used to cook their meals ReeMara tried to relax. Waiting was making her feel sick and restless. Armnell could not help notice ReeMara was upset. What had happened at the last feast could not make the girl so unhappy?

"Tell me what is upsetting you so?" Armnell asked from behind her cooking pots. ReeMara was glad to talk to someone about how she told ReeArk, he was her brother.

Harron had brushed the conversation aside, all he wanted to know was what the men were arguing about; he only wanted to know about the City and it problems.

Harron had only wanted to know what had happened out side the room behind the curtain, Armnell was now asking questions as to what had happened inside the small dark room.

Armnell told ReeMara she had to retreat to the kitchens while the men scuffled in the hall outside. She had seen ReeArk take charge of ReeMara. She did not know what had happened while they were in the concealed room.

"You told him you are his sister, just like that!?"

"What was I supposed to do, he won't talk to me? At a feast it is so loud it was the only opportunity I have had." ReeMara looked so sad that Armnell did not say anymore, she took the poor girl into her arms, before saying:

"ReeMara, there is something you should know. The Iron Man wishes that the new Emperor and Empress bring a child to their union."

How that was going to help the girl, Armnell did not know. Maybe it would help to explain why ReeArk had not come to talk to ReeMara.

Harron found ReeMara crying in the arms of Armnell. Armnell had to explain to Harron what was upsetting ReeMara. He had been reading scrolls of who had begat who. Did he understand what the Iron Man wanted? Start a new scroll, but why? Harron shook his head, he wanted to comfort ReeMara. They were going to have to think of something. Brother and sister could not make children.

The pagan beliefs forbid such a union and from what he had heard about the men following the cross they were not aloud unions with women!

The warriors were making unions with the women that had stayed in the City, moving their new families into homes that had been left vacant by those that had left the City to the Iron Man's armies.

Harron was deep in thought; ReeMara did not speak only played with her food. Armnell had put food for Piper to enjoy but the only one that was eating was Trigary.

CC'raw was not with them he was with the horses. He had gone to find out how they were, as the mood in the wall garden was depressing. He did understand why the humans were so worried.

What CC'raw had not expected was to see ReeArk. He was looking at horses in the large courtyard outside the stables, only the men did not call him ReeArk, they called him Baschi. He was trying to find a horse he liked, but those offered to him did not please him. The Master of the Horse had to send for more horses for ReeArk to look at grooms were running from stall to stall trying to find horses he had not seen.

Just why Soul was pulled out CC'raw did not know, why could the silly horse keep his head down instead of wanting to know what was going on?

It did not surprise CC'raw that ReeArk was drawn to the horse. Soul did not pull away from him; did he think ReeArk was like ReeMara? Was the bored horse going to get into trouble again? ReeArk swung onto Soul's back, CC'raw had to find a perch, watching from a low thermal was tiring. He knew Soul was going to put on a show.

Soul's hooves flashed over the ground, to give ReeArk his due he did stay on Soul's back longer than CC'raw thought. When the youth's body parted company with Soul's back he landed on his feet, he was ready to remount Soul, but the Master of the Horses was rushing towards him with other horses.

ReeArk let them lead Soul away, only because they told him the horse was owned by the Empress. As he turned his back on Soul, ReeArk spotted a bird, CC'raw had the feeling he had been recognised.

"Baschi, we have other animals you will like. Our leader has told us to find you a good horse. We have horses from the Mongol they are renown, for their strength."

CC'raw had to sit there all afternoon as ReeArk tried out horses. The one that was put into a stall next to Soul was one from the Tented Army stock. Fine head with sharp eyes and pointed ears, his coat was the colour of a morning's red sun.

ReeArk had chosen him for his fiery temperament and his speeding hooves. He did not seem to want to talk to Soul or Corn. Bramble called him a snob. The remark did not make the new horse in the stable want to talk to them. The three were not really surprised, as the horse that carried the Iron Man did not talk to anyone, other than to tell them to get out of the way!

That CC'raw did not grumble at Soul for showing off, surprised the three horses, they were a little more surprised when CC'raw told them to watch what they said when the new horse was near them, not that they need CC'raw to tell them that the Iron Man's youth's horse was now stabled next to them. He should not be told about ReeMara busyness. Should he say anything about ReeArk's busyness CC'raw wanted to know what he had to say!

CC'raw was just reaching a thermal he was hoping would take him around the City before gliding back the walled garden, when he noticed ReeArk with a small group of young men. CC'raw saw the young men slapping each other on the shoulder, making mock attacks on each other as they walked along the street. It interested CC'raw to know where ReeArk was stationed, where were his quarters?

The young men disappeared into a house, CC'raw was lucky he found them in the courtyard around a table where wine was spilling from their challises, as was laughter from their lips.

CC'raw found a perch as their shouts for food told him they were going to stay longer. As the young men enjoyed their wine their banter changed from horse play to matters of the hart! If CC'raw had talked about matters of the hart like that his father would have pecked his eyes out. He was glad no one was watching him, he did not want anyone see a crow blush!

When the rowdy group spilled out onto the street CC'raw was pleased. The young men were saying goodnight to each other, ReeArk started up the street with only one guard; they were supporting each other as if one pair of legs was not enough.

One tall fair headed youth and a squally built youngster bound together like a spider, sing songs that would make any crow blush!

CC'raw was glad it was not dark yet, he did not have the eyes of an owl. He was able to see them enter a house not far away from were the horses were kept. As far as the crow flies it was quite close to the walled garden were his ReeMara was.

A light flicked in a small window, it grew stronger as the day light faded.

The little windowsill offered CC'raw a perch. He was eavesdropping on an argument that at first he did not understand.

"Don't touch me!" The dark haired youth said as he backed away from ReeArk. "You are promised to me!"

"Don you know I have responsibilities, Basch has given my hand to that girl. He has his reasons…"

"But, you are promised to me, we have made promises to each other. What can she give you that I cannot? The Iron Man says take her and you jump!"

"Why do you have to be so jealous? She dose not mean anything to me!"

"I have seen you looking at her! Is it her flaxen hair that attracts you, her pale skin? Is my dark skin no longer to your liking?"

"Don stop it, I feel for you as I always have." ReeArk took a step towards but the dark haired youth backed away again.

"I do not feel for anyone the way I feel for you."

"You are only saying that!" Was all Don could say he buried his face in his hands, his shoulders shook, ReeArk slumped on a bed he did not know how to console Don. His feelings for him had not changed since meeting ReeMara. But now he knew she was his sister things had changed. He did not know how to tell Basch that he had given his hand to his sister. Would he believe him? What would that mean to Basch's plans for the reconstitution of the City's commerce?

Basch had seen the girl with an eagle on her arm. People had seen as he had, a woman coming down the steps looking like a goddess. He could understand why his mentor Basch had ordered his companions to take advantage of the moment.

ReeArk could not have known then what he knew now! Would it have helped him if he had recognised who ReeMara as she came out of the grand building? He did not know when it was that he had realised the woman was his sister. He could remember the beach they had been playing on, he could remember sound of hooves pounding the beach, men shouting, crying for the arms of his sister to take him to safety.

That was all before he started his training as a soldier, he would one day take Basch's place as head of the armies, and supporting armies. What Basch wanted from him was for him to bed the girl, use the child to unite the City, show that stability had returned to daily busyness and the City offered fair trading to fair traders. Scholars and men understanding the financial points of trading had left the City was causing problems, not many of their warriors had had scholastic training! It had been a disappointment that the wealthy families had left. Basch had plans that they would have found lucratively interesting, but they had followed that fool of am Emperor!

Now ReeArk was sitting on a bed, his lover was still crying and an ugly crow was sitting on the windowsill!

CC'raw saw ReeArk reach for his sandal before he could aim it at him CC'raw took off into the night.

"How can the people following their religious leaders without prayer stones?"

"You have demanded more gold than was ever assigned to the religious fractions."

"It was the down fall of the old Emperor not being able to satisfy the different fractions in the City." The new Abor was the one that had spoken.

"You take a tax from your members, so they can practise their religion and fill your coffers." The Iron Man was cross with the two parties who only wanted to make themselves weather. "We wish to open the City to all the nations, open new land routs, and encourage the traders that come by with sea. This City will show that the different religions and the pagan practises can live together. People here, all read used to peoples from other nations, with other colour skins, other cultures.

To make a good trading center we need understanding, we need to show understanding. If you cannot come to some arrangement that keeps your arguments behind the scenes, out of the fests to welcome our traders. You will not be invited to attend! I will find men that will address matters as I wish, actors from the plays will take your place. Your voices will be silenced in my darkest prisons where your flesh will rot, where you can find your gods."

The Iron Man's men stood to attention from a shrouded sign their leader had made. The two leaders of the religious fractions seem to lose their important forms as if the air had been taken from them. The man with the cross pointed out that the City owed is stature to its follower's beliefs; its great buildings were to celebrate the new religions.

If the Abor was going to defend the pagan practises by saying the City built on the Seven Hill would never have grown without the pagan worshipers. He was stopped by the Iron Man's men stepping forward. But it did not stop the man with the cross saying.

"The sign of the cross was for all to follow, to offer guidance and promote harmony between all people."

"From the wealth of the people your religions can benefit, I am not interested in saving their souls. I control this city, and I control its resources!" The Iron Man would have said he controlled the amber to control the religious fractions; they need to know who was in control here and not bicker between themselves. He did not need the religious leaders to complete his plans, he could set actors in their places, ban any religious ceremonies. But if he was to show a city open to trading, to ban any practises closed the very markets he was trying to open. Trading with other countries meant showing tolerance over their beliefs, to show harmony between the believers in the City. A sward could whip out a village that would not follow his word; to have men afraid of him had tactical advantages, but now he needed all his skills to set the next part of his plan in motion. The Iron Man waved his hand the ordnance was ended.

"Why not cut of their heads, if they are so troublesome?" ReeArk asked Basch, the Iron Man as the troublesome religious leaders took their leave.

"Two cut the head of a snake in your hand means you have to watch your feet to see where there other snakes are coming from." Basch looked tired. "From the time we first knew each other till now, the skills you have acquired have been for war and controlling warring parties. From now on the skills you need, is to know how to rule this City. You will spend more of your time in studies relating to finances and managing trading."

ReeArk was surprised at Basch's words, before he had enjoyed ReeArk's skill with sward and laughed when he had lent to ride. ReeArk had wanted to tell Basch that he had found a horse to replace his old friend. That dark stallion had been to his liking, why had he been surprised to learn that the horse belonged to ReeMara?

"Did you find a horse befitting your new status?" ReeArk did note Basch's remark, 'New status,' he did not look at Basch when he said he had picked a stallion with a chestnut coat, like a morning sun. Sun Ray matched him in height, and he could gallop with the best. ReeArk was hoping to race him in the next races.

"It is not fitting for you, Baschi as an emperor to be seen racing, if you want to run the horse in a race then find another jockey. Your place is to be seen in control, with the girl by your side. I don't want to see you lying in the dirt in front of the whole City! ReeArk knew Basch to long to argue with him over this point. When Basch presented an order to you, you did not argue, you did not question his authority. ReeArk admired him and when ReeArk had been given the name of Baschi he was proud to take the name of his benefactor. Basch did not have any family that ReeArk knew of. The name of Baschi meant he was the chosen son of Basch.

As son of Basch he would expected to lead men as his benefactor did. Basch had not fully explained what his motives were behind taking this city. The City was bound to attract triad with the donkey trains with their silk and now the access to the open sea. Mongolian horses were being offered in the horse markets, a complete contrast from the horses brought by their Trainian comrades at arms.

The Trainian horses were swift and with a sharp intelligence hard to match with elegance. The Mongolian horses were praised for their endurance and sure hooves on uneven ground.

The Trainian had been the turning point in the battle on the grass plains. Under their banner an eagle holding ball in its talons, they had used their skilled bowmen against the stubborn Legion had caused confusion among their ranks.

The Legion had put up a good fight; they had not been as easy to defeat as the Legion in the northern forests. The Trainian army had come over the mountains; donkeys had continually brought ammunition and supplies that the Grass Lands could not supply.

It was a touch of brilliance to take both armies over the mountains on the same path as the donkeys had used. The very Legions that were supposed to protect the City were left on the Grass Lands with the mountains hindering them. When the Legions realised from their position the route back to the City would take them months, years! They did not have supplies fitting an army nor could the land supply food for such a large amount of men and horses!

Basch had said when they were in Base Camp that the Legions would not follow the mountain route as their resources would not enable them to make such a journey!

Base Camp that was where ReeArk remember seeing that strange crow he was perched on one of the brightly coloured tent polls. And now he came to think of it that was where he had seen ReeMara! She was in the street between the tents, and she was riding that dark stallion. She was dressed as a youth? But he had looked into her eyes, they were her eyes!

"You are not listening to me my lad!" It was the second time ReeArk had seen Basch angry that day, this time it was his fault! "You only have horses in your head!" ReeArk stepped back with an apology he did not want to have to explain which thoughts had been filling his mind when he should have been listening to Basch.

CC'raw did not real know how he was going to report what he had seen! A crow had his responsibilities when it came to thinking about the next generation, every crow and hen took hatching seriously. He was going to find embarrassing to report what he had seen to his young humans.

Two young human males in the same nest were going to make matters more difficult than they all ready were. ReeMara did not say anything and Harron look stunned, Armnell just nodded. CC'raw parched himself so he would be able to answer any questions, but no one spoke.

What ReeMara thought about CC'raw's report she did not say, her face paled when Harron mentioned anything about ReeArk. Harron had found in scrolls referring to older Legions' practices, a paragraph where it said that such relationships between warriors were encouraged. It was Armnell that had to explain such maters to him.

'Warriors with male partners were thought to fight more fearlessly when they thought their partners were in danger.'

ReeMara might have found such information helpful but as she would not talk to Harron about ReeArk's relationships or even about him, Harron could not tell her.

The day was clouded when races were going to be run in the coliseum; the sun was not going to shine on this day. Every one seemed depressed even when horses and grooms were busily preparing for the first race.

Harron had had to listen to ReeMara grumble that she could not ride Soul when he raced. The Iron Man had informed her she would not be allowed to take part; they did not know ReeArk was not allowed to ride Red Sun, jockeys had been found. ReeMara complained the jockey for Soul was heaver than she was, she thought that was unfair. Soul did not seem to mind, he was looking forward to racing Red Sun. Just because he was the chosen horse of the Emperor, weather he was the brother of his ReeMara or not, did not give the young colt the right to stick his nose in the air.

Harron was not going to sniff around the halls behind the Senate today. It was race day, Harron had wanted to find out more about the iron fist, he was puzzled; many of the scrolls he had seen had disappeared from the halls behind the Senate.

But the races were bringing folk together from all over the City, and guest had been invited to enjoy the event.

ReeMara had been told she was to attend, that meant she would have to sit next to ReeArk when the races were run, that did not pleases her at all!

Harron had been jealous of ReeArk, when ReeMara had looked forward to seeing him, but now he felt for ReeMara as she waited for the guards to escort her to the coliseum for the races. It had to be said, having the Empress fussing over her horse got in the way of the easy working of the stable.

Corn and Bramble were enjoying grumbling with ReeMara they could not go with Soul the grooms were only taking the flashy horses from their stables. Bramble wanted to say to a passing groom that he had a mean speed of hoof, but all he got was a friendly pat on the nose! Bramble got an armful of hay offered to him but the best oats had been given to the flashy horses. Soul had said they had tasted really good. 'Fast horses needed fast food!' was all, the apology he had given when he had eaten them all.

When the guards had arrived with the pair of cream horses in front of the cream chariot most folk were glad to see her step into it, her fussing about Soul had upset the grooms and her grumbling had upset Harron, and now Corn and Bramble were grumbling that they could not go to the races!

Armnell was grumbling as the robe ReeMara had on showed signs that ReeMara had been in the stable with Soul.

Harron and Armnell had to follow on foot behind ReeMara and her driver. Armnell was grumbling at the steepness of the road to the Coliseum. Harron wanted to grumble under his breath but he needed all his breath just to keep up as other people were filling the streets. They were excited there had not been races at the Coliseum for such a long time.

The day the Iron Man had presented the new Emperor and Empress to them, they had not forgotten, but today to go to the races with warriors from the Iron Man's armies offered them the chance to show off their new partners. Harron wanted to know if the Iron Man had planned everything, did Iron Man wanted to see his men were happy in their new city?

If the Iron Man planned to expand trading, men and women would be needed to handle goods, unload ships. Handle food and wine. Harron's mind spun with the planning needed to run the City, and now his head spun as the people around him pushed forward to find their places in the galleries around the Coliseum. He could not see Armnell she must find her way to ReeMara, she had to see ReeMara looked pretty.

The sun was still sulking behind gloomy clouds but the people were enjoying the atmosphere, clowns were fooling about as the first race was setup. Harron found the first race boring he had seen from the first moment the race started who was going to win. The horse did not need to be so proud of him self, the others were not in his class. To say the day was becoming boring was true for Harron; now, he would have preferred to have searched among the scrolls than sit here among folk that were loudly making wagers, betting on their favoured horses. Harron almost wished he could sit with ReeMara as the children near him were jumping about and adding to the noise!

ReeMara did not look any happier than Harron felt; she was sitting next to ReeArk. Harron had watched them, before she had tried to catch her brother's eye, but now she did not look at him, she patted Trigary, fed him titbits while the horses were being placed in line for the start of a race.

There was that strange quietness as the horses stood in line waiting for the man with the flag to start the race. Harron felt the tension rise as the flag did. Soul and the new horse Red Sun were among the horses in this race. Their heads went down as soon as the flag started the race, hooves pounded the ground, the dust rose to meet the race goers shouts, the heads that were in the lead were those of Soul and Red Sun, their jockeys did not look as if their instructions were being followed by the two head strong horses as they kept pace with each other. Other horses in the race could only follow them they did not let any horse pass them.

The finish line was getting closer to the horses leading the race. ReeMara and ReeArk were standing to see who would cross the line first, form where Harron was it looked as if they were head to head. Soul could not let the red horse win! Harron put his hands over his face ReeMara would be so grumpy if Soul lost to Red Sun, he could bury himself in the halls with the scrolls! No! They would be feasting tonight Soul had his head in front!

Harron wanted to wave to ReeMara, but than decided not to as ReeArk had sat down and was looking decidedly grumpy.

Soul look pleased with him self when he accepted the winner's wreath. Red Sun did not seem to want the runner's up prize; he looked as grumpy as ReeArk did!

Harron decided he would spend his time in the halls where the scrolls were kept; it would be quieter then here! Harron heard the crowd raw as the next race started.

Harron wandered back through quite streets feeling as glum the day lacked its bright sun light. He past folk's homes he would have stop to look at the trestles usually laden with goods for sale, but everyone was at the races!

Harron was feeling more himself by the time he entered the rooms where Piper sat waiting for ReeMara to return. Piper was surprised to see him:

"I did not expect to see you so soon!"

"I found the races tiresome, after Soul won his race I decided to come back. Would you like to come to the scroll halls with me? You could help me look through the shelves. There are shelves I cannot reach the back of! I think there are mice living there, not that I am an expert."

Piper did not need any excuses to go hunting among the shelves with Harron; she was bored with sitting on the bed waiting for ReeMara to come back. Pigeons did not come into the walled garden when she was there, not after she had tried to catch one! To hunt for mouse with Harron would be better than being bored sitting around here!

Harron's shoulder was a good place to sit on as they walked through the silent Senate, the marble seats did not offer mice a place to live. Piper had nosed her way through the great hall that the Iron Man used to inform his men. Not the Piper was interested in what the Iron

Man had to say, he had hurt ReeMara! That ReeMara did
what he said was a puzzle to her, brother or no brother.
Piper would have bitten his head off like a rat!

They entered the hall where most of the scrolls were
kept; it was gloomy as the normally bright sun light did
not light the hall. Harron took an oil lamp he was going
to light it but Piper wisped in his ear that there was
someone else in the dimly light hall. Why was the Abor
here? What did he want? Harron should not have been
surprised to see Alois, as Armnell called him, in the
scroll hall. He should have been at the races, standing
behind his pagan staff. Harron did not like his expression
of authority nor his pretending he was something Harron
knew he was not.

The Abor Alois was standing in the doorway at the far
end of the hall even though it was gloomy Harron could
see he had scrolls under his arm! Harron and Piper
ducked when the Abor turned. Piper whispered they
should follow him; the afternoon was not going to be as
boring as she had thought!

With or without the afternoon sun there were enough
shadows and doorways to slip in should the elderly man
turned to see if anyone was following him. He was to
busy picking his way through the stony street to waste
time looking behind him to bother. Harron and Piper only
had to keep a discreet distance behind him, when the old
man entered the entrance of the underground place where
Harron had started to explore the day he had found the
sign of the iron fist. Harron and Piper had to change the
way they had been following the false Abor. In the
underground tunnels it was dark with only the light the
Abor had to guide them. Piper decided to track the old
man on her own paws, she was used to hunting in the

dark unlike Harron who was constantly tripping over his own feet.

Piper was not upset to see the flat stones like in the cemetery where they had spent their first night in the City. There were signs scratched on them as Harron had said.

Piper stopped suddenly, Harron nearly stepped on her. The man was putting the scrolls he had under his arm behind a flat stone set in the tunnel wall, the lamp he had in his hand made him look a monster, he was not the only human rat in this city!

Waiting trying not to breath, hoping their hearts beating would not give them away, one steep more the Iron Man's Abor would have seen them if he had turned. Harron's heart was in his mouth, the next instance the Abor was gone! There were twists and turns in the tunnels that had cut the light off the Abor's lamp from Harron and Piper. Now they were standing there not knowing where to go! Harron's eyes were not as good as Piper's in the dark she had to support him in the sudden darkness. Piper was wandering how she was going to get Harron out of this crisscrossing maze, he was griping her by her tail with one hand and trying to feel his way forward with the other. If any one could see them in the dark, they would have laughed!

To let Harron hold onto her tail did prove the best way to lead him out of the dark tunnels, but it was not easy. Firstly he wanted go to where the old man had hidden the scrolls, with them under his arm he was not so easy to guide!

The tunnels crossed over each other so often, some brought them the promise of fresh air only to lead them into air that was stale, or fooled them into dead ends.

Piper was glad Harron did not panic when he fell over a stone that was not lying in its normal place in the wall. Harron was sitting on the ground hugging the scrolls the old man had hidden, he sounded tired, how long had they been groping around? There was no way Piper could tell as they sat there:

"Stay here while I have a look around. I want to know why this stone is across the tunnel; I will have a look around it, while you take a rest."

"I don't want to be left here alone! But I cannot on groping in the dark." Harron did not want to say he did not like being so close to the dead people of the City, it made him feel sick. It could have been the stale air that made him feel ill, not the stones that must have covered their corpse. Leaning against a stone that was not placed in the wall did not help him feel any better! His tired mind worried that the old bones would want to sit next to him, would they want to take the scrolls he had in his arms?

Piper left him asleep still hugging the scrolls! Piper wanted to sniff around without Harron hanging on to her tail! The stone Harron was sleeping against stuck out into the tunnel, Piper wanted to know why. All the others they had passed were set in the wall, it was to dark to see what sign was scratched into each one, but she could feel there was a sign as she had brushed past. p

Piper had expected to have to squeeze past the stone's darkest corner, but there was plenty of room even Harron could get between the wall and the stone slab. Piper had to rub her eyes as the room she found herself in had a low ceiling, slits aloud day light in.

Somehow the stone slab had been pushed through the wall it was supposed to be set in; it had slipped into the tunnel on the other side. Piper decided to explore the room before, she when back to Harron. There were stone slabs set in the wall as they were in the tunnels. The difference was the stones were not as old as the ones she had seen before. Piper though they had not long been placed there. The flowers had faded and dried but had not turned to dust! There was a small stone slab. Piper wondered if humans buried their pups in this place as well!

Steps cut in the wall rose to a door, Piper tried push it open but it did not open for her, she hoped it would when Harron tried it. To get Harron to wakeup was difficult he kept pushing her away saying he did not want the bones to touch him! What bones? She did not see any bones! She did not have a chance to ask as his hands were flapping at her as if she was a disgruntled fly. When Piper got on the stone slab from where she could pull his hair and blow into his ear, he did wake up. But he was acting as if he had drunk all the wine at the last fest! Piper had to bit and pinch him while she pushed him into the room she had found behind the stone.

Harron lay sprawled on his side Piper could only see he did not try to bury his face in the floor, though the air was much better than it had been in the tunnel the floor was dusty.

Harron did not want to move, may be it was better to let him go back to sleep, but they could not stay here forever!

When Harron woke all he could say was his head hurt and where were the scrolls? If Piper had not known humans for so long she would have said something about good manners. But it was not like Harron to be so grumpy, maybe the stale air in the tunnels had upset him.

Piper led the way to the door at the top of the steeps. Harron pulled the door open, more steeps led them into a much smaller room, more like a covered door way, its door when he pushed it open, opened into the very cemetery he had had to spend so much time in when he had first come to the City.

It was quite in the cemetery Harron could see the grass had grown long between the stones, now there weren't any horses to keep in short. Harron thought of Soul, he will be glowing in the light of his win, Harron though it might be a good idea to congratulate the horse; what he did not know was two days had past since he and Piper got lost in the catacombs under the old part of the City.

With the scroll still in his arms Harron was going to step into the long grass till Piper pointed out he could not walk about with them under his arm, not when humans were returning from the races! Harron had to find a place were he could hide the scrolls, after wasting more time in Piper's opinion, the place he chose was not any different than the Abor had chosen, only they weren't behind a flat stone in the catacombs, they were now behind the small slab in the wall of the room Piper had found behind the fallen stone in the dark tunnels.

Harron did not know what he wanted to do first eat or sleep! He drank in deeply the fresh air as he and Piper entered the squear in front of the Bath House. They had been expecting to see people retuning from the races, but it was as quite as the cemetery till CC'raw squawked at them as he swooped towards them:

"I have been looking all over the place for you two! Every one has been worrying about you."

Harron had never seen CC'raw so upset, even Trigary seemed in a fluster. Harron did not mind the silly great bird brush his face with his wing tip, but when it was suggested he and Piper should bath as they smelt like they had been buried in muck, both Piper and Harron said they would not till they had had something to eat and drink. They ignored the other people's holding their noses as they sat at the table in Armnell's kitchen. In fact they did not tell of their ordeal till the next day after a good night's sleep and a refreshing bath!

ReeMara also had something to tell the others sitting in the walled garden:

"When Soul got his head in front of ReeArk's horse I thought I was gripping the arm of the seat, it was not the seat's arm but ReeArk's arm he had to look at me! At the moment he turned to me the Abor waved his stick over us. I felt so embarrassed instead of praising Soul for his win, people were applauding us!

When we were going down to give the jockeys their prizes ReeArk said we have to talk. In the middle of the coliseum did not seem be the place for such a talk. Not when one of the Iron Man's guests asked if I would accept a thousand pieces of gold for Soul! I said ten times that would not be enough for him, as if Soul's head was not big enough all ready, he led his groom away the poor man's feet did not touch the ground.

We were escorted from the races to the feast the Iron Man had arranged for his traders invited to the coliseum. He was not in a good mood as his horse had lost his race and the Iron Man had the lost a wager he had made.

ReeArk and I were left to please ourselves when the traders started to enjoy the wine. Had it not been for one of the men that had been our escort we would have been able to slip away. It was annoying to see him appear from behind columns with wine for us or food we had to try. ReeArk tried to find a place where we could talk away from the attention of our escort.

We slipped into the kitchen thinking we could find a place where we would not be disturbed. Sides of meat were hanging from the ceiling, the hooks made the meat look grossest. It must be the best place to talk, it would have been had the dark haired man with a platter of meat and flask of wine appeared between the hanging carcasses!

I don't know who looked more ghostly the hanging flesh or the unwanted escort.

'Don, why are you making everything so hard?' ReeArk looked as if he was going to hit the man standing with the unwanted refreshments.

It was not an easy moment for me I did not want to say I knew that Don was ReeArk's 'friend' but how could I say how I knew?

ReeArk was standing between Don and me; I thought he was going to tell him, I am his sister. From the look on Don's face I knew why ReeArk wanted to tell him but my gut warned me, the Iron Man must not know!

I don't know what he would do if he knew we came from the Isles in the Mist. She-With-The-Sight had not stopped him destroying every village, killing our family, how many folk died from his men's swards I don't know. I do know She-With-The-Sight wanted to the Isles in the Mist to be hidden.

'I place a command on you; you are to see that the Isles stay hidden behind the mists. If you refuse my command your people well have died for nothing.' Was what She-With-The-Sight had said to the Iron Man! She had said the same to me!

Them I remember the Iron Man saying. She-With-The-Sight had taken revenge on her people; they did not put her in the tree because she was abhorrent to look at, they feared her foresight. The Isles in the Mists will be as she wished shrouded in mists forever.

The Iron Man wanted to stop the amber the sea through on to the beach coming onto the main land. Now I know why he did that."

"He is controlling the City on the Seven Hills! He is in control of any new buildings; whether they are for the religious faction or pagan use. The new trading halls also have to have amber in their foundations and…" Harron was interrupted by ReeMara. Armnell thought they were going to quarrel! What she wanted to know was what had happened between ReeArk and her brother and the young man's lover!

ReeMara looked sideways at Harron who was still thinking about how the Iron Man was ruling the city:

"I did not know how I was going to say to ReeArk that he should not tell Don about us. I was going to have to say something, but what!? Then I saw a mouse, I have never been so pleased to see a mouse! You have never heard me scream so loudly I made everyone jump in the kitchen. Cooks were running everywhere trying to catch that poor mouse! Don was distracted long enough for me to worn ReeArk, not to say we are siblings or from where we come. He did not look surprised when I said that, we still had the problem as to what to say to Don! You do not always have a mouse to save the moment, but when you have two mice and cooks chasing them with their meat cleavers, you know it is time to leave the meat store!

That is why there is blood on my robe, and why we looked flushed when we came back into the hall. As to why the Iron Man was slapping ReeArk heartily on his back and kept winking at me, I don't know.

The one good thing to come out of this evening is ReeArk was told he must visit me in my rooms. He had to agree we need the chance to decide what we should do! He said, he will come tomorrow."

Baschi did not come alone among his escorts, was Don! Armnell did not know how to tell ReeMara that her brother's lover was here as will!

Armnell shooed Don and the rest of the escort out of her small kitchen and she even managed to show them to the door, they were slow to realise they were not wanted in ReeMara's rooms.

Now that ReeMara stood next to ReeArk it was plain to see they were siblings, their blue eyes and flaxen hair! To show them as Emperor and Empress was understandable. But the Iron Man was playing another game!

ReeMara had said She-With-The-Sight was involved in whatever the Iron Man's plan was. To control or even stop the amber coming from the north spoke of a far greater plan than they could try to guess at around the table.

Everyone had sat in Armnell's small kitchen trying to decide what they should do. ReeMara could not have a child with ReeArk, he was her brother. Armnell quest that 'Baschi, ReeArk' did not go to bed with women. She agreed that Don could not be told about his lover's sister.

Should the Iron Man hear their true story it could turn into a melodrama like they used to perform on the stage of the great theatres, before the city's folk left.

Harron had sat there looking down cast, the ferret had tried help. The crow said he wished his father was here, he would know what to do, though his mother Cam was the one to ask about hatching. The eagle had made it clear on one was to touch his ReeMara! Thank goodness the horses were in their stables, to gallop away was not the answer either!

'I place a command on you; you are to see that the Isles stay hidden behind the mists. If you refuse my command your people well have died for nothing." Was what She-With-The-Sight had said back in the twisted tree; if ReeMara had known what the blind woman wanted of her she might have let the Iron Man burn her with the hag in old tree! The joy of finding her brother was still alive was now paled by the command to have a child with ReeArk.

"We agree that the Iron Man is not to know you both come from the Isle in the Mist." Harron looked at everyone around the table. "We all agree that a child from a brother and sister cannot be aloud." Harron again looked around table.

"The Iron Man wants a child, a child to bind his city, to show that this city is the place to raze your families and improve your trading possibilities." ReeArk sounded so like the Iron Man, ReeMara could only laugh!

"Leave that problem to me." said Harron not knowing what he was going to do about such a problem. "ReeArk you should come and see ReeMara regularly, babies are not made at horse races. We want the Iron Man to think something is happening.
And Armnell's cooking is fit for any emperor!

"Will Don become more jealous if he has to escort you here?" ReeMara was worried.

"You will have to tell him, you have to do your duty." CC'raw remarked.

"We can ask him to eat with us!" ReeMara sounded pleased with the idea. ReeArk did not want to deceive Don but as CC'raw pointed out this was more important than a small deception. The Iron Man would know Don was friendly with ReeArk; they both had to think the Iron Man's command was being taken seriously.

Harron had explained he had seen the Abor, 'the old fool.' take scrolls from the halls behind the senate. He had followed the Abor into catacombs and then got lost among the dark passages. He had turned up days later, too tired to explain where he had been. But he had said he had the scrolls the old fool had hidden. They need to know what was so interesting in those scrolls.

When Armnell questioned Harron; he had thought she wanted to know what he was going to about the Iron Man's command. But Armnell wanted to know what was so important about the scrolls Alois had taken from the hall.

Harron realised he would have to get them from where he had hid them. The problem was the elderly man often came to see Armnell. Harron knew he needed Armnell to help him understand whatever the scrolls had to tell him.

CC'raw escorted Harron to the cemetery by air and Piper was on ground control, they took side streets to an entrance way from the squear and its bathhouse. They did not want to be followed. Harron carried a bread basket to bring the scrolls back to their rooms. They did not see anyone on their way to the scrolls hiding place, there were people in the squear as they strode back with the laden bread basket.

Piper had had the good idea of putting bread among the scrolls! The only problem was they were asked if they were going to eat all they were carrying! Harron had to keep his hand over the cloth he had covered the scrolls and bread. He was worried someone would want to take out a loaf, only to find an old scroll.

The table Armnell had cleared of all her cooking pots, it was scrubbed clean, waiting for the contents of Harron's bread basket.

The four scrolls could be unrolled side by side Harron and Armnell could examine them easily. The scrolls did not want to tell them their secrets.

The first scroll had the iron fist sign inked on the papyrus under the sign there was an eye, its shape showed any one studding the scroll it was an eye with sun rays.

The next scroll had the same iron fist under it drawn in a drop of blood was horse's head.

The third also had the sign of the iron fist, but under the sign was a tree with a wide shady crown.

The last had the same iron fist but there was no another sign, it was unlike the others in another way, names had been scratched out!

Armnell could tell they were looking at the family of the Iron Fist. The scrolls told them there were three, four families under the sign. But the fourth did not say why many names had been scratched out nor did it say why it did not have another sign like the first three?

Armnell could tall Harron that the male side of a family took their father's name. Like Basch had given ReeArk the name of Baschi. The sons of the older families were expected to take the rank of their fathers, most families wanted many sons, should, the chosen son not be able to fulfil his father's wishes. Jealous sons had been known to kill their older brothers to have the position in the city their father had held.

ReeMara would have been interested to hear Armnell say the daughters were used to unite families and busyness deals.

Harron had wanted to look at the scrolls with Armnell before he showed them to ReeMara he wanted to have something to impress her with. But he did not know what he was looking at!

The sign was the same as the one the Iron Man had ridden under on the battle field below the cliffs. Why did the Abor wanted to have them? What was the Abor looking for in these scrolls?

Armnell said Harron was coming up with more questions than he had answers for, they had better drink tea; it would help them think better.

The tea was steaming in bowls when ReeMara came into the small kitchen. Harron and Armnell were bent over the table where the scrolls were spread out they did not notice her watching them. Piper got on the table with CC'raw to see if they could puzzle out what was written on the three scrolls.

"The first three scrolls show there are three main families belong to the Iron Fist. The three signs under the fist must mean defiant lines within the family."

Armnell pointed to a mark by names that she said meant female. The other mark they could see must mean male. The other mark by the male or female sign must mean the person was born in the family or was married into it even though the female names did not match all the male names:

"Here shows when women were brought for marriage from other families."

"This sign must mean child died at birth, or an early death. The other sign must mean when an adult had died. Could that be the Iron Man's birth marked here at the end of this scroll?"

Harron pointed at the second scroll with the horse's head in a blood drop. Harron took the scroll in his hand he wished to see how other males with the sign that marked their death had died. What he hoped to learn he did not know, but there weren't any other male entries after the Iron Man's name.

Harron put down the scroll he had in his hand to look at the others. What he did see was the entries had ended, no new entries were marked. There was the Iron Mann's father with a death mark; the Iron Man was son of Basch.

Harron was trying to guess when the last entries had been made, were there any after the Iron Man birth mark, it was hard to tell, if he matched the three scrolls together he could see the scroll of the Iron Man's family was longer than the others.

Harron jumped when he looked up to see ReeMara standing opposite him on the other side of the table. Her face was pale she looked as if she had seen a ghost! ReeMara turned way so sharply that everyone was startled.

Piper found ReeMara in the walled garden. Piper had been with ReeMara for so long, the little red ferret knew not to pry into ReeMara's thoughts.

The sun was sinking below the city walls depriving the little garden of light, when ReeMara returned to the table Harron was still stooped over it. Armnell was not concentrating on the scrolls as Harron was, she was making something to eat, which was not easy without being able to use the table. The crow and an eagle were taking up more space as they watched Harron as he was trying to persuade the scrolls to tell him more than he already knew!

When ReeMara's shadow fell across the scroll Harron was studding, he was not amused as the oil lamps could not take the place of daylight.

ReeMara opened the little leather bag she always had with her, she let the three stones roll into her hand. She placed the eye onto the first scroll; it matched the drawing under the iron fist. She matched the blood stone with its horses head to the second scroll. The green stone that was like the sun and shadows among the leaves in the branches of a tree, ReeMara set below the tree drawn on the third.

Harron had seen them before of cause he had; he had even played with them when ReeMara and he had been kids. The three amber stones matched the signs on three of the scroll! They had just been stones he and ReeMara had played with!

They were the stones She-With-The-Sight had told ReeMara to place under the temple in the City of the Seven Hill. She-With-The-Sight had told ReeMara she must not let the death of her family be for nothing, was why they had come to the City on the Seven Hills.

She-With-The-Sight knew the Iron Man! Harron was trying to piece together all that had happened. She-With-The-Sight was The Sage's twin sister. He remembered the day when he and ReeMara were trying to persuade The Sage to let them leave the Cliff Citadel and bring the stones here. The Sage must have known it was important to let them go, did she know what her sister has planned?

"If she had known she would have told us." About that ReeMara was sure.

"If She-With-The-Sight knew the Iron Man, does that mean The Sage knows him also?" Armnell wanted to know, Harron and ReeMara could only shrug. If The Sage knew the Iron Man she had not said anything about him, with them.

They were sitting around Armnell's table because the Abor Alois had taken and tried to hide the scrolls, now in front of them, Harron point out. They should be asking why the Abor should want to take them! Why did he want to know about the Iron Man's family?

They had planned to listen to what others were saying in the City. Armnell was hoping to gain information from those in the markets she went to for their food. Harron was to nose around the libraries to see what he could find. ReeMara was to see what she could find out in the stables where Soul was with Bramble and Corn. Ferret and crow were also tasked to see what they could find out.

No one expected the gossip to be centred on the rumours that soldiers from the Legions of the ousted ruling senate had been sent to the sea ports, to protect them from forces attacking them. Harron guest that the forces were allies of the Iron Man! Legionnaires were now to be seen in the City and there were problems arising when the returning soldier found his house was occupied by another family, or his place in his household had been taken by a warrior from the armies of the Iron Man.

ReeMara had expected to have to attend events organised by the Iron Man, but with the returning soldiers from the defeated Legions his time was taken up organising tribunals. That the judges favoured the soldiers of occupation did not help the mood of the folk in the City!

Armnell could not find anyone willing to talk about the origins of the City leader, they were to busy discussing other folk's busyness, some of the issues were not verbally discussed; fists or swards were used to decide such matters.

Armnell decided to gain the information from the Abor, himself. After all it was he, Harron had seen hide the interesting scrolls. The question was how to get the Abor Alois to tell her what she wanted to know without letting him know she knew where the scrolls he had hidden were! He must have seen they were no longer in his hiding place.

Trying to explain why she was interested could make him spurious.

"You have improved your position in the City. It was not so long ago we were sitting alone in the Bath House." Armnell hands were working the pain out of the self appointed Abor old mussels. Though the Bath House had returned to public use Armnell was massaging the Abor in the comfort of the little walled garden. It was easer to enjoy a goblet of wine in the shade of the olive trees. Armnell was hoping the wine would make him more talkative.

"You too have taken advantage of the situation you found your self in." Alois said as he groaned with relief Armnell's fingers gave. "I am glad circumstance did not take you away from the city. Where would I find someone with your hands?"

Armnell could only smile:

"Where was I to go? I have been here all my life. When I was taken from my mother to work in the rich family's house, I was too young to remember my origins,"

"Now you are Matron to the new Empress!"

"I took advantage of the situation I found myself in."

"As I did, the family I worked for most of my young life did not give me the chance to prove my self."

Armnell wondered what Alois meant by that remark, she did not want to interrupt him.

"I was employed to help build the catacombs under the city. Of cause most of the catacombs are older that anyone can remember, but as families grow so do their dead; places has to be made. I know every twist and turn in the older and newer catacombs."

He did not say anything for sometime, Alois eyes were closed:

"I had wished to be involved in building impressive houses not crypts for the dead."

Armnell was surprised when Alois said he had seen the Iron Man's family sign in the catacombs.

"I have found the old crypt that I was ordered to build an extension for his family, many years ago."

Armnell did not know how to lead him to say what else he knew about the Iron Man's family, her fingers could only try to ease information from him.

Alois had been interested in the scrolls because he had recognised the Iron Man; Alois remembered the Iron Man had been a child in the city.

That Alois thinks he can better his position in the new city order, by using the information he say's he has found. Now he had told Armnell it was now obvious, others might be interested that Basch had come from the City, not conquered it, as he would like others to think.

This old man, Alois, was only interested in improving his status! But that did not stop him from being dangers, his bones were old but his wits were sharp.

The Iron Man's allies are the army from the Spice Regions. They backed the Iron Man's campaign in the north. The way to the sea was cut of to the old Emperor by other allies coming from across the water. Their men had come inland and put presser on the Legions sent to keep the sea ways free. Their people were taking advantage of the land freed from the control of the old Emperor. The old Emperor's legions did not have enough men to make a counter campaign, they complained the men they needed had been sent on a fools chase in the north. It was not their leaders that were to blame for leaving the City unprotected.

Harron had to admire the Iron Man for the way he dealt with complaints. He offered the complaints, writes to develop trade or start busyness, offers of work halls or storage lagers at reasonable prises and tax reductions in the same way he had offered his allies.

Harron had wondered how he was going to deal with the order the Iron Man had given to both ReeMara and ReeArk, a child from brother and sister was out of the question. Harron knew the Iron Man should not know from where ReeMara came nor she was his Baschi's sister! There was a bird that was known to lay its eggs in other bird's nests! In the back of Harron's mind the bird gave him an idea, but as to how he was going develop the idea, he did not know!

ReeArk's friend Don was insisting he should take tea when he escorted ReeArk on his visits to ReeMara.

Harron could see the crow was not happy when Don made his visits. When he decided to ask him why he was uncomfortable, CC'raw told him, he had seen Don in the company of the Abor! CC'raw had been perched on the roof because he wanted to contact one of his contacts among the pigeons living in that part of the City. CC'raw had seen them together in one of those human houses that wine was drunk.

CC'raw reported that their heads had been close together, they had been talking intently. As CC'raw pointed out he did not have any good reason to follow either one but it did not feel right to him, he did not trust the Abor talking to ReeArk's lover.

Harron did not know which problem he should deal with first!

Now ReeArk made regular visits to ReeMara, with or
without Don, ReeArk's friend. The Iron Man would
sooner or later want a child from ReeMara and ReeArk!
Don was now known to be talking to the Abor. The Abor
had told Armnell he had worked as a young man for the
Iron Man's family in the catacombs. The Abor knew the
catacombs better than his own hands as he had said.
'Harron had found a scroll with some of the tunnels
marked on it, he had been interested in finding away out
of the City till ReeMara had said she did not want to go
without her brother, besides the horses could not use the
tunnels.

The Abor had tried to hide the scrolls about the Iron
Man's family. The Abor knew about the Iron Man's
family, that he intended to use his knowledge to keep his
place at the head of the pagan religions Harron could
understand; Harron now had them hidden safely in
Armnell's kitchen.

Harron and ReeMara knew the signs drawn on the
scrolls matched the amber stones She-With-The-Sight
had given to ReeMara, neither of them knew why she had
done that, but ReeMara was to place them under the
temple at the hart of the City. They had not done that yet,
so much had happened since they had come to the City
on the Seven Hills.

Harron's head was in his hands as he was trying to
think. He had watched the battles below the Cliff Citadel
enjoyed the puzzles of attack and counter attack, re-
enacted them on Mattie's kitchen table with ReeMara,
Piper and CC'raw.

She-With-The-Sight was the twin sister to The Sage.
Harron remembered. She-With-The-Sight lived or had
lived in an old twisted tree whereas The Sage lived in the
Cliff Citadel; she had been ReeMara's and his beloved

teacher. Both were leaders or rulers, one for the Islands in the Mist and the other headed the school in the Cliff Citadel.

The Iron Man had made a deal with She-With-The-Sight; that Harron knew; did the Iron Man know The Sage? Harron could not get the thought out of his mind.

He had watched the battles below the cliffs. They had never felt threatened by the warriors below. Why? It was not a secret they were there, folk brought their children to the Cliff Citadel.

Harron decided to devote his time to the scrolls in the halls behind the Senate; maybe he could find answers there. Days had passed and no one had found anything to help Harron, he was sinking in a cloud or depression.

Harron like CC'raw had seen the Abor and ReeArk's lover together, in the scroll halls. What were they looking for, was it the same as he was looking for? That was the point he had no idea what he was looking for!

Piper was with Harron when he decided to look again among the dusty scrolls. Harron had been through them so many times, it did not mater if you blow away the dust it just settled back down again. Harron did not have to tell Piper that the Abor and Don were also shifting through the halls their smell as strong enough to betray them let alone their foot prints!

'There is not future with out a passed.' Harron was in the habit of saying.

"Maybe the passed we are looking for is not in these halls, maybe we should look in other places!" Piper announced so suddenly even the dusty scrolls shook with surprise. Harron took the ferret up in his arms and was striding off to the stables as fast as he could. When Piper had suggested they should look somewhere else, the real reason was she did not enjoy a mouse hunt among the dust of the scroll!

Bramble and Corn were pleased to see them; they could use a stroll around town. Soul was out seeing to his' mares! Bramble and Corn were glad they were not as popular as Soul was; it all seemed to be a fuss over nothing.

"Where do you want to go?" Corn asked as Harron slipped onto his back.

"Around about the City, please." Piper said from the folds of Harron's robe.

"Corn, if they want to go around town they have something on their minds."

"Bramble, if they have something on their minds they could shear it with us, maybe we could help!"

"Corn, we are not horses just for fest days and holy days we are horses for adventure!"

"Bramble, that we are!"

"Corn, are we or are we not the horses that have crossed mountains, galloped over planes."

"If you lot could hold your muzzles closed long enough we could tell you what is on our minds." remarked Piper under her breath, she knew the two horse were only having fun, but when they got started you just had to let them whinny their way through their jokes or they would be offended.

Harron needed to lighten his mood so maybe a horsy joke would do him good.

"Harron tell old Bramble what is on your mind?"

"You can tell old Corn as well. Who says we are old?"

"Would you like a spring foal to tell you what to do?"

"They don't have the feel of the turf under their hooves."

"We came all that way with those two?" Piper asked Harron it was not going to be easy to lighten his mood, Piper was slipping into the same depression as Harron.

Two joking horses and one depressed human and a ferret with the taste of scroll dust still in her mouth left the order of the stables and entered the hubbub of the City's streets.

It was not unusual to have a bird on your arm but a ferret was not something folk around here were used to so Piper stayed in Harron's robe, when CC'raw joined them, Piper said from within Harron's robe:

"Now we are out of the stables and away from all those long ears you could tell us what our mission is!"

"It was something you said your self, you and I have been looking among scroll in the Senate's halls, where the scrolls tell us of births, deaths and marriages, alliances between families. What those records do not tell us is what happened in those peoples lives." Piper thought Harron was going to say again, 'There is not future with out a past.' But he did not.

"We are looking for other libraries, where scrolls are kept." That was where Harron's enthusiasm faded.

"That is why you need two old hoofers to help!"

"Why do you keep calling us old?"

"No foal has enough gray matter between his ears as we do."

"May the havens help us; the two of them are off again!" Piper would have liked to bite both of them between the ears.

"There is not future without a past." Piper though she might just bite Harron instead.

"We are looking for other places where scrolls could be kept, scrolls that can tell me what those people did when they where alive, not that they were born or died."

"Schools!"

"Houses of the religious!"

"You mean where they put on shows!" Corn remembered how interested Harron was when the men with crosses and oxen had pasted them. He had noticed men filing in and out of large buildings with the same sign on their robes.

Harron was thinking the Abor would not be going into such places, but there were place where the pagan followers went.

"What about the place where the Iron Man talks to humans that have disagreements?" CC'raw suggested. He would have said, 'they must keep records of decisions made, or humans would forget which nests were occupied.' Or something, like that! But Harron was hugging him, knocking the breath out of him:

"Clever old bird!"

"Now he is calling CC'raw old!" said Corn.

"Could an egg come up with an idea like that?" asked Bramble. Even Piper could see the funny side of that remark!

They spent the day sightseeing with the two horses, Harron and CC'raw took in all the buildings that could have a library. The place where the Iron Man was, was too well guarded for them just to walk in, another plan would have to be made to get into its dusty scrolls halls.

One building caught Harron's eye, it was not the tall columns but the courtyard and with children walking in lines behind grownups. It was not so long ago when Harron had also been pulling funny faces behind a teacher.

If you want to know something then ask at teacher, Harron remembered being told, so he slipped from

Corn's back and walked towards one of the grownups
that did not have a line of children.

Harron ask the man where he could find the library, a
large friendly hand pointed to a doorway on the other
side of the courtyard. He might have known when the
grass was soft under his feet. He was not supposed to
walk straight across!
The friendly hand waved to Harron as he reached the
door.

Harron and Piper had expected gloom and dusting
scrolls, not the organised shelving and an airy hall.

A small woman appeared from behind a table that did
not have any scrolls piled on it. In her hands she fingered
a string of amber and she was muttering under her breath.
The string of amber looked as if it had been in use for
many years. The small woman's voice cut into the air
making Harron jump.

"How can I help you? I have a class to teach."
Harron explained he wanted to find out about what had
happened in the City on the Seven Hills before the old
emperor had left.

"You don't want the library you want the archives,
young man. They are across the courtyard."

Harron and Piper were careful to walk around the kept
grass and warned Bramble and Corn not to set a hoof on
it.

Harron and Piper opened a smaller door, its creak was
not welcoming but the tall thin man that greeted them
was. Looking at all the dusty scrolls Harron was sure he
was in the right place but he did not know how to ask let
alone what to ask!

"We have scrolls here naming all the teachers that have
taught here and the names of those that taught them, of

cause. They are named in scrolls under the emperor or empress that were ruling at the time they were here."

As Harron did not know which emperors or empress had been ruling let alone when, he was not sure how it was going to help him.

"Here, we have lists of those that were instructed under the last ruling emperor. Most of our students become teachers, I am proud to say, or are placed in Legions in administration with ranks of importance."

Harron did not have to comment as the tall talkative man continued:

"We lost a lot of teachers and students when the old emperor decided to leave. The older families knew the value of a good education. The new Empress has not even been to see us! Mind you the Dux took most of the good young men for his legion before they were ready."

Harron still did not know how, what to ask! But that did not stop the tall thin man explaining how his scrolls were stored.

"Over here we have scroll listing subjects offered, which subjects were taken up and which subjects were not of use to the emperor of the time."

Harron's depression was returning to bother him and Piper did not feel any better. How were they supposed to know all the emperors or empresses that had ruled in the city?

Had the tall man made a remark about the Dux? Wasn't he in charge of the legions? Didn't he control the emperor's war machine? Didn't the Iron Man control ReeMara's brother!

"Baschiii…" said Harron and Piper together.

"Are yes, the new young Emperor did not study at this center of excellence but his promoter did." Long arms reached to grab scrolls to show Harron. Long arms swiped scrolls from his table to make room for the ones he wanted to show to Harron and his companion peering out form the youth's robe.

There was the Iron Man's name under the iron fist and his name had the sign that said he was male. That gave Piper an idea:

"There is a sign to say the student is male, do females also study here?"

"We do not insist that only males can study as do to the religious houses. We supply teachers to all institutes requiring them!" long arms pushed aside the first scrolls he had brought to show them, to confirm the Iron Man had attended this center.

"Here we have scrolls showing where our trained students were sent."

There must be other cities like this one but what they could be called was like asking for all the names of the City on the Seven Hill's emperors! Depression was setting in again; the names did not mean anything to Harron or Piper. Till a scroll unrolled out before them with the name of the Cliff Citadel on it! It was old but not as old as some Harron had seen.

"All right, all right, can we come again when we have more questions? We do not wish to take up anymore of your time!" Harron was trying not to show he was excited. The tall man was trying not to look disappointed they wanted to leave so soon!

"What was the name of the teacher that was sent there?" Piper wanted to know she was on the table as the tall man unrolled yet another scroll like a wave towards her. She was nearly washed of the table by its force, had Harron not been able to catch her!

"Name… the family name was Medwin!?" Harron said as he strode out of the archive with Piper and promises to return and visit the tall man in his archives.

"What did I see? What did we see when we came out of the archives?" Harron was telling ReeMara and Armnell of their day searching through dusty scrolls. "We saw two horses with flowers in their mouths, not able to find a way to hide their guilt. They had eaten all the flowers from around the courtyard! True they had not set their hooves on the grass.

ReeMara and Armnell were sitting next to each other on one side of the kitchen table. Tea was steaming in its pot; Piper and CC'raw were to be seen through the steam sitting on the other. Trigary was on guard on the wall in the garden, this was a decision that was only for those around the kitchen table.

"I found out that the Iron Man studded at the Centre, I and Piper visited two days ago. In the same visit we saw that the Cliff Citadel had teachers sent to them from here." Harron did not pose to see ReeMara nod. "Fact is the Iron Man must know of the Cliff Citadel and what it stands for. But I could not find any evidence to say the Iron Man knew The Sage.

The fact is the Centre send teachers to other leaning centres and the Cliff Citadel is listed on the scroll Piper and I saw in the Centre's archive.

This information could explain why the Cliff Citadel was not threatened. We never thought to ask why we were not disturbed as we look down on the battles below."

Harron eyes were closed as he looked down onto the grasslands he and ReeMara had left, now so far behind them.

"We were given the name of the teacher that was sent to the Cliff Citadel, Medwin. I have spent the last few days in the hall behind the Senate. This tea will help to wash way the dust! I know now that women name their female children after their own female line, were as sons take the name of their fathers, when a man excepts an unrelated child as his, his name is used. As an example Basch has given ReeArk the name of Baschi.

I had to go back to emperors that most have long forgotten with more dust on them than flowers can grew in grass! To find that Medwin and Basch families have the same foremother, I suppose not a great surprise when folk come from the same city."

ReeMara felt she should say something as Harron had not said anything for a long moment. She was almost startled when Harron unrolled a scroll that all most free of dust but its signs and writing was so faded it was not easy to see it images.

"This sign is used when twines are born; it is a two sided sign it is more often to see that you would think. But mostly to be found when it has been halved when one of the siblings had died. The small lady in the Centre's library told me one of the siblings was likely to die due to the problems mothers had feeding two babies."

No one had interrupted him, it was a great help to Harron as he still could not say what his searching had brought them.

"The sign for a dead twin from this family dose not appear in the scrolls in the Senate. This sign for twins I found at the Centre. This is an application for female sibling students. The tall man told me it was common to apply as soon as a child is born." Harron looked worried he ran his fingers through his hair. "The name of the twin's female line was Medwin!"

"You mean the same name as the teacher that was sent to the Cliff Citadel!?" ReeMara was stunned Harron could only shrug:

The Sage is the twin sister of She-With-The-Sight!?" Harron could only shrug again.

The tea had cooled the aromatic steam had stopped wafting in the air over the kitchen table.

"The leader of the Legions sent to battle must also have known there was a dwelling in the cliffs, they too could have taken advantage of their higher position." CC'raw halted the descending silence.

"I have found out so much but I still do not know what it all means!" Harron did feel better when Armnell put a fresh bowl of tea into his hands. "I still do not understand under which emperor empress I should look under next, what they were at the center at the same time I think as unlikely, The Sage and She-With-The-Sight are a lot older than the Iron Man. They could have taught him but their names do not appear under the same emperors."

They were spending so much time trying find out what could have happened, only to find there were more questions than answers.

Harron had questions of his own, ReeMara knew Harron had noticed, the men in the Tented Army had skin and hair like his, even their noses had the same hook on it. No one could remember who had brought Harron to the Cliff Citadel.

Harron still had the nose, and he still stuttered a little; as no one knew from where he came, he was often teased; children could be hard their teasing had not stopped Harron and ReeMara from be coming friends.

How could she have thought to leave the Citadel without him! ReeMara had confessed to Armnell.

"If he had not been so curious he never would have been motivated to find the answers we need now." Armnell poured more tea into ReeMara's bowl. "I used to look into people's faces to see if I could find out, to which people I belong. There are many people with the same look a Harron. But I don't think the archives in this city will be able to explain his roots.

The records in the halls the Iron Man uses to sort out complaints show when I was brought and sold, but not from were my people came from. Most of the deals and agreements are recorded there." Harron's eyes rolled at the very thought of searching through more scrolls and their accompanying dust!

Armnell and ReeMara turned to look at Harron, it was decided to take him to the bath house if he could not get the dust out of his mind then they could take the dust off his body!

Every one filed out of Armnell's kitchen passed the board guards at to door that lead into the squear and round the corner to the grand building that was the Bath House.

Armnell saw instantly that the bath house was under other management, she would never have let so many soiled towels lye about the floor. But the water was hot enough and the soap and oils smelt fresh.

"I have found out…" said a voice they knew, it was Don's: "ReeArk is riding out with that new horse of his; he still has an eye for that black stallion. With two new stallions in the Emperor's stables to choose from, I would like to see next season's foals."

The man who's back was towards them as that of the Abor's!

"I bet they were not talking about horses, what would the Abor find interesting about horse? His bones would not let him stride a horse!" Piper said as she pushed herself out of Harron's robe. If Armnell was still the mistress of the bath house she would have seen Piper to the door and CC'raw would not have been aloud to perch on the column.

"Shame we did not come a moment sooner we may have heard what they were really talking about." remarked Harron as he stepped into a bath with hot water and bubbles.

Harron remembered ReeMara like bubbles! The first thing she had done was to bathe when she had got to the Cliff Citadel and the first thing she had done was to bathe when they had got to the City on the Seven Hills. And that was why they were here now, with so many questions to answer!

Harron stirred the bubbles in his bath into a pile; then he scooped them up and blew them into the air! The air was full of bubbles, not all of them were his! The whole bath house was full of bubbles! ReeMara was laughing as he was. Harron saw the Abor slip away between the columns. There was another question what were the two of them talking about?

ReeMara was right, bubbles were a good way to clean your body and clear your mind; the Bath House was ring with their laughter.

The building rang with the sound of human voices; a crow had to admit the sound they were making, sounded as if it came from the highest thermals.

CC'raw was in one of the buildings the men with the crosses used. It had high columns and grand arches with domes that towered above the ground. The ground humans had covered with stone so smooth it was like water that mirrored all it saw. He did not like the pictures hanging on the walls. They showed humans suffering horribly and there were crosses with men of stone tied to them.

CC'raw would not usually choose to come to a place like this but he had seen the Abor enter the building! CC'raw had to ask, 'Why would a pagan leader want to go into a building the men with crosses on their robes worshiped in?'

The Abor was known to be continuingly in argument with the leader of the men with the crosses on their robes. Should the Iron Man assign more amber to the religious followers that the pagan, arguments would brake out at feasts, so ReeMara had reported!

Trying to follow the Abor through the building was proving difficult, in such a grand building not that many crows were to be seen to fly between the columns. The pigeons had told him they were not encouraged to fly in the religious buildings.

CC'raw concentrated on being discreet; most of the humans that were not filling the air with sound were on their knees. CC'raw could be forgiven for thinking they might be asleep not lost in meditation. Their meditation was why the Abor could move freely through the men of cross's domain.

Lost him! CC'raw could not go through the small door and the little window in it did not allow him to see into the room behind.

Once CC'raw was on the ground he had to walk towards the door past a group of men with robes that covered their faces. Which was a good thing for CC'raw they could not see him from the corner of their eyes thanks to their hooded robes.

CC'raw wanted to be in the room he had seen the Abor enter, what was he to do knock on the door? With a sharp tap of his beak he braved the door. When it opened he slipped in under the cover of an annoyed robe. He did not see the owner of the robe through an apple at the back of the retreating hooded group!

"May, the heavens forgive, your sins!"

"And yours Father!"

The door banged and the annoyed robe swept CC'raw conveniently under a table, under the very table the Abor was sitting at, his bare feet were not attractive! The feet of the man whose' robe had swept him into the room were so small they could have been a child's.

A bump announced a bottle had landed on the table and the goblets followed.

"Good not to forget old friends."

"So much had changed in the City, so many have left."

"So many new faces!"

"Once we were the dogs in the street…"

"…now we are the street!"

"What do you think of the new Emperor and his Empress?"

"They are only there so Basch can rule the city without taking any risk of direct confrontation from the people. Cleaver move if you ask me, he has understood the risk should his allies fail to defeat the Dux's Legions or the ailing old Emperor want to take back his empire, he can point at the two youngsters. The two youngster's youth and good looks are holding the people in the City together. They are a symbol of a new city, a new order and open trading! Well in his mind anyway. I remember him when he was a street dog; I used to kick his butt!" The Abor was the one talking.

"He was from a difficult family."

"Difficult family! Their wealth did not come from trade as they wanted the Senate to think."

"They gave enough to this house and its cross."

"They gave enough to my houses." The Abor's foot waved its approval, it abruptly stopped then its owner said: "The family took much from other houses; they offered men trained to use force to gain a busyness advantage."

"We made use of the advantages that family offered, and we played our part in seeing his father was stopped; his father's hunger for power was ended with the knife the Emperor had planned for him."

The small feet were swing backward and forwards under the table, CC'raw had to watch the two pairs of feet did not find him.

"And now his son has come to take his revenge on the city that killed his father and banished his family, it was a small price for trying to relieve an Emperor of his empire!" said the Abor.

"Who would have thought his son would have managed to complete such a plan! We never thought the small boy with tears in his eyes could learn to use the sward to back the words of revenge he spoke." said the voice belonging to the small feet.

"Then the Emperor banished himself from the City did he know he would to leave the City exposed to him! Did he know he would send his legions to counter a barbarian had been his pupil?" said the Abor.

"We are still here we are too old to leave. You have taken advantage of circumstances that no one could foretell. As Abor of the Pagans you will not want in your old age." The small feet's voice changed when it said: "What do you want from me?"

"What I want form you is you keep this information from others, we should be careful how we use our knowledge of the City's leader, use it to our advantage!" CC'raw did not like the tone of the Abor's voice: "Like you it is not just my old age I am thinking about."

"You have something you want to tell me?" the small feet were still.

"You know I was involved in building the catacombs. I know where the family of Basch have their tombs; you know that too, I know you were at many of their internments. It would not take Basch long to work out our part in the conspiracy against his family. That he's father was conspiring against the ruling emperor will not help us if he ever finds out our part."

"My dear Abor I think we understand each other."

"Father we could seal our understanding with another goblet of your good wine."

CC'raw had to jump to avoid the Father's little feet when they moved to get more of the wine the Abor was talking about.

Don was feeling a bit too much in demand, the Abor had required he nose out if Harron and ReeMara know anything about the scrolls that he had noticed were gone missing.

From what Don knew about the Abor, there were more fractions that would be interested in the old scrolls the Abor showed interested in. Those from the modern temples and the members of the crosses; could also be interested in the misty past written about this tedious old city.

Don's commanding officer had ordered him to present himself to Commander Basch. The leader had suggested Don should report to him what was said and what ReeArk did when he visited the girl.

This was not what Don wanted to be asked to do! That his Baschi was visiting that girl made him feel sick as it was. To have to report to his lover's elder what his lover was doing did not help!

Don had thought not to heed the leader's demands, but when others had not followed such requests, no one had ever seen them again. Basch had remarked he knew he, Don was often to be seen talking to the Abor but he had not ask him what the Abor wanted from him.

His Baschi had asked him not to be jealous of his visits to ReeMara, but everyone around Commander Basch knew he wanted a child from their alliance! Don could never except Baschi had another lover, Baschi was promised to him. The only good thing was the girl's cook was a wonder, he so enjoyed her meals.

Don was not included in the next meeting between Baschi and ReeMara, he did not know Harron was there nor could he know what was decided that day.

"We have to think of something, Basch has again asked when he can expect a child to be born!" ReeArk was slouching over the table it was as if his sorrow was holding him down.

So the Iron Man is no longer happy with ReeArk just visiting ReeMara, thought Harron. He had given this problem some thought. One solution was to find a baby some where and clam it as from the union from ReeMara and ReeArk. The only problem with that plan was Don. Don was continually coming around, as Armnell said a woman's belly swell as a baby grows inside. Don would notice that ReeMara's belly was smooth. Harron did not trust Don, he could not put his finger on why he was so untrusting of Don, but this was not a solution they could use.

Harron's other plan would need ReeMara's approval, he did not know how he was going to present his second plan, so he started by saying why his first plan would not work.

"ReeArk we cannot even think to try to make a child." ReeMara stood over her brother trying to sooth him; she knew how persistent the Iron Man could be. "It would be better to make a baby with Harron."

Every one's head in the small kitchen turned towards ReeMara, she was used to people looking at her but not in this way. CC'raw and Piper just stood on the table even though was not something Armnell liked when she was cooking and Harron and ReeArk sat there with silly smiles on their faces:

"Well do you have a better idea?" ReeMara demanded.

"That was my second plan!" Harron let his breath out slowly; really glad he did not have to approach the subject, somehow he never though he would find himself in this situation! He had always loved ReeMara, he knew now he would have made a baby with her without the excuse of finding a solution to a difficult problem.

"You make is sound so easy!" Armnell remarked.

"What else can we do, I am watched over wherever I go. The women take note of ever fold in my robe. Others watch to whom I talk. Should I talk to the men of the cross the followers of the Abor whisper behind their hands, the men of the cross press their hands together as if to prevent a pray being spoken out aloud. When traders or warriors are attending a feast, I have to sit next to the Emperor! Babies don't make them selves you know; I don't see another way, do you?

Harron's expression did not change, but his feelings were trying to decide just what ReeMara was trying to say. Her last statement sounded like he was the only man in the city, the remark could have two meanings, could she mean he was the only man in the city for her, or was he the only man in the city.

Nothing else mattered to Harron, he could not think of anything other than ReeMara. They had lain beside each other so many times before, from the time they had left the cliffs they had placed their bed rolls next to each other. They had even held each other under Mattie's kitchen table but now ReeMara was asleep in his arms it was somehow different. Harron could see the stars were in their heaven but tonight they too seemed somehow different!

It was CC'raw that saw Harron came back to earth, what CC'raw had seen and heard could not go unnoticed, the little Father and the Abor had indicated there were secrets they should try to find out about. If 'they' were planning to use what they knew, it would be to their advantage to keep their eyes open.

As Don was often to be seen with the Abor and ReeArk had heard that Don had been ordered to see the

Iron Man office he asked why the Iron Man had wanted to talk to him. Don had not wanted to say, he had waved his goblet and suggested they toast the arts of the cook. Everyone had been in a good mood that evening, they had been happy to agree with him.

But CC'raw had noted that Don was uncomfortable when ReeArk had asked about the Iron Man wanting to talk to him.

"You heard the Abor and a member of the religious group discuss they knew the Iron Man when he was running bare footed in the City's streets!?" Harron had to shake his head.

"They were involved in a conspiracy involving the Iron Man's family, at the time the old Emperor was in commanded of the City and his senses." CC'raw puffed himself to match the importance of what he had said.

Harron was trying to hold onto the feelings he had enjoyed, but CC'raw was not going to let him or anyone escape this discussion. Why was the kitchen the place where the most important discussions took place? Had they not been in the kitchen they would never have heard what their Armnell knew!

No one would have thought Armnell would have the answers to questions that were on their minds, but she had been working in the Bath House next to the Senate for many years, it was understandable she would hear the rumours circulating among the senators.

The Basch family it was rumoured had men for hire, they were to persuade dealers to except bids or deals that were not locative or to the benefit of both parties. Armnell could not help remember how such men had taken control of the slaves use to please the men in the city. Armnell also remembered that Basch's father had been stabbed in the Senate. The rumour had been he had

taken the knife meant for the Emperor. But she had had
the feeling the Emperor had sent the knife into the ribs of
an opponent that was undermining his authority.

It was rumoured Basch's father had tried to wipe out
the other trading families to take control of the city. The
ruling Emperor had banished or put to death the rest of
Basch's family. Armnell had been so young but she
known the ruling Emperor was someone to be respected;
he would not tolerate others testing his authority. He had
been a strong leader till his age had taken his senses.

"Now I understand why the Iron Man wanted to take
this city, if his father and his family were destroyed here
by the ruling emperor. Basch must have planned to
capture the city for himself to revenge the death of his
family." ReeMara said.

"What a plan! We have found ourselves woven into his
plan; our lives have followed his will since we were
parted on the beach!" ReeArk was astounded he thought
he knew his leader!

"It may not be his will we have been following: it
might be She-With-The- Sight's will we have been bound
in." ReeMara was hugging herself; she could feel the
frustration of being manipulated and controlled grow
inside her. What had she done? Was last night with
Harron part of some else's plan? Were the warm feelings
they sheared someone else's will?
Whoever, whatever had been the driving force was now
ReeMara's, she was going to take control of her own
destiny.

Harron noticed ReeMara was somehow different,
wonderful but different. She was happy to come to him,
lie in his arms. She enjoyed their lovemaking and she
kept the bond they always had, but she was somehow

different! Harron realised they could not center on each other, others could become suspicious. ReeArk was often at their kitchen table, and that Don was often with him.

Harron turned his interest to the fourth scroll; the first three explained the Iron Man and his family came from the very city he had gone to so much trouble to conquer. Harron had to admit it was quite a master plan, to take such a large city as this one and in such a calculating way.

Harron knew now the Iron Man must have planned to stop the amber from reaching the city, he had gone to the very island renown for its amber, where ReeMara and ReeArk came from; it was the same island She-With-The-Sight had chosen to rule. Her twin sister was the leader of the Cliff Citadel and it teachers; where Harron himself had been a student.

Until they had learnt their lives had been directed by others, they had thought it was by chance that ReeMara and her companions feathered, hoofed or as a ferret had come to the Cliff Citadel.

The fourth scroll had names scratched out because the Iron Man's father had not wanted anyone to connect his name to the Medwin side of his family. But the Center were he had been schooled had not scratched the twin sisters from their scrolls, if they had been scratched from the scrolls of the Centre Harron would not have been able to find the connection someone had tried to hide.

Harron was wondering who would want to know the twin sisters, The Sage, She-With-The-Sight were related to the Iron Man?

She-With-The-Sight had wanted the boy the Iron Man had taken, not the girl that had found her way to her tree. The fruit of her womb had added to folk that had collected the amber from the sea. Her crows had informed her of her island's busyness; she had known the girl was of her blood. She had known she would send her to do what she had planned the boy should do. She-With-The-Sight had planned to set her blood on the seat of power in the City on the Seven Hills. A calculated revenge for the evil the family of the Iron Hand had used to destroy her foremother, foremother of her sister. She would have been overjoyed to see those of her blood standing in the temple she had ordered the girl to place the three pieces of amber, her blood hand in hand, offered as emperor and empress!

The Sage stood on the highest parapet looking towards the City on the Seven Hills behind the mountains razing into the mist the heavens had used to stop the mountains from reaching the sky. She had wondered at her sister after she had heard what ReeMara had said. To let her go still weighted on her hart, she wondered what had happened to ReeMara and Harron. What could she feel? Could feel her sister thoughts still at the back of mind, though the tree had burnt. Could she feel ReeMara? Was it ReeMara she felt?

Had the battles that had taking place saved the Cliff Citadel from being destroyed?

Had ReeMara and Harron leaving the Citadel something to do with the Tented Armies taking the same way into the mist?

Had The Sage known that the Barbarian leader was from family of the Iron Hand Basch she would have shivered but not from the cold mountain air! She would have understood more of the plan her sister had had, a plan The Sage could only try to guess at. She had not wanted to be responsible if the plan were to falter at her citadel.

The two crows Cam and C'raw had accompanied the little girl and the three horses.
Sea Spray was proving to be a good mare. For the herds of horses on the Grass Lands it was a shame her young stallion had chosen to go with ReeMara and Harron, though knowing he was with them offered some comfort.

The two leader crows had not been able to tell The Sage what her sister had wanted, nor why she had sent ReeMara to her. It was not just for the schooling the girl would receive.

Since the battles on the grass planes had stopped, life had returned to its normal seasonal routines.

The Sage had seen many children come and go from her school, but it was ReeMara that she missed the most her and that strangely intelligent boy Harron.

"How are we going to find the temple She-With-The-Sight said you should place the three pieces of amber under?" It was Harron that asked; he had been looking at them as they drank tea in the little garden next to Armnell's kitchen.

ReeMara's body was showing a baby was on the way, everyone was happy at the news. ReeMara was surprised at the funny foods she found she wanted to eat, other than that expecting a baby was to her liking. Harron fussed over her, Armnell fussed over her, ReeArk came often to see her; she did not have to wait for feast or ensembles.

The three pieces of amber had matched sketches on three of the scrolls. ReeMara had placed the eye onto the first scroll; it matched the drawing under the iron fist. She had matched the blood stone with its horses head to the second scroll. The green stone that was like the sun and shadows among the leaves in the branches of a tree, ReeMara had set below the tree drawn on the third.

To understand that the amber had meaning, the male line of the Iron Man was represented by the stone with the eye. The green stone, matched the tree on the third. The blood stone with the horse's head which families did they represent?

Harron thought it was time he found out which families the two stones represented; would that help him to find out which temple they should be placed under?

Harron was annoying ReeMara, why was he so interested to know where these pieces of amber should go? She so wanted to see them in her baby's chubby fists. She wanted to see her baby play with them as she and Harron had under Mattie's kitchen table.

"The first scroll has the sign of the Iron Man's line but we do not know what the eye represents.

The second scroll again had the Iron Man's line and we can see the Iron Man birth sign clearly, there are no more male lines following him.

The third scroll has his family mark again, it sign was the tree. Female signs are marked on this scroll, could those cymbals mean, no wait they must mean the children they had!" Harron all but through the scroll he had been studding at ReeMara to grab the first he had pushed a side.

"The Eye! This scroll shows the children the women conceived, those that died at birth, look!" Harron was excited:
"Children that did not reach adulthood and those that survived. What can this sign mean?" Harron showed it to ReeMara:

"Looks like two babies to me." even though she did not take a close look at what Harron was pointing at.

"Sisters, two babies, twins…" Harron got to his feet without saying any more; he raped Piper in the scroll she was looking at. He was in such a hurry to get out of the little kitchen's garden!

ReeMara was glad Harron had something to occupy his mind; having someone around you asking questions was tiresome. ReeArk had said he would call in this afternoon to take a cup of tea with her. Armnell was happy to make tea at any time, a fresh pot was steaming on the table next to the three pieces of amber that ReeMara had had with her most of her life. The three pieces had not let Harron enjoy the quite afternoon in the same way ReeMara had wanted to.

In the little walled garden ReeMara felt safe she did not want to place the amber under any temple, she want her baby to play with them as she had done, under Mattie's the kitchen table at the Cliff Citadel.

Harron was heading towards the collage where he had been to ask questions before, CC'raw was sure; he could get there before the land walkers! CC'raw could see Piper's red tail waving from the scroll she was rolled in. CC'raw wished Harron would inform him when he wanted to go on missions!

It was no good asking ReeMara's silly bird to keep an eye on things, Trigary like ReeMara were more interested how they looked nowadays.

CC'raw just remembered in time not land on the short cut grass, there had been a big fuss when the horses had chosen to help themselves to the flowers!

"The old Basch, Iron Man farther, had been found dead in the street near the Senate! His son was sent away for his own safety because it was rumoured that he was in some way behind the plot to kill the old Basch. The family name of the twin sisters is Medwin, they studded here, could well have schooled the Iron Man when he was a student here! One of the sisters was sent to a collage in the mountains away in the north, that much you are sure. We can research that later." Harron posed for breath:

"The other sister also left here, you remember her because she had pale skin and did not like the sunlight, but you do not know where she went!?" Harron was thinking she must be She-With-The-Sight! The first sister must be The Sage!

The Iron Man had stopped amber coming from the far north, He had wanted to control it, to make this city weak. He must have known She-With-The-Sight, the old lady in the tree. He needed her to help him gain control of the islands in the Mist's amber!

Befriending the traders from the east, their trains of donkeys could have bought amber from the silk lands were easy to get under his control!

Harron's mind was buzzing, so much had happened now it made some since to him, this is a greater plan then the battles on the Grass Lands below the Cliff Citadel.

"Oh! There was a scandal in the senate, the Iron Fist's leader tried to take the Senate from the control of the ruling emperor. It was rumoured the emperor send his men to deal with the man meddling in state affairs.

When the Iron Fist's leader was found stabbed to dead in the street. The rumour that went round was it his own son behind the assassination. Who was behind the idea to banish the whole Iron Fist family from the city I cannot say, but when the Senate make a decree of banishment they must know what they are doing. We were very sorry to lose some of our best teachers."

Armnell fingers were easing the pain out of the Abor's body. She felt he came to spy on the youngsters in her care, not just to ease his mussels. When he came he would talk, and if she added some of her herbs to his tea so he would talk more freely than he wanted to and forget what he had said to her as he slept in her warm towels.

Today he said something that made Armnell curious, he mostly talked about his grand roll as Abor to the Pagans, and how he enjoyed irritating the religious groups. Armnell remembered him as an old and frail man that had been left behind unwanted by his master! Now this old man was bragging about his powerful position in the city!

"Who dose the Basch think he talking to? I am the Abor of this city, amber belongs to my rituals. His farther played games of power. The Emperor was right to see he was put to death, my knife was between his ribs and those with me were well paid." His words made Armnell stop smoothing his muscles, to hide her astonishment she reached for more oil before he could grumble. She remembered the scandal in the city when the Senate sent out an order to banish a family.

Never in her life would she have thought it could have been the Iron Man's family! Nor to have the murder of the father of the man now ruling the city under her fingers!

What was she going to do with what she had just learnt, how was this going to help those that were now her family? Her fingers closed round the old mans neck, if he was to hurt them, something in her gut told her the little girl from a beach away in the north and her brother were… what were they? Who were they?

Armnell's thoughts were interrupted by Don, ReeArk's jealous lover hammering at the door, her fingers slipped away from the old man's throat; she left him dowsing as she went to open the door.

Harron after repeating what he just learnt at the collage and with what Armnell had just told him left him feeling flat; not even the tea could pick him up.

Everyone was looking at him from around the kitchen table expecting him to say something.

"What are we going to do now?" CC'raw broke the descending silence. "We cannot leave the city now, not while ReeMara is about to nest."

Just the most sensible thing the crow had said, thought Trigary, he did not say anything he did not want to start an argument not when the humans were so upset.

"Were we to go into battle, I could use what I know to help us, but babies and politics are not my strong points." ReeArk said from behind his tea.

"I don't think this is about battles or babies." ReeMara mover her tea away from her: "this has something to do with She-With-The-Sight."

Harron was so glad she had said that he had the feeling for sometime they were involved in a plan of She-With-The-Sight's making; he had not known how he was going to put his thoughts to the others.

"I think we should keep these findings to ourselves." CC'raw was right till they had time to decide what they should do, it was better to keep the new information to themselves: "The Abor is often here as will as Don, we should watch what we say when they are here."

"Don has been strangely quite when it comes to me seeing ReeMara. Could he be informing Basch about ReeMara's house hold? What Armnell has just said about the Abor could explain why he feels he can risk angering Basch. I know Basch say's he can crush him at any moment, but to have him to destruct the Religious fractions helps him run the city's busyness under their noses."

"The Abor wanted those scrolls, the ones he hide in the Catacombs, why would he want to hide them, he must know what they have to tell."

"He would not want people like us to know."

"Basch would not want them shown about would he? It would not be to his liking if it was known his family was banished from his city. Could have the fourth scroll be the banishment announcement?" Piper asked still remembering the taste of old dusty scrolls in her mouth.

Harron was astounded at what Piper had just said: of cause that would not be something The Iron Man would want the new city senate to know. If he had taken the city by force it would have been different, but he had just walked in!

He was using the same traditions and laws as had the old Senate had used before! Sure they were his men in the Senate, but they were getting wealthy from those trading with the city, opinions were being bought and sold! The Iron Man kept on top of it all with his hand on the amber he controlled its use and how much was a loud into the city.

Harron unrolled the forth scroll, to look at it again. It had the Iron First on it but anything else had been scratched away, the scratching did not tell him anything. Could there be other scrolls to document the Basch family banishment?

Where to start looking Harron did not know. Harron could be certain that the Abor did not have such a scroll as he would have bragged about it to Armnell, when he drank her tea.

Both CC'raw and Trigary were to keep an eye on the Abor, Harron wanted to know what he was doing with his time.

The Abor was often to be seen drinking with Don, Harron had known about them meeting for sometime. The Abor was talking to the Father of the House of Religion, be it behind closed doors Harron also knew. Therefore he could presume that the Iron Man kept an eye on ReeArk through Don. Piper was pushing nuts around the table to represent those Harron was talking about.

ReeMara was also thinking, not about the banishment scroll that was occupying Harron's mind. She was repeating what She-With-The-Sight had told her to do. ReeMara was to place the three pieces of amber under the temple in the City of the Seven Hills. By doing so she would revenge the death of her parents, her family; her village.

What had She-With-The-Sight meant when she had said that? ReeMara took another stick of honey: the baby gave a little kike of approval.

What had it to do with her or ReeArk? The Iron Man had been so insistent that she and ReeArk should have a baby, why? Why had they been so determined to comply too his will? They could have just grabbed the horses and rode out of the city, not let themselves be pulled into this game.

Finding ReeArk was so important to her, so was Harron, she hugged her baby in her.

Maybe she should use the time left to her before the baby arrived, to find out which temple she should place the amber under, even though she did not want to give the pieces up.

The days were hard for Piper and CC'raw with ReeMara looking for temples and Harron looking for banishment scrolls and trying to keep an eye on what was going on in the city.

The Iron Man liked to show a very fat ReeMara of to his traders and visiting leaders. Trigary was of course on guard when she was attending to those duties, but that also meant CC'raw could not send him on other errands.

The horses were not encouraged to run around town but they could report of any unusual comings and goings.

CC'raw was glad when ReeMara was confined to the little garden, Armnell had told the Iron Man not to risk ReeMara health; by insisting she should attend feasts nor to present her in the Senate. CC'raw was quite surprised the Iron Man had accepted Armnell's command; there were not many alive that were able to command the Iron Man!

Today she would present the baby to the Iron Man in the Senate, to day she would dress in the finest robe in the city.

ReeMara did not know if she was frightened or over filling with pride, next to her lay a little girl with dark soft curls, would her nose be come like Harron's?

ReeArk and Harron liked the name ReeAmber, it was just right for the little treasure in her arms.

ReeArk was to walk with her into the Senate; his robe was also to be one of the finest. Armnell saw ReeMara's hair fell down her back, she was not happy when Trigary said he would be going with ReeMara, Armnell gave him instructions not to mess up ReeMara's hair that she had spent so much time on.

The Senate stood as ReeMara and ReeArk entered the grand hall. Trigary had to wait at the entrance with the other birds belonging to those inside. Harron and Armnell had to watch from the gallery that ran the length of one side.

ReeArk and ReeMara approached the waiting Iron Man, ReeAmber slept in the shoal Armnell had rapt her in.

The Iron Man he stood still as the people in the Senate applauded the small group now standing in the muddle of the filled hall.

The Iron Man hand reached for his sward, it was no more that half way out from its scabbard when Trigary rose in the air behind ReeMara and ReeAmber.

The image of a woman and child with a rising eagle made the assembled people cheer.

Trigary was not the only one to see the Iron Man's face was not red with pride, but with anger. Harron and Armnell could only stand and watch as the sword rose in the air. Trigary took the sleeping baby from ReeMara's arms; he then rose, out of the sward's reach above the Senate. He placed the baby in Armnell's awaiting arms.

CC'raw did not see Harron running from the gallery; his attention was on the people in the hall below him. They were cheering and waiving their arms and swards, they must think this is a show organised by the Iron Man. As for the Iron Man, his sward was pointed at ReeMara's hart! CC'raw thought he was going to run her through, ReeArk mover to her side, the Iron Man dropped the point of his sward. ReeArk lead ReeMara away. CC'raw glazed over his wing he saw the Iron Man sward was waving with the same strength as the people's cheers.

"That was the only sensible thing that bird has ever done!"
CC'raw said as Harron and Armnell grabbed things they were going to need. Piper was getting cross with Harron as he insisted they should go and get scrolls from among the dusty scrolls behind the Senate. Harron was stuffing more scrolls then Piper could think they would ever need into a robe. There must be other things more important than old scrolls and did they really need to raze so much dust?

Armnell took armful of robes stuffed them into her large cooking pot. A good knife and the bows and arrows the young pair had come with were rolled into free robe, another cooking pot held all the food it could carry. In another robe she tucked in anything she could lay her hands on, she thought they might need.

Breathless, Armnell stood in doorway where normally their guards had to wait, ReeAmber asleep in her arms. Harron was running with a robe wrapped round the scrolls he had collected. Piper was close behind him when he ducked into their kitchen to take the four scrolls from their hiding place.

Harron lead them to the garden of the flat stones, he told Armnell to wait here but if anyone was to come, slip through the doorway and into the room below. He told her of the way into the tunnel, But, only to go into it if she and ReeAmber were in danger. Piper was not happy when he told her to stay with Armnell. To argue was useless Harron was running towards the Senate.

ReeMara and ReeArk were surrounded by men under ReeArk's command. ReeArk could not take her back to her pretty garden; that would be the first place Basch would look. His men would obey Basch's orders but he did have time to get ReeMara away from the Basch's anger. He could not take her to the rooms he shared with Don. His lover may pretend to accept ReeMara, now ReeArk knew he could not trust anyone.

ReeArk ordered his men to escort them to the foot of the steeps of the temple Basch had chosen to show ReeMara and himself to the people, not long after they had arrived in the city.

There fine robes and ReeMara's hair swelled in the playful breeze. The men stood to attention as they ascended the stone steps, where the stone pillars took over the duty of being their guards.

The heat of the past moments was lost in the dark of the place ReeMara was standing in, she could feel ReeArk was be side her. They were below the temple she and ReeArk had been reunited! Her hand went to the little leather pouch she always had hung around her neck,

Armnell knew better that to make her take it off. The
string of creamy white amber hung over her robe.

ReeArk was making her walk forward in the dark.
How long they walked, ReeMara could not say, for the
moment they were safe in the bowls of the earth.

She-With-The-Sight face was clear in ReeMara's mind
as were the words she had spoken. ReeMara let the
leather pouch with the three amber stones slide out of her
fingers into the darkness.

Harron heard people talking as he slid into the gallery
above the still gathered Senate. He wanted to hear what
they had to say. Did they know the Iron Man had waved
his sward in anger? How was he going to get ReeMara
and ReeAmber out of the city now the Iron Man had
shown them to his Senate members?

Harron's mind was caught in the anger the Iron Man
had showed towards his child, ReeAmber and ReeMara.
The folk here were talking as though the whole incident
was just one of 'his' shows made Harron all the more
angry. Harron knew he had to be careful, he did not know
how the Iron Man would react to what had just happened
in his Senate.

People were leaving when Harron saw Aloes slip
through the shadows below him, what did the said Abor
want? Harron could not think of an answer but the Abor
did give him an idea.

The Senate was light by wooden stakes dipped in fat,
once burnt they were replaced. There were used light
stakes waiting to be collected in most corners.

'Ruled by one of the banished!' and the Iron Man's
closed fist sign stood out on the strangely white pillars.

The letters were large and straight as any guard, Harron would have written more but people were beginning to return to the lobby.

From within the lying stone garden, only the sound of ReeAmber stirring in her baby sleep disturbed the strange quietness. Armnell saw Trigary circle over head before he landed next to her:

"ReeMara is with ReeArk, they have entered that place on the hill. There were two many of ReeArk's men about for me to duck between the pillars. I did not get a chance when the Iron Man's men challenged ReeArk's guard to say where they were. Both sides did not seem to know what they were supposed to do; orders were flying about, ReeArk's men held their spears stopping me or CC'raw from getting under the low roof. So I came back here while CC'raw is looking for Harron.

Armnell sat up when from behind the wall the sound of men at arms' spears banging against their shields took away the silence. Piper ran towards her with Harron close behind. They swept up all the things they had with them as they ran to where Harron pointed.

A little door hidden in the wall hid them from the armed men entering the flat stone garden. Harron did not let them stay in the darkness of the room behind the door. He pushed and pulled them past a stone figure. It was not easy for Armnell and her ample figure holding a baby and robes and cooking pots to get through, she was breathless when she got herself together in the dark passage.

"Cover ReeAmber's face, the air in here is foul. I was sick the when I was here. We must not stay here, Piper can you lead the way?"

With a grumbling eagle and a crying baby, Armnell treading on Piper's tail they made their way in the darkness. Harron had the only light they had, he only look back to say which way they should turn.

Piper could not tell if Harron knew they were under the Senate's great hall. The sound of heated discussions and stamping feet she could feel in the stones of the tunnel they were in. Was that the sound of clashing swards?

ReeAmber cry for her mother cut the air sharper than any sward, Armnell could not stop the child's cry as it cut through the air again.

In the Senate hall the cry rang around the pillars with their blackened message. The Abor did not hear a young child's voice but that of someone much older. From the look on the Ruler's face he must have heard it too.

The Abor kept his lips together he did not let a smile betray him. He knew the Basch's family had been banished from the city and why. He had had his part in the old emperor's plan, but as to who could have marked the pillars?!

The scrolls he had lost in the tunnels did not explain the families' banishment their names had been removed from one. He had stopped worrying about who could have found them. That stupid boy Don had not found the scrolls in ReeMara's apartment. If the Basch had found them he would have cut of his head long ago.

Orders were being given to remove the marks off the white pillars. Voices were again being razed, asking for an explanation to their meaning.

ReeMara felt the cry, her body ached she knew her baby needed her but it was She-With-The-Sight's face she saw in the darkness. ReeArk did not need to be told they needed to find the others; the baby's need would wear on ReeMara.

ReeArk had seen the two birds flying above the points of his men's spears. Sitting in the dark trying to think what others could be doing did not help him decide what their next move should be. He felt ReeMara stiffen next to him, she did not scream even though she had drawn in air.

Rodents used the underground passages Piper's eyes did not betray her; he would have pushed her away if she had not whispered.

"I am glad to catch up with you two! Stay here while I get the others." Piper's tail tickled ReeMara's nose, the breath she had been holding escaped in a sneeze. "The tunnels have a strange way of conveying sound. We don't want anyone to know we are here." With that her eyes disappeared from in front of them.

For all Piper had said it was difficult to more down tunnels with robes and scrolls cooking pots a grumping eagle and a baby. The baby would not be content with Armnell's little finger to suck for long. Now Piper was not leading the way, left Armnell tripping over her own robe instead of Piper's tail.

Harron found holding the scroll with some of the underground tunnels marked on it and the small pot of wax and keep it a light, trying to say the least. The underground ways under the place where ReeMara had taken her brother's hand in front of the Iron Man's crowd were not on this scroll he had to find another. They had to stop while Harron sort for the scroll he needed.

Armnell would also have thought Piper was a rat, If Piper had run up her robe as a rat had tried to do earlier, one of the cooking pots had knocked it off, had it not clanged against the wall it would have been lost in the darkness.

"I have located them; they are not far from here. I told them to stay where they are; it is easer for me to ferret my way back to you."

ReeMara was glad for the light Harron's wax lamp gave, ReeAmber was held snug next to her in her robe she had rapped round them both. That they were sitting under the very place she had been reunited with ReeArk! Now they were with ReeAmber and Harron and a grumpy bird, it struck ReeMara as funny! Was it really to do with the three pieces of amber or was it to do with those now sitting near her. Again ReeMara saw She-With-The-Sight just as she had been in the tree so long ago. The three pieces of amber she did not have anymore, she had given them to the darkness, but she did have her family around her! What would the old woman have to say about that?

The Senate's members stood without vocal comment as the Iron Man's men tried to remove the dark marks from the whiteness of the columns; their message was not as easy to remove. This was the first time his authority had been in question since he marched into the City on the Seven Hills.

The men now standing in the Senate had been given their positions by the Basch, the Iron Man. But they enhanced their incomes by accepting payments from those wishing to trade in the city.

Just as to who could have whispered the rumour about the old Basch that had been murdered by his own son and the son had left the city soon after, the Iron Man was not able to tell! Who would have known that he and his family had left the city? There were not many that knew about the family's banishment. One he had left burning in her tree on a misty island and the other thinking she was safe in her cliffs over the battlefields beyond the mountains to the north.

Basch wanted to question the woman he had ordered to look after the girl he had chosen for Baschi, she had been here a long time; she was not to be found. To have her ownership scroll might bring him closer to the truth when he was able to integrate her.

Yes he had walked back into the very city that had thrown him and his kin out. It had never been his plan to take the city by force. He could not make a plan that would force the old Emperor to abandon the city it had been a turn of fate. The old Emperor thought more of his wealth than he did of the City, he had left it unprotected. It would have suited the Iron Man better if the old Emperor had asked him to favour his City; just to walk in to a city that had been left had not given him the satisfaction a revenging son could have had.

"You came back to this City to take revenge on the exiled Emperor, knowing you could set you own blood in his place." The Iron Man just grinned at the Abor: "You and I brawled in the streets when we were youths. You think I have no power over you. But I do, the banishment has not been lifted."

The Iron Man's sward was with easy reach of the old Abor through, the Abor only held his place because he had given it to him. That he was only an actor he had known all along, but what the man had to say was not from a play.

The Abor face was so close to the Iron Man's, but still the Iron Man could not place him! The Abor was talking about the places where the Basch's, his father's remains had been laid under the city.

"The girl you united with your youth, are brother and sister! His lover discovered their story; she is the sister of the child you took from a raid!" The Iron Man's mind wandered back to day he took the village near the beach; stopped the folk from collecting the amber. Could he remember who was there when he pulled the boy onto his horse? He could only remember his sward flashing and his horse speeding through the shallow water.

Was she the little girl that had stood between him and She-With-The-Sight? The winter had been hard outside the tree no one could have survived!

The Abor's face was still close to his and his breathe was foul. Guards were uneasy as what they should do. Their leader's sword was in his hand, pointing at the Abor of the Pagans' throat. They let their breath out as the Abor's blood ran down the stone steeps.

Had the Abor decided to confront the Basch in the Senate and not on the steeps outside he would not have been able to wash his blood away as easily, nor blame his death on another pagan follower.

What had he meant by saying 'You are setting own blood in his place?'

That remark puzzled CC'raw he had seen the Abor die at the hand of the Iron Man. He had been searching the city for any sign of his friends. Trigary had taken the baby out of The Iron Man's reach. CC'raw also believed the razed sward had not been to greet ReeAmber!

CC'raw would have remained puzzled if he had not remembered following the Abor into the building used by the members of the new religion. The conversation he had overheard he needed to remind Harron of as soon as possible! The Abor had implied he had been involved in the murder of the Iron Man's father!

Without an eagle or a ferret CC'raw had to ask help from the three horses in the stables. Maybe they could find out what was happening. Corn and Bramble were shifting from one hoof to the other no one had been to see them for so long. Soul was hiding himself in his stall, the mares only wanted him for his good looks, what he really wanted was some one to talk to.
Bramble and Corn jokes bored him. So when CC'raw landed next to him he was happy to see him but when he heard what CC'raw had to say he was horrified!

"I don't know if we can just wonder around the city, the last horse to come back to the stable said there are many armed men in the streets, they are looking for someone. Could they be looking for…?"

Bramble and Corn did not look bored anymore not after hearing what CC'raw had to say. Bramble and Corn could be relied upon to find out what the other horses in the stables knew about what was happening in the streets. CC'raw could see men running with harness and saddles.

From the birds perching on a low building out side the stables CC'raw leant the Iron Man had given orders to find the killer of the Abor. Had CC'raw not seen with his own eyes the man fall at the point of the Iron Man's sward he would have believed the need, but to hear an order had been given to find the murder increased CC'raw's fear for his missing friends.

All CC'raw could do now was to perch near the horses and hear what the returning horse had to say. It might help him to know which parts of the city were being searched.

ReeMara and Harron hugged ReeAmber in the dark they did not want to keep what was left of the little wax lamp for when they really need it. To know Armnell and

ReeArk were next to them in the dark helped a bit. The hear Trigary grumbling somehow helped sooth their nerves even if it did not help Piper's:

"We can not sit here indefinitely; it is cold and dark, as Trigary says, you cannot even spread your wings." CC'raw would be a useful bird to have around now, with his commonsense. What they needed now was commonsense; sitting in the dark was not going to help.

Piper made everyone jump when they heard her tearing a robe into strips, she placed the ends into Armnell's hands with the suggestion she should tie them together. Armnell took spare strips and bound their things into easier to carry bundles. Armnell also made a sling for ReeAmber to be carried in, to have your hands free when you are moving about in the dark will be helpful.

Really Piper did not know what or where they should go, to have everyone busy tying strips of robes together made the darkness feel less unfriendly, and the grumpy eagle less irritating.

Harron thought Piper's idea was good the only question was where were they to go? She was right they could not stay here. He had to see to their needs. It might be a strange place to go, but back to the little cemetery was the best idea he could think of, as from there they could with luck reach places they knew could provide the things they would need.

Harron and ReeArk had tried to discuses in the dark how they could get out of the city. They would need the horses but as soon as they disappeared from the stables everyone would know! The little room in the cemetery wall was the best option they could think of. They could save the little wax lamp as Piper could find the way there without its help.

If anyone could have seen them they would have thought they were a group of blind folk being lead by a ferret they would not have seen the grumpy eagle as his head was under ReeMara's robe. He was now sulking as he could not sit on ReeMara's shoulder. 'Eagles are too big to sit on shoulders in low ceiling tunnels!' was the nice way she told him he had to walk.

The way Piper took them seemed to Armnell to take much longer that than it had to get to wherever they had met in the dark. The strip of robe tightened around her wrist as she lost her footing; trying to regain her balance she tested the air with the hand with the cooking pot. What she did not expect was the wall she touched crumble away! She fell into the space the pot had made: she could not say the air was fresh, though it did have a smell she recognised.

Everyone drew in their breath when Harron light the little wax light. The room they were in was returning the light!

Amber of every colour returned the light, warm and true. Pieces larger than a man's fist with animals and flowers held in them, tree leave green and gold, the colour of blood or as white as snow. The piece of black on the floor close to ReeMara fitted into her the palm of her hand. It was not dark but full of all the colours around her.

Harron held up the lamp it showed the hall they were in was lined with shelves each with the best quality of amber to be found. ReeArk could have told them from where each type came from but he was astonished at the amount.

Without speaking they filled in as best they could the hole Armnell had made when she fell into the Amber Hall.

The blackness of the tunnel contrasted the wonderful return the amber had given. With the last of the wax light Harron marked on a scroll where he though they were, Piper could only shrug at Harron's mark, she would be able to find this place again.

The news above ground was not to CC'raw's liking. The Iron Man had told the Senate, the death of the Abor was attributed to those with the Emperor and Empress. His men were looking for them. He declared he would stop anyone leaving or entering the city till he found the culprits.

The leader of the Pagans murder must be found! He called on the different houses of religion to offer support to the houses of the pagans in such difficult times.

There was one man that found the Basch's accusations difficult to believe. He had brawled in the city streets with the Abor when they were youths. He knew the Abor's part in the death of Basch's father. He drew his robe around him and covered his head as he left the Senate.

CC'raw diced to follow the man leaving the Senate before the Iron Man had spent his rage at those he had gathered there.

CC'raw flew with ease behind the man, he kept his head was covered as he walked, he did not even look about him!

CC'raw had been here before; he had followed the Abor to the very door the robed man was unlocking. CC'raw had had to find away into the small but comfortable room among the great pillars, when he had wanted to hear what the leader of the religious and the Abor had to disuse.

The point of the Iron Man's sward had slain the Abor, if the Iron Man had known that the Abor had been among the assigns that had killed his father, the punishment would not have stained the steps of the Senate!

CC'raw stood in the door way not really knowing what he should do next when a sandal was kicked under the table the second sandal did not want to leave the small foot as easily as the first now under the table. CC'raw did not usually help humans take of their foot wear but it was as good excuse to enter the room.

It was not until the pair of feet were resting on a small stool and the wine in the challis had been drunk did the man in the robe speak.

"To have a crow assist me makes me curious to know what a crow wants from me!"

"I have witnessed the death of the Abor it was committed by the Iron Man's own hand. We both have heard him accuse others. I do not wish my friends to carry the blame."

"He has stated members of the Empress' household are reasonable."

"The Empress did not like his sward pointed at her child, if the eagle had not been there his sward would have torn the child in two."

The religious leader wanted to ask what had that to do with the death of the Abor. Everyone had thought the eagle carrying the baby away was a show power planned by Basch! Now this bird was saying he had overheard him and the Abor when they had talked about the assignation of the Basch's father, and the Abor's part in it. Life was different in the time when the old Emperor was ruling!

"I was under this table when you were…"

"How did you get into my office without me seeing you?"

"I knocked on the door, when you opened it I slipped under your robe."

"And, I through an apple at the monks thinking they had knocked on my door!"

"I know you are not convinced by the Iron Man's beliefs."

"The religion I follow has its own beliefs; a city like this has beliefs and has to except other beliefs. That is why Basch chose to place a figurehead for the people to believe in, to unite the different beliefs. The Emperor and the Empress to have child was part of that plan."

"The Emperor and Empress are siblings! He stole a boy from a beach, to be emperor; left his sister to die with the rest of the villagers. He could not know the girl he chose to be Empress was the boy's sister he had left to die.

We tried to get ReeMara to leave the city, but her wish to not to lose her brother again held her here. The child she offered the Iron Man was sired by Harron the scribe. The Iron Man must have seen the baby's likeness to Harron, it explains his anger and drawn sward."

CC'raw did not know how much he should tell the Leader of the Religious, whose table he was sitting on. But his friends need help, and help from someone with power to protect them. And! If Armnell was right; ReeArk and ReeMara and now ReeAmber were apart of the Iron Man's line.

What was it his mother had said about laying eggs in an others nest? 'Watch where you hatch your eggs, in another nest the hatchling may not be the bird you have expected!' now made sense to him. But life with The

Sage in cliffs had not shown him the wisdom of her words.

To find help for his friends was one thing but it was another to find them. He had flown over the city many times! He had been back to the garden with the stones hoping they would be there. The horses had not reported anyone had seen them, even though the Iron Man's men had sent his men and horses many times through the city.

"Find your friends; I am not with out resources." It could be to the Religions advantage to offer them sanctuary, the Leader was thinking. To have the Emperor and Empress as his guests would give him an advantage over the distribution of amber.

"We cannot sit around here in the dark, where is that ferret?" Trigary was the one grumbling, but everyone else where beginning to feel the same. After finding the hall of amber the small wax lamp had give its last light, Piper had left them to see if she could find the way back to the garden of flat stones. She had not expected to find CC'raw sitting huddled on a stone near the door to the catacomb, he looked so lost!

"I thought I would never see you again! No one on the ground has seen or heard from you. I have no way to find you or help you when you are underground!"

"Everyone is all right, it was too difficult to try and find my way here with the others stumbling in the dark behind me. It will not take me long to bring them here, we should be here by sundown."

"Piper the Iron Man is still searching the city his men are everywhere. The Iron Man has killed the Abor; I saw it with my own eyes! Before the Abor died I heard him say to the Iron Man 'You are setting own blood in his place!'The whole city knows the Basch family were banished. Someone wrote 'Ruled by one of the banished!' in the Senate."

Piper could see how stressed CC'raw was, but the others were sitting in the dark somewhere below them.

"Look, I will get the others you wait here for us and then you can tell them what you have told me.

The religious men's voices chants rang between the tall columns, their sandals slapped along the warn stones of the streets. The incense they carried wafted over the normal day's cooking smells. The hoods of their robes they wore were drawn over their heads. There were so many followers that the Iron man's men could not ride through them.

One monk had to stop voicing his chant as he had to grab his robe before it fell from him. A large horse had put his hoof on it! The rider of the horse was one of the Iron Man's men:

"What is going on here? There has not been any rights to celebrate given to day!"

"This is a holey day of remembrance! We cannot upset the saints, can we?!"

"No we can't, but how am I going to get my men past your monks? How am I going to get my horses past you and those waving incense and crosses?"

"You could always ask the saints to let you through, but they cannot hear you with all this chanting going on."

"I have my orders."

"Maybe you should pray!"

"I don't know how your saints can help me!"

"My brothers can pray for you, just put a remittance in my hand."

"Look brother! I have my orders!"
"And I have my prayers my brother."

CC'raw had watched with amusement what was
happening at the back of the religious procession. Trigary
was watching from behind a stone figure. He saw four
figures with robes like those of the passing monks slip
out of the walled cemetery and join the men waving
incense and crosses in the air. Their chanting hid any
baby's cry. Now ReeMara was among the monks he
could not pick her out from the air. CC'raw had said
when the humans had left the street below them they
would fly directly to the great house of the religious.

The chanting and singing and the swaying of incenses
left a trail of smoke, the Iron Man's men and their horses
found the smoke caught in their throats, they could only
draw back from the smoking mass.

From the air it did look strange, like some great beast
winding its way through the streets below. The steps to
the religious building were lined with monks with the
cross on their robes their hands clasped together in
prayer. Just for good meagre the leader of the religious
had ordered three large drums to be placed between the
coulombs. The men that beat them added to the chanting,
it became the pulse of the great best that was now
entering the building.

Trigary and CC'raw were most imprested they would
have to tell Harron later. But there was a but to all of this,
the Iron man's men were still running around the city
looking for those hidden in the chanting mass below
them. The sound of the drums stopped so suddenly the
silence almost deafened the two birds as they entered the
great hall of the religious. The monks that had been part
of the great beast took off the hoods to their robes;

CC'raw was worried that his folk would want to do the same. They were supposed to join the chanting monks but from where he and Trigary were they could not see them.

CC'raw got Trigary to land where no one would see them, then walk to the office of the Leader of the Religious. Trigary was not happy at having to walk he grumbled all the way to the small door! CC'raw found it strange to think he had knocked on this door before, firstly as a spy and now as a conspirator in the Leader of the Religious plan.

"Basch cannot restrict religious seminaries; that the saints needed a remembrance day today and that my good sectary had forgotten to send a scroll to the Senate cannot be counted against the Religious!" The Leader of the Religious opened the door the two birds hopped in, glad to see their friends were assembled in the Leader's office. ReeAmber had slept through the whole event in ReeMara's arms but now they were here she decided to let them know!

It was not difficult to make everyone comfortable, behind the Leader's office were small rooms, one was a kitchen! Armnell was soon busy making something to eat. There was enough wine stored in another, with smoked bacon hanging from the roof.

The Leader of the Religious said cells had been made ready for them, Harron was not happy at the idea of a cell he had been held in prison when he had first arrived in the city.

"I will not leave! For all the Iron Man has done to us I will not give in to him." Harron was not the only one looking at her as she stood with ReeAmber in her arms, the eagle had at the very moment she had stood up to speak spread his wings behind her. The Leader of the Religious could not fail to notice her defiance. "Our parents paid with their lives as many others have, just please the whim of the Iron Man! I will not walk away! We will show him what it means to lose all you value." ReeMara saw all in the Leader of the Religious office were looking at her strangle. "We will take all the amber stored in his halls. Without the amber he cannot control the city!"

In the silence that followed what just ReeMara had said; she felt her words had fallen on deaf ears; she sat down as if the weight of her words were too heavy.

"Have you any idea as to how you are going gain axes to the halls of amber you speak of?" The Leader of the Religious asked.

"We know how to access the hall of amber!" ReeArk said almost under his breath. Harron was not sure they should be talking about the amber hall in front of the Leader, even if he was offering them sanctuary.

"We could walk in and take it all, but can we carry so much and where could we store it?" Nice to have a practical ferret when you need one, thought CC'raw as he perched himself next to her on the table. When Trigary suggested he could air lift it away! CC'raw wanted to say something but Piper said everyone would see him carrying amber over the city. What they needed was a plan to take the amber from under the Iron Man's nose, and a place to keep the amber hidden.

"Places of safety can be found in my realm, this temple of religion has many assets we can exploit." The Leader of the Religious stated. "No one shall speak of the deeds we will ask them to do. There are monks in this religion that have given their voices their God, vowed not to speak, a vow useful in times like this." The Leader of the

Religious looked at ReeMara and ReeArk: "Had they known you were entering the Religious Halls their greeting would have been more fitting for an Emperor and Empress. But I had to whip up a saints day to hide your entry in my halls! If suspicion should fall on anyone of them, they cannot tell of my deeds." He said when he saw Harron head turn towards him.

The men the Iron Man had sent to search the city did not know how much amber was stored under the city, that gold and silver were stored was common knowledge, they excepted it as payment. That there were catacombs under all the temples was also common knowledge. The idea to search the catacombs was born because no sign of those they sort had been seen on the streets.

The Iron Man had band the daily markets, people had been ordered to stay in their houses, forbidden to gather in any of the open meeting places. Why the house of the Religious had been aloud to celebrate all saint's day, at such a time as this was not questioned, no one dared to ask their leader Basch questions.

The catacombs did not allow solders with uniforms, horse and helm to march through them. The search had to be done on foot; the horses were taken back to their stables.

None of the men searching the catacombs realised the hall of amber had been empted of its riches.

The small group of men that had been ordered to enter the empty hall could not have known what had been stored in it. Their ignorance could not explain Basch's anger when he stood on his empty halls. The three halls one leading into another had been striped of the amber he had stored. The small hole in the wall of the one he was

standing in, explained how his amber had been stolen.
But it did not tell him who had done such a thing!

Harron knowing the Iron Man would be outraged once
he discovered his stores of amber had been emptied. The
role the Iron Man had played in ReeMara's live; the birth
of his daughter and in his own life Harron gave him the
impetus to think of ways to nerve the man that had done
them so much harm, lead them in ways they would not
have chosen for them selves. He knew ReeMara wanted
to bring the Iron Man down!
'The blood of the banished will rule the empire!
It will not be your body's blood that will hold the
empire.'
This was now written on the forth scroll that Harron
had found, the one that had had names written on, before
someone had scratched them away. Harron looked down
at the words he had written. If the words he had marked
the Senates' pillars had angered the Iron Man then these
words would not let him rest. Harron closed his eyes to
see a face in his minds eye, was it the face of She-With-
The-Sight? From what ReeMara had said it could be. The
face he saw was smiling, it made him shiver.
Harron looked back at the words he had written to find
he was smiling. ReeArk would know how to get this
scroll to the Iron Man.

CC'raw had followed ReeArk's directions but the
room was empty except for the bed in it middle, that
someone live in this room was marked by scrolls lying
without order on the floor.
The almond tree opposite the Iron Man's private
quarter provided the best perch while he waited for the
Iron Man to return. CC'raw had placed the old scroll

Harron had given him on head of the bed, where the Iron Man would be sure to find it.

It had been a good idea to get the horses from the stables, ReeArk's stallion had to except Corn and Bramble hassling him out of the stables. Normally he and Soul would have razed their heads arched their neck as they pasted the mares in their stable. To day they had slunk out, then let the monks CC'raw had brought with him harness them like pack horses!

Four horses laden with goods went unnoticed through the streets of the city. The Iron Man's men were looking for humans not horses! Horses entering the courtyards of the religious temple were not challenged, even if the goods they were carrying were for the religious kitchens. Fresh food was not easy to get now the Iron Man had closed the city's gates to traders.

CC'raw was interest to see how the Iron Man would react to the scroll. But the man did not seem to need to sleep! It was just before the sun sent its light into the sky over the city when CC'raw was knocked out of his tree by a flying sandal!

The Iron Man's voice shook his senses awake; it was when men entered the yard where the almond tree grew CC'raw decided to take the offensive sandal with him. The men did not seem to notice a crow hovering with a sandal over the yard they were searching, the Iron Man's voice held their attention firmly to the ground they were searching.

CC'raw did not see the Iron Man hold his head in his hands the scroll was on his lap. The words Harron had written held him on his bed.

'The blood of the banished will rule the empire!

It will not be your body's blood that will hold the empire.'

The dreadful man whose blood he had spilt on the steeps of the senate had had knowledge of his family's banishment. He had been seen entering the apartments of the girl. The Iron Man's informants had said he visited the old slave he himself had ordered to look after the wretch he had chosen to be Baschi's consort.

He had not understood their likeness, had meant they were brother and sister when he first saw the girl coming out of the Bath House.

He should have taken the girl when she had tried to defend that vile woman. The woman's vision had spoken of a child with blue eyes and flaxen hair that would confirm his rule.

Was it his pride that had seen he had taken the boy and not the girl? The Island in the Mist had been the source of the best amber, the very amber that had been removed from his halls!

The face of the old woman whose tree he had burnt with the fires he set appeared in his mind, her smile did not cool his temper.

This was one of the four scrolls that had gone missing from the offices of records. He himself had scratched away the names on it. He had wanted to use it to prove or disprove his connections to the City. But it had slipped away from his control. He could plan a campaign of war with swards, lay the path to battle but to plan with the written word he had not able to take the advantage. He had seen the advantage of circumstance many times, but this time he had let it slip through his fingers.

The Iron Man decided to let the city start trading again, stop his men from disturbing everyday busyness. The way forward was not with self pity. If those he wanted

had gone into hiding so be it, but they would pay a price!
He would accuse them of the murder of the Leader of the
Pagans.

Scrolls of warrant were pressed on pillars around the
town. The Iron Man had men stand in the markets telling
folk that the 'Basch' was offering a handsome reward for
any informing the whereabouts of those that had
abducted the Empress and Emperor. Their descriptions
could have matched with the Empress' scribe and the
woman could have been Armnell! The men on the streets
did not mention a baby.

It was not unusual to see monks in the streets, no one
noticed Harron studding the scroll of warrant nor did they
see him press another massage next to it.

'The blood of the banished will rule the empire!

It will not be your body's blood that will hold the
empire.'

The people in the street that could read did not
understand the message in the same way as Harron meant
it; the message was to annoy the Iron Man. Anything that
would aid the Iron Man to lose his temper would help
Harron plot against him.

The idea to hold court in the High Temple had not
been his, though to use the amber they had taken away
from the Iron Man had been. ReeMara had agreed they
should use it as the Iron Man intended. Traders and those
that wanted to build in the City needed it as will as to
Religious and Pagan temples.

The Leader of the Religious was happy to see his needs
and the needs of his temple were attended to. He sent his
monks to meet the traders waiting to enter the trading
centres, to see any new supplies of amber entering the
City were brought to his temples stores, before the Iron

Man's men could take charge of the amber, they were slow to notice that the usually amounts were not arriving.

The monks gave the traders bring their amber to the city the same mark they had been given by the Iron Man's officials, they did not thing to question it, they had had to wait for the gates to be opened due to his order to close them. They had not received an explanation as to why they had had to wait out side closed gates.

When the monks told them conditions of trade had not changed, only those that they traded with had, busyness for all traders continued as it had before they did not think to question the city's change of authority.

The mark the monks used was not different to the one the Basch used! Harron had seen the smile on the face of the Leader of the Religious when they had been deciding what action they should take.

ReeArk had pointed out that the traders would become suspicious if the trade mark was changed. The Leader of the Religious had many that could make copies of it.

ReeMara and ReeAmber were safe from the Iron Man's furry in the Religious Temple. Harron had been able to request she and Armnell were guarded, as far as Harron was concerned not just to keep her safe from the Iron Man but stop her from trying to take her revenge alone. As the temple had its own bath house he hoped she would stay here.

Harron kept ReeArk busy by insisting he oversee the amber that the monks were bringing into the halls of the Religious.

Harron with a monk's habit to throw over his robe and with Piper and his knowledge of the tunnels under the City they were able to move about as they wished.

Harron was able to start a rumour in any part of town he liked. The Iron Man's men had said to look out for a thin man and a round woman with dark skin in connection to the murder of the Leader of the Pagans. Fat scribes and thin dark women were just as likely to commit murder. And, wasn't it convent for the Basch that one of his opponents had been killed! Not that he wished to imply anything!

Trading was not disturbed by the rumours running around town but the Iron Man was. He had lost control of amber coming into his city. Whenever his men saw monks trading close to the city's gates they folded their tables and moved away! Even when his men escorted the traders to his busyness halls he was not receiving as much amber as he did before! He had the idea to confront the traders before they entered the city but they were unwilling to trade out side the safety of the city walls even when his trade mark was offered as security.

Armnell was pleased to have a little kitchen to her self and the cells they had been offered were as comfortable as they could be made. She had a pleasant tea stemming in bolls on the small table she had just scrubbed:

"Now look you two!" she was speaking to ReeArk and ReeMara, they were staring into their bolls as if they were lost in its steamy mists. "Things have changed and changed to our benefit. The Iron Man has lost some of his steam; without the amount of amber he cannot control the city the way he used to. Harron's idea to start rumours to counter his can only frustrate him more."

ReeMara had been holding council with the traders till now it had been just a game, a game to get in the Iron

Man's way. She could see the advantage of paying for their quarter at the Halls of the Religious. It meant that the Leader of the Religious Temple could only advise them what they should do. Armnell had been the one to see a fair trade had been made. The leader of the Religious did not seem to care they were only folk the Iron Man had chosen to be Emperor and Empress. If he known they were of his blood line maybe he would have seen fit to execute them all. But ReeMara could understand that it suited him to back them as they were prepared to see his halls benefited from their alliance.

The Leader of the Religious was also happy to keep the balance with the pagan followers it pleased him to supply them from his stores of amber and had negotiated with Armnell and Harron so that he could also benefit in this way.

"To use the profit the amber is making to befit the city in some way, would be befitting of an Emperor and Empress." ReeMara heard Armnell say. ReeArk thought she meant soldiers should receive more training. That was not what Armnell had in mind: "The monks have in this religious temple a place where their people can find treatment for their ailments. Their healing rooms could be opened to the people of the city."

CC'raw could see the cleave plan behind Armnell's idea. If the Iron Man tried to say the Emperor and Empress were not for the city's humans the very fact they were openly behind an idea such as this would take the steam out of his words.

The Iron Man's warrant scrolls that said there was a handsome reward for any informing the whereabouts of those that had abducted the Empress and Emperor, would have be to ignored. The Empress and Emperor could not be abducted if as they were openly trading with the amber!

Armnell could see ReeArk and ReeMara could not see throw the steam of their tea as they sat there, so she said:

"The Iron Man cannot send in his men into a place were the sick are being cared for, any more than he can enter the halls of any of the religions. We will place the open treatment halls in the Temples of Pagan as well as the Religious! "

"Such rules did not stop him before!" ReeArk was interrupted by CC'raw:

"On a battle field! But now he has to use the rules he has set, this is a city where trading is encouraged from many lands. He cannot say he will not trade with anyone of them as each brings deferent goods here. There are three things that they all have in common gold and silver and Amber. That is why he cannot walk in and knock tables over. He cannot come in here and demand you handle only with him."

"The leaders of the religions do not have goods to trade." remarked ReeArk.

"They have dreams to sale!" Armnell toped up the bolls of tea. "How do you think the religious hall became so wealthy?"

"We cannot leave this place of sanctuary!" ReeMara thought of open grass planes, the sea splashing on the beach.
But She-With-The- Sight face was before her as she closed her eyes. ReeMara could almost feel the three pieces of amber she had been given by She-With-The-Sight in her hand, she had left them somewhere in the dark under the high temple.

Things had changed as Armnell was saying, but this was not the revenge she had planned. A sward in the Iron

Man side, to see his blood spill like so many she had seen would have been a better revenge that the one they were planning.

There was something she did not fully understand, She-With-The-Sight and the dear Sage were connected! The Iron Man had taken ReeArk away with him, was it she he had wanted? Should it have been her that had grown up with the Iron Man not her brother? He had made them Emperor and Empress insisted they continue their blood line, controlled them like puppets in the market place.

Maybe Harron was right the words he had written meant something to her too!?

Maybe Harron was also right when he said the best way to revenge her parents was to see him brought down by his own rules not the sward she had planned. Giving the three pieces of amber to the darkness under the temple had led them to find the underground halls of amber. Amber from her home by the sea was making it possible for them to take most of the trading away from the Iron Man! ReeMara's sadness lifted a little when Harron entered the little kitchen with Piper. ReeAmber giggled when Piper's tail tickled her. ReeMara looked around the kitchen; her brother was sipping his tea. Harron was hugging ReeAmber. Piper was curled up in her lap. Trigary sat on top of the door, his head under his wing, just like he had done when he was first hatched! The horses were grumbling about their new stabling, the monks' horses were not so keen the share their tales as the soldiers' horses had been about the battled fields they galloped on. But, they were her family! It was time to start thinking in another way; these were the family she had to think about now. Armnell, pored more tee into her boll, ReeMara put her arm around her. The hug she gave her was not just for her but all of those in the kitchen.

It was time to talk to the Iron Man or use the sward as she had planned.

No one stopped her from walking into the chamber the Iron Man was holding council, the guards saluted her as they all ways had. She silenced the guard who was about to announce her presents with a wave of her hand. As she stood in front of the Iron Man those that were holding council with him withdrew from the chamber.

Now she was alone with the one man that had done so much to her and those around her, she could not find the words she wanted.

"Why should my council not accuse you of the death of the Leader of the Pagans?"

"You want them to know the games you play? The old man was a fool! He died from the point of your sword, before you could make him account for his part in your father's death."

The Iron Man eyes showed he had understood the meaning of what she had said even though his facial expression did not change.

"Is that all you want to say to me?"

"I want to accuse you of the death of my parents, the destruction of my village, for the loss of my brother. I want to accuse you of mass slaughter. Curse you for the lives you have wasted in order to achieve your aims." ReeMara waited to hear what he would say, when he did not take his eyes away from her face ReeMara took a step closer to him, she almost spat her words at him:

"Your sward was pointed at my child! I will not let your plan of revenge harm her." The sward in her hand under her robe felt as if it had a will of its own. If it had not been for the smooth piece of amber in her other hand, the piece she had found on the day they had discovered his halls of amber; she would have used it to sink it into his flesh, as he had done to Alois on the steps of the Senate.

ReeMara wanted to laugh; she wanted to laugh as she had heard She-With-The-Sight laugh in the tree all those years ago. No sound came out of her throat it was stopped by the thought, who had manipulated her? She-With-The-Sight had played her part in bring her the City of the Seven Hills.

The sward felt ready to play its part, she could hear She-With-The-Sight laugher ringing in her head.

ReeMara dropped the sward as if it was hot, she would not follow an others will, too many people had died! The City had families like hers; their lives should not be governed by one man's whims. To risk her life when ReeAmber needed her, to risk Harron's life, lose ReeArk again! This man's life was not worth it.

"They were not the Iron Man's men. I saw her leave the Iron Man's chambers he did not order them to arrest her. He sat with his head in his hands as she left." CC'raw was distraught. He had not had the chance to tell anyone ReeMara had left the sanctuary of the Religious Leaders' halls.

ReeMara had not told anyone what she had planned she had just got up from the table and left the cell they used as a kitchen, then, she was gone! CC'raw had found her just as she was entering the Iron Man's compound.

"His guards just let her in! By the time I got close to them she had turned her back on him. I saw the sward lying on the floor. I do not know who dropped it. I wanted to scold her for leaving without telling us but a covered wagon drew up next to her. I could not beat away the arms that pulled her in!"

CC'raw was hopping from one foot to the other. One of the arms had knocked him out of the air; he had lain winded on the ground: "I did not see where they took her, they have not left the city, of that I am sure. I have asked every bird to see if a covered wagon has left. Not one has reported seeing such a wagon leave."

Harron could see CC'raw needed comfort, not to be worried by the thought ReeMara could have left the City. Who could have taken her, if it was not the men guarding the Iron Man then who?

Had Harron known his counter rumours were hindering finding where ReeMara was, he would never have uttered them. The most resent rumours in the markets told she, ReeMara was behind for the murder of the Leader of the Pagans. The Iron Man had stared such rumours. And he, Harron had pointed out how it was convent for the Iron Man one of his opponents had been killed! The Iron Man would find it convenient to hear the rumours were centring on ReeMara.

ReeMara found her self at the base of a flight of steps, they wound upwards. The hands that had pushed her through the small door had not been unkind. They had kept their voices low, she had not heard people speak like that for so long; it was almost lost in her memory.

When the door was shut the darkness held her, she could hear bare feet on the stones outside move away. The following silence the lead her to feel her way up the winding steps. The day light would have hurt her eyes but she climbed out of the darkness into a new darkness. To know she was in a tower of the Halls of the Pagans did not lift her heavy hart nor did the night's darkness help her, she only had the lights of the city folk to comfort her though the long night.

Two long days and nights went by ReeMara saw no one. Someone had banged on the door below her, but when she had climbed down no one was there. A basket with food and something to drink had been set on the first step for her.

The end of the second day ReeMara was dozing with her back against the wall of the tower looking at the city between her feet when a voice asked her if she would come down.

Three figures stood waiting for her, they had covered them selves with plain gray robes, one was offered to her, she took it without comment.

Four figures moved among the pillars of the pagan hall. ReeMara had not expected to be taken into a small cell near the pagan kitchens! The three men offered her a place at the table, a fish stew was steaming in a pot. Lamps were burning by the time the door was shut.

The three men had taken of their gray robes; their flaxen hair was like hers.

"You are not members of this pagan religion these are not your halls." ReeMara accepted a challis of wine. Still on one spoke: "If no one will speak I would be happier to enjoy this sew in the tower." ReeMara did not know if she was frightened or annoyed or amused! She had the feeling they did not know how to begin to explain why they had abducted her, they must know she was the Empress.

The oldest of the group of three was the first to speak:

"I hope you do not feel mistreated." He did not wait for her to answer. "There have been crimes committed against our people that need addressing."

"The Senate is the place to address you grievances."
ReeMara saw the two younger men were uneasy at her
remark.

"The Senate has those with whom our grievances
stem."
ReeMara put down her whine. She asked for tea, Armnell
sorted out problems with steaming pots of tea, if these
men had a grievance then tea was what she needed not
the mists of wine.

"Men came to our island, our villages were destroyed
those that could not find sanctuary were slaughtered like
cattle, men women and our children. Those of us that
survived the slaughter were not strong enough to change
them. The winter held us, we had to see we had enough
to eat the winter was hard on all of us.

With frozen seas the sun stones could not reach the
beaches we did not have anything left to exchange with
those on the main land." He stopped, ReeMara shook the
gray robe from her head took the cord from her hair freed
her hair from its plat let it fall over her shoulders. The
string of amber the Iron Man had instructed ReeArk to
give her, she placed on the table:

It was not tea the men needed, but a swig of strong
wine!
The men were looking at ReeMara and her flaxen hair
and the string of sun stones on the table.

Was she a daughter of the Islands of the Mists, were
they came from?

Was the woman she spoke of the horror that had lived
in the tree? It was said she had lived with their folk till
the day's light had banished her to the tree. Older folk
had told of her white skin and twisted body when she had
been among them. Her daughters had not looked like her
and her son's had been strong. The old woman had not

accepted food from the villages their offerings had been left unheeded.

Great crows had controlled the skies around the part of the forest where her tree stood.

"Was it you the old woman in the tree sold to the Iron Man? He set fires to burn the forests. His plan of destruction has left the Islands in Mists that could not repair the hurt he has done."

ReeMara broke the silence that had fallen between them:

"I was taken to She-With-The-Sight, cared for by her crows. I hated her and loved her, she told me to leave the island to come to the City on the Seven Hills to revenge the death of my parents. I saw the Iron Man hurt my brother. I had to take refuge in a cave near the beach with a mare and her foal. Leaders of her crow flights and a ferret kept me company through the long winter. I had crossed the channel when the Iron Man set his fires. I saw it burn, I thought I heard her laugh.

I saw The Iron Man's plan of destruction was not just for the Islands in the Mist. With two other horses I found my way through his battle fields to the Citadel in the Cliffs.

I was a child alone, the horses with me and Piper the ferret could not keep me safe from the battles on the grasslands below. The two crows lead a flight of birds that could watch the land below. I never questioned why the warring sides did not attack the Citadel. We were besieged but we lacked nothing. I did not know The Sage was from this city nor did I know she was the sister of She-With-The-Sight!

The scrolls Harron found in the halls behind the Senate show they are of the same family as the Iron Man! The closed fist is to be seen in many places around the city.

ReeMara did not tell them of the pieces of amber She-With-The-Sight had told her to place under the temple, things had started to change once she had dropped them.

"I have let the sward I had intended to use fall to the floor, before you abducted my. I had planned to kill him. So many have died, I wanted to spill his blood in revenge!" she looked at the three men sitting around the table: "Look I have a baby that needs me, I need to get back to her and there are others that will be worrying about me. If you have come here then the way is open from the north. You have not come with an army!? We have all ready taken advantage of his lose of amber; the Island in the Mist has the most powerful amber."

"The Iron Man, Basch, planned to bring the city to its knees by stopping amber getting here. To take the city by depriving it of the amber it needs was part of his revenge.

He had been acquiesced of the murder of his own father. He as a young man was trained in the arts of war. When he and his family where banished from the city for the death of his father.

His father, the Basch had plotted against the old emperor. The old emperor had seen fit to send assigns to deal with a member of the Senate that was undermining his rule.

We know this because the Leader of the Pagans had disused his part with the Leader of the Religious"

CC'raw nodded his head at what Harron was saying. They did not have to say that the leader of the religious had also plaid a part in all of this.

That the new leader of the pagans had been chosen for the width of his girth not his power to lead, he had accepted under the influence of the best wine the city had to offer. No one was willing to take the place of Alois the self made leader of the Pagans, the Iron Man had himself murdered the last leader.

"We cannot just kill the Iron Man. If we should do so the City will fall. There will be war between the lands more will die then we have ever seen before. The land set to waste like we never want to see again!" Harron had been speaking, he paused before he continued:

"The Iron Man had warred against other lands to hold back the trading of amber so he could take control. He has now made this city the center of trading between lands he set against each other. He has opened the city to traders form all over the continent. He even took the sea ports way from the old Emperor control. He did not have to take this city by force as the old emperor feared for his own wealth; he left the city to its own fate."

"The Iron Man, Basch had seen that the old emperor legions were deployed too far away to come to the aid the City on the Seven Hills, he kept them in battles fields and causes that used up the resources the City had. Legions upon legions have been destroyed. People have had to pay a high price for the Iron Man's revenge not knowing why." ReeArk slumped on his stool: "If we kill the Basch then every land we are trading with will want to control this city, each nation will want to rule here! Now do you see why we cannot let you kill the Iron Man?"

Everyone in Armnell's small kitchen was looking at the three men huddled on the bench.

ReeMara knew how they felt; this was why the sward had fallen from her hand. How could she leave this city knowing others would die? Knowing there would not be a place for ReeAmber to grow up in. Knowing that her parents had died for nothing if she let them kill the Iron Man!

It seemed strange to be standing outside the Iron Man's chamber with the three men that had abducted her the last time she was here! She had never wanted to see him again after she had left his chambers. The sward she had taken to kill him was lying on his table. He would not take it and use it against her, of that she was sure. To kill her would create a similar paten that would disrupt the city. Her death would also leave ReeAmber in his hands! But ReeAmber was far too young for him to teach her all he had taught her mother!

As he sat there ReeMara could see he was showing signs of his age, the strain of the battles he had fought were written on his face.

As she stood there she realised she did not know what to say to him! How was she to tell him it was all over? His blood would rule but not from his flesh.

"I cannot call you father, though you have taught me all I know, I cannot call you my leader as I hate what you have done. I have come to take my place." ReeMara saw the men with her draw their swards, she saw ReeArk enter the chamber with his in his hand! She could hear She-With-The-Sight laughing it was louder than her hart beat could hide.

Behind ReeArk were his men. Harron came and stood beside her ReeAmber was in his arms:

"This child is of your blood, the child you wish to reject!"

"You have taught us how to run this city." ReeMara said softly as she took ReeAmber in her arms. "Your death is wanted by many. But your death will destroy everything you have built." ReeMara was shaking; She-With-The-Sight laughter was breaking her self control. She was no longer speaking to the man in front of her. She was speaking to She-With-The-Sight:

"I will not let you do this. Your wish for revenge is more than evil!"

The Iron Man took her sward from the table, was he going to take on everyone in his chamber? Harron saw ReeMara and ReeAmber were out of its reach. He swung the sward in his hand and knocked the sward from the Iron Man's hand, it was no longer pointing at the Iron Man's hart!

ReeMara turned she was feeling sick, the very man she wanted to see dead was the man she must see was kept a live!

She-With-The-Sight scream of betrayal shook her free of her sickness. ReeMara did not want to rule the city, but to let an evil take over, to destroy more than even the Iron Man could. She-With-The-Sight was more evil than he.

ReeMara, her reasons were to keep her child, her family alive! Keep alive those around her.

"I order you my lands men, to protect the life of that man with your lives!" She was pointing at the Iron Man. "I cannot undo what he has done. No more destruction will come from his ill will."

Nor from the will of the woman crying in her head, she would not hear She-With-The-Sight again.

ReeMara hugged ReeAmber to her as she opened her eyes everyman in the Iron Man's chamber had laid their sward at her feet. ReeArk took her arm and Harron guided her into the great hall outside the Iron Man's chamber. At ReeArk's signal men laid their swards on the ground their heads bowed as she past. ReeMara did not understand then the army was hers, the city's to use, all she wanted was a cup of tea, sit in Armnell's kitchen and hug Harron and ReeAmber.

Pederson the oldest of the three men that had abducted her stood in the doorway of the small cell Armnell used as a kitchen. He was twisting his robe in his hands:

"Mam?"

"I am so sorry I ordered you to guard the life of someone you hate!"

"Mam, when his life was ended in the way we had planned my people in the north would not have the possibility to trade. I understand that now. To be able to trade freely will better help the people of the north over come the evil that man has brought upon us.

"Has he?" ReeMara and Pederson turned to look at Harron:

"Don't look so surprised, with his campaign he has removed all that got in his way. By doing so he has also opened the way for nations to trade freely with one another and he has provided a place for fair trading, a city where waterways and roads cross." Harron could tell they were having difficulty in understanding what he was saying: "I do not know if he has realised his campaign of revenge on this city go rid of a system that was chocking and corrupt! Oh yes he has used us! He has used us all!" He took ReeAmber from ReeMara; ReeAmber was not finding his speech as interesting as the others were.

Pederson sank onto the bench; he was younger but had the same stature as the Iron Man. He had come with two other men to assonate a man that had brought death and destruction   to his home lands.

There was no hope to defeat an army he had hoped with two other men to defeat one man. They had planned to smite him down at the next games.

While they had taken sanctuary in the House of the Pagans they had learnt the Iron Man would accept delegations from traders. Should they be offering amber and amber from the northern coasts they would be sure to get an ordinance with him.

"Of cause we have sun stones, amber with us. We brought some of the best the north has to offer." Pederson large hands covered his face: "We had not planned to take you, Mam. But when we saw you leave the halls of the Iron Man, you fitted the description we had of the Empress, with you we knew would be able to get closes to him." He placed his large hands on his knees: "Jan and Sapson are guarding him. Your brother has offered his support."

There was something else on his mind ReeMara could tell.

"So many lives were ended at the point of his swards, many families are lost forever. I cannot look into their faces and say from whom you came. If you say the woman in the tree came from here, she was part of our family, then, I have to except he is also part of the Islands in the Mist, a part of me."

ReeMara patted the island man's hand she knew how strange it felt. To feel how near and yet, how far away their home land was and what connected them!

"I wish I could go back to the Island in the Mist."

"He left nothing, those left have built mounds to mark those that died. New villages have started to collect the sun stones as before. We have built with stone the woodland have suffered from the fries the Iron Man men set before they left."

"There is much we need to do!" Harron broke the silence Pederson and ReeMara shared. He wanted to explain they need to see roads were built to the north, other roads were needed, wagons were able to carry more then the donkey trains could. Oxen were to slow but horses! Landing points by the river could be made to take bigger boats.

ReeMara saw the man that had been so strong, so powerful, writher on his bed, his skin as white as She-With-The-Sight had been. His limbs twisting and contorting like wet wood in a fire. A chalice was spilt on the floor; it was not the powder of amber used for ailing stomachs in the pool of wine!

The Iron Man would die there was nothing anyone could do.

The horror of death was on his face, the horror of war was in his eyes, he could not speak. ReeMara did not know if he wanted forgiveness for his wars, had She-With-The-Sight been in her mind she could have her hate to deal with man's death.

The Iron Man's chamber had been closely guarded, but now as he lay twisting ReeArk and Harron bared the door no one was aloud to enter. Armnell took ReeAmber away this was not a place for a baby. Jan and Sapson stood as broken men watching their charge succumb to the poison.

This cannot be! The man was dieing, his death would mean destruction. ReeMara saw Pederson step forward his sward swing in the air the light from the lamp caught on its blade as it swung down to cut the head from the body of the Iron Man.

"Not even a dog should die like that!"

In the long moments that followed Harron was breathing heavily his mind was full of the consequences of what had just happened. No one must know; no one must know the Iron Man was dead! Not now!

Harron said everything must remain the same no rumour of what had happened in this room was to escape its walls.   ReeMara's lands man he ordered to stay where they were. ReeArk was instructed to see his men did not enter the chambers.

Some one wanted the Iron Man dead, someone would be watching. They must not know their poison had killed. Harron did not suspect anyone in the chamber, had the Iron Man wanted to take his own life he would not have used such a poison, a poison that burnt his sole out. The poison had come from outside the chambers.

Harron turned to Pederson and said:

"Long live the Iron Man. The Iron Man must live! With his robes, with his armour we can keep his image alive. Darken your hair keep you away from those that really knew him. No one at the games will know what has happened here."

Harron knew the way the Iron Man like to create a show, with robes and swards they could shield their substitute.

So good was their substitute that no one suspected there had been a change of leadership, that ReeArk and ReeMara took on more of the duties the Iron Man had seen to was excepted without comment.

ReeArk saw his best men were reasonable for Pederson and his two men. Everything was checked that entered the Iron Man's chambers, their food was prepared by Armnell. Wine flashers were examined to see they had not been tampered with.

Harron thought it was time to investigate who was behind the poisoning of the Iron Man. He thought of the Leader of the Religious, it was unlikely he would have wished for the Iron Man death. He had access to the best amber; he had The Iron Man's amber in his halls. He had an influence over how much amber the Leader of the Pagans could receive.

The new leader of the Pagans only thought of his belly. Who was behind him?

He had been too busy trying to keep ReeMara alive! Protect her and ReeAmber from the Iron Man.

Harron had known there were under ground ways to and from the Iron Man's chambers, just as well he had not told ReeMara or it might have been her sward that had seen to his demise. If others knew of the underground ways to these chambers he did not know, but no one had disturbed the entrances for a long time.

Getting ride of the Iron Man's body was made easer by using the entrance to the underground system. Piper was able to lead the party that carried it to where the Iron Man's family had been laid to rest in the times of the old Emperor. Ironic to think father and son now lay side by side, both had been murdered for their interference in the running of the city.

The City was humming with its usual rumours such as who was trading with whom! The games had given folk new heroes! No one was talking about the death of the Abor. The new Abor's girth had people talking! But Harron did not have any idea as to who was behind the murder of the Iron Man.

Harron now knew it had been a mistake not to listen more closely to what was going on in the city, if he had taken more care to hear what was going on and not trying to influence the rumours may be he would have heard something that could have helped him now.

When Don stood before the door Harron did not know what to make of his wish to see him. Harron had thought of Don was no longer ReeArk's lover! That he had often been seen talking to the murdered Abor did not put Don in a good light.

"I have come to say it is known that the Basch is not the Basch."

"Why is the Basch not the Basch?" Harron could not help asking.

"Because his robes are being clumsily used to dress another!" Was Don's reply, Harron had to admit men that liked men looked at the way they dressed! To be found out over such a simple thing as away someone dressed.

"Don no one will believe you."

"It is rumoured in the Halls of the Pagans that three men came to see the Basch. They asked for sanctuary, three men from the north."

"An interesting theory you have. Don." Harron was trying to think fast. "Why come and tell me?"

"Because I want to better my position."

"We had better look more closely at the Pagan halls and who is running them." Said ReeArk after he had heard Don had been to see Harron: "We must see that ReeMara is not upset not now she is with child."

What they had really wanted was something to cover any rumours coming form the Halls of the Pagans, make any rumours coming from there less believable.

One thing Harron did find out was She-With-The-Sight had seen the rape and murder of her mother. He had found that out when looking among the scrolls in the Halls of Justice. It could explain the hate behind the things She-With-The-Sight had done.

Harron would have liked talk over with ReeMara, she was happy looking after ReeAmber and existed at the through of a new baby, she needed to forget the strain of the last weeks.

ReeArk liked to mother ReeMara as will as Armnell did. Harron was happy to think another child was on its way, he loved ReeAmber so and her mother.

The feature of his children also depended on seeing the city did not fall into the wrong hands. To say they were lonely was not true but their circle of those they could trust was small.

Now that Don had said he knew the Basch was not the Basch, the circle could not get any larger.

Harron was overjoyed to hold the twins in his arms. A little girl sucked at his finger tip, the little boy's hair was dark like his. ReeMara was hugging ReeAmber, the toddler happy to see her mother; she had not been aloud to stay by her mother when the twins were born.

ReeRon was like his farther, ReeMara loved him. ReeAra was the sweetest baby girl ever! Would she have her mother's eyes? They had taken a house on a hill where they could look down onto the city. The walled garden was a safe place for the children Armnell could watch them from her garden kitchen.

CC'raw was perched near the nest his chicks were squabbling for the food he had brought. Three healthy young crows had hatched from the eggs his partner had laid, she did not have a gray head as he had, throw one of his sons did.

CC'raw could understand Harron's pride as he watched his hatchlings.

The horses had returned to the stables they had been before, CC'raw had told them they were needed there, they were to report all they heard, even the gossip among the humans would be of interest to him, the things humans told their horses!

Though no one had spotted the difference between Pederson and the Iron Man, when he appeared in public; CC'raw wanted to know if any differences had been noted in the barracks. The talk was mainly about the Iron Man's loss of reason. The Iron Man had had the habit of keeping a small guard around him, they had lain their swards at ReeMara's feet the day she had been to see the Iron Man.

They had seen, been told insanity had taken the Iron Man; he had pointed the sward at his own belly! ReeArk had instructed the guard not to talk about the Basch's show of insanity. He did not have to tell them they needed to be loyal to the Empress and Emperor, they would risk losing their place in the city; lose the income they were receiving for their services; lose their spoils of war.

The traders were now asking favours from the Emperor and Empress, ReeArk did not think there would be problems arising from Pederson's disguise. The Senate was not disturbed by the Iron Man's reduced attendances. They were gossiping about senate members' affairs and not about the Basch!

ReeArk saw that there was a need for a chairman and he appointed one, that he was one of his men did not seem to bother the senate members or their affairs.

There was gossip was spreading about a strange incident that could not easily be explained. CC'raw heard a group of humans that had been slaves, but too old to be sold to new owners, they had been found dead!

They had washed robes and cloaks for other humans, to provide their daily comforts. The steam from their soapy vats had become a useful guide when flying at night.

When CC'raw had preached above their wash house he noted how the bodies lay twisted, their features distorted. It was not soap that was around their mouths, and their skins had had a white sheen to it. 'Not unlike the body of the Iron Man.' CC'raw had seen the body the day they had laid it to rest near to Iron Man's family volts.

The other point that was disturbing CC'raw was he had seen a flight of crows, when he had approached the wash house, not unusual in the city but they had had gray heads, like him self and one of his hatchling!?

For Harron to openly investigate the death of the Iron Man had not really been possible. How could you ask revelling questions when the victim was striding about the city? The only thing he could find out was the amber powders the Iron Man had used for his indigestion had come from the market.

It had come from the usual trader, who was very proud of the finely marled amber he was selling. He had sold it to the Iron Man in person.

Harron and CC'raw had looked at the man's stall the little packets of amber powder were easy to spot among his wares. It could have been easy to swap a packet of poison. But from what the trader was saying there was no reason to suppose anyone had.

Harron knew amber powder helped grumbling tummies, the Iron Man had mixed it himself; his men were not aloud to asset him with his ailments. No one would use a poison on themselves as it was such devastating way to die, there were poisons that took away your life as you slept.

Every day life had babies and hatchlings voices calling for food, Armnell and ReeMara were running around seeing to this baby's need or that baby's need. The only cool parent was CC'raw, Armnell provided his partner with the best food available for his hatchlings.

CC'raw was not the only one with time on his wings, Trigary had decided to find a hip chick for him self, he was not really interested in trying to find the flight of crows that CC'raw was talking about but they could fly out together.

Trigary and CC'raw had planned not to drop in at the stable where their friends were as the morning offered the best flying thermals over the city and the surrounding land.

"He was the best chariot builder the city had to offer." Red Sun was saying: "His chariots have been used in all the races, they have wind dynamic kick boards; wheals that can be fitted with slash swards! The drivers swear they can keep their balance even in the most difficult turns."

"A racehorse dose not need a chariot." Soul was not as upset as Red sun at the news of the unexpected death of the chariot builder.

"We had pulled one of his chariots, haven't we Corn?"

"They put us to a chariot I have to say it was a dream. I so loved the colour of the harness. But when we got back the stable manager made such a fuss about us pulling it, we made sure we did not stand in the harness lines again, didn't we Bramble?"

"It would have been fun to have another go with such a flash wagon, Bramble shall we try to be harnessed to one again?"

"We could try but I don't like the idea of being harnessed with another pair of horses, they may want to go faster than us, Corn."

"Speed is not everything nowadays, Bramble is right. The young horse of to day thinks speed gets you there the fastest but speed cannot take you the furthest!"

CC'raw was not interested in the chariots but he was interested in hearing their builder had died inexpertly. He and Red Sun left Bramble and Corn whickering on about the problem with young horses to day. Soul would have come too but he had promised to visit the new mares, they came from the north so he had heard.

Trigary did not want to ride on Red Sun's back he took to the air he was hoping to slip away to look for his 'hippy chick', as CC'raw was talking to Red sun he might not notice if he whinged himself away.

The halls of the chariot builder were easy to spot from the sky. Trigary saw crows flying low away from the main building they cast a dark shadow over the courtyard he was thinking about landing in. They had gray heads like CC'raw but he did not think it was strange at the time.

CC'raw and Red Sun stood together in the courtyard of the chariot builder they could see Trigary hovering over them. The dark shadow of a flight of birds past fleetingly over the yard, then they were gone.

They could not see if there was anyone that they could have called suspicious. The chariot builder's men could be recognized by their short robes they stood around not able to work after learning their old master lay dead.

The Religious Leader had sent two of his monks they wore their habits their heads bent in pray. The Leader of the Pagans had sent more humans than the Religious Leader, they were placing emerges in odd corners and waving incense about the place.

The human's face was distorted so was the body, the embalmer had not been able to lay the body out flat. CC'raw shuddered when he saw the human's white skin tone.

CC'raw pecked Red Sun, there was a figure almost a shadow leaving the courtyard. Moment they moved to follow it had gone. It was no good asking Trigary to look out for it as he was busy. The great eagle was stopping another bird from dropping out of the sky! They were spiralling down with a speed would be difficult to control when landing. Their landing was not fitting for such a solemn moment. The chariot builder's household were disturbed by the two birds decent. Red Sun and CC'raw had to forget trying to catch a shadow. They had to rescue Trigary and the bird he had gone to so much trouble to save from curtain death; they now had to be saved from the brooms that were about to beat them for trying to disturb the dead.

Back in Armnell's villa kitchen Trigary was in as need of comfort as did the bedraggled eagle he had rescued, she was not the youngest of birds.

"I have never seen a human die like that before! I have been with him from my hatching." The tea Armnell had given her made the unhappy eagle feel a little better: "I have never seen a human die like that!"

"Can you tell us what happened to your master today?" CC'raw decided to ask. Armnell smoothed the bird's feathers to encourage her to drink and reassure her.

"He had complained about the men not working, the wood he had been sent not being of the usual quality he had expected, he complained that his belly hurt him. They gave him his red wine. I have never seen a man die like that before!" she took a drink of the tea: "When he needed me I was more interested in seeing off those prying crows."

She was falling asleep she put her head under her wing, just what Armnell had planned. Trigary was also nodding off when he said:

"I saw a flight of crows, now I come to mention it; they had gray heads like yours." He too was asleep. It irritated CC'raw that he could not question him.

"The chariot builder was one of the few that did not leave the city with the Old Emperor. I knew him he was often in the bath house. Why did you and Trigary go to his halls?"

CC'raw could only shrug, he did not say why, everyone at the stables had been upset at hearing of the unexpected death of the chariot builder. Armnell gave him some of her tea, he was soon asleep. His last thought was of the gray headed flight of crows.

Now Armnell's kitchen had three birds sitting in it. There was a lot to do with the twins and their mother and ReeAmber needed her too. And CC'raw's hatchlings were asking for more food every day! Armnell did not really have time for Trigary and his new friend.

CC'raw was happy to see Trigary was infatuated by the older eagle, she knew so much about the city before the old emperor had left. When he had asked her why the chariot builder had not left with the Old Emperor? She had said, he had said. 'The old emperor did not need chariots he needed wagons for his goods. That he would be better off staying in the city; he only needed to wait till a new order came. They would need chariots to show of their prowess.' He had been right!

Armnell was always telling everyone not to except food or drink from anyone other than her. CC'raw was glad he was not the only one to be suspicious, but of what were they suspicious of neither of them knew.

CC'raw had discovered that Pederson and his two men had brought the mares Soul had been interested in meeting the day the chariot builder had died. That they came from herds from the north did not mean as much as the gray headed crows he has seen did. He was a gray headed crow and he came from the Cliff Citadel, his parents had come from the Island in the Mist. He had a hatchling, his head was also gray.

Armnell broke into his thoughts by asking him what was on his mind. They were watching Trigary fussing over the eagle he had brought back to her kitchen. The twins and ReeAmber were with ReeMara for an afternoon nap. CC'raw did not answer as Harron came into the kitchen with dust on his robe. Harron would not talk about the tunnel he was constructing when there was a stranger in the kitchen, even if the stranger was Trigary's friend Minny.

The tunnel was to take them from their villa to the old tunnels under the city. Harron had not wanted a villa that was marked on any of the scrolls he had found. He had made sure their villa was not presented on any of the older scrolls. Harron was mindful of everything that was going on in the city. He and Piper had decided that they could not be the only ones to know about the underground ways under the city, to have a private entrance that only they knew about would be to their advantage.

CC'raw was telling Armnell about the other gray headed crows that had been seen in the city. Harron had been used to seeing gray headed crows all his life, black headed crows were something that belonged to the city and the cliffs. He did not understand why CC'raw was so disturbed by them. But when they started to talk about the strange deaths of the wash slaves and the chariot builder he too was disturbed by their remarks.

"I saw the wash slaves' bodies their bodies looked similar to the Iron Man's. That is where I first saw the flight of gray headed crows."

"The chariot builder had that strange white sheen on his skin." Trigary remarked.

"And there was a flight of Gray headed crows there too!"

"Iron Man died from a horrible poison."

"It was the same poison that killed the wash slaves and the chariot builder!"

Harron and Piper sat with Armnell at her kitchen table with CC'raw. Trigary was perched next to Minny. Minny was not the hippy chick he had set out to find but she was happy to accept his offers of food.

"We had better tell Pederson and Jan, Sapson."

"Don should also be brought into our confidence." Harron saw everyone in the kitchen look startled: "He has seen it is to his advantage not to spread rumours. He saw the changes in the Iron Man."

"Is that why you gave him an impotent assignment!?" ReeMara stood in the door with a giggling baby in her arms; ReeAra did not want an afternoon nap. ReeMara had been listening to their conversation.

"He wanted to benefit from his theory." Harron said.

"I thought he wanted to be near me." ReeArk said from behind ReeMara and his niece. He took the giggling baby from ReeMara.

"It would be better to have him where we can keep an eye on him and in his office he can inform us of any deaths were the victims deaths match those we have been discussing." Harron pointed out.

"I will see that Pederson, Jan and Sapson know." ReeArk would have said more but Armnell interrupted him:

"They had better move into the villa with us." Armnell could not put her finger on what was bothering her. The slaves she had not known but they had been in the city as long as she had, they had belonged to a trader that had bought and sold slaves for those looking for pleasure. He had sold her! It was all so long ago.

"My Master liked his pleasures; he would often go to those halls when his wife was out of town. He liked to go to a trader that brought interesting slaves into the city."

Minny could not be talking about the same trader as Armnell thinking about!?

"He left the city when the Old Emperor did. I suppose he did not think a new order would need such pleasures as he had to offer."

"May be he knew they would find out he had stolen the people he sold." Remarked Armnell, CC'raw and Armnell gave each other a knowing look.

"I will bring the Iron Man to my chambers no one will think it strange if Basch moves into the chambers of Baschi." ReeArk made everyone jump.

"But Don will!" Piper remarked.

"He dose not have to move in there as well dose he!?" ReeMara did not like the idea. Don had sat in Armnell's kitchen table thinking ReeMara and ReeArk were lovers!

Don had also been there to see if a baby was to be expected.

ReeMara had to giggle when she thought about it, Don was ReeArk's lover, or had been.

"If it is not just a strange coincidence there have been unexplained deaths in the city, then we have to consider Pederson is in danger." Trust Harron to think like that thought ReeMara, but she had to agree with him. They need to take better care of Pederson.

"The twins loved it! ReeAmber sat up front as if she was the driver; I know ReeMara was holding on to her!" Corn could not control his enthusiasm. "Armnell twisted their robes so she could hold onto both toddlers, I have always wondered why they had robes with tails, all you have to do is put your hoof on it and you have your runaway toddler!"

"It was long time ago when we were foals. I have forgotten what fun it is to gallop about the world kike your hooves in the air."

"Bramble, we cannot do that when we drive out with the children!"

"No Corn we cannot! But we can enjoy taking them about town. The harness maker has made a lovely harness we look so smart. The young three crows sitting on the back of the coach dos give us a certain style."

"Bramble, they seem to have grown every time we see them!"

"Corn that is what our mares said about us!"

"Long time ago, Bramble."

"Not so long ago or we would forgotten Corn."

"Are you two going to twitter on all day?" CC'raw wanted to know. He was proud of his three sons even though they had not been so easy to keep an eye on when they want to learn to fly. He and Lady could not rap a robe around them!

Just to take hold of the flapping tail when they got into difficulty when they were trying out different flying movements, it would have saved many broken feathers and bruised prides!

CC'raw's flight of crows sat behind their father. CC'raw was caught in the same mood as Corn and Bramble, he remembered when he was a fledging flying over the Cliff Citadel:

"Are you going to stand there remembering how it was when you were young, or are you going to take this coach back to the barracks and stop blocking the road?"

"Since when have you become so bossy CC'raw?" The two horses wanted to know.

"Since I have a flight of youngsters to knock sense into!"

ReeRon was marching on his toddler's legs out of the door from the villa; he had got rid of his robe. Corn could not see the child from where he stood with Bramble. Arms out stretched ready to cling on to Corn's hind leg he would have done if CC'gray had not flown down and pusher the toddler on to his bottom. Corn did not kick kids CC'gray knew but he may have reacted in surprise.

The wail from ReeRon brought ReeMara to the door, when she saw ReeRon sitting and crying in the street she did not have to ask what had happened:

"I am sure Corn and Bramble will take us out again." She gave the two horses a pat before she picked up ReeRon. ReeRon twisted his fingers in Corn's mane only to cry louder when he was told to let go.

"It is a hard live when you are young Bramble."

"You could be right there Corn!"

"It would be good to have eyes at the back of your head Bramble."

"Ah! You don't need that when you have a good young crow with you."

CC'raw pride showed as he took off, his three sons rose into the air with him.

Someone had seen the incident in the street outside the villa. Someone had hidden in the shadow of the wall.

Pederson with Jan and Sapson took the villa next to Harron and ReeMara; it was more comfortable than ReeArk's chambers. ReeArk made sure that there was a guard present at all times. It was particle to have guards around both houses.

Pederson and his two friends were like uncles to the children, squeals of fun could often be heard coming from the garden. Armnell from her kitchen could keep an eye on all their fun.

The three men from the Islands of the Mist enjoyed her cooking so much that new robes had to be ordered for them all! Corn and Bramble would take ReeMara and Armnell and the children to the markets for food and house hold goods and when the weather was good out into the fields for pick necks with their three uncles and their guards.

The weather was so good it became to hot in the city's streets, most folk chose to leave the city for a day or two or at least send their older children out into the fields to help with making hay or bringing in ripe crops.

Bramble and Corn loved the idea to take the children to see the Sage. ReeAmber was about the same age as ReeMara when she first arrived at the Cliff Citadel. To ReeMara to make such a journey seemed imposable, it had taken her years to get to the city now Harron and Pederson were saying it would only take a few weeks! If the summer was going to stay so hot then it would be a good idea. ReeMara so wanted to go to the Cliff Citadel to see The Sage and Mattie, most of all to see Beana! Beana had been the best mother to her, she so wanted Beana to see her children.

ReeArk decided to stay in the city as head of its army he could not go and leave his men nor could he leave the traders and the Senate even if he was only a figure head.

Piper had also decided to stay in the city. She did not want to make a long trip again; her red coat had taken on a salt and pepper look, were the years taking their toll?

Harron decided he would go with ReeMara and the children as Soul said he wished to see his mother.

The only one that did not want to leave the city was CC'raw he did not want stop his three sons going with ReeMara, it would do them good to see how a well disciplined flight worked. Not that they were bad lads only they did squabble over who flew next to who! C'raw and Cam would be happy to keep an eye on their first fledgling's squabbles!

In one such squabble the three youngsters had had to make an emergence landing. They landed in a hep on top of a stall selling ground corn! In the cloud of flour their dark feathers had turned white, the flour trader's wife had screamed and then fainted because she thought they were ghosts! They had screamed because to them she looked like a ghost through the falling white flour!

Those in the market had not been able to set things right they were laughing too much that and the fact flour made everyone cough. His three sons had walked away together their heads down trying not to be seen!

CC'raw also did not want to leave his Lady as she was broody was she thinking of nesting again?

CC'raw gave Trigary strict instructions on looking after ReeMara and the children and he was to keep a close eye on his three sons.

Armnell was going with the group CC'raw and his Lady liked her cooking so much, Armnell had to tell him not to worry she had found someone to see to ReeArk's and Pederson's needs.

ReeMara had thought the tripe would be tedious with the children but it was not, they loved to see everything as they travelled in the wagon Corn and Bramble had chosen for the trip, ReeAmber pretended she was their driver.

Soul and Harron, Jan and Sapson with their mares from the north ran races with the guards ReeArk had insisted should accompany them.

The bath was full the room was ringing with happy voices! Soap and water splashed very where! The three young crows were enjoying the fun. Harron was throwing soap bubbles at anyone that moved! That Beana should come into the bathroom at the moment he had thrown the biggest bubbles in the air, Harron could not have known, Beana was covered in them and there were more on their way.

Beana could not scold anyone not when she saw ReeMara emerge out of the steam with a wriggling ReeRon in her arms. ReeAmber and ReeAra were gathering bubbles to throw over their father. The only dry person was Trigary, he was watching from the safety of the window sill.

Armnell was happy she was not sharing the same bathroom! It was so nice to have someone prepare a bath for her. The bubbles in her bath were hers she was not going to throw them at anyone. Just to sink into them and listen to the happy screams of laughter was just right for her. Not to have to see to visitors and their horses, cook large delicious meats for everyone. But when Beana cries of joy mixed with ReeMara's sobs, Armnell had to get out of her bath to see everyone was all right. Tears of happiness ran down ReeMara's cheeks, ReeAmber and ReeAra were hugging Beana as if they knew her all their life. ReeRon ran to Armnell to pull her into their bath room Harron had to grab a towel quickly!

Three wet crows were trying to walk out without being rubbed dry by large towels and willing hands.

There was more laughter and tears of joy, this time the steam was from Mattie's tea pot. The bubbles in the bathroom had made the floor wet but no one cared! Everyone was sitting around Mattie's kitchen table; the very table ReeMara and Harron laid out the Iron Man's battles.

Mattie had got a little bottle of something out to celebrate the occasion.

When The Sage came back from her trip on the Grass Land below the Cliff Citadel she found Mattie's kitchen was full of strangers and they were having a party! She was about to get cross with the visitors for making so much noise, till she saw ReeMara in the middle of the mayhem Beana hugging her to her, three children were in their arms.

It could not be Harron! He was hugging a crow and a mug of Mattie's tea. The other men The Sage did not know but they were obviously in ReeMara and Harron's party. So must the woman with dark skin, she also was hugging a crow and a mug of Mattie's tea!

Laughter and tears was again spilling and filling Mattie's kitchen, The Sage was in the middle being hugged and kissed by ReeMara and the children; ReeMara and Harron's children!
There was so much to tell but for now The Sage had her arms full of children and young crows!

The horses were also in the middle of the heard that lived at the Citadel, they had to tell their tales, over and over again, where they had set their hooves?
Soul found he had half brothers and sisters, his mother would not leave his side.
Youngsters gathered around Corn and Bramble waiting to hear every word they had to say.
"We were treated like heroes, Corn!" Bramble said later.
"We are heroes, Bramble!"
"Soul had all the mares looking at him, Corn."
"He always dose Bramble."
"From the look in their eyes it is more than tales they want to hear, Corn."
"But we are still heroes, Bramble."
"Yes Corn, we are heroes!"

The Sage office high in the cliffs seemed smaller than ReeMara remembered it to be the last time she was there, Trigary filled the window!
Mattie's tea steamed in mugs on the table, this time the tea did not have the something extra from one of Mattie's little bottles! The other places were filled by Harron and The Sage.

Harron was telling The Sage of their adventures. For ReeMara it was as if she had never been away, for once in her life it was as if everything was as it should be.

The Sage was beginning to understand what her sister had had in mind; she was both fascinated and horrified at what Harron had to tell her. Could ReeMara and the Iron Man and herself have the same forefathers!? What had it meant to She-With-The-Sight to see the murder of their mother? Had she really made such plans of revenge? The Iron Man had taken ReeArk!

The Iron Man was the old Basch's son, she had known him as a scruffy boy in the street; he had lead armies that had defeated legion upon legion of the old Emperor's regime!?

He was not responsible for the banishment of their family; his father had plotted against the old emperor.

"I have a job for you both while you are here." The Sage always had jobs for everyone ReeMara had been was hoping for a holiday: "You have so much to tell, you should write it down, just as you remember it, just as you have told me.

The last time you were in this office I never dreamed you would be sitting here telling of such events. Then, I could not even guess what would await you once you left the safety of the Cliff Citadel. Now I do not wonder why the Citadel was not attacked by the armies. The Legions could not have helped us. It was not long after you both left the Tented Army disappeared up into the mountains. Now leave me." She put her arms around both her children, yes they were both her children, their story had brought her much sorrow and great joy. She needed time to think through all they had said.

The City was hot, so hot that CC'raw had found himself a perch on one of the towers of the Halls of the Religious. His wings he had let hang beside him so his feathers to catch any breeze.

It was not the heat that was the city's real problem the lack of water was. It had not rained for so long that the city's wells were running dry. The canalization needed water as parts of the city were beginning to smell.

ReeArk has set his men the task of bring water to the city, but it would never be enough to rinse out the drains, the humans took their washing to the river. The water level was so low there were many new beaches and dried mud banks.

Traders had to bring their goods to the higher banks manually, slaves had to struggle with the heavy loads; the only thing that was good was the price of male slaves went up.

CC'raw knew the city had another problem. He should have been the only gray headed crow in town. He had seen the flight of gray headed crows leave a dried mud bank. When he had dropped down to see what they had found interesting. CC'raw had discovered the bodies of slaves that must have gone there to wash off the day's dirt. Twisted and contorted like the bodies he had seen before, he had shivered at the sight of their whitened skin. They had been young the other victims had been much older. The smell of stale water in the cracked pool had made him reach.

ReeArk had ordered their bodies to be burnt. ReeArk had hoped that would stop any rumours but as everyone was grumbling about the heat to have the death of the young slaves to ponder over was a distraction.

There must be a connection between the gray headed crows and the mysterious deaths. CC'raw was glad his son was with ReeMara and Harron. He was the only gray head crow. He could try to join their flight. His lady was not happy at his plan she was sitting on their brood waiting for their hatchlings. Minny had just laid her first egg and was so excited.

ReeArk was too busy to listen to CC'raw's idea he had to concentrate his men to deal with the city's water problem.

Pederson was busy with his duties as the Iron Man even if he was only to be seen in the background. Armnell had found a really good cook, but he was a bit temperamental though he had appointed his lover to take responsibility for any meals the hatchlings would need.

Don was ready to listen to CC'raw but he could not see there was a connection between the deaths of the older humans and the young slaves. Even when CC'raw pointed out they had the same look of death on them.

'Water that had been standing in this heat would not be safe to drink without boiling it first. It really was the responsibility of their owner to see they had safe drinking water.' Was what Don had said, CC'raw asked him to keep a list of any deaths that showed any of the same symptoms!

CC'raw could not try to join the flight of gray headed crows when they cruising, they would notice a stranger. His only chance was when they were in full flight. But he had not seen them for days!

The water shortage was the cause of more than the drains stinking. Outside the old city wall were huts used for keeping newly arrived slaves. It was little more than a makeshift camp, their water wells were the first to dry up. The slave traders should be accountable for the water their busyness need, but the traders were more worried about their private households. Their orders for water did not take in the need of their slaves.

Maybe the sickness came from a newly arrived slave, or the lack of water meant they did not have enough to wash with!

Don told CC'raw the people in the camps were dying; they had suffered from sickness and dehydration.

CC'raw was glad to hear the Senate had taken his advice when he had said. 'The dead should be burnt, notices should be posted that attention to cleanliness should not be neglected during the water shortage. Humans should boil water be for use.' Armnell had often scolded ReeMara when she first was nursing ReeAmber when she did not make sure everything around the baby was clean.

The Senate went one step further they ordered the doors in the city wall should be closed. To stop anyone from the sicken camps entering the older part of the city.

Not only were the humans sick but now they were cut off! No one thought to see they had water, food, wood for a fire!

When CC'raw pointed this out to ReeArk he had the Senate ordered the traders should provide their slaves with the basic things humans need.

Don and ReeArk stood in front of stores meant for the camp, the traders had said they did not have men enough to bring it to where those in the camps could get it!

"I also do not have enough men to move all of this. They are fully employed with bring in water." ReeArk was worried something had to be done.

"The traders are putting in complaints their goods are perishing. They want compensation for their losses!" Don showed ReeArk a scroll he had been given.

"They don't want much do they!? They bring their slaves here; tell us to see to their needs so they can make a fat profit."

ReeArk was beginning to get annoyed; it was not his busyness to see to the slave traders' demands: "Tell them it is not my place to see to their goods, if they are worried about going into the camp, they should through these supplies over the wall."

CC'raw sat on the ledge in the wall to watch the owners of the sick humans through much need supplies down to the camp. They shouted orders to anyone able to walk.

They were to make fires.

They were to burn the dead.

They were to boil water they were going to drink.

They were to cook their food.

CC'raw noted most of the humans did not understand what was being said. There wasn't anyone that could show them. He had taught his sons the importance of keeping mind and feathers clean, 'let them get out of balance, you could not fly.'

Feathers that were not regularly preened did not keep you in flight.

"The heat, the lack of water and now the rats! That rats, could be bring the sickness into the city, the slaves are confined to the camp. Maybe we should require the traders to compensate those who are sick!"

CC'raw had heard a member of the Senate say. The sickness in the slave camps had breached the city walls. Markets traders have not stopped bring their goods to the markets as they were doing good busyness with their sickness relief mixtures.' It had been noticed the very young were at risk, so were the elderly.

CC'raw was feeling he was not of any use to man or beast as he sat on his perch trying to catch a cooling breeze. Lady had her feathers full with two fledglings they were dark headed like her, CC'raw was pleased to see.

If there were gray headed crows up to no good over the city he was happy he was the only one, what did he mean? Don had asked. CC'raw had not known what to say.

What had the senator said? 'He had hoped the dark cloud that had crossed his window was rain. He had found the bodies of twisted contorted rats on the ground. The other senator had suggested he should not drink so much wine!

CC'raw had wanted to question the senator, questions like did they have gray heads, but the senator was looking deeply into another bottle of wine.

CC'raw head was full of clouds if only it would rain! He did not have time to contemplate the weather as a flight of crows were flying low over the west wall. They past under the tower perch where CC'raw was sitting, he stopped feeling sorry for himself; he only had to drop down and join their tail wing!

CC'raw had not expected to be flying over the east wall down to the sandbank where the young slaves' bodies had been found!

He did not want to be stopped as an intruder. As they passed over the sand bank CC'raw picked up a dead and twisted rat by its tail, he carried it in his foot as the others did. The flight then swooped upwards turned back to go over the city.

The idea to drop dead rats into the city's streets would never have occurred to CC'raw. A squawk came from the bird before him as an arrow pierced his side. He and his rat thudded on the ground. Children were running to see what they had shot. CC'raw could not warn them.

The flight had not stopped to see to a fallen bird they flew over the east wall back to the sand bank.

"Don't take any part of a rat in your beak." Was the order CC'raw heard. "Don't preen your feathers with the foot you carried a rat, when we have returned from the next drop, bathe in fresh sand."

"He says every time." said a board crow not far from where CC'raw was.

"It is his responsibility." CC'raw heard another say.

"Why can we not eat the rats we catch, all this flying around makes me hungry."

"You want to eat something that will twist you till you die!?"

"Don't think of it, I have to explain to her why we have lost one of our flight members, a human fledging is one thing but a stupid bird is another."

"We could eat them before they twist!"

"Silly bird and risk angering her!"

Who was 'her' who was she they were talking about? CC'raw could not ask. He was a crow but he did not speak the same way as they did. He understood them but the moment he open his beak they would know he was not one of them.

CC'raw could not see who or what through other dead rats onto the sand bank, he was in the air with a dead rat's tail held in his foot like the others.

"I was able to spiral away after the next drop." CC'raw was perching on the edge of ReeArk's window sill.

"We have to find ways to get more water into the city, the number of sick is increasing, though the number of deaths is not. If that is not enough the city has to deal with a plague of live rats that could or could not be bringing the sickness into our walls and now you say a flight of crows are dropping dead rats all over the place!? If you were one of my men I would put you in a closed cell!"

"If I had not been part of a flight that was dropping rats over the city I would be able to agree with you. The rats have died the same way as the Iron Man, just look at this one."

ReeArk could not dinghy the rat's dead body did have the same look as the Basch, to say it had a whitish tone to its skin was difficult it had a black coat, he did not want to touch it. When complaints started to flood the Senate he had to take CC'raw seriously.

The crows had been seen dropping dead rats on the city, not everyone would be drinking too much wine.

When the weather changed and rain started to fall hopes in the city were high, the smell changed from extremely unpleasant to dank and wet! Now the Religious were complaining that the Pagans had over done their request for rain. Though how humans' dancing could make the skies produce rain was beyond CC'raw. He was also sure pray, was also not a way to control the weather.

If it was not for the plague of live rats life could get back to normal. Normal, it was not normal to have gray headed crows dropping dead rats all over the place!

For CC'raw it was a difficult time. He could not freely fly about the city. If he did he had to avoid being hit by stones or arrows. Humans are strange they made bets as to how many gray head crows could be knocked out of the sky, rats and all!

CC'raw was in Don's office with ReeArk, matters of the city were being disused.

"You will never believe how many petitions have been made to sell rat poison!" Don told ReeArk and CC'raw. "I would never have though that rat skin would be of interest to traders or that other cities find it a luxury! There must be rats in every city! I wonder what make the rats from here so desirable?"

CC'raw wanted to say it must be the colour but he had just put his head in Don's ink well, the door to the office had burst open, augury men were advancing towards the table CC'raw was sitting on. One had a gray headed crow swing upside down in his hand and in the other he had its dead rat! This was not a good moment to be gray headed crow. CC'raw sat there with black ink dripping from his feathers.

If the men that had burst into Don's office had not been so augury they might have spotted the drops of ink on the large table between them and Don.

ReeArk was amused to see the traders slam the dead rat on the table next to CC'raw:

"Gentlemen we have problems with the waterways, the drains need attention after being for so long dry. The sickness is still causing problems to folk in the city. Rats are running around the streets and now you want my men to shoot crows?"

ReeArk turned to look out of the window. The city looked clean and shiny after a welcome shower of rain.

"Birds like this are dropping rats, dead rats into the streets. I have seen it with my own eyes." The man shook the poor bird. CC'raw felt sorry for it. He would have said something but this was not the moment to draw attention to himself; not with ink dripping from his feathers.

Don put wine on the table he filled the glasses full, CC'raw was glad to see the augury men draw up seats.

They wanted the City Office to do something the Senate had sent them here.

CC'raw would have sent them back to the Senate. The gray headed crow was cowering in the corner. CC'raw would have advised it to put its head in the ink pot, he had taken a sip of ReeArk's wine to get the taste of ink out of his mouth, he might have taken another he was not sure! One thing he was sure of the room was going round. He walked across the table right under the men's noses his inky foot prints crossed the partition they had brought from the Senate. They did not seem to mind he was patted as he pasted, one man that kept saying he had never seen rats falling out of the sky. More wine found its way into his glass he seemed happy, more wine filled everyone else's.

When CC'raw fell of the table he did not expect to find another man asleep on the floor! The sound of discussion above him spurred him towards the bedraggled crow in the corner. The dead rat shot past his head just before he could reach the by now terrified bird. CC'raw could not at that moment think why the terrified crow though he was a devil. It could have been the trail the ink made on the floor or the dead rat thumping the wall above his head.

CC'raw wanted to get this sorry crow out of Don's office so he could interrogate him before one of the drunken men thought to kill it.

"I hope it is the wine I think I can see two crows!" CC'raw heard a man say, between hic ups.

"No brother, there are more! And there are flying rats!" Someone found it funny, the thought of flying rats.

"That is why we have come here to complain about flying rats."

"You will be telling me crows are dropping dead rats on the people of the city next!" It was a voice CC'raw knew.

"Strange things do happen you know."

"Not in this city." said the voice CC'raw knew, CC'raw was close to the door, it was opened for him by the first man that had spoken.

"Thank you." CC'raw said as he dragged the confused crow the augury men had brought with them behind him.

"My mum always told me to open doors for others." CC'raw heard from the other side of the door the man hic up again, there was a muffled bump it must have been the man slumping to the floor.

ReeArk told him later the other men wanted to come after the big crows that had just left the room. But the man's body blocked the door way.

CC'raw was having to push his prisoner into the safety of the water closet if he had chosen the men's loo it would have been all right, but when one of men needed to relive himself he took the wrong door. He found himself in the water closet reserved for ladies.

The scream CC'raw gave would not have convinced anyone that had not had a glass of wine; that this was the ladies connivance, but it was good enough to convince the man now tripping over himself trying to get out!

The bird next to CC'raw fainted. A lady who wanted to use the convenience fainted at the sight of two crows the nasty man must have left in the ladies room. The man turned to help her but when he tried to support she screamed only to faint again. CC'raw dragged his fainted crow behind him.

"Just pull her by her hair, women just love it!" CC'raw said as he past the pair on the floor.

CC'raw was glad ReeArk picked him and the unconscious crow up when they were in the hall outside. ReeArk did not say anything as he took them to his chambers. CC'raw was not sure why he and ReeArk were laughing so much now the door was closed, no one would see the tears in their eyes.

Trying to interrogate the young crow was not easy. It was so frightened. CC'raw was not sure of what or who it was frightened of.

'Don't poison the bird. I crow swear to do my duty to the flight. I crow swear to her!'

"He kept saying he would swear to her." CC'raw told ReeArk. "I don't understand what he means. Really he is too young to be a full member of a flight. He cannot even tell me where he was hatched."

"To put him through more stress by asking him more questions will only bring the same results. When I had to get information from men like him, I saw they were well feed, slowly got their confidence. When I say slowly it can take months. To cut off his head will not bring us anything!"

As the door opened and Pederson and Piper entered the chamber the poor crow had sunk into the corner nearest to him.

"Who wants to cut heads of today?" Pederson saw the desperate crow cowering in the corner. "He looks like one of the Crows from the Island in the Mist, But, CC'raw you said you were hatched it the Cliff Citadel. I thought gray headed crows only were to be found in the north!" Pederson did not stop to hear what CC'raw say:

"Piper and I have been in the drains. We took a couple of your men with me, ReeArk. Piper is the best expert we have on rats!"

ReeArk looked at Piper; Pederson could be right, what better person to discuss the rat problem with then a ferret!

"I have been so occupied with rats above ground I have not given time to looking at the problem from underground."

ReeArk invited Piper to come and sit on his table next to CC'raw. The crow in the corner was trying not to be a frighten crow in a corner, he was making his way to the unguarded door.

ReeArk had to smile when Pederson shouted with his best Iron Man's voice at the crow who was trying to disappear through the door.

"Bring that crow to me." Pederson had been practising not only to look like the original Iron Man but to sound like him, since ReeMara and Harron were away he had taken on some of his 'old' duties.

He must not be doing to badly from the smile on ReeArk's face. The smile faded when the two men carrying the crow entered the room, they smelt! 'Odour of Drains' Piper called it. The two men had been ordered to stay with the Iron Man they had not had a chance to bath. They were grateful when ReeArk dismissed them, the young crow was not. He was back in his corner.

"I like him." Pederson said: "He reminds me of my home lands. Has he been able to tell you anything?"

"'Don't poison the bird. I crow swear to do my duty to the flight. I crow swear to her.' Have been the only words we can try to make sense of. Do they mean any think to you?" Pederson was not a loud to answer Piper did:

"The rats that they have been dropping have died from the same poison used on the Iron Man. Of that I am sure."

"The slaves from the wash house and those I found on the sand bank died also from that poison! As did the coach builder." Added CC'raw: "He said, don't poison the bird. He is talking about poison!? The rats I dropped with the flight he has sworn to; were poisoned. The only thing that dos' not make sense to me is who is her? What is her? He has sworn to!?"

It was no good asking him now as he was lying on his back with his legs in the air, trying to look dead. He might have got away with it if he could keep his legs still, they were shacking.

"What are we going to do with him?" Pederson went over to the crow's corner: "We could send him back to his flight."
The legs trembled so much the bird had twist to sit on them. Everyone was surprised to see him faint! Pederson left him, to recover in his corner:

"Funny bird! Talking of funny, the rats I saw, we saw." Peterson turned wards Piper: "When we were looking at the drains in the northern quarter, the live rats we saw; were eating the dead rats people have thrown there."

"Why did you not tell us before?" CC'raw wanted to know.

"We don't have fainting crows in our chambers every day."

"We were shocked and puzzled when we saw rats eating the rats that have been thrown all over the city." Piper cleared her throat. "Pederson and I were planning to build a force of ferrets to tackle the problem of the city's rodents. But I cannot ask a fellow ferret to risk their life. The live rats we saw eating the dead rats started to show symptoms of poisoning!"

"Did you see what happened to them!?" ReeArk was interested to hear what Piper had to say.

"We had to leave the drain we observed this incident in, as the air was becoming unsuitable for the humans with me." Piper looked almost smug, ferrets could move about in drains where humans could not.

"You said you would not ask another ferret to risk their life when it came to destroying rodents. Would you ask them to inform us as to where they are? It might help us to know where they are!" ReeArk did not yet know what he really wanted to know. Piper was looking at him; one thing was clear they did need to know what was happening under the city.

Piper took to the idea of organizing the city's ferrets with pride. CC'raw was proud to organize feathered friends to watch the skies. Flying rats or live rats they did need to know where they were. The humans and ferrets were told not to touch the rats, if they felt threatened to beat them with brooms.

"I cannot say, you say, you can see the twins shear knowledge, if one is hurt the other one will cry even if they are not in the same room. I have not felt her presents for many years, but thoughts come unbidden into my head I thought they were my thoughts. I too was disturbed by our mother's death." The Sage drew breath: "She-With-The-Sight's hate comes from the rape our mother, and that our mother was murdered to stop her from speaking out against Basch's father. He was the one that took our mother. That is why it was said Basch was made responsible for his father's death. The truth behind the old Basch's death was he had schemed against the old Emperor."

"The scroll I found did not say who had committed the act against your mother." Harron was trying to understand what The Sage was suggesting. Was The Sage trying to tell him that She-With-The-Sight might not be dead, that the thoughts and feelings ReeMara had could be likened to the twines?

"Is She-With-The-Sight with the sight is still alive?"

The Sage was after all She-With-The-Sight's twin sister. He had often watched ReeRon and ReeAra, even when they were only playing one knew what the other wanted! But ReeMara and She-With-The-Sight were not twins!

"She-With-The-Sight has gone to so much trouble to see her blood line was mixed with the fresh blood from the northern islands, she was not to know it was ReeMara and not ReeArk she should have given to Basch. She must have hoped for twins as they have the senses she can best use."

"ReeMara said she felt she was being driven to murder the Iron Man. We both felt our lives were being controlled, decisions we were making were to bring us to that moment!

Why should you listen to someone that must be dead!? But if She-With-The-Sight were still alive! ReeMara must have thought she had'madness' in her head!

When we left this office we never thought we would be able to come here again. To be here with our own children so they can see where we were when we were children. I see, if you are right we have to do something." Harron did not know if he was making sense or not. The Sage nodded.

"It is the twins she wants!" They said both together it was a horrible realisation she wants the twines.

"She thinks the twins that will revenge you both. If She controllers the twins from her blood, your blood line she can revenge what has been done to you." Harron did not know if he was right, he and The Sage were staring at each other.

"Sage do you know- can you feel where she is?"

"No. It is her strongest emotions I feel."

"Does she know where ReeMara is?"

"Her plan was to send her to the city."

"Have you asked ReeMara if she can say where she is?"

"No I have not asked her that, ReeMara said she would not listen to She-With-The-Sight. I thought then, when she was confronting the Iron Man, she wanted to explain why she had not used her sward on him. Did ReeMara want to explain that to..." Harron wanted to ask another question, The Sage could see he was trying to put a question into words:

"If she can put thoughts into your and ReeMara's minds can you put a thought in hers?"

The Sage did not know how to answer, if she could answer. She-With-The-Sight was her twin sister, like ReeRon and ReeAra it was between them:

"It must be so; I have never questioned it before."

They both jumped when they saw ReeMara standing in the way with a tray of tea from Mattie kitchen. From the way she looked they could not tell how long she had been standing there. But when she spoke they knew she had heard everything they had said:

"We must see she does not set her hands on the twins! What will she make them do if she does!?" ReeMara put the tea on The Sage's table she was shacking. "They are only children."

"We were only children."

"We must stop her. I will stop her!" Harron had seen her augury, happy and sad, but when she stood like that there was nothing you could say to make her change her mind.

"Harron you have been asking if The Sage or I can say where she is. No I cannot feel where she is, I know where she is! She-With-The-Sight is in the city." ReeMara was walking towards the door, Harron stopped her.

"Who killed the Iron Man, I did not, even though I went there to do so. Pederson took his head off because he was dying of some poison." She looked Harron straight in the eye: "Who would want him dead? She did. So where is she? She is in the City!?" Harron understood; he wanted to say something ReeMara stopped him by saying:

"The twins must stay here! They must be protected from her. She is in the city. We must get her before she can do any more harm."

"There were similar deaths after his." Harron pointed out.

"To kill others have stopped you from thinking he was the only target." The Sage said: "I have been wondering why she should want to kill those slaves; they might have made fun of her when she was a child. The coach builder may have looked at her they way men look at women, I do not know. She may have wanted to tell you she was in the city."

Plans had to be made, ReeMara and Harron wanted to get back to the city as quickly as possible. The children would stay with Beana and Armnell, though they needed Armnell as she knew the city so will. ReeMara would not think of leaving her children without Armnell even though she knew they loved Beana as she did.

Fast horses were needed Soul said it would be better if he and another stallion were to carry Harron and ReeMara. Bramble and Corn wanted to protest till ReeMara said she wanted them to stay at the Citadel to make sure no one got into the Cliff Citadel through the herds of horses. They were to get to know all herd members note from where they came from and tell Mattie of any they found suspicious. The guards ReeArk had insisted accompany them were ordered to stay in the Cliff Citadel; their duty was to The Sage and the safety of the children.

Harron had wondered why ReeMara had insisted Bramble and Corn stay with the herds of the Cliff Citadel, Trigary had pointed out She-With-The-Sight could not fly! ReeMara had not wanted to say, there were younger and faster horses.

Trigary did not wait to hear if ReeMara thought he was to old he was staying with her and Harron.

She need to come out of the dark, put fine robes on if she was to start rumours in the City. She knew the real Basch was dead. It might be time to kill his imposter! Give the blame to an ambitious Empress. Blame her! The Empress has used poison to gain the city.

When the fire had spread over the island, flames had licked at her home. Her skin still carried scars of its hunger. She had had to let the seasons turn, spring and summer, autumn and winter. How many times must the seasons have turned before she had set forth? The child she had chosen needed many seasons to be able to do as she was bidden.

From above she looked like the charred trunk of the tree she was clinging to. She had waited till the sun had warmed the sea its colder water would kill her.

Crows hang in the wind over the human drifting on the log, they did not dare speak they could not understand why she should want to leave the island. Not now she had the island to herself. All this had been her wish! How were they to see to her needs? How were they to see to her wants?

Humans had disrupted the life on the other side of the sea. Villages had been burnt out like those on the island. Hard winters had seen to the remains of war, only wolves had profiteered by the carnage.

How was she going to get to the place she wanted? The humans they saw were struggling to survive; a burnt woman unable to walk on her twisted limbs would not receive their pity. If pity was offered they would have given her, her death.

The blind ox had been a stroke of luck! The gray headed crow had seen the birds hanging above the thicket waiting for the animal to die. He was entangled in brambles; there was no flesh on his bones, perhaps that was why the humans had not slaughter him!

The crow called for his flight to get the animal out from the grasp of the thorns. She was pleased with the crow's find; the ox would server her porpoise well. He could carrier her, but to sit on him hurt her so. The crows were not able to tie to her to branches for him to pull. The best was to cling to his horns let him pull her. Her voice and their viscous beaks guided his cloven hooves.

Where battles had been fought the land were strewn with its waste. The small two wheeled wagon they found could be hung on the ox, the wagon's flat boards could hold the crippled woman. They let the stream wash earth onto the covering rags to protect her body in the wagon.

Her need for sustenance was covered by the plants the land had to offer. The plants she kept with her did not make the wagon smell any better nor did the bones she hung over its sides. Any humans that saw them did not stop them. The ox with the circling crows smelt of death, the bundle of rags were of no interest.

Now she was here! The time it had taken her to get here did not matter to her. The word on the street was halls were to be opened, halls where the sick could go. She could bring her plants to good use. She would be able to more about the city without being clanged, get close to those she wanted to watch!

One of those halls had offered her rest; her crows had found shelter in its high pliers. They had slaughtered the ox and burnt his carcass; they had feared he carried disease. She knew he was not to be feared, but he had served his purpose.

The city offered her darkness to walk in, tunnels to crawl in; temples to hide in. She knew the city well she had played here when her body was young.

She could not know all that had happened to the city, but she saw the girl was the Empress.

The body she had found where it had been hidden had made her lips twist into a smile. She did not have to guess whose it was. The poison had struck where she had wanted.

ReeMara had shut her out of her hart, if she had not done so she could have felt her presents in the city. To be like a snake that could spit its venom where it will, pleased her, he was not the only one to die. Others have deserved to taste her revenge!

The city would know what destruction meant, her sister did not want such revenge, but she did. Their family had had to leave; they had been banished from the city for something he had done. She had waited long years to see the man that had done her family so much harm body rot in the catacombs.

Now all she wanted see was all he had made lay broken, and see the city destroyed as thanks for such harm he had caused. He had been reasonable for their mother's death. To be banished for his father's murder was not a fitting punishment.

He had wanted the boy but she had known the girl was the stronger. The girl had placed the amber where she had been told, the eye of his soul lay with the blood red piece its horse could gallop in the summer tree's shadows.

The girl carried a child in her arms, another in her belly they would play their part in destroying the city.

The girl has had twins! She wanted the children, twins like her and her sister. The crows did not have the sense to take the babies just pick them up and bring them to her. She would destroy the girl and take the twins!

ReeArk had not expected to see ReeMara and Harron in his chambers that morning. Nor had he expected to hear them say She-With-The-Sight was in the city! How could she be? To him she was just a story! Now she was real and a threat too! As if he did not have enough problems in the city.

ReeArk had told them about the problems the city had been troubled with while they were away. Piper and CC'raw were the experts to ask about the rats. Live rats were still a problem they were living in the drains, they would come out to steal food. People had been told to burn their rubbish not to leave anything a rat would be interested in the open. If the rats had brought in the sickness it was still recommended to cook all foods.

ReeMara and Harron seemed to be pleased when ReeArk told them that CC'raw was coordinating other birds to watch for any movement from gray headed crows carrying dead rats.

Piper was in charge of the city ferrets keeping an eye on what live rats were doing underground.

ReeMara was glad the children were at the Citadel, there had not been a water shortage or sickness. CC'raw had told them there had been other humans that had suffered from a poison. ReeMara was sure it must be She-With-The-Sight's poison the rats were being killed with it. Did she want to poison the whole city?

Before they got everyone together ReeMara wanted to find chambers for Jan and Sapson they had made the fast ride with Harron and herself. The young stallions and Soul were being taken care off in the stables. ReeMara did not want to go back to their villa, the children were not there! Nor was Armnell, who was going to cook for them?

Pederson had all the answers:

"Firstly these chambers are large enough for all of us. Secondly, the cook Armnell found has not managed to shrink me belly. And thirdly if we are to find She-With-The-Sight
We need to keep together. This place is easy to guard, ReeArk's men are all around us. A little old lady will find it hard to get past them."

ReeMara did not like to think what the little old lady might or might not find hard to do. She never thought of She-With-The-Sight as a little old lady.

ReeArk counselled they should gather in his chambers, this was not a matter for the Senate. She-With-The-Sight was their private problem even though she was using the city.

The crow, Crow Rat that had been brought into Don's office had followed CC'raw wherever he went, he considered himself CC'raw number two. CC'raw's three older suns were at the Cliff Citadel, they were never to let the children out of their sight. His two new fledglings had black heads like their mother. CC'raw he was confident his Lady would see to their early training. So to have Crow Rat to assist him was useful.

There were things they had to do. One was to keep an eye on the sand bank; CC'raw wanted to know when dead rats were thrown there. Whoever was throwing out dead rats started to throw them out at night, he could not see in the dark who or what was putting the rats on the sand bank. And it was not every morning the gray headed crows found dead rats to drop into the streets of the city.

City owls took watch for CC'raw, till one silly bird eat a dead rat and died the same horrible way as it the rat. CC'raw could understand they did not want any harm to come to their chicks. Trigary would have to take up the post.

The other thing CC'raw had to do find out why the rats were staying in the city. That they had come into the city when water and food were short, he could understand, but now the humans were more careful with their rubbish surely the rats would want to return to the open fields they must have come from. Don still had to deal with complaints from humans about the rats; he also had to sort through their patents for rat traps.

CC'raw was feeling torn between his Lady and their fledglings and the problems of coordinating the birds of the city. It had been some days since he had heard of any gray headed crows flying over the city dropping the poisoned rats.

Piper had reported that rats were still entering the city! The Senate had been persuaded to build defences against the rats. Youths were being rewarded for the amount of live rats they could catch. If they found dead twisted rats they were to be burnt. But that was all the Senate would do, they felt it was up to the city's armies to deal with the plague.

CC'raw sat staring down at the sand bank Crow Rat was perched next to him. Piper was exploring the sand bank below them, there was nothing to be seen that could help discover who could be throwing poisoned rats here. There was not a bird in the sky only two friendly crows watching her.

There was an opening under a crumbling wall, sand had been built up to hide it; an animal could enter the underground here. Piper beckoned to CC'raw to drop down:

"Look there is an entry here! I do not want to investigate alone."

"You think we should go in and investigate?" CC'raw did not like the look of the hole she was showing him. CC'raw turned he almost tripped over Crow Rat as he was standing close behind him: "Crow Rat I want you to stay on guard till the sun goes down, if by then we have not returned you are to tell Harron where we have gone." He could see the young crow was not happy about staying near the sand bank from where he's flight had been ordered to pick up the dead rats to drop on the city. "Should a flight of crows land here use a perch better suited to cave nesting birds as a safe observation post. Do not get muddled up with them, we know what they will do, what we need to find out how they are being supplied."

Crow Rat knew why they were here he did not want to even think of entering the hole on the wall. If he had to stay here he would use that cave nesting perch before anyone could turn up! CC'raw looked back to see the youngster's head looking out of the entrance of the cave:

"Funny young crow that one, but I think we can rely on him!" CC'raw said as he followed Piper into the darkness.

It was dark and dank water dripped down the walls the ground was also wet; the air did not smell fresh once they had followed the tunnel's twists and turns. He was not worried they would get lost as Piper was the best expert he could be with; even so this was not his element. How long they had walked in what to him was a maze of tunnels CC'raw did not know. What was guiding Piper he also did not know, she was following something he did not understand. It was not that he could not sense what she sensed. There was the sound of activity, of movement! The floor of the tunnel did not show resent disturbance, rats had been using this way.

They never would have expected to see what they saw when the tunnel brought them over a large cave like hall. Rats were milling around on the ground below them. These rats were moving strangely, round and round. CC'raw had never seen anything like it! He looked at Piper if she was shocked she did not show it. They were both shocked when a loud sound stopped the rats from moving. Something larger than a rat was coming down a tunnel on the other side of the hall.

CC'raw could not see what it was. Piper indicated to him to press himself against their tunnel's floor, they must not be seen. Piper stole glances at what was happening below, she saw rats stamping on each, killing each other to get the food being thrown to them.

It had been quite for sometime Piper dared to look again at what was happening on the halls floor. Those rats that were still alive were priest against the outer walls. One side of the hall the ground had been cleared of the rat's bodies. The sound of movement made Piper move, she grabbed CC'raw by his wing he was pulling her half running back down the way they had come.

They were moving faster that whatever was come behind them. Whatever was following them was carrying something.

CC'raw and Piper burst out of the hole Crow Rat was watching from his observation point above the sand bank. He would have gone down to greet them, but they were looking for places to hide!

When Crow Rat saw what they were hiding from, he only let his eyes pier out of his observation point.

Rats, large rats were placing dead rats on the sand bank! They were large mindless, blind to what they were doing!

From where Crow Rat was he could see a cloud of crows flying over the wall. He had seen the dark mass before; he had had to promise to it! He could not look at it then he could not look at it now.

Crow Rat's eyes could not be seen anymore looking from the cave nesting perch CC'raw had to pull him out. Piper used her tail to fan air into his face.

"It is all right now they have gone!" CC'raw wanted to reassure the fainted bird. "We saw what went on the sand bank." Piper stopped him from saying any more:

"We need to get to ReeArk's chambers as soon as possible!"

"They were killing each other to get to the food that was being offered them!" Everyone in ReeArk's chamber was looking at Piper as if she was mad.

"No, no we both saw what was happing in the hall we found from the sand bank. And Crow Rat can confirm what happened on the sand bank." CC'raw was standing next to the ferret that was trying to tell those in the chamber what they had seen:

"We had to lay flat on the tunnel floor we could not take the risk of being seen. From where we were that was what we saw!"

"We must go in there and destroy the rats nest!" Pederson rose from his seat. His hand was on his sward!

"You would need a legion to deal with so many, how would we get enough humans into the tunnel, the tunnels are too small for most humans." Piper pointed out.

"The rats are being destroyed." Harron stood up. "The point is why? Why kill, why poison rats? Why drop them on the city?

Harron put scrolls of maps and plans of the city on the table in front of everyone. ReeArk had ordered more large tables to be brought to his chamber for Harron's scrolls.

"Here is the sand bank. It is on the east side of the city, from what your birds are saying dead birds are being dropped everywhere." Harron was more that puzzled. "You could just drop the poison into the water channels if you wanted to poison the population. But she is not. She has a plan. What does she want to do?"

Don had not report the deaths of guests at a wedding because he did not think their deaths were connected to the poisoned rats. But when he had taken a statement from the remaining family he had the idea to ask them what they had done with the dead rats they found.

An old man had said he feed those he had found to the pigs. The very pigs that were being fattened for the betrothal! Other guests that had survived had spoken of fights that had broken out at the fest. There was still wine that had not been drunk. Don had to go and find the remaining guests as Harron wanted to know, had they been ill afterwards, had they eaten the fest's meat?

The report came from the south of the city that dogs had attacked each other. Dogs that were trained to guard sheep! They could not be stopped from tearing each other apart.

When the report came in that a company of young army requites had behaved in a similar way as the dogs a week before, their commanders could not stop them from killing, they had blindly slaughtered each other till there was only one man left and he had turned his sward on himself.

ReeMara was trying to understand what could be going on in She-With-The-Sight mind, that she must be under the city was clear to her, but, the city's underground was a large place, almost a world of its own! Harron's maps and plans were not helping her to think what She-With-The-Sight could be planning. That she was planning something was clear to her. Why the rats? The rats had become aggressive, eaten each other! The guests at the wedding had become aggressive! And now the new requites had behaved like the dogs!

It was not ReeMara's habit to attend the Senate but that evening she decided she would attended the Senate as they were planning to debate the strange happenings in the city. To have gladiators tear each other apart was what the people wanted, that was mostly show! To have normal folk destroying each other was not something a trading city needed.

ReeMara and Jon and Pederson stood in the outer hall where food and drink was waiting for the Senate members to refresh themselves. The two men wondered why she did not walk into the debate that was nosily taking place in the senate hall. They saw ReeMara take the meat from the platter give it to a dog that was glad to have a snack, if ReeMara was right he would not be so grateful if he knew why she had given him such luxury food his master would not think to give him. Another piece she gave to another dog he was more interested in going to sleep in a corner. In the same corner was a cook he was holding his belly, his eyes were red.

"Take him back to his kitchen." ReeMara said, but before they could he burped, and then again loudly there was a smell of wine in the air. Jon and Pederson tried to take hold of him, they almost dropped him.

ReeMara did not really know what to do with the man. He could not stay in the outer hall where the food for the senators   was waiting for them. The cook started to sing between his burps. With the cook sing and burping the three of them did not see the dog from the corner help himself to a plate of meet. The other dog saw no one was looking and copied the first.

That the hapless cook was there to see the senators' dogs did not steal from the table became clear later. But the dogs were not interested in the food they were eyeing each other, they were dogs that were bred for hunting, that they were fighting so viscously surprised everyone watching.

The owners of the dogs could not get them apart. Snarling, teeth holding onto whatever they could; tearing clothing or flesh, the two senators had to stand back nothing was going to stop them, the dogs did not respond to any commands.

Jon and Pederson drew their swards advised the gathered senators to stand back.

ReeMara did not want to look at the dogs torn and battered bodies. She saw from the corner of her eye a senator put a piece of meat into his mouth, she slapped him so hard he spat the piece of meat on the floor! By way of an apology ReeMara said: "The dogs were eating that!" he did not understand what she meant. His figure was well rounded did she mean he should not eat the dogs food? He was even more confused to see the Empress gather up all the dishes with meat on them order the drunken cook to help her take them to the kitchens.

The head cook was distressed to see the Empress carrying dishes and his undercook look as if he was drunk walked behind her with more plates shaking in his hands. The two armed men running to join the Empress had blood on their swards. ReeMara calmly said:

"I want you to get all of meat you have prepared for tonight's senate dining table. No man or beast must eat it. And get this fool out of my sight."

The head cook was almost bent over double as he tried to comply with the Empress' demands all at once. He did not know what to worry over first, his bad cook or the Empress not liking his dishes. No one had ever complained and he had been in these kitchens ever sense the new order had taken over. He was glad the Empress turn when her consort entered his kitchen. Harron did not please him though! He was asking so many questions!

"I want to know what meat this is and where you got it, who slaughtered it, where it was slaughtered. What it was feed with?"

How he, the cook was supposed to know all the answers to the questions Harron ask he did not know! It was his job to cook dishes for his senators to enjoy and to oversee the right wines were survived. He shank away to find out all he had been asked.

Harron grabbed another man in a cooks robe.

"This is lamb?" The man nodded.

"This is duck?" The man nodded.

"This is beef?" The man nodded.

"This meat is from swine." The man nodded, he was still nodding when Harron pushed the first three plates of meat off the table; he was still nodding as the platters rolled away.

"This is the only animal that eats meat?" Harron wanted to know, needed to know.

The Master of Cooks and the Master from the Slaughterhouse were standing in front of ReeMara and Harron, they had been ordered to present themselves in ReeArk's chambers.

"Is the swine the only animal that eats meat?" Harron repeated the question he had asked in the Senate's kitchen.

The two masters looked at each other. ReeMara thought they were going to look at each all afternoon. It was the master from the slaughterhouse that spoke first:

"Swine eat all organic matter."

Harron had to think how he was going to ask so they could answer his questions:

"I want to know if other animals eat meat. I want to know if we humans eat their flesh?"

"Some people eat cat, the cat eats meat." said the Master Cook, Harron could see they still did not understand what he wanted.

"Dogs are bread that people eat; the silk traders call them Cho Cho."

"Don't they eat cats as well!?"

"Rat meat is used to feed slaves."

ReeMara drew in her breath before she said:

"We fear the rats that have been poisoned. Whatever the poison is, it kills the rat. If that rat is eaten by another rat it can become aggressive. So aggressive it kills another!"

"That is what we believe happened to the dogs in the Senate dining hall last night. They had eaten meat, that we know; ReeMara gave it to them It could have been human blood staining the marble floor. We have to keep the Senators safe.

We have to warn the people not to eat any rat. Destroy any animal that could have been feed rat meat, in the first instant you cannot tell if it has been contaminated."

The Master of Cooks face went pale he was listing in his head all the luxury meats there were that the senators asked for. Crocodile, it was fed with meat like rat! Lion, all the big cats! The bear eats meat too, snakes! In fact the rat was an important part of the food change. To make people aware of the poisoned rats was not going to be easy! The Master of Cooks and the Master of slaughter the house left to instruct their underlings.

It was Don that suggested if rat meat was so important people should bread them themselves. He thought the idea was so good he disappeared to organise the preparation of licenses.

"That is what this city really needs is licenses to bread rats!" Harron snorted.

"It might not be such a bad idea everyone will be made aware of the rat problem!" ReeMara soothed him. Harron Looked at her:

"You know we might not have a rat problem."

"What do you mean?"

"The rats Piper and CC'raw saw were destroying each other. She-With-Sight must know how the poison works. She knows what effect it has taken directly. She has dropped dead rats all over the city knowing a dog would eat one or a pig would be thrown one. You heard the Master of Cooks, say rats are given to the slaves to eat. The wedding guests Don told me had died; they had been fighting with each other. Then the new recruits! You saw the dogs in the senate fight each other to the death or would have done if Jon and Sapson had not used their swards. What she wants is to turn man on man! Here in the city!"

Harron and ReeMara held each other, the very thought was so horrible. Thank goodness their children were safe with The Sage.

Piper and other ferrets were keeping an eye on was happening underground. They did not go where rats were gathering they did not want to be caught up in their fighting. They were hopeful Harron was right about the rats destroying themselves.

CC'raw was interested as to where the flight of crows could be. The flight of gray headed crows had not been seen for sometime over the city. They could not have all been shot down by the bowmen. He had to stay well out of the way or stick his head in an ink pot! He was glad his gray headed son was with his human's children.

The flight of gray headed crows must be in She-With-The-Sight's control. If they really knew, but then how could they? A flight member did not question he's leader. If they had sworn allegiance to her!

They had to be somewhere? A flight did not just disappear.

The city did not have the old traditions of flights of crows as the Island in the Mist or the Cliff Citadel. CC'raw could go and ask other birds, there were pigeons and swallows but they were more interested in seeing to their fledglings than reporting on the whereabouts of a flight of gray headed crows.

Eagles would have been useful but they insisted on staying with their humans. Trigary had come out to help CC'raw, but had only grumbled about the weather.

CC'raw and Crow Rat took to the skies; there was a warm thermal they were enjoying. Apart from the young swallows that were using the gently thermals to practices their flying skills, there was nothing to see from the sky.

They had been often to the sand bank in hope of seeing the flight there. They had perched on towers on columns on pillars but not seen a single crow black or gray headed!

They had not thought to go to where the city humans though their rubbish. Not since Harron had said the rubbish should be burnt.

The smoke did not have a pleasant smell, it drifted this way and that, as the breeze played with it. At first the dark shapes were not recognisable, not as birds. The breeze cleared the smoke away from eight slumped figures, their feathers bedraggled. They must have tried to darken their heads with the black coals from the rubbish burning around them, it made them look rejected and old. They did not move when CC'raw and Crow Rat joined them. They did not even raze their heads to look at CC'raw when he spoke to them:

"Where is your mistress?"

"What mistress? We have not mistress."

"Where are your leaders?" CC'raw signalled to Crow Rat not speak. "Where are the other members of your flight?"

"What you see is all that is left! She did not protect her flight she sent us to the points of the arrows aimed at us. She did not want to offer her flight safety, she told us to eat her rats!"

Crow Rat shook as he turned to CC'raw. CC'raw was also shocked at what the bedraggled birds had said.

ReeMara was surprised to see ten crows sitting in a row on the table in the kitchen in the chambers ReeArk were using. That CC'raw and Crow Rat had control of the strange group did not help in the next instance, it was a blur of black feathers! An angry cook had charged into his kitchen with a broom in his hands, he was not interested in sweeping the floor!

Now there were ten disgruntled birds sitting in a row on the wall outside. ReeMara had to calm the crows and the cook; she helped him remove black feathers from his table while he muttered, 'birds did not have a place in an artist kitchen.'

The crows were happy to eat the food ReeMara had been able to persuade ReeArk's cook to give them. She missed Armnell and Mattie they would never have made a fuss about birds being in their kitchens. Now she missed her children!

The eight new gray headed crows looked better for the meal they had eaten. CC'raw and Crow Rat told ReeMara where they had found them and what they had said, and how difficult the flight from the smoking rubbish dump had been to persuade to come with them. Firstly the birds were not in good flying condition due to being undernourished. Secondly humans had tried to knock them out off the air. Thirdly they were nervous to fly over the City!

ReeMara knew the crows had been members of She-With-The-Sight's flight. They could not be left unprotected in a city that had suffered from She-With-The-Sight plans. But what was she to do with them? When CC'raw suggested they should go to the Citadel the very idea upset her! Her children were there! She-With-The-Sight must not know where they are. She-With-The-Sight had managed to get to the city she would somehow get to the twins. That she had misused the birds did not mean they would not tell her where the twins were. From the look of them thankfully it would be sometime before they could fly that distance.

CC'raw's Lady was the one that took control of the bedraggled flight her last fledglings were ready for more serious flying instruction which CC'raw could see too while she saw to the rehabilitation of the undernourished group. While they had gray heads they were to stay in the chambers garden. ReeMara could blacken their heads as she had done for CC'raw and Crow Rat. Not that would help much as crows in genial were not popular in the city at the moment.

ReeMara had not wanted spend the morning sorting out crow problems, she had wanted to look at Harron's scrolls, those that showed the underground ways and known catacombs. Known catacombs! There could be underground ways that had not been marked on any scroll. The Sage had told ReeMara, as children they had played in the catacombs.

ReeMara thought She-With-The-Sight would go to places she knew as a child. The Sage had spoken of the catacomb her family had used. It was where they had laid the Iron Man's body. ReeMara had been to see if anyone was living there, no one had disturbed the dust for sometime only a thighbone that had become wedged between a flat stone and the wall was left of the body they had laid there.

ReeMara held the bone in her hands, to look at it made her think of the man it had belonged to. He had destroyed so much, had he been used as she had been by She-With-The-Sight?

ReeMara had spent so much of her live wishing to end the Iron Man's life. How was she going to find away to stop She-With-The-Sight from ever finding her children? They must never be used as she had been. Was she becoming like She-With-The-Sight? No she only wanted to protect her children.

The new crows had not been able to tell her much. They had been ordered to land on the sand bank so they could pick up the dead rats their flight leader seemed to know where they were to drop them; it had been hot and tiring work.

They had been fledged since their flight had arrived in the city, so they could only tell what their elders had said about how 'She' had come from the north to the city. It was strange to think She-With-The-Sight had managed to get a flight of crows to bring her to the City on the Seven Hills!

ReeMara could only stare at the scrolls Harron had used before, there was a little mark that showed where the tunnel he had built from their villa and the underground ways was. Harron wanted away out from their villa that no one other than they knew.

ReeArk broke into her thoughts:

"The Senate wish to hold a meeting, I think we should attend." More ReeArk would not say.

The hum of voices stilled as ReeMara and ReeArk entered the great hall. When a senator from the east side of the city spoke ReeMara was shocked:

"The question is who is responsible for the crows that have been dropping dead rats into the city? It is bad enough to be plagued with live rats!" The Senator from the east did not mention the live rats had come to the city due to the lack of rain fall on the land. The sickness had been attributed to the rats. Harron could have been right when he thought the lack of water had lead to water or food becoming contaminated. He had been the one that had suggested people pay more attention to cleaning their things, to boil their drinking water etc.

Somehow ReeMara felt the Senate were looking at her as if she could answer their questions.

"Then we were told to burn the dead rats not to feed them to any animal we would choose to eat!" The Senator was interrupted by a senator from the other side of the city.

"Should we be looking for the person that has ordered dead rats to drop inside our walls?"

"It is known that the Empress has a gray headed crow in her house hold."

ReeMara did not say there were another nine sitting with CC'raw on the garden wall behind ReeArk's chambers.

"Fights have lead to many deaths around the city."

"Animal against animal!"

"Man against man!"

"Who would want such a thing?"

ReeMara could not answer the question.

"Senators, my I have your attention? Whoever is responsible for rats being dropped on the city at this time I cannot tell! I hope it will reassure to know the plague of rats is under control. The poison that has killed the rats; those that were dropped onto the city, have been digested by live rats; those that have been attributed to carrying the sickness. Once they became contaminated, they turn on each other."

Harron pursed to see if his explanation was being accepted, no one seemed to want to interrupt:

"The problem we now face is if we consume meat that has been contaminated with the same poison we too can become aggressive."

A senator remarked if they were to find the owner of the flight of gray headed crows they would know who had brought such grief on the city's people. ReeMara felt sick she did not own the ten birds on the kitchen wall but most people would think they were hers.

In the tunnel below the Senate She-With-The-Sight together with her twin sister had listened to many debates. Her laugher could have been heard if anyone had been listing. The girl was being accused of bring harm to the city! Whispering words into recipient ears was bringing its rewards. Once she had the twins she could control the city or take revenge on it, just as she wished!

The debater argued that if the gray headed crows were dropping rats, dead rats that were being consumed by the plague of live rats, then it was fair to argue that the gray headed crows were protecting the city citizens. There had been a warning about eating meat that had been contaminated. The Empress and Emperor had seen that the city people had been informed of the suspected contamination.

ReeMara sat in the chamber's kitchen she realized just how close she had come to being accused of being a threat to the people of the city! Empress or not, her rank would not have saved her from the people's anger. What good would she be to her children if the Senate had made another decision!?
Harron put his hand on her shoulder:
"They are our children ReeMara. We will see they are all right." For such a rumour to reach the Senate there must be a person that has spoken it! ReeMara did not need reminding.
"It is time we turn our attention to finding She-With-The-Sight. She is trying to turn the city against us. She will want to use our children."

"Use the special contact twins have." ReeMara could not forget.

"You said you have not heard She-With-The-Sight since the day you when to kill the Iron Man." Harron did not want to upset ReeMara. Had ReeAmber been a boy the Iron Man might not have rejected her. The sward he had razed had been to kill her not to celebrate her birth. Trigary had swept the endangered baby out of harm's way.

The Senate had thought it was one of the Iron Man's planned shows; their cheers had allowed them to leave the Senate and escape the Iron Man's anger:

"ReeMara it is not just twins that understand someone else's thoughts, we understand each other we don't have to use words." ReeMara knew he was trying to tell her something.

"You have many times said she was inside your head, that you would not listen to her anymore." Harron took ReeMara in his arms. "If we are going to find her you should listen to her." ReeMara was shaking:

"If I listen to her she can hear me. She will know where our children are!"

"Not if you don't let her. Not if you don't open your thoughts to her. The Sage told me there were thoughts she did not share with her sister, you don't have to share your thoughts with her. Just listen to her. The children are in our thoughts, you don't worry about them they are safe with The Sage and Bean, you just miss them."

"There is not day not a moment where I don't miss them I think about them all the time." Tears of love were running down her cheeks. ReeMara looked up into Harron's eyes to see he too had tears in his eyes.

Are! She is there! Why does she want hear me now!? I was good enough for her then! She listened to me. The tree was her home I cared for her as if she was my child. Without me she would not be where she is now! She is part of me.

The darkness was holding her; the old tunnels were her home. She had played here. The girl would not find her here.

She wanted the girl to find her! The twins must belong to her. Unlike her sister she could control the girl. Her sister had not been able to control the girl. The girl had known not to make a child with her brother. The twins were hers not the girl's. The girl had no right to take the twins out of the city.

"Did you think I would not know when there had been changes made in the tunnels? I have known my way about the city long before you were born." The dirty robe did not disguise the crippled woman it only hide her tortured skin from Pederson's eyes:

"Have you come to see my rats? It is sad to see them die."

Pederson would have dismissed the woman as mad but there was something about her. The large crow sitting beside her did not take his eyes off him. The crow as waiting for him to move; just a twitch of his fingers and the crow would have known he wanted to use his sword.

"You think you can take the place of Basch's son?" Pederson was surprised to be asked such a question from an old woman that must be living under the old city.

"Killing him was such a pleasure." She said.

"I did not take pleasure in killing a man that was suffering."

"Is there is no pleasure in killing rats?"

"There is no pleasure in killing."

"Basch's son took pleasure in killing."

"He destroyed my village, killed my people. I came to the city to take revenge on him."

"My poison destroyed your pleasure!"

"My sword was swifter."

"You are an imposter."

"A harmless imposter." Pederson did not know what the woman wanted. She spoke with words his people used. She was the woman that had lived in the tree! His hand griped the hilt of his sword.

"He is swifter than your sword." The crow did not turn to look at the woman: "He will be the last thing you will see. He can have your eyes, I will kill you later."

Pederson had to let his sword slide back into is scabbard. The vile woman was moving back into the dark.

"She said I was an imposter, she would kill me later. She knows her way around under the city!" Pederson slumped in his seat.

The kitchen in ReeArk's chambers was full and the cook was not happy that people wanted to disuse the latest happenings while he was preparing meals. And now they all wanted tea!

Harron turned to ReeMara, why had 'she' sent ReeArk two dead rats? The rats had been found on his bed with the necklace of white amber the Iron Man had given ReeMara when he had joined to ReeArk.

ReeMara turned the piece of amber she had found in the Iron Man's amber halls. How had She-With-The-Sight had got it? ReeMara could not think when she had last seen it.

The white smooth oval stones with their smoky or hints of island mist had been with her in the villa, she could not remember if Armnell had taken them with them when they had taken the children to... when the city had become so hot.

The piece she had in her hand was whatever colour ReeMara wanted but it did not help her remember where she had last seen the white amber necklace.

This had started on a beach, a beach where amber had been thrown in the shore by the sea. What did She-With-The-Sight want to say? Why take the necklace? Why the dead rats on ReeArk's bed? In the darkness of the tunnels she could move wherever she wanted. She could not find the twins, they were not here.

CC'raw was not surprised to hear She-With-The-Sight had a large flight leader to protect her. The eight he and Crow Rat had found were discreetly watching from the chambers garden wall. If 'she' had kept a flight leader he would be a bird they would have to watch out for. It had been to dark in the tunnel Pederson had not been able to say if the leaders head was gray.

Piper wanted to know why Pederson had been alone in the   tunnels. He did not answer her question.

The bird, the flight leader was spotted flying low over the city. He seemed to be looking for something, someone, but from the way he was moving he was not in a hurry. When he did land he was on a wall that guarded the stables.

The flight leader found the horses he was looking for. They were the horse that had accompanied the Empress when she first came to the city. She had grown into an empress but these horses had become old. They would not be taking anyone quickly away from the city. 'She' wanted to turn the man she had spoken to in the tunnel; he would cut down anyone wishing to leave the city. 'She' would offer him all he desired.

'She' had told him she had made the Iron Man; she after all had made him the flight leader. One crow to rule them all, one crow to take all!

He could peck out the eyes of the horses, all the horses! One crow against all! As one crow he could do nothing, she had seen to that! What was a flight leader without a flight to lead? He had been blind, not those around him he had listened to what she had said. He would guard her as she wished but now his eyes were open, she needed his protection; she needed him.

He turned from the stables, he lifted into the air. He was seen by a ferret, was her coat was white with age? The ferret could not get him even if she tried.

Piper watched the crow she did not need to be told who he was, CC'raw had been informed. It was up to him to follow She-With-The-Sight's decoy by air.

ReeArk had been moved from his rooms, after they had found two dead rats and ReeMara's necklace.

She-With-The-Sight may wish to show she had her hand over the city. Mice that did not nest in the same place each night were not so easy to catch.

"You saw her crow drop down behind the Senate. There is an entrance to the catacombs there." said Harron: "She is under the Senate."

Pederson could understand why Harron would think she would place herself under there.

ReeArk knew the ways under the Senate well he had often used them when he was with the Iron Man. She-With-The-Sight would know he was familiar with their darkness. No she was not resting there, of that he was sure.

ReeMara did not allow herself to think about her twins, her children. Harron had said 'You don't have to open your mind to She-With-The-Sight, but to hear what she is thinking could help us.' The twins, she wanted the twins, the twins were the power she wanted not ReeArk, nor her.

ReeMara looked around the chamber, CC'raw and Piper, the men from her home land in the mists. Harron was standing next to ReeArk. She was turning the city on its self She-With-The-Sight would destroy it all just to get to her children.

Harron nodded to her, 'our children are safe.'

ReeMara now knew she had to find She-With-The-Sight. Only she could stop She-With-The-Sight, she should have stopped She-With-The-Sight's plans then- How could a little girl stop a woman that lived it a tree, how could she have known then what it all would mean? ReeMara could not ask anyone for help, what did could she ask them to do?

ReeMara slipped out of the meeting. There were things she wanted to prepare. On the table was the piece of amber she had taken from the Iron Man's hoard; it have a bit of amber that belonged to him seemed fitting for the plan she was putting together. That it could change colour was comforting to her. A narrow pointed blade lay next to it, in a leather sheath. But the small clay pot with a wax seal to hold its' contents was the thing ReeMara wanted the most of all. It held a potion made from the rotting corps of the dead rats that had been found in ReeArk's chambers.

It seemed fitting to distract the poison from them; their bodies had little liquid left in them for ReeMara to press out. What they had given her was enough to fill the small pot in her hand. ReeMara did not know if there was enough to kill She-With-The-Sight.

ReeMara hoped by showing it to the old woman to keep her mind, not to forget why she was there.

ReeMara knew the old woman would try to twist her thoughts, how many time had she been able to do that?

ReeMara took off the long robe, got sensible sandals to protect her feet. She tucked the amber and knife into the belt she wound around her waist over the short robe she had chosen. The pot she put into a small pouch and hung it around her neck taking care it was not free to swing as she moved.

Near the bed ReeMara saw the string of white misty amber she still could not remember when she had last seen them. Did remembering really matter? But! They had been placed on ReeArk's bed with the rats.

It took ReeMara eyes time to adjust to the darkness under the Senate. She stood there remembering what had happened in the halls above her. The Iron Man had tried to take her first born from her. And now She-With-The-Sight wanted to take the twins from her.

ReeMara wished then she had told Harron what she was going to do. It was not his battle, they were his children.

Not knowing where to start looking for She-With-The-Sight, ReeMara wandered through the catacombs with its' familiar passages the cities family marks cut into the stone.

ReeMara did not want to carry a light she wanted to use the darkness as She-With-The-Sight did.

ReeMara could see the faces of her children, happy and smiling, playing in the little walled garden that belonged to the villa where they had all been so happy. It would not be difficult to find her way there! Nor to find the passage that lead into the villa from the catacombs.

Something brushed her leg; it was the soft coat of a ferret. ReeMara did not need to ask who it was. Piper spoke from the gloom:

"Don't go alone, I will come with you. You want to keep your children safe, safe from her. My children are living in this city. I want to keep them safe from her."

Another voice that ReeMara knew spoke out of the darkness, it was CC'raw:

"My fledglings were hatched in this city. I want to keep them safe from her."

"But this is something I have to do alone."

"Not without us!"

ReeMara wanted to turn back and take these hopeless friends back to their chambers.

"We have come this far with you we will not leave you now." ReeMara could feel tears run down her cheeks. What could she say if she turned back they would only wait till she tried to slip away again, their voices in the dark would surprise her again.

Piper nor CC'raw were surprised when ReeMara lead them to the villa where they had lived. The door into the street was locked. They had to return to the darkness of the catacombs to find the way into the villa. How silly not to have thought to bring a key!

The villa darkness was broken by shafts of light that cut through the shutters. The strips of light were played with by the dust that stared as they slipped into the kitchen. Armnell had kept pots and preserves on the shelves that hid the entrance to the underground tunnels.

The smell that met them was like that of rotting leaves and wood. There was no one there. They did not open the shutters, ReeMara set a bench by the table to sit on; she would wait.

They did not talk Piper sat on the table her kept eye on the shelves hiding the entrance. CC'raw had taken a perched over Armnell now cold cooking place.

The daylight fayed no longer did the sun send shafts of light to make patens on the floor. No one had moved.

CC'raw could see his fledglings flying about in the garden, swooping in and out of the shadows.

Piper stretched lazily out on the table; under her were youngsters playing, they rolling into soft balls to stop another sibling from pulling their tails.

ReeMara could see little hands reaching out to grab the soft balls of playful ferrets.

They had not noticed the woman sitting on a stool in the corner. Had she been there all the time? Why had they not noticed her before? Not seen her enter the kitchen.

She sat there looking at them, watched them realising she was there. It was as if they had always sat together in the kitchen, water should be bubbling for tea.

"What do you want from me?" She-With-The-Sight's voice was as it had been when ReeMara was a child.

"I want nothing from you. I want to bring you, your death."

Piper was surprised ReeMara had said what she intended to do.

"You think death is a gift you can bring me?"

"You could have had all you wanted. It would have been given to you. You could have had you grandchildren at your knee and your great grandchildren.

We would have worshiped you for what you know, your experience, your wisdom."

ReeMara looked at She-With-The-Sight; ReeMara dropped her voice to match the mood of the sunless room:

"You let your rage blind you; you sent a man to kill the very seed you wanted to sow! You set the Iron Man on a road that would kill him, deface him in front of his peers. You have taken your revenge on this city because his farther raped your mother; her death was to stop her from speaking out against his father.

My mother's death, the village's destruction was so you could get her children, me and ReeArk. You used us to work your revenge. Did you think we would hear each other when we were parted? We are not twins.

That is why I bring you your death, the twins are my children. I will protect each of my children from your venom."

ReeMara put the piece of amber on the table, next to it the knife, the little pot she kept in her hand. ReeMara was silent, she did not know what the next moment would bring, she wanted to take the knife in her hand to make a little scratch, spill a little of the pots contents onto opened skin.

'You are going to kill your grandmother!'

'She wants to take my children.'

'You want to kill my sister.'

'She wants to take my children.'

'She will use them as she has used us.'

'She placed war before the Citadel, set fire to the Grass Lands'

'She put the land to the point of the sward.'

'To take revenge!'

ReeMara stopped their voices from saying any more. 'I will protect my children.'

"She-With-The-Sight, I too feel the sorrow you feel, you made so many pay for your pain."

The crow's wings sent dust into the air as they swept across the table. ReeMara's knife fell to the floor near Piper felt something brush past her, the piece of amber rolled away.

CC'raw move to defend ReeMara, was the lead crow going to attack her? The lead crow was bigger that CC'raw, his talons were stretched to strike at anything that got in his way.

"I made you what you are!"

"I want to hold you in my arms." ReeMara reach out to take her grandmother into her arms, CC'raw pushed her away.

"You are nothing without me!" She-With-The-Sight stretched her arms towards ReeMara.

"They are my children!"

"You are my child."

"Kill her!" The talons of the crow slashed across the old hag's face. CC'raw drove ReeMara back; she wanted to help the old woman as she fell. She-With-The-Sight's twisted hands went to cover her face her twisted body writhed on the floor. ReeMara had not noticed the little clay pot drop to the ground she did not see the crow take the pot! She did not see the crow smash the pot, spill its poison into the wheals he had in She-With-The-Sight face, her hands could not hold the poison. As it dripped from her fingers she screamed:

"You are my child."

"They are my children." ReeMara whispered: "This city and they deserve better than your revenge."

Harron and ReeArk took ReeMara into their arms away from the slumped figure. The broken pieces of amber were left unheeded on the floor.

Amber that matched the signs in the family that governed the City on the Seven Hills, were not reported to have been found, but it was said that one day they would again be need to unite a sick world.

1) The eye, that looked into your soul, orange sun colour.
2) Deep blood red with horse's head of mist and a milk
   tooth from a foal held in it.
3) Green shadows, sun light in summer forest.

The Empress and her family were remembered as fare leaders.

Travellers from the planes.

Book one in a tales of
a Herd.
Ark Of Hoof Print

Hoof Prints- Travelers on the Plane.

Horses' hoof prints are driven from the grass plains, by the storms and flames of fire. The Blue Mountains are where herds of horses have from the beginning of time sheltered from the seasons' storms.

The horses have to leave without finding many other who have survived the storms.

She-With-The-Sight and her cruel owl try to hold the survivors from the great herds to feed to their shrouded needs.

Book two in a tales of
a Herd.
Ark Of Hoof Print

Hoof Prints- Tail of a Herd.
   Normal life was to end on 'The Day'.
Horses had been working with humans for so
long!   No one remembered not doing so.
From that day on those that had not been
evacuated have to find a way to overcome the
strange results of the experiment in their
 Closed Lands.

The Tale of Tails

Book Three in
the Ark Of Hoof Print

Hoof prints-Tail of a Tail.

The land that had been closed for so long is now open to sightseers. Mara lived with a herd of horses when she was a baby, after her parents were killed in the accident, till she was rescued by other members of her family.

Her father was a rescue driver in the War Zone. It was all Mara dreamed of, becoming a rescue driver with a team of horses, like her father.

A program controlling the Com-Pax that runs everyday life has been stolen! The missing program has been found by the Co-Driver of a Team of ponies who were taken from the Closed Lands!

The program must not fall into the hands of those that wish to have control of the 'Black Gold'. It is in the interest of Oil the War Zone is enlarged.

A Twist in the tale.

Book four in
The ark Of Hoof Prints

Hoof Prints- A twist in the tale

.

What the program is planned to do is clear.　　　It must be stopped from causing damage to the folk in the dunes.

A new Oilfield would explain the plan to increase the War Zone. Who is behind such a program, a program that can control the weather in each zone?

There is another reason the team have been chased over the Blue Mountains and across nations.

A reason that know no one could have ever guessed hidden behind the cover 'Moor' used to hamper their chances of preventing the program from continuing the war!

Amber Ark

Book six in

Ark of Hoof Prints.

There is no Future without a Past.

Is being
written at this moment.